TORIKAEBAYA MONOGATARI

TORIKAEBAYA MONOGATARI

*A Japanese Tale of
Gender-Swapped Siblings*

Translated, with an Introduction and Notes, by
ROSETTE F. WILLIG

And a New Introduction by
GUSTAV HELDT

STANFORD UNIVERSITY PRESS
Stanford, California

Stanford University Press
Stanford, California

Cataloging-in-Publication Data available upon request.
Library of Congress Control Number: 2025037962
ISBN: 9781503646261 (cloth), 9781503646544 (paper), 9781503646551 (ebook)

Cover design: Daniel Benneworth-Gray
Cover art: *Two Pigeons on Autumn Branch*, Ohara Koson (Japanese, 1877-1945)

The authorized representative in the EU for product safety and compliance is: Mare Nostrum Group B.V. | Mauritskade 21D | 1091 GC Amsterdam | The Netherlands | Email address: gpsr@mare-nostrum.co.uk | KVK chamber of commerce number: 96249943

For my mother
LUBA FRIEDMAN
in loving memory

Contents

Introduction

GUSTAV HELDT

THE TWELFTH-CENTURY Japanese narrative *Torikaebaya monogatari* is both a worthy successor to *Genji monogatari* (*The Tale of Genji*)—often called the world's first novel—and an entirely innovative piece of prose fiction in its own right.[1] Insofar as it draws on the latter's vocabulary, characters, and scenarios, Rosette Willig's engaging translation of this tale offers readers of English an opportunity to experience that literary masterpiece without having to tackle a thousand-plus pages. Yet *Torikaebaya* manages to achieve much more than simply condensing elements of its predecessor. It is a seemingly unique account of the complications that arise when a high-ranking aristocrat has his daughter and son by different mothers swap identities so that they can secretly embark on adult lives as a man and woman, respectively. Consequently, its plot revolves around the ensuing gap between the siblings' sexed bodies and others' perceptions of their genders.

As a result of the siblings' gender swap, *Torikaebaya* creates a singular blend of tragicomedy, familial love, and oblique social commentary that also slyly subverts the gendered identities and tropes structuring *The Tale of Genji* and previous *monogatari* (court romances) written in the Heian period (794–1185), an era in which fictional prose and other vernacular Japanese cultural forms of literature, painting, architecture, and clothing flourished at the imperial court. Moreover, the existence of two versions—an "older *Torikaebaya*" (*furu Torikaebaya*) and a "newer *Torikaebaya*" (*ima Torikaebaya*)— make it the earliest extant Japanese narrative to have been successfully updated in a later adaptation bearing the same title as the original. That it managed all this with aplomb is evidenced by the tale's reception in its own time, while its status as one of the few two-hundred-plus Heian *monogatari* to have survived intact attests to its enduring appeal in later centuries as well. For all these reasons, Willig's rendering of this remarkable work of fiction merits a wide audience.

Representations of gender fluidity appear with notable frequency in premodern Japan.[2] Perhaps the most well-known example outside the country is that of the *onnagata*, male actors who play female roles in Kabuki. Instances in which beings transform from one gender into the other (as opposed to those in which they combine elements of both) are already visible in the earliest myths. In such cases, the transformation ends once the immediate goal is met (such as disguising oneself from an enemy). By contrast, the siblings in *Torikaebaya* live as consistently as possible in accordance with adult genders different from those they are initially assigned as children. The uniquely committed nature of this embodiment helps explain why the tale repeatedly describes their situation as "unconventional" (*yozukazu*), as well as why modern terminology can potentially help us articulate its distinctiveness. The word "transgender" is of course inevitably anachronistic in this context, not only because there is no equivalent in the tale but also because it encompasses a range of possibilities for gender fluidity that were not all in existence prior to modern medicine. Consequently, the intention here is to tailor the term's use to the circumstances of the siblings (and similar characters in other narratives) by employing it to refer to persons who have transformed their lived experience from male to female or vice versa to the fullest possible extent through modes of expression that are both corporeal and cultural, such as hair, cosmetics, clothes, activities, and mannerisms.

The shifting identities inhabited by *Torikaebaya*'s twin protagonists make it necessary for this introduction—like the tale's narrator, commentators, and translators—to determine how they should be appropriately designated. I have elected to refer to the siblings as "daughter" and "son," not in order to imply their childhood genders are aspects of their identities that are essential, natural, or inevitable but instead to underscore their father's key role in establishing the plot— something suggested by its distinctive title. Whereas the names of most *monogatari* are nouns (often ones identifying their chief protagonists, such as Genji), *torikaebaya* is a complete sentence combining the verb *torikau* (to switch) with the particle -*baya* (if only I could). The resulting utterance could be rendered into English in such ways as "Would that I could change them," "If only I could have things the other way around," "I wish I could swap my children," and (in Willig's rendering) "If only I could exchange them."

This wistful lament occurs to the father twice: first, out of frustration, when he finds himself unable to dissuade his daughter from behaving like a boy and her half brother from acting like a girl (see p. 16 in Willig's translation); and then, as he recalls this wish while weeping for joy, when they switch back into their original genders (p. 164). Yet this second swap, which is precipitated by the daughter's unbidden pregnancy, leads her at times to later rue the loss of her former freedoms as a man, perhaps suggesting she still wishes at points to switch once more back into her masculine gender. Indeed, the daughter is often viewed as the chief protagonist due to the extensive depiction of her angst-ridden travails as both a man and a woman. *Torikaebaya*'s title thus appears to encapsulate its contents in a bittersweet fashion by reminding its readers that the potentially endless possibilities for switching gender in Heian court society are ultimately circumscribed by a patriarchal system in which noblemen could always choose to exercise power over the bodies of others should they ever feel the need to.

Gender crossings in *Torikaebaya* also resonate with multiple transitions contained within the history of its transmission. The most immediate of these shifts concerns its status as a tale that was transformed from an older version into a newer one (the latter possibly a female retelling of a male-authored original). In literary historical terms, *Torikaebaya* transmitted the language of *The Tale of Genji* while introducing transgender versions of its characters. In political terms, the age in which it is initially mentioned represents a transition from the Heian period, in which the imperial court held sway, to the Kamakura period (1185–1333), in which its members shared power with samurai—a historical shift characterized at times as the triumph of virile warriors over effeminate aristocrats. Finally, its modern dissemination through multiple media offers various views of gender and sexuality in contemporary Japan.

EARLY HISTORY

On the basis of circumstantial evidence, recent scholarship has tentatively proposed that the older version of *Torikaebaya* was completed no earlier than 1055 before being substantially revised between 1165 and 1198. This broad span of time corresponds roughly with a period known to modern historians as *insei* (cloister government), during which the Fujiwara-clan regents, who had previously presided over the imperial court in the name of child rulers, now found themselves sharing power with retired sovereigns, who had accrued substantial wealth after ostensibly renouncing the secular world.[3] Initial references to the tale, however, occur soon after this political arrangement was confronted with the need to accommodate the first shogun, Minamoto no Yoritomo (1147–1199), who began overseeing all samurai in 1185 from his *bakufu* (military-camp government) based at Kamakura after having won a years-long conflict with rival warriors, known as the Genpei War (1180–1185).

Torikaebaya is first mentioned by title in the penultimate measure of poem 621 in the *Saneie shū* (Saneie Collection; ca. 1183–1186). This *waka* (a classical poetic form consisting of thirty-one syllables in five measures with the syllabic meter 5-7-5-7-7) is accompanied in the anthology by a headnote that describes it as being "about love through reference to the name of a tale" (*monogatari no na ni yosuru koi*):

> koyoi waga
> afu tefu yume o
> mitsuru kana
> torikaebaya na
> tsuraki utsutsu ni
>
> (Tonight we
> met up in a dream
> beheld by me.
> If only things were switched,
> however cruel in reality!)[4]

Despite its relatively straightforward surface meaning, the poem leaves us with more questions than answers, particularly since the identity of its speaker is not necessarily that of the nobleman Fujiwara no Saneie (1145–1193), who composed it. Even a conventional reading in which the dream concerns a liaison between a man and woman still leaves it unclear which genders to assign to the speaker and addressee. Nor is it evident why switching places in the waking world would be harder for either party to endure. The outcome being wished for is also uncertain: Does the speaker want to replace an imagined liaison with an actual one or to swap identities with the addressee? Such ambiguities make the *waka* poem an apt means of alluding to a tale in and around which certainties repeatedly fade from view.

Roughly a decade after the tale's title inspired Saneie's poem, several *waka* from the older version of *Torikaebaya* appeared in *Monogatari nihyakuban uta-awase* (Tale-Poetry Match in Two Hundred Rounds; ca. 1193–1196)—a text which pitted poems from *The Tale of Genji* against ones from later *monogatari*.[5] The afterword by its compiler, the renowned *waka* poet and scholar Fujiwara no Teika (1162–1241), attributes its contents to tales possessed by Sen'yōmon-in (1181–1252), a daughter of Go-Shirakawa (1127–1192; r. 1155–1158) and adoptive mother of Shijō (1231–1242; r. 1232–1242) who had recently become a cloistered empress in 1191. More than twice as many *waka* poems from *Torikaebaya*—six of which are explicitly identified as belonging to the newer version—subsequently crop up in the thirteenth-century poetry anthology *Fūyō wakashū* (Collection of Windblown Leaves; 1271), whose contents were drawn from tales possessed by the cloistered empress who commissioned it—a consort of Go-Saga (1220–1272; r. 1242–1246) named Ōmiya-in Saionji Kitsushi (1225–1292).[6] The poems in these two texts are all that remain from the older version, while their headnotes offer a handful of plot details. One such prefatory comment in *Fūyō wakashū*, for example, indicates the daughter originally became a minister's principal wife rather than an emperor's chief consort.[7]

The origins of both anthologies suggest that the female counterparts of retired sovereigns, known as *nyoin* (cloistered empresses), were particularly interested in preserving *Torikaebaya*.[8] Perhaps one reason why these senior women in the imperial family valued the tale has to do with its inclusion of a female heir apparent (referred to as the Imperial Princess or Crown Princess in this translation), who was possibly inspired by a daughter of Toba (1103–1156; r. 1107–1123) named Akiko (or Shōshi; 1137–1211). According to the historical chronicle *Gukanshō* (ca. 1219), the death of her half brother Konoe (1139–1155; r. 1142–1155) led their father to consider making her successor.[9] Instead, in 1161, she became a cloistered empress while still unmarried—as was also the case with both the female heir apparent in the tale and the owner of the copy that Teika consulted. Although these events might suggest one version of *Torikaebaya* was written around the same time, Akiko herself does not appear to have ever been officially designated as the heir apparent.

The newer version's absence from Teika's poetry match could indicate *Torikaebaya* was revised less than a decade after he had compiled his collection of *monogatari* poems. The first reference to this updated edition of the tale appears in a section of *Mumyōzōshi* (Untitled Book; ca. 1200–1201)—helpfully included as an appendix in Willig's translation—which also gives us our fullest picture of its reception close to the time it was rewritten.[10] Cast as a discussion among a gathering of women on topics ranging from *monogatari* tales and *waka*-poetry anthologies to accounts of notable female figures, this singular work of female literary criticism was probably written by a biological grandchild and adopted daughter of the renowned *waka* poet Fujiwara no Shunzei (1114–1204) named Fujiwara no Shunzei no Musume (literally, "Fujiwara no Shunzei's daughter"; ca. 1171–1252). Like her biological paternal half uncle Teika, the author's interest in fictional narratives can be traced back to Shunzei, who famously urged poets to thoroughly familiarize themselves with *The Tale of Genji*.

The women in *Mumyōzōshi* criticize the older version of *Torikaebaya* for, among other things, depicting the siblings' transformations in an unconvincing manner, as well as for being unpleasantly lurid in its descriptions of the daughter menstruating and of her giving birth in a male official's garb. It also describes the newer version as a rare example of a *monogatari* that has been improved upon, particularly due to the greater plausibility with which it now depicts the siblings' gender switches. As *Mumyōzōshi* itself notes, such an evaluation departs from the tendency at the time to view more recent cultural forms as lesser imitations of past models. While the newer version could therefore be considered novel simply by virtue of having been deemed superior to its predecessor, other aspects of the tale as we now have it can be seen in the same light. The daughter's occasional discontent with having to relinquish her life as a man, for example, offered an innovative means for satirizing masculinity at court. By including a female heir apparent, moreover, *Torikaebaya* created an alternate reality set within the vague "Once, we know not when" (*itsu no koro ni ka*) (p.13) that it opens with.[11]

RELATED TALES

Despite the acclaim *Torikaebaya* garnered in its own time, most of its later history remains a mystery. We must therefore turn to other narratives resembling it and *The Tale of Genji* in order to get a sense of why it was one of the few Heian-period *monogatari* that endured. Many of these other texts suggest early audiences were especially drawn to the final ten chapters, in which Genji's illegitimate heir, Kaoru, replaces him as the chief male protagonist. Unlike his putative father, Kaoru's religious scruples and self-doubts prevent him from wholeheartedly chasing after women, perhaps also because his own illicit origins make him loath to procreate or because the three sisters he courts in turn are increasingly imperfect substitutes for their father, a man who Kaoru is drawn to in ways that are potentially homoerotic.[12] Regardless of the reason(s) for his ambivalence, it departs from the expectations that lead most men in *monogatari* to aggressively pursue women.[13] In more general terms, these chapters—primarily set in Uji, a location just outside the capital, which also figures in *Torikaebaya*—are populated by characters resembling him who are less likely to embrace conventional romance and more alienated from those around them, leading in turn to lengthier depictions of their internal deliberations.[14]

All these elements in the Uji chapters are reproduced to

one degree or another within several later tales. Two that have survived in fragmentary form are often thought to have directly influenced *Torikaebaya*.[15] Their likely author, Sugawara no Takasue no Musume (literally, "Sugawara no Takasue's daughter"; ca. 1008–1059 or later), is best known for the *Sarashina nikki* (Sarashina Diary), which among other things chronicles its protagonist's obsession with reading *The Tale of Genji*. One of these two tales, *Yoru no nezame* (Awake at Night), is distinguished by lengthy interior monologues marking divides between characters' internal and external lives—a technique also extensively deployed in *Torikaebaya*. The other narrative often attributed to the same author is *Hamamatsu chūnagon monogatari* (Tale of the Hamamatsu Middle Counselor), whose hero is involved in an asexual relationship with a woman resembling the ones engaged in by Kaoru in *The Tale of Genji* and by the transmasculine daughter in *Torikaebaya*.

Two tales that are roughly contemporaneous with *Torikaebaya* also showcase protagonists who diverge from feminine norms. *Ariake no wakare* (Partings at Dawn) is centered on a girl who is raised by her father as a man after he consults an oracle.[16] Here, too, the transmasculine daughter is involved in an asexual marriage with a woman characterized by mutual empathy, reciprocity, and communication.[17] And here, too, she voices nostalgia for her former life as a man prior to attaining the most exalted position accorded women at court when she becomes mother to a crown prince. Another twelfth-century narrative, the short story "Mushi mezuru himegimi" (The Young Lady Obsessed with Crawling Creatures), concerns a girl who questions the need to observe feminine norms of behavior and presentation that she views as artificial.[18] Regardless of whether or not these two texts came after *Torikaebaya*, they make it evident that nonfeminine heroines were familiar figures at the time.

Tales featuring relationships similar to those in *Torikaebaya* can also be seen in later centuries. The same homoeroticism

fostered in the all-female entourage of an unmarried princess
that enables the transfeminine son to impregnate the female
heir apparent in *Torikaebaya* is depicted more explicitly in the
thirteenth-century story *Wagami ni tadoru himegimi* (The
Princess in Search of Herself), in which a jealous female attendant curses her royal mistress when the latter shifts her affections to another lady-in-waiting.[19] The female ruler in this
story may also have been inspired by the female heir to the
throne in *Torikaebaya*. The Muromachi-period (1336–1573)
story *Shinkurōdo monogatari* (Tale of the New Chamberlain) is named after yet another transmasculine daughter—in
this case, one whose personal wish to become a man is reluctantly endorsed by the father out of his desire for a son who
can attract the emperor's favors. The emperor subsequently
lavishes his affections on this new chamberlain, who, like the
daughter in *Torikaebaya*, reverts to a female identity after becoming pregnant. The hero in another story from the same
period, *Chigo ima mairi* (The Acolyte Now in Attendance),
is a Buddhist temple acolyte whose wetnurse disguises him
as a lady-in-waiting so that the youth can gain proximity to
a noblewoman he is smitten with.[20] Like the female heir apparent's ties with the transfeminine son who attends on her
in *Torikaebaya*, this same-gender relationship ends with a
pregnancy. Intriguingly, the tale also features a supernatural
creature known as a *tengu*—the source of the siblings' initial
dispositions in *Torikaebaya* and a kidnapper of the acolyte
here—perhaps reflecting a common belief that these winged
goblins were prone to meddling in the lives of young humans.

Torikaebaya may have even influenced the medieval period's
literary practices as a whole due to the newer version having
been, if not the first of its kind, the first successful example of
one to survive. As the earliest such *monogatari* extant, there
is a distinct possibility that it spurred on similar revisions
of older tales in later times, including an early thirteenth-
century version of the tenth-century *Sumiyoshi monogatari*

(Tale of Sumiyoshi), as well as later medieval iterations of the tenth-century *Ochikubo monogatari* (Tale of Ochikubo), the eleventh-century *Sagoromo monogatari* (Tale of Sagoromo), and *Yoru no nezame*. Many other Heian-period tales now only exist in complete form as later retellings created between the fourteenth and sixteenth centuries, including such works as *Ama no karumo* (The Seaweed Harvested by Seafolk), *Iwaya* (The Boulder Cave), *Suzuri wari* (The Broken Inkstone), *Shinobine* (Muffled Weeping), and *Hashihime* (The Lady at the Bridge).

TORIKAEBAYA IN MODERN JAPAN

Torikaebaya resurfaces in the early modern era, during which knowledge about Japan's past literary heritage was produced and consumed through print technology and scholarly instruction by an urban population that grew increasingly numerous, literate, and wealthy over the course of the Edo period (1603–1868). The tale's antiquarian appeal in this context is demonstrated by its preservation in over eighty manuscripts representing the earliest surviving examples of the text. Their close resemblance to one another further indicates a pronounced interest in faithfully reproducing the story's entire contents at the time. These handwritten texts are the products of social networks through which copies were borrowed or transferred between literati engaged in a wide array of cultural pursuits or between teachers and disciples of *kokugaku*, a nativist intellectual movement that sought to uncover an originary Japanese identity through the philological investigation of early vernacular texts. Manuscripts made in the Bunka-Bunsei period (1804–1830) in particular begin to boast scholarly apparatuses in the form of indices, plot synopses, genealogies delineating parents and marriage partners, and definitions for individual words based on their usage in other Heian texts.[21] During this same period, the tale also influenced commercially popular print fiction by inspiring a gender switch between the two chief protagonists in the second half of a story by Ryūtei Tanehiko (1783–1842) that he initially titled *Shin Torikaebaya* (A New *Torikaebaya*) before publishing it as *Yakko no Koman* (Koman, the Tough; 1807).

Torikaebaya was viewed more ambivalently when long-standing attitudes toward sexuality began to contend with Western ones informed by Christianity after Japan became a modern nation-state in the Meiji period (1868–1912).[22] An especially notorious instance involves the scholar Fujioka Sakutarō (1870–1910), who denounced the tale as "obscene" (*shūwai*) in his *Kokubungaku zenshi* (Complete History of National Literature; 1905), reserving particular revulsion for a philandering male character's pursuit of both the transmasculine daughter and their wife, Yon no Kimi (or Shi no Kimi).[23] Nonetheless, *Torikaebaya* attracted attention before and after this moralistic condemnation. In 1889, a loose novelization by Jōno Saigiku (1832–1902) was serialized between January and July in the literary magazine *Shinshōsetsu* (New Novels). Shortly thereafter, the first modern annotated editions of the tale were subsequently produced in 1890, 1891, 1903, and 1909.[24]

Although the earliest translation of *Torikaebaya* into modern Japanese was produced in 1927 by the scholar Yoshizawa Yoshinori (1876–1954), the most famous one is by Nobel laureate Kawabata Yasunari (1899–1972), which was initially published in 1937 and then subsequently in 1948, with the postwar version including depictions of the emperor's sexuality that had been censored in the previous one.[25] The following year, the scholar and novelist Takagi Taku (1907–1974) put out a work of historical fiction entitled *Onozukara monogatari* (Tale of a Spontaneous Occurrence; 1949) whose transgender Heian-period characters were inspired by *Torikaebaya*. A fictive stage adaptation of the twelfth-century tale also plays a role in the 1957 short story "Onnagata" by Mishima Yukio

(1925–1970).[26] Subsequent reinterpretations of the original in modern Japanese include *Ihon Torikaebaya monogatari* (Another Version of the *Tale of Torikaebaya*) by Niihara Sumie in 2001 and one Kōdansha published in 1993 by the acclaimed novelist Tanabe Seiko (1928–2019), which proved so popular it was reissued by Bungei Shunjū in 2015. *Torikaebaya* also inspired adaptations in other media, such as the manga series *Za chenji!* (The Change!; 1983–1985), *Yume no ishibumi* (Monument of Dreams; 1984–1997), and *Torikae baya* (If Only We Switched; 2012–2018), along with the anime film *Kimi no na wa* (Your Name; 2016). It also provided source material for the play *Yukariko: Torikaebaya ibun* (Yukariko: The Curious Story of *Torikaebaya*), staged by the all-female cast of the Takarazuka Revue in 1987 and then subsequently in revised form in 2010. Overall, responses to the original vary widely—from nostalgia for premodern forms of male homosociality to celebrations of heteronormative nationalism and sympathetic portrayals of transgender individuals.[27]

Scholarship on *Torikaebaya* also began to grow appreciably in the second half of the twentieth century. Yoshida Kōichi, Kuwabara Hiroshi, and Suzuki Hiromichi laid the groundwork for future research by organizing the surviving manuscripts into three or four distinct lines. Suzuki—the doyen of late Heian *monogatari* who supplied the edition Willig's translation is based on—further characterizes *Torikaebaya* as a form of "allusive variation" (*honkadori*) on *The Tale of Genji*, likening their textual relationship to the practice of citing older *waka* in new ones, which was codified by the same Teika who had matched poems from the two tales.[28] In fact, it could be argued that *Torikaebaya*'s relative neglect in the twentieth century was due at least as much, if not more, to the impression that it was derivative rather than depraved. In this regard, its treatment differs little from that accorded to other so-called *giko monogatari* (pseudoclassical tales), a genre created in the twentieth century to describe late Heian and early medieval narratives that replicated the language of *The Tale of Genji*, often with the added implication that this imitative quality is symptomatic of social and cultural decline.[29] Needless to say, such an evaluation fails to account for the aforementioned ways in which *Torikaebaya* was both innovative and potentially influential in its own right.

It is impossible to do justice here to the exponential growth in Japanese-language scholarship on *Torikaebaya* that has taken place since Willig's translation came out. Over sixty academic books and articles devoted to it have already been produced in the first two and a half decades of this century (a number roughly equivalent to that for the last five decades of the previous one), with the total number published midway through this decade already approaching those for the entirety of the 2000s and 2010s each. In addition to considerations of how gender is represented in its text, the range of topics they explore include comparisons with other vernacular fictional narratives (such as *The Tale of Genji*, *Hamamatsu chūnagon monogatari*, and *Ariake no wakare*), recurring tropes (such as the moon, tears, music, and maternity), and depictions of individual characters (especially the daughter). One particularly telling indicator of *Torikaebaya*'s changing status has been its inclusion in updated iterations of two standard annotated series representing the classical Japanese literary canon— volume 26 of *Shin Nihon koten bungaku taikei* published by Iwanami Shoten in 1992 and volume 39 of *Shinpen Nihon koten bungaku zenshū* produced by Shōgakukan in 2002— after having been absent from the original editions of these series issued between 1957 and 1976.[30]

GENDER IN *TORIKAEBAYA*

Even accounts of *Torikaebaya* that seek to avoid explicitly moralizing language must grapple with the inherent challenges posed to our understanding by the extensive and intricate depictions of sex, gender, and sexuality in a premodern text lacking those conceptual categories. In describing the siblings, for example, Suzuki resorts to such terms as *seiteki tōsaku* (sexual inversion), a nineteenth-century psychosexual pathology; *sei tenkan* (sex change), implying anatomical alteration; and *ruiji handanjo* (pseudohermaphroditism), an early twentieth-century sexological category combining male and female traits.[31] Another term employed by some scholars to characterize the tale, *taihaiteki na sei* (decadent sexuality), reflects presumptions about cultural and social malaise at court during the transition from classical Heian Japan to its medieval successor. According to this gendered view of the period, a stagnant world of effete aristocrats who preferred traditional cultural (i.e., feminine) pursuits to the exercise of raw power gave way to a dynamic history of change led by vigorously assertive (i.e., masculine) samurai under the shoguns.[32]

From the late 1970s onward, Japanese-language scholarship has also employed more ostensibly neutral terminology to analyze *Torikaebaya*, including *chūsei* (androgyny), *dōseiai* (homosexuality), *iseiai* (heterosexuality), *iseisō* (cross-dressing), *shintaiteki seisa* (anatomical sexual difference), and *jendā* (gender).[33] Pioneering work by Takeda Sachiko, for example, noted that (1) both male and female standards of physical beauty were coded as feminine at the time, (2) the unisex nature of Heian undergarments and preference for loose-fitting robes covering most of the body would have facilitated passing as either gender, (3) homosexual desires are as integral to the plot as heterosexual ones, and (4) *Torikaebaya*'s representation of gender crossing differs from Western narratives like Shakespeare's *Twelfth Night* insofar as both male and female characters engage in it simultaneously.[34] Nevertheless, the need to rely on such neologisms as "heterosexual" points to a persistent epistemic divide between our world and that of the tale.

Similar issues accompany *Torikaebaya*'s treatment in a

groundbreaking article by Gregory Pflugfelder published nearly ten years after Willig's translation.[35] Employing the categories of sex, gender, and sexuality to analyze the story, he observes that *Torikaebaya* represents gender as something that is as easily learned as it is unlearned—with the siblings remaining paragons in either case—while also recognizing sex characteristics, such as pregnancy or facial hair. Pflugfelder further argues that any such latent distinctions between sex and gender are complicated by the range of erotic forces at work in the narrative for two reasons. First, the siblings' secret awareness of the divergence between their sexed bodies and their genders leads them to experience desire differently from their partners. Second, characters of the same sex or gender in the tale can be attracted to one another but not simultaneously on the basis of being both the same sex and the same gender. The complexities that arise from this situation are illustrated by the pivotal scene on pages 82–84, in which the philanderer who forces himself on the daughter is initially aroused by her embodiment of a quintessentially male form of attractiveness combining a masculine guise with feminine facial features.[36]

At the same time as *Torikaebaya* draws attention to the fluidity of gender and sexuality, the narrative direction in which they flow is channeled through the political concerns, status hierarchies, and familial structures by which court-centered narratives defined their aristocratic protagonists. Like *The Tale of Genji*, in other words, its main plot can be seen as revolving around the implications (intended or otherwise) that the chief protagonists' desires hold for determining the line of succession. As Kimura Saeko notes, the resolution of the story is thus not so much a matter of the siblings reverting to their original genders per se as it is the ways in which this switch enables them to ensure the political prominence of their descendants when the daughter births a future emperor and the son then becomes his regent.[37] Willig's references to "sexual complications," "sexual problems," and "sexual deviation" in her introduction can be viewed in a similar light. That is to say, the disinclination of the young siblings to conform to the genders they are initially assigned is chiefly problematic insofar as it prevents the father from deploying their adult bodies in pursuit of the ultimate political goal shared by most men of his rank: becoming the maternal grandfather of an emperor.

In addition to politics, other cultural and historical factors merit consideration in attempting to understand how bodies and desires are constituted in *Torikaebaya*. Rajyashree Pandey argues that even the supposed immutability and universality of anatomical difference upon which such categories as "sex," "gender," and "sexuality" are based is a product of the post-Renaissance West, which is incommensurate with a premodern context—informed in part by Buddhist ideas of impermanence, reincarnation, and monasticism—in which bodies were amenable to transformation rather than being set in stone with the result that neither "man" nor "woman" were stable categories. In medieval Japan, bodies were instead understood as psychosomatic processes and dynamic sites at which persons interface with their surroundings through shifts in the flow of psychophysical energy (*ki*) and their social relationships, among other factors. Thus, it is the linear forms of hair, clothing, and calligraphy constituting their outermost extensions in *monogatari* like *The Tale of Genji* that provide the primary means for rendering gender intelligible and for generating erotic desires at particular moments involving particular interpersonal dynamics.[38]

The same challenges posed by *Torikaebaya*'s premodern context can also afford opportunities for reading it in new ways. At the time he was writing, Pflugfelder asserted that modern American society "can accommodate a switch in gender only if it is accompanied by a corresponding modification of the anatomy."[39] More recently, however, scholars in many countries have embraced "trans" as a category encompassing not only transexual identities but also transgender, nonbinary, and cross-dressing ones that represent nonnormative alignments between bodies and genders as a transhistorical phenomenon (albeit experienced and expressed differently in different periods and places).[40] As Pflugfelder himself notes, the words *otoko* (man) and *onna* (woman)—like their nongendered counterpart *mi* (body/status/self)—are frequently qualified in *Torikaebaya* by other words indicating their contingency, whether through nouns describing their appearance, figure, or form (*sama, arisama, sugata,* and *yō*) or through verbs indicating change or performativity, such as *naru* (becoming), *kawaru* (changing into), *torinasu* (making into), *manebu* (imitating), *onna-bu* (acting womanly), *narau* (getting used to being), and *narikaeru* (reverting). Such provisional modes of personhood represent gender at the Heian court, like its titles of office, as a form of social identity that was capable of being more fluid than fixed.

WILLIG'S TRANSLATION

Willig's translation of *Torikaebaya* was published a few years after one in German and several decades before subsequent versions in Russian, French, and Spanish.[41] Like these other renderings into European languages, hers was faced with the challenge of applying pronouns to a text written in a premodern form of Japanese that rarely employed grammatical subjects and, in any case, lacked equivalents for either "he" or "she." Vernacular prose instead preferred to mark individuals by their social relationships with others, as expressed through honorific language or the bureaucratic posts they occupied at court. In *The Tale of Genji*, for example, its namesake is typically identified by the offices he is consecutively promoted to: middle captain (*chūjō*), major counselor (*dainagon*), chancellor (*dajō daijin*), and so forth. In a similar vein, *Torikaebaya* refers to its twin protagonists over the course of the story, sometimes both siblings consecutively, as young lord (*wakagimi*), young lady (*himegimi*), younger sister of the gentleman-in-waiting (*jijū no imōtogimi*), chief imperial handmaid (*naishi no kami*), lord of fifth rank (*tayū*), lord master (*daibu no kimi*), middle captain (*chūjō*), middle counselor (*chūnagon*), major general (*taishō*), junior consort (*nyōgo*), empress (*chūgū*), empress dowager (*kokubo*), minister of the center (*naidaijin*), minister of the left (*sadaijin*), and regent (*kanpaku*).

Contemporary readers confronted with this plethora of appellations usually rely on consistent designations for each character in order to track their development. Although such heuristic devices amount to little more than convenient fictions in a cultural context that departed from modern concepts of the self as autonomous and uniform, the sobriquets adopted for this purpose originate in the texts themselves, often perhaps because they contain ironies that hint at the characters' narrative arcs. The chief protagonist in *The Tale of Genji*, for example, is known to modern Japanese readers as Hikaru Genji (literally, "the radiant ex-royal"), identifying him by his paradoxical status as the son of an emperor who can never succeed his father despite his divinely dazzling qualities. Likewise, the modern Japanese names for the son and daughter—either Otokogimi and Onnagimi ("the nobleman" and "the noblewoman") or Wakagimi and Himegimi ("the young lord" and "the young lady")—appear in *Torikaebaya* and gesture to some of its narrative ironies by reflecting the genders assigned to the virtually identical siblings as children but not those assigned to them in early adulthood.

As with the other characters in her translation, Willig utilizes a similar strategy for transmuting official titles into personal names through their transliteration when she initially refers to the daughter as Chūnagon and the son as Naishi no Kami. This choice takes its cue from the narrator, who informs the reader early on, "Hereafter I shall refer to the children as the others had come mistakenly to do; the son I shall call the daughter, and the daughter the son" (p. 16). The same titles are also used to identify the siblings in *Mumyōzōshi*, which occasionally further specifies that they are applied to Naishi no Kami "as a man" (*otoko no*) and Chūnagon "as a woman" (*onna no*). In adopting these designations, Willig employs gendered pronouns consonant with the official posts they represent: the son as a chief imperial handmaid (*naishi no kami*) becomes "she," while the daughter as a middle counselor (*chūnagon*) becomes "he." When the siblings swap identities, Willig notifies the reader on pages 164–165 that Naishi no Kami and Chūnagon will refer to the daughter and son, respectively, going forward. The result is a remarkably deft technique for making the characters consistently recognizable on the basis of their gender identities rather than their sexed bodies.[42] Readers already familiar with similar conventions in this century are therefore more likely to find a sentence such as "It did not occur to him that he might be pregnant" (p. 95) less jarring today than would have been the case at the time Willig translated the tale.

It seems fitting to conclude with a consideration of the original name Willig gave her translation, both because doing so circles back to the opening account of *Torikaebaya*'s title and because the titles that begin books can often represent later stages in their development. In choosing *The Changelings*, Willig was able to achieve several aims. Since the original title constitutes a complete sentence, a literal rendering preceded by "the tale of" (for *monogatari*) would inevitably sound unwieldy in English. Nouns, by contrast, are more succinct and can also indicate who the story is about (as is true of most *monogatari* titles). Moreover, her choice alludes to the supernatural source of the father's dilemma, which originates in a spell turning the son feminine and the daughter masculine that is cast by a *tengu* as karmic retribution for unspecified deeds in a previous life (whether on his part or theirs is unclear). *Torikaebaya*'s version of this Buddhist logic—one often deployed in premodern Japanese narratives to explain the challenges individuals faced in the present as the fruits of past actions— also resonates with European folklore regarding changelings. They, too, can be a form of punishment meted out by goblins, and they, too, can be virtually perfect or identical with the children they are exchanged for—apart from initially minor differences that eventually prove momentous.

The persistent gendered proclivities of *Torikaebaya*'s siblings similarly seem at first to represent relatively minor divergences in children who are otherwise visually identical with one another and with the ideals of Heian court society, in which aristocratic boys and girls shared the same hairstyles and clothing prior to the coming-of-age ceremonies they underwent in their teens. These divergences promise to be significant for their father in the long term chiefly insofar as they will bar him from employing their bodies to amass power through politically productive procreation. Given such a state of affairs, it is all the more meaningful that he is initially content to prioritize what he perceives to be their personal predilections over parental ambitions informed by conventional social expectations. When we consider that others' whims have all too often forced trans people in our own time to relinquish their happiness, their dignity, and their lives, this remarkable tale of wistful switches offers a vital reminder that love, recognition, and affirmation, regardless of the consequences, have always been conceivable as well.

NOTES

The author wishes to thank Rosette Willig for making herself available to discuss her translation, as well as Margaret Childs, Christina Laffin, Grace Lavery, Rajyashree Pandey, Joan Piggott, Hiroaki Sato, Sachi Schmidt-Hori, Joseph Sorensen, Dylan Kyung-lim White, and Anri Yasuda for their comments and suggestions.

1. Japanese surnames precede given names unless the person is being cited as the author of an English-language publication or appears as such within it.

2. For a wide-ranging account of this phenomenon, see Sachi Schmidt-Hori, "Nonbinary Genders in *Genji*, the *New Chamberlain*, and Beyond," in *The Tale of Genji*, trans. Dennis C. Washburn (W. W. Norton, 2021), 1282–95.

3. For an overview of this historical period in English, see G. Cameron Hurst, *Insei: Abdicated Sovereigns in the Politics of Late Heian Japan, 1086–1185* (Columbia University Press, 1976).

4. Fujiwara no Saneie, *Saneie shū*, in *Shikashū taisei*, ed. Wakashi kenkyūkai, vol. 3 (Meiji Shoin, 1974), 116. All translations by author unless otherwise noted.

5. Two of the six poems listed as entries have headnotes that include the *waka* they respond to. Both the first of these six and the one it replies to also appear in the newer version of *Torikaebaya*, making six *waka* from Fujiwara no Teika's poetry match unique to the original edition.

6. Three of the thirteen poems in *Fūyō wakashū* that are from the older version of *Torikaebaya* previously appeared in Teika's poetry match.

7. For one comparison that focuses on the transmasculine daughter's wife, see Masao Karashima, "The Two Versions of the *Torikaebaya monogatari*: With a Focus on Material Relating to the Fourth Daughter," *Acta Asiatica* 83 (2002): 50–68.

8. Women who became *nyoin* included princesses, consorts, adoptive mothers, birth mothers, and grandmothers of reigning emperors. On the considerable resources they could possess, see Sachiko Kawai, *Uncertain Powers: Sen'yōmon-in and Landownership by Royal Women in Early Medieval Japan* (Harvard University Asia Center, 2021).

9. Delmer M. Brown and Ichirō Ishida, *The Future and the Past: A Translation and Study of the "Gukanshō," an Interpretative History of Japan Written in 1219* (University of California Press, 1979), 98.

10. For a complete translation, see Michele Marra, "*Mumyōzōshi*: Introduction and Translation," *Monumenta Nipponica* 39, nos. 2–4 (Summer–Winter 1984): 115–45, 281–305, 409–34.

11. Although the sixth of the eight female sovereigns in Japan, Kōken (718–770; r. 749–758 and 764–770), did officially hold the title of *tōgū* (heir apparent), it is unlikely *Torikaebaya* is referring to her since the story is set after the capital had moved from Heijō-kyō (Nara) to Heian-kyō (present-day Kyoto) in 794.

12. This characterization of Kaoru is taken from a larger exploration of the psychological complexities *The Tale of Genji* shares with Proust that are identified in Doris G. Bargen, "The Search for Things Past in the *Genji monogatari*," *Harvard Journal of Asiatic Studies* 51, no. 1 (June 1991): 199–232.

13. For a wide-ranging account of these masculine norms in *monogatari*, see Margaret H. Childs, "Coercive Courtship Strategies and Gendered Goals in Classical Japanese Literature," *Japanese Language and Literature* 44, no. 2 (October 2010): 119–48. How best to characterize such behaviors in their own time remains subject to debate. For one approach that draws on both literary and historical sources, see Hitomi Tonomura, "Coercive Sex in the Medieval Japanese Court: Lady Nijō's Memoir," *Monumenta Nipponica* 61, no. 3 (Autumn 2006): 283–338.

14. On the depiction of these characters' interiority, see Amanda Meyer Stinchecum, "Who Tells the Tale? 'Ukifune': A Study in Narrative Voice," *Monumenta Nipponica* 35, no. 4 (Winter 1980): 375–403.

15. For translations of these tales, see Carol Hochstedler, *The Tale of Nezame: Part Three of "Yowa no Nezame Monogatari"* (Cornell University China-Japan Program, 1979); Thomas H. Rohlich, *A Tale of Eleventh Century Japan: "Hamamatsu Chunagon Monogatari"* (Princeton University Press, 1983). Synopses of both works are helpfully provided in Charo B. D'Etcheverry, *Love After "The Tale of Genji": Rewriting the World of the Shining Prince* (Harvard University Asia Center, 2007), 165–74.

16. For a study and partial translation, see Robert Omar Khan, "*Ariake no wakare*: Genre, Gender and Genealogy in a Late 12th Century Monogatari" (PhD diss., University of British Columbia, 1998).

17. Daniele Durante, "Cross-Gender Female Same-Sex Love as Women's Solidarity in *Torikaebaya monogatari* and *Ariake no wakare*," in *Percorsi in Civiltà dell'Asia e dell'Africa*, ed. Federica Casalin and Marina Miranda, vol. 1 (Sapienza Università Editrice, 2021), 37–55.

18. For a translation of *Mushi mezuru himegimi*, see Robert L. Backus,

trans., *The Riverside Counselor's Stories: Vernacular Fiction of Late Heian Japan* (Stanford University Press, 1985), 41–69.

19. For a fuller account of *Wagami ni tadoru himegimi*, see Donald Keene, "A Neglected Chapter: Courtly Fiction of the Kamakura Period," *Monumenta Nipponica* 44, no. 1 (Spring 1989): 1–30.

20. For a translation and study of *Chigo ima mairi*, see Sachi Schmidt-Hori, "The New Lady-in-Waiting Is a *Chigo*: Sexual Fluidity and Dual Transvestism in a Medieval Buddhist Acolyte Tale," *Japanese Language and Literature* 43, no. 2 (October 2009): 383–423.

21. Nishimoto Ryōko, "Dare ga yonda no ka: Edo jidai no *Torikaebaya* kyōju," *Nihon bungaku* 54 (2005): 60–63.

22. For an overview of this change, see Gregory M. Pflugfelder, *Cartographies of Desire: Male-Male Sexuality in Japanese Discourse, 1600–1950* (University of California Press, 2000).

23. Fujioka Sakutarō, *Kokubungaku zenshi: Heianchō hen* (Iwanami Shoten, 1923), 634.

24. A more extensive list of modern Japanese translations and annotated editions produced up to 2002 can be found in Noriko Kubota, "Orlando and Literary Tradition in Japan: Sex Change, Dressing and Gender in *Torikaebaya monogatari*," in *Woolf Across Cultures*, ed. Natalya Reinhold (Pace University Press, 2004), 167–77.

25. On the contexts surrounding Kawabata's two renderings of *Torikaebaya*, see Masaho Kumazawa, "Disturbing Gender Norms: Yasunari Kawabata's *Otome no minato* and Translations of *Torikaebaya monogatari*," in *Gender Fluidity in Japanese Arts and Cultures: Critical Essays*, ed. Dean Conrad and Sayuri Hirano (McFarland, 2025), 32–50.

26. For a translation of this story, see Yukio Mishima, "Onnagata," in *Death in Midsummer, and Other Stories by Yukio Mishima*, ed. J. Thomas Rimer, trans. Donald Keene (New Directions, 1966), 139–61.

27. Rafael Montón Gómez, "*Torikaebaya* Unravelled: The Modern Adaptations of *Torikaebaya monogatari*," *Asiadémica* 18 (2023): 402–27; see also Michiko Oshiyama and Kohki Watabe, "Interpretative Negotiation with Gender Norms in *Shōjo Manga* Adaptations of *The Changelings*," *Journal of Adaptation in Film and Performance* 12, no. 3 (December 2019): 179–93.

28. Suzuki Hiromichi, *Heian makki monogatari kenkyū* (Daigakudō Shoten, 1979), 88.

29. For one example of this view, see Keene, "Neglected Chapter," 3.

30. Another annotated edition of note published between these two is

Tomohisa Takefumi and Nishimoto Ryōko, eds., *Torikaebaya*, Chūsei ōchō monogatari zenshū 12 (Kasama Shoin, 1998).

31. See, e.g., Suzuki Hiromichi, *Heian makki monogatari no kenkyū* (Hatsune Shobō, 1960), 293–306; Suzuki Hiromichi, *Heian makki monogatari ron* (Hanawa Shobō, 1968), 113–37.

32. Thomas Keirstead, "The Gendering and Regendering of Medieval Japan," *U.S.-Japan Women's Journal* 9 (1995): 77–92, esp. 78–82.

33. One outlier is Kawai Hayao, who draws on Jungian psychology; see Kawai, *"Torikaebaya": Otoko to onna* (Shinchōsha, 1991). For an abbreviated version of his approach to the tale in English, see Hayao Kawai, *Dreams, Myths and Fairy Tales in Japan* (Daimon Verlag, 1995), 123–40.

34. Sachiko Takeda, "Menswear, Womenswear: Distinctive Features of the Japanese Sartorial System," in *Gender and Japanese History*, ed. Wakita Haruko et al., vol. 1, *Religion and Customs / The Body and Sexuality* (Osaka University Press, 1999), 187–209.

35. Gregory M. Pflugfelder, "Strange Fates: Sex, Gender, and Sexuality in *Torikaebaya monogatari*," *Monumenta Nipponica* 47, no. 3 (Autumn 1992): 347–68.

36. On this male beauty standard, see Schmidt-Hori, "Nonbinary Genders in *Genji*," 1287–90.

37. Saeko Kimura, *A Brief History of Sexuality in Premodern Japan* (Tallinn University Press, 2010), 46–58. Kimura's reading of *Torikaebaya* reflects a larger distinction made between forms of sexuality at court on the basis of whether or not they produced political power. Because both siblings' first children are illegitimate, for example, they represent a nonproductive form of reproductive sex.

38. Rajyashree Pandey, *Perfumed Sleeves and Tangled Hair: Body, Woman, and Desire in Medieval Japanese Narratives* (University of Hawai'i Press, 2016). The body's outermost extension in such texts could also possess olfactory and auditory dimensions in addition to visual ones.

39. Pflugfelder, "Strange Fates," 353.

40. Chris Mowat et al., "Historicising Trans Pasts: An Introduction," *Gender and History* 36, no. 1 (2024): 3–13. In an Asian context, see also Howard Chiang, "Trans Without Borders: Resisting the Telos of Transgender Knowledge," *Journal of the History of Sexuality* 32, no. 1 (January 2023): 56–65.

41. Michael Stein, *Das "Torikaebaya-monogatari": Übersetzung und Bearbeitung* (In Kommission bei O. Harrassowitz, 1979); Maria Toropygina,

"Torikaebaya monogatari," Ili putanitsa (Hyperion, 2003); Renée Garde, *Si on les échangeait: Le "Genji" travesti* (Les Belles Lettres, 2009); Jésus Carlos Álvarez Crespo, *Si pudiera cambiarlos: "Torikaebaya monogatari"* (Satori Ediciones, 2018).

42. One exception is the philanderer Saishō, who refers to Chūnagon as "she" in the translation when he confuses the son with the daughter he previously impregnated (p. 206).

Preface

THE TRANSLATION is based on the text in Suzuki Hiromichi's *Torikaebaya monogatari no kenkyū*, the Koten bunko edition of the tale, and the Shintenshahan gentenshirizu reprint of the manuscript housed in the Imperial collection. In the reprint of the manuscript, the tale is divided into four books rather than three, but there seems to be no major significance to this difference, and I follow the three-part division of the other two texts. Apart from this, the variations in the texts are minor.

I would like to thank E. Dale Saunders, Barbara Ruch, and Hiroshi Miyaji of the Japanese Division of the Department of Oriental Studies at the University of Pennsylvania for their help and guidance over the years. I also acknowledge my debt to my husband and daughter for their patience and understanding.

R.F.W.

Introduction

A CLASSICAL TALE of unknown date and authorship, *The Changelings* (*Torikaebaya monogatari*) is the story of a brother and sister whose natural inclinations lead them to live as members of the opposite sex. Their difficulties in concealing certain physical attributes and the complications they face in their sexual encounters are fully chronicled. Eventually the hero and heroine take each other's place in society and thus return to their true sexes.

The unusual plot, with its emphasis on the physical, has caused *Torikaebaya monogatari* to be either neglected or maligned during much of its existence. It seems to have circulated for a hundred years or so,[1] and then to have gone unnoticed from the late thirteenth century until relatively modern times. Significantly, there are no printed editions of the tale predating the Meiji period (1867–1902), and of the manuscripts, what few remain are of fairly recent vintage.[2] Such notice as the work did eventually receive focused on its putatively erotic and decadent nature. In 1807, when Ryūtei Tanehiko published a storybook about a female disguised as a male and a male disguised as a female, he explicitly noted in his preface the similarity of his tale to *Torikaebaya monogatari*. By this

[1] On the question of when it was probably written, see pp. 3–4 below.
[2] Suzuki 1973: 363–65.

1

time, apparently, *Torikaebaya monogatari*'s reputation as a piece of erotica was well enough established that Ryūtei could in this way imply that his own story was at least suggestive. This, of course, took place in a period during which fiction and poetry were not taken seriously, no matter what their literary worth. However, even after the scholarly re-evaluation of native literature elevated *The Tale of Genji* and *Tales of Ise* to the status of major classics of literary merit, *Torikaebaya monogatari* remained enshrouded by an aura of indecency and perversion. The only advantage it derived is the questionable one of having been rescued from obscurity to become the subject of attack, occasionally quite vehement, by straitlaced Meiji scholars.

The tale received its first positive and earnest consideration by a modern scholar when Kawabata Yasunari published a translation shortly after the conclusion of the Pacific War. A number of other translations followed, so that the tale became easily accessible to a wider reading audience and first began to be understood for what it was, or, at least, for what it was not, namely an immoral and pornographic production. The renewal of interest culminated in important studies by three Japanese scholars: Morioka Tsuneo (1967), Suzuki Hiromichi (1968, 1973), and Hisamatsu Sen'ichi (1971). Yet these scholars, even at so late a date, appear to have been unable or unwilling to abandon the morality issue. It looms, in fact, as their central concern; all three have sought vigorously to defend the work—to minimize the "decadence" of its theme and to explore not only its literary qualities but its morality, which they have invariably succeeded in finding. Even granting that they have felt obligated in some sense to compensate for the abuse the work took at the hands of their Meiji counterparts, the continued emphasis on the morality issue is unwarranted.

It is clear that morality was not at all a matter of concern to the author or to early readers of *Torikaebaya monogatari*.

Mumyō zōshi, a frame tale believed to have been written sometime between 1196 and 1202 that provides valuable discussions of the literature of the period, contains critiques of two different versions of the tale (see Appendix). In neither critique does the *Mumyō zōshi* author find fault with the basic story line of the sex switch of brother and sister, nor does he criticize either version for a lack of morality. On the contrary, he is at pains to say, of the later of the two versions, "One does not feel it to be an offensive and absurd plot that such a sex reversal occurs." Indeed, his criticism is directed wholly at what he deems to be unrealistic or poorly executed passages, and not at the treatment of unusual matter in and of itself.

The *Mumyō zōshi* commentator's attitude toward the two versions indicates that both were relatively well-known works in his time, and from the inclusion of their poems in poetry anthologies of the period, namely *Shūi hyakuban uta awase* and *Fūyō wakashū*, we may infer that the tale was not only popular, but admired for some of its literary qualities.[3] The relative literary success of *Torikaebaya monogatari* is unusual for a tale belonging to the class of *giko monogatari*, or "tales imitative of the classics," works generally held to be of inferior quality.

HISTORICAL CONTEXT

Placing *Torikaebaya monogatari* in historical context requires a brief presentation of the theories on its dating and authorship. The existence of two versions of the tale, one known simply as *Torikaebaya* and the other as *Ima torikaebaya* (Present-day *Torikaebaya*),[4] exacerbates the dating prob-

---

[3] *Shūi hyakuban uta awase* was compiled by Fujiwara Teika (1162–1241). *Fūyō wakashū*, which dates from 1271, is a collection of over 1,400 poems taken from what are presumed to be post-Heian period *monogatari*, or tales.

[4] The addition of the word *monogatari* to the title was apparently a subsequent development. Other works refer to the older version of the tale as *Ko torikaebaya* (The Old *Torikaebaya*).

lem because, despite numerous studies on the subject, the relationship between the two versions remains unclear, as does the relationship between the extant version and its predecessors. The preferred view, and plainly the most logical, to which even a cursory reading of the *Mumyō zōshi* description tends, is that the extant tale derives directly from, if it is not identical to, *Ima torikaebaya*.

Most attempts to establish ranges of dates for the completion of both the original *Torikaebaya* and *Ima torikaebaya* are based primarily on considerations of the *Mumyō zōshi* commentaries and of poems attributed to the two tales in *Shūi hyakuban uta awase* and *Fūyō wakashū*. There have been analyses of many sorts: of language usage, in terms of both general tone and specific words;[5] of the manners and customs depicted, such as the blackening of teeth and plucking of brows;[6] of the work's place in the history of literary development in general;[7] and of references to the tale in other works, along with the nuances of the terms used in discussing it.[8] Most of these approaches are highly speculative, and none yields very specific or accurate conclusions. Taken collectively, however, they do provide something more than the vague descriptions that were previously used, such as late Heian, late *insei*, or early Kamakura. From these studies, it now appears that the original *Torikaebaya* was written sometime between 1080 and either 1100 or 1105, and *Ima torikaebaya* sometime between 1100 or 1105 and 1170.[9]

[5] See Nomura 1944: 226 on the late-Heian tones of *bai torite* and *hikibai* (both meaning "to snatch") and *sonare* (growing accustomed to some special aspect of nature). See also Takano 1956 on the use of the word *kisaki* (Empress).

[6] Katayori 1938. See also Ikeda 1931: 41.

[7] Fujioka 1974: 280–81.

[8] See Morioka 1967: 493–94 on the term *ima no yo* ("nowadays"), used to describe *Ima torikaebaya* in *Mumyō zōshi*, as compared with the term *kono goro* ("present times"). Suzuki 1973: 288–97 enlarges on this discussion and includes a consideration of the relative meanings of *furuki* ("old") and *mukashi* ("olden day"), terms also used to categorize works of literature in *Mumyō zōshi*.

[9] Suzuki (1973: 299–325), in an attempt to narrow the range of possible years for *Ima torikaebaya*, has proposed 1116 as the earliest probable date, though he freely confesses to considerable uncertainty about his conclusions.

Still more elusive are efforts to draw even the most general conclusions about the work's authorship. Not only have scholars not been able to name any likely candidates; they have yet to agree on the sex of the *Torikaebaya monogatari*'s creator. Meiji scholars tended to argue for a male authorship simply because they found it inconceivable that a court lady could have fashioned so distasteful and degenerate a plot. This argument has now been refuted, however, by Suzuki Hiromichi, who has pointed to several passages from works known to have been written by women in which there is a similar focus on the physical.[10]

Yet the arguments for a female authorship are not all that convincing, either. It is true that *Torikaebaya monogatari* is written in a peculiarly women's style, but the *Mumyō zōshi* criticism of the poor use of language in the original *Torikaebaya* may well suggest that a male not nearly as talented as the author of *Tosa nikki* attempted to imitate women's writing.[11] Since the *Mumyō zōshi* indicates that the style of *Ima torikaebaya* was much improved and the tale purged of its more distasteful and unrealistic sections, it is conceivable that a woman rewrote a work originally written by a man. Yet another possibility is that it was written by a woman who had actually experienced something like the sexual complications of the heroine of the tale. This would account for the blend of masculine and feminine elements in the work, and however bizarre or unrealistic this theory may seem, it cannot be totally ruled out, for *monogatari* very often contain autobiographical elements.

Fortunately, the ambiguities surrounding the dating and authorship of *Torikaebaya monogatari*, though not likely to be resolved in the near future (if ever), do not affect our ability to establish the tale as being solidly within the *giko monogatari*

[10] Suzuki 1973: 326–27.
[11] Hisamatsu 1971: 635. *Tosa nikki*, the earliest extant Japanese diary (936), purports to be the work of a woman but was in fact written by a man—Kino Tsurayuki (868?–945).

tradition. By definition, *giko monogatari* are works written in imitation of Heian-period tales, and most date from the Kamakura period, though some are of later origin. Generally, they are characterized by a high degree of imitation, especially of Murasaki Shikibu's *Tale of Genji*; a lack of originality; a nostalgic and pessimistic tone; and the frequent treatment of the bizarre or the lewd. The decline of the nobility is held responsible for this deterioration of the *monogatari* form. Unlike the new and vital *monogatari* of the Kamakura period, which deal with the warrior class that rose to power during the twelfth and thirteenth centuries, *giko monogatari* continued to be written by and for a declining aristocracy, and thus tend to reflect both in content and in manner of execution the court nobility's ever-growing despondency, escapist bent, and lack of positive energy or creativity.

The aristocracy recalled with nostalgia the period of its greatest prosperity and *The Tale of Genji*, which both depicted that world and marked the height of the *monogatari* as a literary form. *Giko monogatari* thus betray considerable borrowing of the classical language of the Heian period as well as thematic elements from *Genji*. Depictions of Wakamurasaki as a nun or the negative aspects of the somber indecisive Kaoru are particularly popular and very apropos to the mood of the Kamakura nobility. Buddhism, dreams, the desire to retreat from the mundane and real world, are common themes. Love remains an important concern, but more often than not the emphasis is on disappointments in love and a subsequent retirement from the active world. Unfortunately, *giko monogatari* authors on the whole seem to have lacked the range and perception of Lady Murasaki. In contrast to *Genji*'s complex network of multiple themes and the author's skillful handling of numerous characters of varying degrees of importance, most *giko monogatari* have a paucity of themes and characters and a relatively simplistic approach to their development. The

resort to licentious subject matter may well reflect the author's
need to compensate for deficiencies in talent.

Typical of the genre, *Torikaebaya monogatari* has a com-
paratively simple structure; a very limited number of characters; an unusual, in this case sexual, problem as the basis of
its plot development; a nostalgic acceptance of the past as
superior to the degenerate present; and, above all, numerous
elements imitative of *The Tale of Genji*. Its imitativeness is
readily apparent in the clear parallel between its heroine, the
female Chūnagon, and *Genji*'s Kaoru. Among the secondary
characters, Saishō resembles Prince Niou of *Genji*, the Yoshino Prince resembles Prince Hachi, and the Yoshino Princesses resemble the daughters of Prince Hachi. The similarities
between the Uji sections of *The Tale of Genji* and *Torikaebaya
monogatari* could not be more striking, and a considerable
number of other segments possessing specific counterparts
in *Genji* have been distinguished.[12] Some echoes of *The Tale
of Genji* may be secondhand, and it is possible that such
commonly used devices as the forgotten fan or the mistaken
identity in the dark do not have any one particular source.
Occasionally, *Torikaebaya monogatari* betrays the influence
of works that were themselves *giko monogatari* and clearly
patterned after *The Tale of Genji*, notably *Sagoromo monogatari* and *Hamamatsu chūnagon monogatari*.[13] There are
also references and allusions to *saibara*, folk songs popular
during the Heian period, and to an impressive number of tales
and poetry collections.

PROBLEMS OF INTERPRETATION

Torikaebaya monogatari was at least sufficiently successful
in entertaining its medieval readers to secure its survival while

---

[12] See Miyada 1940 for a list.

[13] Suzuki 1971: 356–73 details the many similarities between *Torikaebaya monogatari* and *Sagoromo monogatari*.

most other works of the genre faded into oblivion. It is difficult to determine, however, the reason for its success and the precise view the medieval reader took of the hero's and heroine's sexual problems. The reactions of readers of this translation, only some of whom specialize in Japanese literature, confirmed my suspicion that the modern Western reader tends to interpret *Torikaebaya monogatari* as essentially comic, the role switch being seen as somewhat similar to the common comic device of deliberate disguise as used by Shakespeare in *Twelfth Night*. Of course, the *Torikaebaya monogatari* characters do not simply adopt a disguise temporarily for a specific purpose, but find themselves rather in the more complicated position of being temperamentally more suited to the pursuits of the opposite sex.

In some respects *Torikaebaya monogatari* can certainly be seen to fit the comic mode. Its plot can be seen to reveal the exaggerated absurdity and improbability conducive to comedy. Furthermore, it fits Northrop Frye's description of the "theme of the comic" as "the integration of society, which usually takes the form of incorporating a central character into it."[14] The female Chūnagon needs to be, and ultimately is, incorporated into society, as is her brother, both of whom can be seen to function together as a single hero-heroine entity. The "discovery" that permits the comic resolution is the pair's forced acknowledgment of their true sexes and assumption of their appropriate social roles. Finally, the narrator of *Torikaebaya monogatari* takes the reader fully into his confidence, permitting him to enjoy the irony of the situation in which Saishō constantly approaches the female Chūnagon for help in satisfying his longing for Chūnagon's "sister," Naishi no Kami, whom we know, but Saishō does not, to be a male. To the extent that the role reversal and the different levels of knowledge possessed by the various characters and reader provide an added dimension to otherwise conventional situa-

[14] Frye 1971: 44.

tions, it is even possible to view the work as deliberate parody. And indeed, though there is no readily apparent tone of
general ridicule, the very fact that *Torikaebaya monogatari* is
a *giko monogatari* supports the parody idea.

For all of this, however, there are strong arguments against
the comic view. The *Mumyō zōshi* commentary, our only
evidence of contemporary reaction to the work, betrays no hint
that the sexual deviation at the heart of the tale was considered
absurd or improbable. In fact, sexual problems of the sort
described in *Torikaebaya monogatari* were considered at the
time to be grave maladies, resulting from bad karma and
requiring much earnest prayer. This serious approach to *Torikaebaya monogatari* is reinforced by the emphasis in *Mumyō
zōshi* on the realism of the tale and the qualities of the characters; and the commentator frames his discussions of these
subjects in the same terms as he uses for such undeniably
serious works as *The Tale of Genji*.

The non-comic view is bolstered by the amorphous nature
of genres during the period—the fact that often only the thin-
nest veneer of fiction distinguished *monogatari* from autobiographical forms, and that the motivation behind the creation
of the poetry included in all literary forms in varying abundance was fundamentally autobiographical.[15] Whether or not
this fact will reasonably permit the conclusion that the *Torikaebaya monogatari* story must therefore be autobiographical, or at least biographical, it certainly increases the like-
lihood that the problems arising in the role reversal were
meant to be considered realistic sources of intense emotion.
The poems indeed are, surprisingly often, effective outpour-
ings of love or grief.

This is not to say that *Torikaebaya monogatari* has no comic
elements or even that a largely comic reading of the tale is
impossible. It seems clear that a certain amount of humorous
treatment was intentional, designed to enhance by contrast the

[15] See Cranston 1969: 90–129, for an interesting discussion of Japanese genres.

emotion-laden episodes, those moments of pathos, as when mother and child separate, that are generally the focal points of *monogatari*. But where modern Western and medieval readings are likely to differ, a general awareness of possible medieval interpretations of the tale permits an intelligent balancing of the competing views.

Whether one ultimately opts for an essentially comic or for a serious interpretation does not affect the pleasurable reading experience afforded by *Torikaebaya monogatari*. Not only does the tale raise intriguing questions for the student of classical Japan interested as much in its social fabric, mores, and ideologies as in its literary arts; it also provides even the most casual reader with a surprisingly fluid, logical, and entertaining narrative. That the work is relatively simple in structure, particularly when set against the complexity and psychological acuity of the overshadowing *Tale of Genji*, does not at all detract from its effectiveness, but rather lends it a certain considerable charm, a directness, and an uncluttered air.

The Changelings

Book One

ONCE, we know not when, there was a man called Sadaijin who served as both Acting Major Counsellor and General.[1] He was altogether remarkable in features, learning, attitude, character, and reputation. Nor were his circumstances such as to bring him any dissatisfaction. Yet he was constantly plagued by a secret grief.

Sadaijin had two wives. One belonged to the Minamoto family and was the daughter of a Minister of State. Though he felt no great love for her, he did think of her affectionately, for she was the first to whom he had pledged his troth. Further, she had given birth to a peerless son, radiant as a jewel, and this made it especially difficult to part from her.

Sadaijin's other wife was the daughter of a Middle Counsellor of the Fujiwara family, and she had given birth to a most beautiful daughter. Both son and daughter were rare and ideal children, and Sadaijin spared no effort in their upbringing.

Neither wife was particularly charming. Both failed to meet

---

[1] A Gondainagon and a Daishō. Whenever possible I follow Reischauer 1937: 87–105 for titles of rank. Though the man is not here called the Sadaijin (Minister of the Left), I use that title as his name, since that is the rank to which he eventually rises and the title by which he is known throughout most of the tale. I will similarly anticipate titles for other major characters in the interest of providing one name for each person, rather than follow the original in changing the characters' names every time they are promoted.

Sadaijin's ideal, and he regretted this. But now with both son
and daughter growing up so nicely he found it difficult to forsake either wife and could not help feeling an attachment for
them.

Both children had exquisite features, and looked so much
alike that one could easily be mistaken for the other. It was,
in fact, fortunate that they were brought up separately,[2] for
there would have been problems had they been raised together. Their faces, identical for the most part, differed only
in that the boy's revealed a certain elegance; he was endowed
with a refined and noble look. The girl had a bright and proud
countenance, infinitely attractive. Its charm touched all about
her. To this day their features have never been equaled.

As the children matured, the boy became surprisingly shy.
Not only did he avoid the eyes of any lady-in-waiting who was
the least unfamiliar to him, but he even felt ill at ease and
embarrassed in the presence of his father. At length, his father
put him to the study of letters[3] and taught him appropriate
subjects, but the boy, in his embarrassment, could not fix his
attention on any of them. Always hidden behind curtains,[4] he
painted, played with dolls, and was absorbed with such games
as matching seashells.[5] His father, astonished at such proclivities, constantly criticized him, until finally the wretched and
intimidated boy was reduced to tears. After that he was seen
only by his mother and his wet nurse or extremely young

[2] Each mother lived with her child in a separate pavilion.

[3] *Onfumi*, more specifically, the study of Chinese classics.

[4] *Michō*, also known as *kichō*, movable partition curtains behind which women
sat when receiving visitors. Generally they were about three or four feet tall and six
or eight feet wide. For a detailed description, see Ikeda 1967: 160–61.

[5] All of these were amusements for girls. *Hiina asobi*, translated as "played with
dolls," was the precursor of the doll's festival on the third of March; it entailed the
making of dollhouses with various furnishings for small paper dolls. See Ikeda 1967:
546–47. The game *kaiooi*, another indoor pursuit for girls, evolved from *kai awase*,
the matching of shells. In both, the shells, which had pictures painted on them, were
divided into two groups, and the point was to pair up shells from each group. The
girl who matched up the greatest number of shells won. For a detailed description
of the game and its rules, see *Seikai dai hyakka jiten*, 4: 421.

children. When ladies-in-waiting with whom he was not so familiar came near him, the excessively shy boy clung fast to the curtain screening him. Sadaijin found this most peculiar and upsetting.

On the other hand, the daughter was already quite mischievous by this time and was outside constantly playing kickball and shooting arrows[6] with the young male attendants. When guests came to the reception hall[7] to compose poems,[8] play flutes, and sing songs, the girl rushed to join them, and ably played the koto and flute with them, though she had not been taught the art of either. She recited Chinese-style poems and sang songs. The courtiers and noblemen who visited the mansion admired her and treated her with affection, and they became her teachers.[9] They were all of the same mind, musing that though they had heard the child was a girl, they must have been misinformed. Of course, when she met with her father she was more restrained and did not display her unladylike behavior. But while her father was dressing or attending to some guest, she would promptly join the rest of the men and lark about with them quite as she pleased. At such times it was impossible to control her, and so her companions simply assumed she was a boy. They took such pleasure in her company, becoming as fond of her as she was of them, that her father

[6] These are male pursuits. The ball kicked in the popular game *mari*, or *kemari* as it is more commonly known, was somewhat like a football. The men stood in a circle and attempted to keep the ball from touching the ground. "Shooting arrows" translates *koyumi*, small arched bows.

[7] The *shinden*, or main building of a nobleman's mansion, was divided into three areas. The *sunoko*, an open veranda built of narrow boards, surrounded the building on all four sides. In the center, a significant portion was given over to the *moya*, part of which was used as a sleeping area. The long, narrow areas between the *sunoko* and the *moya* were called *hisashi*; the floors of these areas were higher than the veranda level but lower than the *moya* level. The reception hall, or *on'idei*, referred to here was a portion of the *hisashi* set up for the reception of guests. For a discussion of these structural features, see Ikeda 1967: 146–58.

[8] *Fumi tsukuri*, which refers to the composition of Chinese poems.

[9] "Courtiers" translates *tenjōbito*, officers of the fourth, fifth, and sixth ranks who had the right of entrée into the inner court. "Noblemen" translates *kandachime*, another term for *kugyō*, officers of the third rank and above or Imperial advisors of the fourth rank.

let them go on thinking as they did. Within his heart, of course, Sadaijin was sad. "If only I could exchange them," he mused, "my son for the daughter and my daughter for the son."

Despite this recurring thought, Sadaijin tried to console himself, for the children were still young and would probably soon revert in good time to the behavior of their own sexes. In the meantime, things continued as they were. Finally the children passed the age of ten, but their deportment remained unchanged. As the years passed, Sadaijin wondered what could be done, but all he could do was grieve. He waited for the children to become aware of their abnormality, but as the months and years went by and he realized that they would doubtlessly not return to normal, he felt the situation to be even more unusual and unprecedented.

Because of Sadaijin's important position, it was unseemly for him to philander about as he had once tended to do, and so he had a spacious mansion built and settled himself and his family into it. He installed one wife in the Western Pavilion and the other in the Eastern.[10] He himself took up residence in the lavish main hall. What a pity, though, that neither of his wives was the kind of woman he would have liked to be married to. So that neither would be jealous of the other, he spent fifteen days a month with each.[11]

Hereafter I shall refer to the children as the others had come mistakenly to do; the son I shall call the daughter, and the daughter the son.[12]

[10] The nobleman's mansion consisted of several buildings connected to each other by long covered corridors. In the center, facing south onto a landscaped garden, was the main building. The *nishi no tai* and *higashi no tai* were pavilions located respectively to the west and east of the main building. There was a building to the north, usually occupied by the principal wife, and to the rear of this, the servants' quarters. Other buildings might be added as needed to the north of the original complex. For a diagram of the layout of pavilions and garden, see Ikeda 1967: 147.

[11] The reference here is to the lunar month, the idea being that since the months had thirty days, Sadaijin would spend the same amount of time with each wife and show no favoritism.

[12] The reader is cautioned to take note of this author's aside, because the switch in terminology can make for difficult reading in the early going, where no names are

One tranquil spring day during a period of ritual abstinence,[13] Sadaijin went to visit his daughter in the calm of midday. Behind her curtains as usual, she was passing the time
quietly playing the thirteen-stringed koto.[14] Her ladies-in-
waiting were clustered here and there, playing *go*, backgammon, and other games;[15] they looked very bored.

"Why do you stay buried indoors like this?," Sadaijin exclaimed, pushing aside the curtain-screen. "Go and see the
beauty of the flowers in bloom! Your ladies seem terribly bored
and peculiarly dreary."

Because of the length of her hair, which exceeded her height
by seven or eight inches as she reclined on the inner platform,[16]
the girl suggested an autumnal scene with luxuriant pampas
grass. Her delicately trailing hair was not as magnificent as
that described in the old tales as "the unfolding of a fan,"[17]
but certainly it was attractive. Sadaijin looked at her thinking
that even the Shining Princess of old was probably not so
lovely and beautiful as this child, and his eyes filled with
tears.[18] He approached the child. "How does it happen that

---

used. A passage like this one, from p. 19, "it doesn't look as though I can forcibly
turn him back into a girl," can be pretty baffling unless the change is kept firmly in
mind.

[13] *Monoimi*, a period of abstinence undertaken as a means of purification before
praying to the gods for protection following some evil omen, astrological warning,
strange occurrence, or the like. During this period the person was confined to the
home. For more on abstinences and taboos generally, see Morris 1969: 107–8,
136–43. See also Frank 1958.

[14] The *sō no koto*.

[15] "Backgammon" translates *suguroku*, a gambling game; considered less elegant
than *go*.

[16] The measure used, *sun*, was roughly one and one-half inches; thus her hair was
actually closer to ten inches longer than her reclining height. The inner platform, *yuka*
or *hamayuka*, was a raised section of the room used as a bedroom. It stood about
20 inches above the *moya* (see note 7) and was surrounded by curtains.

[17] This probably refers to old *monogatari* in general, but it also refers specifically
to a passage in the Wakamurasaki chapter of *The Tale of Genji*: "Her hair, thick and
wavy, stood out fanwise about her head." (Translation from Waley 1960: 84.)

[18] The Shining Princess is the central character of the mid-tenth-century *Taketori
monogatari* (Tale of the Bamboo Cutter). It is the story of Princess Kaguya, who was
born inside a bamboo shoot and raised by an old woodcutter and his wife. The Princess
brings her adopted parents fortune, rejects a series of suitors because they fail in the
tasks she sets for them, and finally is recalled to the moon, whence she came.

you have become so beautiful?," he murmured, and with tears in his eyes, he began combing her hair. Looking embarrassed and distressed, the girl broke into perspiration, and her face glowed the color of pink plum blossoms. She looked on the verge of tears and seemed to be in such great distress that her father wept even more as he gazed at her tenderly, all other thoughts gone from his mind.

Sadaijin's daughter was reluctant to use cosmetics, and so did not wear any. Yet her complexion was as beautiful naturally as if it had been deliberately made up; and her side locks, dampened by perspiration, fell in a cascade of curls, as if someone had set them. She was lovely and charming. A too liberal use of white powder is unbecoming; her appearance was perfect without it. Though only twelve years old, in her development she was neither backward nor inferior to others in anything. She was tall and slender,[19] and infinitely captivating. Her appearance was set off to advantage by the pale and subdued pattern of the luxurious silk robe[20] she wore over six delicate layers of white underrobes lined in pale violet. She was elegant from the tips of her sleeves to the hem of her robe.

"How sad! Shall I bring her up carefully to become a nun and let her devote herself to religion?," mused Sadaijin, gazing at her. His tears of sorrow clouded his heart with sadness.

> What were they like,
> My sins[21] of olden days,
> Those sources of my pain?
> Even as I wonder,
> This life's grief grows greater still.

When next Sadaijin visited the Western Pavilion, the won-

---

[19] This description is of her stature while seated.

[20] *Uchigi*, an everyday robe worn indoors. For a discussion of the changes in these robes over the years and their variety, see Ikeda 1967: 217–19.

[21] *Tsumi*. Though I use "sins" for lack of a better word, that term does not accurately express the complex meaning here, where *tsumi* is used in the Buddhist sense and implies retribution for transgressions in former lives.

derful and clear sounds of a flute greeted him. As he heard the
lilting notes echoing in the skies, Sadaijin's heart grew restless
and uneasy. He realized that this child too, like the other, was
not normal. Once again he was thrown into confusion. But he
assumed a casual air as he peeped in at his son, who respectfully
sat upright and laid his flute aside. Over robes of various
colors,[22] he was wearing a pale green brocade hunting outfit
lined in light blue, with violet brocade trousers lined in red.
His face was round, his complexion extraordinarily beautiful,
and his eyes lovely. His radiance filled the air all about. It was
as though his charm overflowed right down to the hem of his
trousers. When Sadaijin saw this beauty, so stunning that he
could not tear his eyes away from the lad, he was so moved
that the tears he had shed and his grief were both forgotten,
and despite himself he smiled slightly.

But then he became despondent again. "Oh, how sad! If he
had been carefully brought up as the girl he really is, how
splendid and beautiful he would be!"

This child's hair was not so long as the other's. It fell just
slightly short of his seated height, with its ends like the "unfolding of a fan." Each time Sadaijin saw this hair and all this
beauty, he could not help smiling. Yet his heart was dark with
sorrow. There were so many fine young boys all around,
playing *go* and backgammon, laughing gaily, and amusing
themselves with ball games and bows and arrows. It was all
very strange!

"How dreadful! But should the child remain like this? There
wasn't anything I could do earlier, and it doesn't look as
though I can forcibly turn him back into a girl now that things
have gone so far. It may be best to let him become a priest—to
have him stay clear of people and devote himself to the life
hereafter."

His children probably entertained no such thoughts.

[22] *Sakura*, white underlined with light violet, and *yamabuki*, pale yellowish-brown
underlined with yellow. This description is meant to contrast his colorful appearance
with the subdued impression given by his sister.

"Since it is their fate to be the way they are, perhaps something will turn up for them. It's meaningless to have both of them forsake the world to no purpose and take holy vows if they're not entirely devoted to such a resolve," thought the distressed Sadaijin. Again he realized how cruel and unparalleled the situation was.

A child of this sort, it would seem, would naturally lack self-discipline. Sadaijin's son, however, was splendid. From this time on, he showed great promise and excellent ability as a scholar;[23] he was growing up to be a future advisor to the throne. His koto and flute resounded extraordinarily sweetly throughout heaven and earth. For those who listened to his voice as he chanted sutras, songs, and poems,[24] truly once again "the handle of the ax would rot and one would even forget one's birthplace."[25] There was absolutely nothing in which he was in the least deficient. Yet his confusion in the one matter of his sexual identity seemed deplorable to his father.

In time it became widely known that Sadaijin's son was outstanding in both abilities and appearance. The Emperor and the Imperial Prince found it most surprising that though he excelled in every way, he had not yet been presented at court[26] and did not socialize there. Again and again they asked Sadaijin to send his son to court, but Sadaijin, feeling more and more despondent, and worried about what the Emperor and the Prince might think, responded that his son was still

[23] *Zae.* The emphasis is on Chinese studies.

[24] *Shi* refers exclusively to Chinese poetry.

[25] The reference is to the legend known as *Ranka*, which is recorded in such works as *Jutsuiki*, a collection of curious tales whose themes are derived from Chinese collections of a similar nature. A woodcutter named Ōshitsu, stopping to watch some children playing *go* and singing, so forgot himself that he lost all track of time. By the time he recovered himself, the handle of his ax had rotted away, and when he got home, no one he had known was there any longer.

[26] That is, he was not permitted to enter either the Shishinden, the building in the Emperor's residential compound in which official business was conducted, or the Seiryōden, the Emperor's private residence to the northwest of it.

a child and could not be presented. The Emperor thought that
the father was probably just being modest, not wanting to
show off his child. He insisted on conferring as high a grade
as the fifth rank on the child, and time and again he requested
that the manhood ceremonies be held, that the boy be dressed
as an adult and prepared to come to court. In the circumstances, what was Sadaijin to say? There was no way he could
avoid sending him. Since things were as they were, he resigned
himself to the reversal of the children's sexes. It was apparently the result of sins in their previous lives. He was convinced that the children were fated to behave as they did, even
if it was in this confused manner. And so that year he hastily
prepared for the coming-of-age ceremonies for both son and
daughter.[27]

When the day for the ceremonies arrived, Sadaijin's mansion
was splendidly decorated. His daughter was present with her
mother. The girl's grandfather, of course, tied the sash.[28] It
was unusual to have so simple a ceremony, but not surprisingly, Sadaijin felt uneasy before others. Outsiders hearing
about the event—since the children's predicament would
never have occurred to them—understood simply that they
had mistaken the boy for the girl and the girl for the boy, that
they had got things the wrong way around. The few who
knew the situation well kept it quiet, for it was not something
they wanted to talk about. As a result, on the whole, no one
in society knew about it, and this was most satisfactory.

Udaijin, Sadaijin's elder brother, was the one who placed
the headgear on the boy at his ceremony.[29] With his hair done

[27] There were separate ceremonies for boys and girls. The girls', called the *mogi*,
could be held at anywhere from twelve to fifteen years of age; on this occasion the
girl donned a train for the first time. The *gempuku*, the ceremony marking a boy's
initiation into adulthood, usually took place around his twelfth or thirteenth year.
For details on both ceremonies, see Nakamura 1965: 125–49; and Fujiki 1960:
206–8.
[28] A ritual part of the *mogi* ceremony.
[29] That is, the headgear worn by nobles in full court dress. As with the tying of

up for the occasion, those who had known him before found
that the boy looked quite different; his beauty was greater
still. His appearance was unequaled in all the world. It was
natural that Udaijin should admire him. This nobleman had
daughters only—four of them. The eldest was the Emperor's
concubine and the second, the concubine of the Imperial
Prince. Since nothing had been arranged for his third and
fourth daughters, he would certainly have liked to see one
married to Sadaijin's son.

The congratulatory gifts brought and sent for the occasion
included every conceivable item of incomparable beauty.

Because Sadaijin's son, Chūnagon, had received the grade
of fifth rank as a child, he was called Tayū.[30] But before long,
when the new appointments were announced that fall, he
became a Chamberlain.[31] All the people at court, from the
Emperor and the Imperial Prince to the lowliest gentlemen
and ladies, who had so much as glanced at this boy felt they
would never tire of looking at him, so exquisite was he. Since
he was the child of one so noble as Sadaijin, it seemed natural
that the Emperor and the Imperial Prince would love him like
no other. In the music he produced from the koto and flute,
in the compositions he wrote, in the art of poetry, even in his
light and dexterous handling of the brush, he was beyond
compare. His features, of course, and his beautiful manners
as he mingled in society from this time onward were ideal. He
was clever in his perception of the state of the world and the
affairs of noblemen. In each and every way he so excelled that
he did not seem of this world. Sadaijin finally became resigned
to it all, feeling that it was surely fated for his son to excel even

---

the sash for the girl, the placing of the headgear on the boy's head for the first time
was a ritual part of the coming-of-age ceremony.

[30] Tayū designates the fifth rank. In the interest of clarity, I introduce the name
Chūnagon (Middle Counsellor) here for the boy, though he does not attain this rank
for some time to come. (See note 2.)

[31] Jijū, an official in the Nakatsukashō (Ministry of Central Affairs). The *tsu-kasameshi* ceremony, the appointment of new officials by the court, was held twice
a year, at the beginning of spring and fall.

though he was actually a girl. The situation could not be
altered. So gradually he consoled himself, thinking only of the
joyous and beautiful ways in which his child excelled as a
male.

While the boy was still young he did not understand much
about his body. Satisfied that there were surely others like him,
he continued to conduct himself as he chose. Gradually, however, he learned about other people, and after much thought
came to realize that he was very different. Even so, though he
thought much on the subject, there was nothing he could do.
He grieved, asking himself why he was unusual and different
from others. He restrained himself, kept his distance from the
other men, and was somber. His reticence when mingling in
society was admirable.

At that time the Emperor was in his forties and most prepos-
sessing. The Imperial Prince was twenty-seven or twenty-eight,
and was of dignified and regal mien. Both had heard that
Chūnagon's sister was lovely and held in high repute, and they
earnestly requested that she be presented at court. Her father
put them off on the pretext that his daughter was hopelessly
shy, and dismissed the notion from his mind. But he was
terribly upset, hoping against hope that somehow she might
actually serve the Emperor and Prince.

The Emperor had one daughter, whose mother, the Empress, had died. In his affection and anxiety for her, he brought
her up with great care, never letting her out of his sight. Neither
the Emperor nor the Prince had had a son, a very grave matter;
and both had prayers said ceaselessly. Udaijin's eldest daughter was very dear to the Emperor, but because she was not the
daughter of a Regent or Chancellor,[32] she could not become
Empress. Night after night the Emperor worried about his
daughter. Since Chūnagon was becoming so beautiful that he
seemed not to be of this world, the Emperor considered

---

[32] Sesshō, a Regent for an Emperor during his minority; Kampaku, a chief advisor
to the throne.

making him the Princess's companion and having him look after her. Every time the Emperor saw Chūnagon, his eye was drawn to him particularly. Perhaps because the Princess's attendants had tended to spoil her, she was still very young and innocent. The Emperor therefore felt that Chūnagon, accustomed as he was to being with his lovely sister, would probably find the Princess not to his fancy. Since Chūnagon was not yet in a position of importance, the Emperor thought he would wait and consider the idea when the youth's position was more elevated.[33]

It somehow came to Sadaijin's ears that the Emperor was considering this, and he was alarmed. If only, he thought, the situation were not what it was, what an honor and joy this would be. Regretful and wretched, he nonetheless received the news with a faint smile.

Chūnagon was intelligent and even though young, he was fine and seemly. Whenever the ladies-in-waiting saw him at court, they became self-conscious, and deliberately tried to attract his attention so as to somehow elicit a word from him. Chūnagon realized he was unusual, but having adopted the male role, he could not hide. He had no choice but to mingle with the court. Yet why would he be attracted to ladies-in-waiting? He therefore acted with the utmost sobriety and calm, and many a forlorn lady was the result.

At that time the Emperor's uncle, known as the Minister of Ceremonies,[34] had an only child, Saishō. Chūnagon's senior by only two years, Saishō was of course not so handsome, but compared with the average man he was most refined and elegant. He was an unparalleled gallant. Slender and graceful, he was interested in every woman he saw. He fervently wished that somehow he might win both Sadaijin's daughter and Udaijin's fourth child, both widely acclaimed for their beauty.

---

[33] Another interpretation of this sentence is possible: "Since his daughter was not of significant stature, he thought he would wait and consider the idea when she grew to be more impressive."

[34] Shikibukyō.

While his suits were being presented through the appropriate
go-betweens, he wrote passionate letters and was racked with
impatience and worry. But in view of his fickleness, both girls,
thinking that the exchange of even a single word might be un-
propitious, shunned him, and neither replied. Saishō grieved
bitterly.

In the meantime Chūnagon remained very serious. Nothing
excited him. He was subdued and seemed dejected. Yet every
time Saishō saw him, so handsome, so pervasively charming
and beautiful, he yearned for a woman comparable to this
man. He imagined that Chūnagon's sister would no doubt be
like him, and indeed as a woman all the more lovely. He had
to see her. In his misery he spoke frequently with Chūnagon,
and overcome with feeling, he would weep bitterly without
concealing his tears. His face then surpassed all others and
was truly beautiful. The sympathetic Chūnagon spoke with
him more affectionately than with others, but he could not be
entirely frank and candid. Each time Saishō spoke of his sister,
the distressed Chūnagon, quite aware that the girl was unusual, kept his guard up, becoming taciturn and unresponsive.
Saishō was resentful and brooded without concealing his
tears. Each time Chūnagon saw this distress in Saishō he
wanted to reply:

> I know a sorrow
> Unmatched by any other,
> But does this sorrow
> Flood my eyes like yours with tears
> That stream down upon my face?

But then Saishō would probably ask what he meant. Since
there would be no way to reply, Chūnagon treated him coldly
and resolutely withdrew.

While all this was going on, the Emperor had been ill for
some time. Thinking it proper to abdicate, and feeling that
there must have been precedents in olden days for his actions,

he gave up his throne to the Prince and appointed his daughter Crown Princess; he himself went into retirement at the Suzaku-in.[35] Chūnagon's grandfather had now reached the age of seventy, and believing himself gravely ill, he took the tonsure. Sadaijin then became the Minister of the Left and Regent. Chūnagon, promoted in turn to peership with the third rank, became Middle Captain.[36]

Udaijin was disappointed that his eldest daughter, the Emperor's concubine, had been unable to rise to the position of Empress. Since he could hope for nothing better, he decided to take Chūnagon as his youngest daughter's husband: he was of exceptional character, and there was no hint of his being the least bit fickle or frivolous. When Udaijin spoke of this to Chūnagon's father, Sadaijin thought it ludicrous. But he despaired of getting across to Udaijin how unlikely it was that such a marriage could succeed, and so he consented. "For some reason the boy doesn't seem in the least to have awakened sexually," he said. "But anyone can plainly see that he is an earnest lad."

When Sadaijin told his wife, she said: "The innocent girl will not find fault with his strangeness. We will have him visit her, and they will simply talk together and behave like a normal couple in public. He will make a good guardian for her," she added, laughing.

Chūnagon's parents were uneasy because he was still so young, but since it was appropriate for him not to have to visit the girl yet, they were reassured and had him write a letter to her. Chūnagon had no understanding of such matters, but in the company of his male companions he was accustomed to constantly hearing tales of love. So thinking this to be a love letter, he wrote:

[35]Suzaku-in is both the Cloistered Emperor's name and the name of his residence. The reference to a precedent above probably has to do with the appointment of the daughter as Crown Princess.
[36]Chūjō.

Is this then love's path,
Entangled and bewildering,
Painful and dark?
Embarking at the mountain's foot,
How clearly do I go astray![37]

His handwriting was indescribably beautiful. Considering his youth, his parents wondered how he had written so well. They were moved, and their eyes filled with tears. Since Udaijin had persuaded Sadaijin to take this action, he urged his daughter to reply and, with some difficulty, made her do so:

Which path will you take
From the foot of these mountains?
Will you go astray?
I too know not which way to go,
To the mountains here or there.[38]

Chūnagon sent a stream of letters after this, and since it was Udaijin who had promoted the marriage, he set the wedding day. A noble and well-intentioned man, Udaijin was taking Chūnagon, a Middle Captain of the third rank, as husband for his daughter, who had been brought up with exceptional care. Under these circumstances, the ceremony was not to be commonplace, merely passable, in any respect. The Major Counsellor died at that time, and Chūnagon was promoted and made Acting Middle Counsellor and Head of the Left Guards.[39] He was handsomer than ever, more than the word splendid can describe.

Saishō, promoted along with Chūnagon, became a Minister

[37]The theme of this poem is taken from a poem in the *Kokin waka rokujō*, IV, Love, no. 9 (*KKT*, 9: 394): "To the newcomer / Who enters deep within, / The Mountain of Love, / How bewildering it is, / How easy to lose one's way." Both Chūnagon's poem and Yon no Kimi's response, "Which path will you take," appear in the *Fūyō wakashū*, Love I (*ZGR*, 14: 57); and in the *Shūi hyakuban uta awase*, Right, no. 84 (*Gunshō ruijū*, XI: 304).

[38] That is, since your heart may stray to others, I do not know what to do.

[39] Gonchūnagon; Saemon no Kami, head of the Left Division of the Outer Palace Guards.

of State. But hearing that one of the ladies to whom he had given his heart, Udaijin's fourth daughter, Yon no Kimi, was inconstant as the fickle smoke of the salt furnaces,[40] he pretended not to know about the joyous occasion.[41] When he happened to meet Chūnagon, he was somewhat withdrawn, as if overcome with grief. Chūnagon wondered with amusement why Yon no Kimi rejected Saishō, who loved her so, for him.

Chūnagon was sixteen years old, Yon no Kimi nineteen. She was immature in neither mind nor body. For all her tender years, she was satisfactory in every way, as lovely as one could wish. Her parents were more partial to her than to her sisters. This made her proud; and she felt in her heart that the highest position of Empress ought to be hers. She was thus terribly disappointed, and though she did not let it show, inwardly she sorrowed, "I never thought I should grieve so."[42] But Chūnagon was very handsome and his behavior pleasing; he unfailingly spoke to her with real affection as their familiarity grew, and she came not to scorn him. Under the same bed robe,[43] they appeared to join in intimacy; no one fully knew that a single barrier remained between them, and that their union was not consummated. Chūnagon did not conspicuously hover affectionately about her in the vulgar fashion of the day. Theirs seemed to be a lovely and pleasing relationship.

It seemed to Udaijin, however, that Chūnagon was not, as he had thought him to be, so contented that he would never weary of Yon no Kimi. Yet Udaijin did not blame him. "Since

---

[40] This is a reference to a poem in the *Kokin wakashū*, XIV, Love IV, no. 708, Anonymous (*NKBT*, 8: 242): "They are boiling salt, / The maidens of Suma. / The smoke is blown by the wind. / It swirls about, trailing / In unexpected places."

[41] The joyous occasion may refer either to Chūnagon's promotion or to his marriage, probably the former.

[42] The phrase used here may have alluded to a poem, but this is uncertain.

[43] *Yoru no koromo*, a large kimono that was not worn, but draped over a couple when they slept.

he is still very young, his attitude will surely change," he reasoned to himself. "Still he seems to feel a certain reserve for some reason." And he treated Chūnagon with the greatest affection. Besides, it never occurred to the youth even to dream of philandering. Other than visiting his father's residence or taking part in the musical entertainments at the Imperial Palace, he never absented himself from his wife at night. But four or five days each month he was unable to conceal the strange ailment about which he could do nothing.[44] "I am afflicted by evil spirits," he would say, as he secretly went off to his wet nurse's village to hide. This worried people, who wondered what it was all about.

On the fifteenth day of the ninth month, when the moon shone brightly, Chūnagon, having been in attendance at a court concert, was on night duty. The Emperor's concubine, Umetsubo,[45] was to go to the Emperor's rooms that night. Though Chūnagon did not especially want to see her, he nonetheless concealed himself by the wall leading to the ladies' quarters[46] and looked on. The late night moon lit every nook and cranny. A lady carrying a lamp came out, her gauze-like outer garment transparent over thick underrobes, her hair beautifully cascading over it. All the ladies-in-waiting looked lovely, their gauze cloaks over lustrous robes flung loosely over their shoulders, reminding Chūnagon of the sky as it just then shimmered with moonglow. It was graceful and beautiful the way the ladies went to wait upon the Emperor, elegantly holding up their portable screens. "If only my heart and body were normal!," thought Chūnagon in dismay. "I would surely have access to the Emperor's rooms like this. How absurd! It seems unreal that I should show my face and mingle in society as the male I am not."

[44] His menstrual period.

[45] Udaijin's second daughter, earlier described as the then Imperial Prince's concubine.

[46] The Fujitsubo, north of the Seiryōden and west of the Kokiden, one of the five residences in which the Empress and the Imperial concubines lived.

Were I the moon,
Thus would I brilliant shine
Over the clouds.[47]
Oh what sad fate is this
That it may not be so!

"Ill-fated indeed. If only my sister had been like other girls and mingled like this, all would have been fine. Had that been the case, I might have assuaged my own grief about myself by looking after her when she visited the Emperor."

He went on alone, pondering his problem, wanting to leave this place and lose himself deep in some mountain. Thus for some time his eyes followed Umetsubo, and as he continued to think on these things, his voice rose up, lovely and clear, and he sang out "Moon of the Hōrai Grotto."[48]

Saishō too had been in attendance at the evening concert. Still ardently pining for Chūnagon's sister, he wanted to see the incomparably handsome brother and reproach him for not acting as go-between. Though as usual that would be in vain, he thought a meeting might comfort him. When the concert was over he did not leave, but went in search of Chūnagon who, he supposed, had hidden himself away in some corner. It was then he heard a voice that left him bewildered. Looking to the spot where it came from, he saw Chūnagon, who appeared very small in the lustrous patterned magenta silk cloak that he wore hanging loosely from his shoulder over his trousers. But he looked youthful and handsome and so fine that he was radiant in the moonlight. His bearing showed him to be more depressed than usual. His sleeve, wet with tears, exuded an extraordinary perfume, different from the usual. He looked most attractive to the man gazing at him.

---

[47] "Over the clouds" was a common metaphor for the Imperial Palace.

[48] This is from the *Wakan rōeishū*, I, Autumn, Chrysanthemum, no. 271, Kansambon [Sugawara no Fumitoki] (*NKBT*, 73: 116): "It is after the purple orchids in the orchid garden have swayed in the storm. / The frost glistens in the moonlight at Hōrai Grotto." Hōrai Grotto, the name of a place where a Taoist hermit lived, is here meant to refer to the Imperial Palace.

"No woman could listen unmoved were he to speak but one word to her," thought Saishō, feeling more envious and ashamed of his own appearance than ever. But he stopped Chūnagon nonetheless and voiced his grievances about his hopeless love.

Saishō's captivating and delicate beauty was not without charm for Chūnagon even then. From the start the two had not spoken familiarly with one another on anything. But even in his excessive reticence, Chūnagon was moved and found it hard to dismiss Saishō.

"You keep saying these things about my sister, but as pretty as the words may be on the surface, I am afraid that, like the dayflowers, you are easily changeable.[49] At times I do feel sorry for you, but I can't let my own feelings influence my judgment. It's pointless and sad for you to be at me about it constantly." Distressed at the situation and at the feelings he had experienced earlier, Chūnagon was most depressed.

"What can be bothering him that he, in a position in which he would seem unlikely to feel this way, should grieve constantly?," Saishō wondered as he eyed him. "He keeps behaving so terribly seriously. That too must come from some real concern. I haven't heard that his wife is deficient in any way. He's doubtless grown accustomed to her. Might he be distressed over something else, some other lady? Could it be about the recent matter of the Crown Princess? Even so, for someone like him, that wouldn't present any difficulties. Oh, such a reserved man is so pitiful!"

Saishō considered the situation from every possible angle, hoping to fathom what was troubling Chūnagon. "I would search your thoughts and grant your wishes though it meant putting myself in your place. But you refuse to confide in me," Saishō said reproachfully.

"But you're not me. If we discussed the problem, you'd

[49] This is an allusion to a poem in the *Kokin waka rokujō*, VI, Dayflowers, no. 301 (*KKT*, 9: 562): "The hearts of men, / Those who in this world dwell, / Fickle are they; / As readily do they change / As the dayflower its color."

probably consider it something that could be easily solved, a
matter of faithless love," said Chūnagon, smiling, at a loss for
a response.

> Though no special care
> Gives me cause to worry,
> Each time I see the moon,
> I wonder how long this pain will last,
> And sadness fills my heart.

His voice was radiantly beautiful. Flooded with tenderness
for him, Saishō wept profusely, as was fashionable in those
days.

> Oh so true it is,
> In this inconstant world
> Nothing stays the same.
> Why then forever fret,
> Ever buried in your cares?

"If I found out that your sister definitely would not have me,
I would want to lose myself deep in the mountains, for I am
always aware of my great sinfulness," [50] said Saishō, speaking
of his feelings.

"When you do decide to leave the world, don't leave me
behind!," replied Chūnagon. "As the months and years go by,
I am more and more convinced that I would not like to go on
somehow living this way, but I still can't resolve on quitting
the world."

They spoke sadly throughout the night, and when it grew
light they both left the palace. "In many ways Chūnagon is
magnificent; I would especially like to see his refinement in a
woman. How beautiful she would be!," thought Saishō, and

---

[50] Here I follow the suggestion of Professor Tsutomu Kakimoto of the University
of Osaka in reading the phrase in the negative and as referring to never seeing the
sister. A more common interpretation reads: "If once I had ascertained what it is that
is troubling you, I would want to lose myself . . ."

in sensing his own affection for Chūnagon he dreamt even more of the sister. He yearned with all his heart for her, but when it seemed that the girl would not accept his love, he wondered sadly what to do.

Now, at this time the Cloistered Emperor was living apart from his daughter, the Crown Princess, and so was unable to be near her and look after her. No one about her seemed reliable or trustworthy, not even her wet nurse. The Princess herself was weak and childish. As a result, the Cloistered Emperor was most anxious and worried about her. He had heard that Sadaijin had abandoned all thought of taking a husband for his daughter or of presenting her at court, and so wanted very much to have her become the Princess's guardian. Sadaijin came to court, and while he and the Cloistered Emperor were speaking at length on a variety of matters, the Emperor asked: "What have you decided about Chūnagon's sister?"

Sadaijin became nervous, wondering whether the Emperor still had in mind his usual interest in his daughter's presentation at court. "I haven't thought about it at all. She is surprisingly reserved and shy even with me, though I am her parent. When she sees me, she breaks into perspiration and even feels unwell. In view of the way she is, I think the only way is to direct her toward the religious life," said Sadaijin, weeping.

"He didn't say she would actually retire from the world," thought the Cloistered Emperor. Looking at Sadaijin compassionately, he said: "She shouldn't retire from the world. I have no one reliable to look after the Crown Princess, and not being close at hand I am worried about her. Have your daughter come to the palace and be her companion. In any event, if your daughter does not abandon the world, she will surely become Empress."

Thinking about what had happened to Chūnagon, Sadaijin felt that probably his daughter was destined for a similar

course. He was confused, finding it both joyous and odd. "She
may be able to mingle in society as much as is required of
someone in this position," he thought.

"I'll discuss this with the child's mother," he said as he took
leave of the Emperor.

Sadaijin told his wife about it. "Well," she said, "I can't
decide what should be done."

"When we consider what has happened in Chūnagon's
case, wouldn't it be best for her to do as the Cloistered Emper-
or suggests? If we comply with his request, she will surely
become Empress, as he indicates. It seems so wonderful I
never dreamed it would happen."

Sadaijin felt agitated just thinking about the future and had
prayers said at a number of temples. The Cloistered Emperor
requested that, if it made no difference to the father, the
daughter be presented soon, and so Sadaijin had her brought
to court on the tenth day of the eleventh month. Of course
nothing was lacking at her presentation. She was splendidly
attended by forty ladies and eight children and lesser servants.
The position in which she was to serve was not a usual one,
but because it would have been unreasonable for her to serve
without a title she was called Naishi no Kami.[51]

She was installed in the Sen'yōden, since the Crown Princess
was in the Nashitsubo.[52] For some time she went to the Princess only at night when she would not be clearly observed, and
they lay together behind the same screen. From what Naishi
no Kami saw and felt, the Princess was very young, refined,
and composed. Though terribly shy and withdrawn, Naishi
no Kami could not withstand the charm of the Princess's

[51] Naishi no Kami (Principal Handmaid) was normally the highest position in the
Naishi no Tsukasa (Palace Attendants' Office) and carried with it the responsibility
of petitioning the Emperor and relaying messages. In the court hierarchy Palace
Attendants ranked immediately below Imperial concubines. Here the position is
simply given to the daughter as a title, and she has no particular duties to perform.

[52] The Sen'yōden was a building for concubines. The Nashitsubo, also known as
the Shōyōsha, was another of the five ladies' residences and often housed Imperial
Princesses.

innocence and frankness, and in attending her night after night she must have become much too bold.

The Princess was amazed at this unforeseen development. But there was nothing the least bit loathsome to her about Naishi no Kami's appearance and manner—indeed, the girl seemed surpassingly lovely and graceful. The Princess, thinking that there must be some reason for this behavior and finding the girl an earnest and good companion, clung to her and loved her as no other. Before long Naishi no Kami was serving in the Princess's room during the day too. Together they practiced their calligraphy, painted pictures, and played the koto. Night and day the Princess kept Naishi no Kami at her side. After those idle days when she had been reserved and shy about everything, Naishi no Kami felt dazed by it all.

Saishō, even now, did not abandon all thought of Naishi no Kami and could not help yearning for her. "As long as she was secluded in her lonely inner room there was no way I could ever think to get near her," he mused. "But now that she is in court service, it's wonderful. I'll stay around the Sen'yōden night and day and wait for a glimpse of her. Her dignified bearing and her reputation are truly magnificent. When will my wish be answered—when will I be able to make her my wife?"

When the Emperor paid his visit to the temple for the annual Gosechi ceremonies,[53] the patterned robes of Saishō and Chūnagon looked particularly splendid amidst all the plain purification robes worn by the others. Saishō cut a tall, manly, brilliant figure. Supple and sensual, he looked fascinatingly handsome. Chūnagon was stunning, his radiant beauty, his

[53]Professor Kakimoto takes the *chūin* here to refer to a temple on the palace grounds where the Emperor usually went to pray. The Gosechi ceremonies were held annually on four days of the eleventh month, the days of the cow, tiger, rabbit, and dragon, with a fifth performance on the evening of the day of the tiger. Four girls of good family, three the daughters of high court nobles and one the daughter of a provincial governor (except during the Great Thanksgiving Festival after an enthronement, when there were five girls), were selected to perform the Gosechi dances at these ceremonies. See Fujiki 1960: 192–93.

dynamic charm, were so transcendent one could gaze at him endlessly. Though he looked and acted like a man, he was yet so soft, lithe, and winsome that he dazzled the eyes. The ladies-in-waiting all about found him fascinating.

If there was the slightest indication a lady, though but average, was around, Saishō did not just ride by, but stopped each time and said something to her. Chūnagon, however, defying the ladies' glances, would look back at Saishō, who kept stopping, and ride on. Everyone's eyes followed him; it was if they were saying, "If this were the Hinokuma River, he would let the horse drink awhile."[54]

From behind, one of Chūnagon's escorts apparently had something to say, and when he indicated as much, Chūnagon asked what it was. "At the first door of the narrow corridor of the Reikeiden,[55] someone called me over and asked me to give you this," his escort said, taking out a very elegant-looking letter. Chūnagon looked at it, having no idea who it was from.

> A meeting with you—
> Always hard to arrange.
> My heart would not rest
> When I saw your print robe,
> Fleetingly, as you rode by.[56]

The handwriting was very lovely.

"Strange. Who could it be from?," mused Chūnagon, smiling. Yet with all the commotion about, he did not answer. But it would be a pity to have whoever she was think him unkind,

---

[54] The reference is to a poem in the *Kokin wakashū*, XX, Songs for the Gods, no. 1080 (*NKBT*, 8: 326): "Rapidly flowing, / The Hinokuma River; / At its bend stop, / Let your horse drink awhile / That upon your figure I may longer gaze."

[55] The Empress, Princesses, and Imperial concubines lived in the Reikeiden.

[56] There are three *kakekotoba* or puns here. Because I follow Professor Kakimoto's suggestion to read *karisome ni miru zo*, and not *karime ni* as Suzuki does, the *some* of *karisome*, "fleetingly," puns with the verb *someru*, "to dye" or "color." The other puns are *kataki*, meaning both "difficult" and a wood block for printing, and *shizu*, "quiet" or "calm" and a specific type of woven cloth.

and so when the day's events were over and everyone had
settled down, he lingered in the vicinity of the narrow corridor
of the Reikeiden under the late night moon, which shone
bright and clear.

> Still distant as the mountains
> In the patterns of my robe
> Is our meeting.
> From afar, with heart aflutter,
> Who was it who espied them?[57]

No one spoke as he recited this poem. Just as he was wondering if anyone was there, at the first door, from which the letter
had been sent, a voice replied:

> It was I who saw you,
> And my heart was not mistaken
> In appraising your charms.
> But unworthy as I am,
> I shall not tell you my name.

Her retort was uncommonly lovely. Chūnagon drew near.

> Asakura maiden,
> If you do not tell me your name,
> How am I to know you?
> How, throughout this night,
> Are we to exchange love's vows?[58]

"It is I, the one of the print robe," Chūnagon continued
teasingly. Now that the lady saw him more closely, he looked
so endearing and charming that he seemed all the more in-

[57] This poem contains a play on *tōi*, functioning both for "distant mountains" and
for "seen from afar."

[58] Asakura is a *makura kotoba*, or pillow word (a fixed epithet, often providing
image and/or sound effects). The old Imperial Palace was located in Asakura, which
is in Nara prefecture. The name is used to allude to a poem in the *Shinkokin wakashū*,
XVII, Miscellaneous, no. 1687, Emperor Tenji (*NKBT*, 28: 344): "In Asakura, / In
the Log Palace was I, / When she walked by. / Whose child was she, who as she
passed / Spoke her name aloud?" I read *yo* to mean "night" (not "world," as Suzuki
does).

triguing. He stood there calmly, and the lady was uncertain and worried about what he was going to do. But Chūnagon, unlike some, would not force himself on her. This lady, he thought, must be someone like the younger sister of the Imperial concubine. He saw that she was not just a lady-in-waiting. So having spoken enough to be courteous, he left furtively, for he heard people approaching.

Many women, having glimpsed Chūnagon like this, would speak to him, unconcerned about the wife waiting anxiously for him or about the rumors people would spread. Chūnagon would chat with them occasionally—if they seemed to be of high rank and beautiful—but only enough to be polite. Otherwise, if they were just low-ranking ladies, he behaved nonchalantly, ignored them, and remained distant and reserved. Some thought something lacking in him, like a flaw in a jewel. On the other hand, many found it amusing that Saishō, in contrast, constantly went about searching for, visiting, and courting ladies.

The year ended. And though the hazy sky of the first days of the year looked just like a spring scene, snow, a remnant of the old year, fell lightly. It was enchanting. Sadaijin went to the Sen'yōden, and Chūnagon was there too. Chūnagon and Naishi no Kami, during their childhood at home, had not been at all close because of the competition between their mothers. But their father would tell them: "You have no other brothers and sisters but yourselves. I don't know what the future has in store for me. You are both unusual, and I think it would be better if you would go through life counseling with each other rather than with others." After the children had grown up, they were allowed to stay together behind the same bamboo blind.[59] But Sadaijin's daughter was so very shy she still would not permit her brother to come around the screens surrounding her elevated platform. However, after she came to the palace, her brother assisted her in her comings and

[59] *Misu.* For a description, see Fujiki 1960: 138.

goings, and in so doing they grew close. Naishi no Kami too had learned about the world. Perhaps she had just gradually grown used to him and calmed down. She now spoke to him endearingly, separated from him by only a small movable silk screen.

Bearing in mind that he was himself unusual, Chūnagon looked at his unbelievably beautiful sister and was overcome with sadness. "Oh," he thought, "if only she, at least, might be normal!" Naishi no Kami too felt her heart throb every time she saw Chūnagon. Similarly troubled, although it was to be expected, they did grow very close, their compassion for one another strong.

Naishi no Kami's sitting space in the Sen'yōden was decorated with curtains of luxurious red and purple silk brocade and with small movable screen-curtains, three layers thick. The ladies-in-waiting wore five pale-red robes lined in plum red over unlined kimonos. In addition some wore red and purple silk brocade tunics, and others three layers of pale green robes. In the midst of these many ladies clad in every possible hue sat Chūnagon, respectful and dazzling, with the deep red shades of his purple brocade trousers glinting beneath his tunic. More than usual, his brilliance, his encompassing charm, his captivating winsomeness, seemed unparalleled.

When Sadaijin saw his son, he smiled despite himself and forgot his cares, though in all these years the cloud of the child's unusual appearance had never been lifted from his heart. He peeped behind the screens. Over strikingly beautiful red and purple silk brocade robes, in colors of progressively greater intensity from top to bottom, Naishi no Kami was wearing an all-red robe, and this was crowned with a formal silk brocade robe,[60] white on the outside and deep purple within. With her face masked behind a fan red on one side, purple on the other,

---

[60] A *kouchigi*, brocade lined with plain silk. For a description of this everyday robe, see Ikeda 1967: 228–29.

she looked so like Chūnagon one could hardly tell them apart. It was as though someone had made a copy of Chūnagon's beautiful face. The girl's somewhat more refined and delicate beauty was indescribably lovely. Her shining, perfectly arranged hair hung gracefully down; and the ends, extending roughly two feet beyond her height as she sat, were set off by her white robes. She looked like a picture. Each time Sadaijin saw her he was overcome by sadness. Had she been ordinary, he would not have minded so much if she was flawed. Then even if she were to enter the religious life deep in some remote mountain he would probably regret it less. But with both children so extraordinary, tears of grief and sadness came easily.

It had grown late, and the moon was shining brightly. "How good are you at playing the koto?," Sadaijin asked Naishi no Kami. "I'd like to hear you accompany Chūnagon on his flute." Urging her to play the thirteen-stringed koto, he handed a flute to Chūnagon. As always, the lovely notes of his flute were enchanting as they rose clearly, resounding in the distant clouds.[61] It was difficult for Sadaijin to restrain his tears. And then the sounds of the koto joining in, in no way inferior to those of the flute, were infinitely entrancing. Saishō, who had not left the vicinity, stood and listened. "How splendid both this flute and this koto sound! The talents of this brother and sister are not of this world. Naishi no Kami is surely as beautiful as she is talented," Saishō thought, and in spite of himself his tears fell.

He could not bear it. Aloud he quoted, "The rain drips from the eaves,"[62] and he appeared in the vicinity of the arched

---

[61] Here again "the distant clouds" is a metaphor for the palace.

[62] This is a line of a *saibara*, or folksong, entitled "Azumaya." It is divided into a husband's part and his wife's reply: "The rain drips from the eaves on the roof of the summer house. / I get wet standing here. Open the door! / If there was a bolt or lock I would fasten the door, but there is none. / Push open the door and come in. I am your wife." (*NKBT*, 3: 384, no. 6.)

bridge.[63] Chūnagon quickly exchanged the flute for a lute[64] and played "Open the Door and Come In." Saishō's heart throbbed as he answered: "There are no curtains hanging here, and I feel so forlorn."[65]

But Sadaijin was sitting there looking stately, and there was nothing Saishō could do. Disappointed, he grew grim. Other courtiers and noblemen came up to Sadaijin and met with him; but even then, all Saishō was aware of was the sound of the koto he had just heard ringing in his ears. "Even if she took her eyes off Chūnagon, who so excels in everything, and looked my way, would the sound of my koto-playing linger in her ears however well I played?," reflected Saishō, resentful and reserved. Chūnagon offered him a lute, but he merely declined it.

Though Saishō was certainly not the equal of Chūnagon, the ladies thought him most superior to others generally. He seemed very endearing and charming.

Since Naishi no Kami too was now living within the palace compound, Saishō occasionally heard her playing the koto. He could think only of the song "Waves Striking Against the Crags,"[66] and lament that the opportunity to fulfill his love did not seem likely to arise. As he gazed at the mist-swept moon, his heart left him to roam the skies. Sunk in gloom, he thought that speaking to Chūnagon would comfort him, as it usually did. He quietly proceeded to Chūnagon's residence without a large number of forerunners. It was unusually quiet there, and a retainer informed him that his master had left for

---

[63] A nobleman's house typically had a stream or artificial lake on the grounds that was surmounted by an arched bridge for decorative effect.

[64] *Biwa.*

[65] He is alluding to another *saibara* entitled "Wa ie": "In my home the curtains, large and small, hang down before my bed. / I would have you come and be my husband. / Of fish what would you like to eat—abalone, sea urchin?" (*NKBT*, 3: 415, no. 60.)

[66] This is a line from a poem in the *Shika wakashū*, VII, Love I, Minamoto no Shigeyuki (*KKT*, 4: 148): "Driven by the wind, / The waves crash painfully / Against the rocks; / Such is my longing for you / That thus shattered I feel."

night duty at the palace. Coming there had been pointless, and
Saishō was disappointed. He gazed blankly about, wondering
whether or not to go on to the palace.

Suddenly the faint sounds of a thirteen-stringed koto coming
from within the house caught his ear. "That would be Chūnagon's wife," he thought to himself. "She too moved me deeply, but like 'smoke from the salt kilns' that blow in unexpected
directions, she impulsively married another."

Even now in his heart he had not completely given her up,
and he was distressed. He crept up to the house so as not to
be seen and peeped inside. Seated near the outside edge of the
house, Yon no Kimi had rolled up a rattan blind. Wearing so
many layers of kimono that there did not seem to be a body
within them, she looked frail and beautiful, delicately lovely
in the moonlight.

"Even the beauty of the famed Naishi no Kami has its limits;
how can she surpass Yon no Kimi?," thought Saishō, as soon
as he heard her play. "Yon no Kimi is highly acclaimed for
her beauty, but I scarcely imagined that she would be so
lovely. Truly extraordinary!" He felt his soul leave him and
enter Yon no Kimi's sleeves.[67] He could not leave her. Reason
abandoned him.

"I'll go in to her tonight," he resolved. Since it was very late,
everyone had either gone to bed or was in the garden strolling
among the flower shadows. Yon no Kimi was alone. Leaning
on her koto, she gazed at the moon, quite lost in thought as
she recited to herself:

> A lovely spring night.
> Yet because it is I
> Who gazes upon it,

[67] The idea of the soul leaving the body and entering a beloved's sleeve was
common during this period. The phrase used here echoes one in the *Kokin wakashū*,
XVIII, Miscellaneous II, no. 992, Lady Michinoku (*NKBT*, 8: 303): "Not for a
moment / Did your company weary me. / I feel it is gone, / My soul no longer with
me. / Perhaps it entered your sleeve."

The moon has darkened, become
The shadow of my distress.[68]

"Her parents love her so," Saishō pondered, "much more
than their many other children. Her husband is a fine man.
He never indulges himself with other women and is completely reliable. Is it possible that despite all this something is
troubling her?"

When he had heard her poem, it became all the more difficult
for Saishō to leave, and pushing aside the door, he boldly
walked in. The ladies in attendance, assuming it was Chūnagon, were not startled. Saishō abruptly approached Yon no
Kimi and said:

> Surely my heart,
> Unable to forget you,
> Has visited there—
> The moon that appears to be
> The image of your distress.

Yon no Kimi was taken aback when it became clear that this
man was not her husband, and she hid her face in her robes.
Saishō put his arms around her and led her behind a screen.
She cried out in fright, and nearby, Saemon, the daughter of
her wet nurse, heard her. Startled, Saemon wondered why
Yon no Kimi would cry out if she were with Chūnagon.
Investigating, she saw that Yon no Kimi was in an indescribable state, and it was evident, moreover, that she was silently
weeping.

"Your distress pains me so," Saishō said comfortingly.
"You were cruel enough to abandon me, but my enduring
love for you and our destiny have brought this meeting about.
Regardless of your feelings, there is nothing for it now. Just
be calm."

[68] This poem appears in the *Fūyō wakashū*, Spring I (*ZGR*, 14: 6).

When Saemon heard this, she knew who the man was. It was startling, but really there was nothing she could do. She would reveal nothing to anybody.

"Chūnagon is not with Yon no Kimi," she reported to the others. "I will stay with her. Why don't the rest of you spend the night watching the moon and the flowers?"

"If only there were someone with whom we could share this lovely night,"[69] said the other young people as they went out to amuse themselves.

Yon no Kimi had grown accustomed to being with Chūnagon, and thought that men did nothing with a woman but talk in a placid and restrained way. Now, she was in tears and on the point of swooning at Saishō's unreasonable and inconsiderate behavior. To Saishō she seemed remarkably lovely. It pained him that he might not be able to see her so easily in the future.

"How strange Chūnagon is. I thought it was because he loved Yon no Kimi so much that he was so steadfast, but it must be some sense of religious obligation that has kept him from consummating the marriage." Saishō found so many things strange.

The night, too short for lovers' trysts,[70] passed more quickly than usual this time. Saishō felt he could not tear himself away; but with Saemon fretting and worrying, he had no choice, and departed in tears, promising to see his beloved again. It was all like a dream.

> So close are our bonds,
> There will be no one if not you.
> At Mitsuse River,

---

[69] The phrase they use is from a poem in the *Gosen wakashū*, III, Spring III, Saneakira (*KKT*, 3: 184): "So lovely they are, / The moon and flowers tonight; / Oh, for someone, / Someone to show them to, / Someone to share my feelings."

[70] The allusion here is to a poem in the *Kokin wakashū*, XIII, Love III, no. 636, Oshikouchi no Mitsune (*NKBT*, 8: 228): "They are long, / It was thought indeed, / Because they are / The autumn nights for lovers / Who have met since days of old."

Who will guide me across?
Who will say when we meet again?[71]

"It is pointless for you to persist in not understanding my love for you," said Saishō, but Yon no Kimi did not reply. After speaking to Saemon about the startling event, he returned home. Even then he could not tell if it was all only a dream, and the tears ran down his face.

Yon no Kimi herself was even more stunned, so dazed that she did not know what had been real and what not; she felt faint and did not arise. Her ladies asked if she felt ill, and were concerned. When Chūnagon returned from the palace, Yon no Kimi, increasingly miserable and wondering how she could face him, hid her head in shame. Chūnagon asked why she was behaving this way, and a lady told him that Yon no Kimi had been unwell since last night. Feeling sorry for Yon no Kimi, Chūnagon lay down beside her and said: "How do you really feel? I haven't heard anything about this until now." As he ministered to her gently and graciously, Yon no Kimi suddenly recalled Saishō's extraordinary behavior of the night before and became choked with emotion.

Yon no Kimi's mother too was alarmed at her daughter's affliction. Prayers were offered and rites of exorcism performed, and with one thing and another, everything was in an uproar. Chūnagon remained with Yon no Kimi. Consequently, Saemon did not show her the letters that came constantly from Saishō. With no word of reply, Saishō's anxieties multiplied. Life seemed unbearable, and he felt he could not go on this way. "Had I felt such misery over the years, would I still be living now?," he thought, baffled by many things; but

[71] The Mitsuse River, or as it is more commonly known, the River of Three Crossings (Sanzu no Kawa), is the equivalent of the River Styx. By Buddhist belief, a person must cross the river on the seventh day after his death, and the virtue or sinfulness of his deeds in earlier lives determines which one of the three crossings, each of whose currents present a different degree of difficulty, he must use. See Shinmura 1971: 923. The *mitsu* in the name Mitsuse is a *kakekotoba*; it is both the number three and a form of the verb "to see."

there was nothing for it. He sent off letters to Saemon a thousand times a day, till there would have been no place to put them on Mikura Mountain.[72] To the young and inexperienced attendant, Saishō had seemed deeply pained that dawn when, looking indescribably elegant and alluring, he had wept and lamented as though his life had ended; this had left its mark on Saemon's heart. His endless stream of letters was touching, and because she had a weakness for affairs of the heart, Saemon was sorry for him and could not abandon his cause. Each time she sent him the same reply: because Yon no Kimi had been preoccupied and ill since that dreamlike episode, and because Chūnagon was with her constantly, she could not deliver his letters.

Saishō assumed that this was really happening. He recalled how Yon no Kimi had been on the verge of fainting, and his resentment at the unanswered letters vanished. Yearning for her, and sad, he did not feel like getting up and going out either. Night and day he grieved bitterly.

"Now why on earth," he mused, "hasn't Chūnagon consummated his marriage with his wife when he seems very much in love with her? If he knew what happened between her and me the other night, he would be angered and weep. He's very handsome and attractive, but apparently he has abstained from sexual relations, thinking it wrong to force himself on his wife. He goes on acting as though love really exists between them. He's a strange and unusual man. Will he ever become intimate with her?" Choked with emotion, he thought, "I will devise some way to steal her away. This might be possible if she loved me even a little and would exchange a few words with me, but I can't force myself on her. She's so young and frail in manner and appearance, and is probably very much in love with that handsome and elegant husband

---

[72] *Mikura* is a storehouse. The allusion is to a poem in *Kokin waka rokujō*, II, Mountains, no. 42 (*KKT*, 9: 299): "So great is my love, / My body cannot contain it. / Mikura Mountain— / Even if I moved it there, / There would not be room enough."

who talks with her. She no doubt remembers me as unfeeling and hateful." He could not hold back his tears. As he saw the moon and remembered the poem she had recited, "The Moon I Gaze Upon," he felt distraught.

Chūnagon could not just stay at home, for there was nothing particularly and identifiably wrong with Yon no Kimi. Intending to go to his father's and to the Imperial Palace, he said to her: "I worry about you when I go out since you continue to feel unwell. Do try to get up and resume your normal activities. We've grown so close that when I sadly reflect on how short a time I am meant for this world, it is you more than anyone else who keeps me from the religious life of the priest.[73] Seeing you constantly ill makes me even less able to go on living. I am very depressed."

He stroked her hair, and the expression on his lovely, radiant face with its tearful eyes was extraordinarily touching. He went on speaking to her with nothing the least bit domineering or coarse in his attitude, nothing for which Yon no Kimi felt she could reproach him. And yet because of her painful secret relationship with Saishō, she continued to assume she ought to feel estranged from Chūnagon and refused to respond to him. She covered her head and wept even more.

Chūnagon did not understand. "Could it be that someone has told her I don't love her enough?," he thought, distressed that she was sad and miserable. "I'll be back soon," he said. To her ladies he added: "A number of you should stay with her. This mysterious affliction must be the work of ghosts or wraiths." And he left.

When Chūnagon arrived at the palace, Naishi no Kami's ladies found his visit refreshing after all this time, and they chatted about what had happened over the past few days. A lady named Saishō no Kimi smiled broadly and said: "I won-

[73] The term *michi no hodashi* used here is from a poem in the *Kokin wakashū*, XVIII, Miscellaneous II, no. 955, Mononobe no Yoshino (*NKBT*, 8: 294): "Enter I would / Upon that mountain path; / Invisible there / The misery of this world. / Yet those I love stay me."

der how Saishō has been. It's annoying to have him always reproaching me. I am not a lover's guide.[74] It's very trying being a 'capital bird' who brings news of someone's lover.[75] Maybe he has found a sweetheart of his own. It's so nice that I haven't heard from him for a while now."

"I've heard that he has been ill," replied Ben no Kimi, another of the ladies. "It's true that there's been no word from him for quite some time now, and he used to come calling so constantly it was annoying. How sad."

Chūnagon was surprised to hear this. When he left the palace he went to visit Saishō. Saishō was distraught at this turn of events, and he met Chūnagon with deep trepidation.

"For days I have been busy with someone ill and stayed at home," said Chūnagon. "But I was bored and went to the palace. Someone there told me you were ill and hadn't been to court in some time. I was surprised to hear it and came over to see you."

Saishō felt his face turn red, and he became even more uncomfortable. "It's nothing to make a big fuss over. When I have this trouble, I can't usually get about at all. I stayed home to take hot baths. Who's this person you mentioned who's ill?" As he spoke he seemed to forget himself and say more than he should. Though he deliberately spoke as though all this was unimportant, he paled and appeared haggard and despondent.

Usually whenever Saishō saw Chūnagon, he would ramble on tiresomely about four and twenty things, but now he said little and was sick with worry. He seemed truly not himself

[74] The expression *sato no shirube,* "a guide," is from a poem in the *Kokin wakashū,* XIV, Love IV, no. 727, Ono no Komachi (*NKBT,* 8: 245): "Of the village / Where live the fishermen / I am not a guide. / Why do some reproach me then / For not showing them the bay?"

[75] The *miyako dori,* or city bird, is an allusion to a poem attributed to Ariwara no Narihira that appears in both the *Ise monogatari* (*NKBT,* 9: 117, Section 9) and the *Kokin wakashū,* IX, Songs of Travel, no. 411 (*NKBT,* 8: 186): "City bird, / Since such is the name you bear, / I will ask of you: / She whom I hold most dear, / Is she there or is she not?"

and out of sorts. Chūnagon felt sorry for him, but since he was
worried about Yon no Kimi being ill, he was anxious to return
to her and so simply smiled and said: "You really don't look
your usual self. You've grown so thin that 'it would be shameful even before the still pools beneath the waterfall.'[76] But it's
not a physical ailment. It's some malady of the heart." Chūnagon had guessed correctly, and Saishō felt himself blush,
but at the same time he could not help smiling.

"Have you only now noticed how haggard I look?," he
parried, not looking very distressed, and so Chūnagon left.

In the dim haze of evening, Chūnagon looked so fine he
outdid the cherry blossoms in their gorgeous color. Following
him with his eyes, Saishō thought: "What can she think of me
when she has grown used to seeing him night and day. It's
natural that she should remain indifferent to me." He felt
more and more disconsolate as he continued to think about
his plight, and his tears flowed. He passed a sleepless night.

Saishō did nothing but sorrow and fret, and unable to
restrain himself even in public, he pressed Saemon to help
him. She, being weak-willed, yielded to his importunings.
Whenever Chūnagon was on his usual night duty at the palace, she would lead Saishō, as in a dream, to Yon no Kimi's
apartments.

"If Chūnagon were ever to hear anything at all about this,
how could I go on living?," Yon no Kimi brooded each time,
the tears coursing down her cheeks. Yet at each of these
fleeting meetings, the weeping and distraught Saishō seemed
enchanting and attractive. As time passed, Yon no Kimi was
obliged to recognize his sincerity.

Impressive though Chūnagon was, he was not intimate with

---

[76] The waterfall image is from a poem in the *Kokin wakashū*, XVIII, Miscellaneous I, no. 928, Mibu no Tadamine (*NKBT*, 8: 289): "Waterfall, / Down gushing
from on high, / Forcefully falling: / So old you seem to have grown, / Not a single
strand is black." This image was used in a similar way in the Hatsune chapter of *The
Tale of Genji*: "Her [Suyetsumu's] hair, which once looked so full, had lost its beauty
in recent years, and it was all the more embarrassing when compared with the pool
beneath the waterfall." (*NKBT*, 15: 385.)

her and displayed affection only when others were present; otherwise he was placid and decorous. When Yon no Kimi compared the two men, she felt that Saishō, so deadly in earnest and concerned, certainly loved her. Yet she was terribly embarrassed, and she worried about what would happen if anyone ever had the slightest cause to suspect their relationship. Still, it was only this secret liaison that she now fully appreciated; and yet she realized it was cruel to do so.

Yon no Kimi did nothing but worry, and the days passed with no relief from her anxieties. She did not comprehend what was happening to her, but after three or four months, everyone saw that she was pregnant. Her father had inquired about her, observing that she had been ill for no special reason these past months. Could it be that she was pregnant? As long as her attendants were not certain, they offered no confirmation. But then the ladies who attended Yon no Kimi in the bath saw that she was with child, and they told him.

Udaijin was overjoyed and broke into a smile. "We still haven't had any prayers said," he observed as he bustled about. "Chūnagon loves Yon no Kimi so much he doesn't run after other women; he has real affection for her. How could we blame anyone so handsome even if he were thoroughly inconstant? Faithful men who never stray are hard to find, and Chūnagon ought to be set up as a model for the world. If only the child would resemble him, it would add all the more to the glory of my family."

Udaijin went on speaking in this vein, tears standing in his eyes. Then, smiling broadly, he went to Yon no Kimi's room and sat in front of the screen behind which she was seated. Though she was in intense pain and lying down, she arose when she heard her father approach. Udaijin, looking delighted, drew near. "How are you really? I have just heard of your condition. We must have prayers said." He wept with joy. Yon no Kimi thought this strange. She continued to be distressed, for ever since that unusual night with Saishō she had felt

pained and uneasy. If she was really pregnant, what would
Chūnagon think? She thought how terribly dreadful she
would feel then at meeting him in their usual way, and she
broke into perspiration.

"You're much too shy," her father said, looking immensely
happy.

Returning home, Udaijin saw to everything. There was
nothing he did not think of, including various fruits and other
items. He told his wife to go to Yon no Kimi straightaway,
but she replied that the girl would surely feel embarrassed, and
not to speak about her pregnancy so openly.

"You seem to neglect her, whereas you were certainly concerned about your other daughters,"[77] said Udaijin. "I wonder
if there are women who don't realize they are pregnant until
the symptoms become quite so clear as this? The hopes I have
cherished for years have been fulfilled, and my worries are
over." Then he summoned the wet nurse. "Perhaps Chūnagon
has not managed to take in what has happened. Today is a
good day. When he comes in this evening give him a hint."
Just as Udaijin was speaking these words, Chūnagon walked
in. "You see, it's not even late at night yet. How trying it
would be if he were callous or frivolous. Even if a woman were
to become Empress it could be no better. It is marvelous
simply to be cared for by this man. It was a wise idea taking him as my son-in-law," said Udaijin, full of self-praise,
speaking of this and that to no one in particular. It was very
touching.

The wet nurse, Nakatsukasa, while preparing Chūnagon's
meal, did hint at the developments Udaijin had so happily told

[77] The text here literally reads: "You were certainly concerned about the [wife of
the] Major Captain and the concubine(s). Earlier, we were informed that Udaijin's
eldest daughter was a concubine of the Emperor, that his second daughter was a
concubine of the Crown Prince, and that nothing had been arranged for his third and
fourth daughters. Though "concubines" may refer to the two eldest daughters, it is
not easy to assume that in the interval the third daughter had become the Major
Captain's wife. It is possible that "Daishō" is an error for "Ōgimi," the eldest
daughter, and concubine refers to the second daughter.

her to convey to his son-in-law. Chūnagon's heart leapt in surprise. As he listened, his face suddenly turned red. Naka-tsukasa interpreted this as embarrassment. Though an adult, he looked so innocent and so enchantingly handsome.

Yon no Kimi felt forlorn. Beads of perspiration and tears became one, and she pulled her robes over her head. Chūnagon lay down beside her as usual, but what could he say? "I am different from everyone else," he thought, "yet I continue to lead a normal life, though I fear with an uneasy heart it will only be for a short time. I wonder into what depths of grief[78] my mother will be plunged when, for no particular reason, I forsake her who loves me as dearly as anyone. Nor does my father cast me aside as someone unwanted. It upsets him if he doesn't see me for even a day. Turning my back on them will surely make my sin all the greater. Yet time has passed, and I have not come to a definite decision, and now that this ridiculous incident has come up, I feel wretched. People call me flawless, but now, because of all this, there will probably be some who will think me a fool—a man who doesn't even know his wife is unfaithful. It is so sad! People would surely think it strange that while we've been together I still have not touched Yon no Kimi. My wretched life is an embarrassment. Since I was not planning to remain long in the world, I intended to live alone until I took my vows; how regrettable that I ever married." He pondered on through a sleepless night. Now, he felt, he must surely renounce the world.

"Who could the father of this child be? An affair has taken place and I, totally unaware of it, frequented the court and mingled with everyone. A certain man must surely have thought me foolish." It grew light while Chūnagon was lost in thought, and neither he nor Yon no Kimi was anxious to arise. They were lying back to back. Chūnagon, deciding to

---

[78] The phrase used here is from a poem by Fujiwara no Kanesuke that appears in the *Yamato monogatari* (*NKBT*, 9: 252, Section 45) and in the *Gosen wakashū*, XV, Miscellaneous I (*KKT*, 3: 322): "How lost and confused, / Though it not be in darkness, / Is a parent's heart, / When the road it travels / Is one of love for a child."

get up and leave, roused Yon no Kimi, but she pulled her robes even further over her head.

"This is unbearable!," he exclaimed. "I felt that you were being strangely standoffish lately, but I was too innocent to suspect anything; I simply worried because I wondered what you thought of my unusual behavior. It is piteous and naturally distresses you. But it would pain me greatly if your father questioned my love for you, not knowing of my misery. What are you going to do now? Who has loved you more than I? I have never philandered with other women; I have simply remained by your side. I deeply regret and am ashamed of my foolishness in having assumed that no other would be so faithful."

He spoke tenderly, with embarrassment hinting at the difficulties of his position, but inwardly he thought, "Who is to be blamed?" He could not help feeling intrigued by the situation, probably because he was not really jealous.

Chūnagon, with a smile radiant beyond description, gazed at the reclining Yon no Kimi. The intensity of her emotion brought bitter tears. Unable to think of any soothing words, Chūnagon called for a lady to come. He washed his hands and face in a basin of water he had brought to him and chanted a sutra. In his heart, he was very agitated.

"There is no reason, really, for me to feel hurt," he told himself, growing more resigned to his fate, "but it's very embarrassing that people are probably taking note of me and thinking me foolish and strange. Why did this mishap have to occur? Is it because, after all, I have continued to live in this world?"

He seated himself and chanted the sutras with great intensity. Giving himself up to this activity somewhat eased his troubled heart. Yon no Kimi was still reclining and, listening to his fervent chanting, found it hard to bear. She could not face him; she was too distressed. How could others know what she felt in her heart?

Meanwhile, Udaijin, delighted at the joyous news of Yon
no Kimi's pregnancy, lost no time in mentioning it to Chūnagon's father. "Very strange and certainly unexpected,"
thought the amazed Sadaijin. "Chūnagon mingles at court
dressed as a man, unsurpassed by anyone. He knows he is
unusual, but this alone should not be cause enough to grieve
him, and yet as time has passed he has come to look very
worried. Is it this strange pregnancy that is troubling him?"
He would have asked Chūnagon himself, but since it might be
very embarrassing for Chūnagon, though Sadaijin was his
father, he was hesitant and could not bring himself to put the
question. In public Sadaijin asked about the pregnancy and
looked pleased and proud, as a father usually does. Chūnagon, however, felt thoroughly embarrassed about what his
father might be thinking.

"When I go out and mix in public there is surely a certain
man who notices me and thinks me both foolish and strange,"
he thought. As a result, he became even more aloof, as remote
as the distant clouds.

Chūnagon now openly displayed his belief that this world
was but a transient one. For months he had been exchanging
pledges of deep love with Yon no Kimi. They had always been
loving to each other, and had come to think and feel alike. The
marital vow that had joined Yon no Kimi to someone so
unusual was regrettable.

"Oh, I hope no one suggests I am straying with other women
as men frequently do," Chūnagon had once thought. He had
been afraid to think what Yon no Kimi might feel when he was
on duty at the palace night after night. He had loved her
deeply. But now, having learned of her relationship with another, he thought that she had probably come to realize what
a strange relationship theirs was. He was embarrassed, lost all
interest in her, and felt estranged from her. If he continued to
treat her as affectionately as ever, he would look foolish. Yon
no Kimi thought his reaction justifiable and could say noth-

ing, though she was overcome with embarrassment and sorrow. No longer did they ever speak intimately together, looking each other in the face, and their relationship grew cold.[79]

Chūnagon interpreted Yon no Kimi's growing distance to
mean that the one with whom she had fully consummated her
love had taken his place in her heart. He was disconsolate and
resentful, no longer behaving toward her as he had before.
Laying aside mundane affairs, he became more and more
absorbed in Buddhist devotions. Even when he was with her,
he would remain outside her curtains devoting himself night
and day to his austerities. He began to visit his father's home
and to stand night duty at the palace more often. Many found
this behavior odd, for they assumed his love for Yon no Kimi
would increase now that she was to bear his child.

"It's strange," Udaijin and his wife mused sadly. "Chūnagon is always at his devotions and no longer comes to his wife
at night. What can it mean?" Aware of their worries, Yon no
Kimi felt helpless and wretched. "If only I could somehow do
away with myself, die!," she frequently thought.

Saishō heard all about Yon no Kimi's condition from Saemon, his sympathic guide, and her descriptions made him feel
even more tenderness for his beloved. Realizing the depth of
their ties now, he wanted to flout the rules of society, to ignore
public humiliation, and to steal her away and hide her. But
though his impatience grew, this course of action he could not
follow. He looked terribly worried.

Chūnagon noticed that Saishō was behaving differently and
seemed burdened with care. "I have heard," he recalled, "that
Saishō was once deeply in love with Yon no Kimi. He must
surely be the one who has been carrying on this secret affair
with her. No one besides me is likely to realize it. But if it is

[79] The phrase used here, *naka no utoku mo*, which refers to feeling estranged even
when within the same nightrobe, is taken from a poem in the *Shūi wakashū*, XVIII,
Love III, Anonymous (*KKT*, 3: 489): "Together we were / Under one nightrobe for
cover, / Yet so far apart, / So estranged even that night, / Our vows of love unful-
filled."

true, he will be watching me more intently than any other and probably be both embarrassed and jealous, wondering secretly about me." He was thoroughly confused.

"Yet this is something that is hard to know for certain. Why should I force myself to go on living in this distasteful world? How unfortunate that this had to occur while I myself remained hesitant to take the religious vows out of concern for my parents' feelings."

Little by little his desire to seek out that mountain path where life's uncertainties cannot be seen grew.[80]

At that time an Imperial Prince, the third son of the late Emperor, lived at Mount Yoshino. He excelled in all things. He was thoroughly versed in scholastic matters and in the arts of divination, astronomy, dream interpretation, and physiognomy. In olden days, qualified men were sent to China once every twelve years for study. But because people had deteriorated greatly in appearance and character in recent years, no one went there any longer. The Yoshino Prince, however, was so superior that when he put in his fervent request to go, he was permitted to do so.

Those who received him in China admired and respected him. "Many Japanese," they said, "have come here, and in our country too we have many sage men, but there has been no one so learned as he in the many teachings and arts." A governor took him as a husband for his exceptionally well-bred daughter and treated him with affection.

The Prince's wife gave birth to two daughters, one right after the other, and then died. "Though she was of a different country," he thought, "she was not remote nor did I feel her to be unusual. I don't know about the women of this country, but of all the ladies I have seen in Japan—court attendants, the Empress, the Emperor's daughter—none was so beautiful as she."

[80] Since mountains are the sites of many Buddhist temples, there is a strong association in Japanese literature between mountain paths and paths into religion.

The Prince, loving his wife very much, had given up all thought of returning to Japan. To say that he was deeply saddened at her death is not to describe what he felt. He wanted to remain in China and realize his original plan of renouncing the world, but leaving his daughters, the mementos of his wife, was also sad. While he worried about what to do, his father-in-law, the governor, grieved so for his daughter that he grew ill and breathed his last.

When the governor died, the Prince found himself more and more alone and felt he could not go on. Just then he heard that a court noble had plans to make him his son-in-law. But feeling that he could not marry again, he dismissed the proposition. His refusal was resented, and the Prince learned that there was even a scheme to kill him. His life was of little value, he felt, yet it was sad to throw it away in some foreign country. Honored and loved, he had forgotten his native Japan, but now that it was difficult and frightening to go on living in China he began to feel he wanted to return.

It would be sad to leave his daughters behind. But it was said that women could not cross the China Sea because the legendary Nanishū could not cross it when Sasemaro did.[81] And yet what was he to do? Should a Dragon King intercept their ship, the Prince felt certain that he would not regret abandoning his life beneath a traveler's sky. He consulted the children of the dead governor, and then left as though in flight with his daughters. Did the Dragon King have a change of heart? Even this ominous creature never stopped their ship, and propitious winds seemed to favor their departure.

When they arrived home, the Prince did not want his family to become a topic of conversation. Not wanting to have it said that he had had children by a Chinese woman, he kept his daughters carefully concealed when he got to the capital. It was

[81] A reference to the *Sasemaro densetsu* (Legend of Sasemaro). A variant of this tale appears in the *Hamamatsu chūnagon monogatari* (NKBT, 77: 161). Some versions confuse the name Sasemaro with Sademaro. Suzuki 1971: 261–85 examines some of these legends.

different here from the country to which he had grown accustomed, and being so far from the clouds toward which the smoke of his wife's pyre had risen, the Prince brooded over the sad events, lost in his memories.

The Prince cared lovingly for his daughters, but he felt he could never share intimacies with or marry another woman. He stopped wanting to altogether, though he went on living with an aching heart. Then—it is not known how it happened —the rumor began to spread that the Prince was planning something that threatened the future of the court, and that he thought it desirable to become sovereign. The Prince was flabbergasted to hear—was he dreaming?—that he was to be banished to some remote mountainous region.

"This has all happened," he thought, "because I stayed here as a layman and did not take religious vows. My heart having left this world, it was unsuitable and wrong of me to continue to care for my daughters and remain in society. I went on thinking that I would raise the girls until they knew more of life. This was regrettable."

Thus resolved, he took the tonsure at once. He and his daughters went to the lovely region at the foot of Mount Yoshino, into nowhere, unseen and unknown. From then on they lived buried away quite alone in the mountain's snows, growing used to listening longingly for the chirping of the birds.

The beauty of the Prince's daughters was sadly wasted here. They would idly strum the koto in an authentic Chinese manner, far better than most others, as the Prince watched them, moved and sad. He wanted only to go away deep into some mountain, but he felt he was not free to leave this wretched world behind because of the sad plight of his friendless daughters. Being so well versed in the arts of divination, he knew that in the course of time someone would appear to guide them, though for a short while, on the road to adulthood, and so he decided to wait for this person who was destined to come.

In the meantime, Chūnagon felt increasingly that he should retire from the world. Whenever he made his way into a mountainous region, whether to view cherry blossoms or autumn leaves, he wondered if there was not some place there that might answer his needs, some place in the shade of a valley or on the top of a mountain peak where he could hide, his whereabouts unknown to anyone. Someone then spoke to him about the Prince of Mount Yoshino: "His hut looks like that of a sage who has completely abandoned the world; the streams and the forms of the rocks are all of a sort never seen in the capital; a place that brings peace of mind and contentment."

"If I were to turn my back on the world," thought Chūnagon, after hearing all this, "it would be quite dreadful and painful to approach just any group of mountain ascetics and become the disciple of one of them. But this Prince is clearly no one ordinary in either disposition or appearance. This is something I have never thought of before."

"What is your connection with the Prince that you know so much about him?," he asked the person who had spoken about the Prince.

"My uncle is his disciple and never leaves the area. On days of religious observance, I assist him and so see the Prince when it is suitable," the man answered.

"How very fortunate. For years I have wanted somehow to become acquainted with this Prince and visit him, to study the seven-stringed koto that they no longer play here,[82] and to ask about various passages in the classics that are difficult to understand. I was afraid, though, that someone living in such a remote place would find this disagreeable, and I have felt reluctant to ask. I would like you to find out if he would agree to receive me; if so I will come very secretly to see him."

[82] This is the *kin*, which is known to have already fallen into disuse by roughly the year 990, in Emperor Ichijō's reign. Unlike the thirteen-stringed koto (*sō no koto*) and the six-stringed koto (*wagon*), the seven-stringed *kin* had no bridge and was therefore more difficult to play.

Chūnagon was very earnest. The man told him that his request was a very simple one, and Chūnagon said: "In that case, do go and see the Prince soon."

The man went to Yoshino. He told the priest, his uncle, all about what Chūnagon, the son of Sadaijin, had said.

"In the past," said the uncle, "important people had called or written of their desire to come, but the Prince did not want it to be thought that he still had worldly ties, and so had refused to pay any attention to them. As a result, no one seems to have come these last four or five years. Still, I don't know what he will think of your request. I will definitely find out and let you know."

The priest left his nephew for a moment and went to speak with the Prince, relating what was said and adding that the message had been specially conveyed by his nephew.

The Prince pondered for a little while and then said: "Chūnagon is surrounded by such splendor that nothing but beautiful butterflies and flowers should please him. But then why does he say his thoughts dwell on distant mountains? It may be that he is the destined one. How very delightful! Have him come."

Looking very pleased, the Prince wholeheartedly agreed to the meeting. The priest thought it strange, but appreciated that the Prince probably had his reasons.

"I thought it very unlikely that he would agree," he went back and told his nephew. "I assumed that you would go home disappointed, your visit fruitless. But the Prince said it was all right."

His nephew was pleased and, upon his return, he told Chūnagon of his success. Chūnagon, feeling that his wishes had finally been answered, was overjoyed. Chūnagon swore his messenger to secrecy, imploring him never to reveal what had occurred.

"The Prince would probably think it rash of me," he thought, "if I were to turn my back on the world immediately after I first saw him. He probably would not agree that was a good thing. This first time I will return after just seeing him and pledging my faith to him not only in this world but in worlds to come."

Before setting out he made a few comments to put people off the track: "Someone interpreted my dreams as very disturbing and said that I ought to stay at a mountain temple for a week or so to have purification services held. I feel restless when my whereabouts are known, and people coming to see me would distract me from my devotions."

Formerly, whenever Chūnagon had to be away from Yon no Kimi for two or three days, the two had affectionately told each other of their anxieties, and their relationship, such as it was, had seemed a close one. But since Chūnagon had learned of Yon no Kimi's pregnancy, he no longer behaved this way, fearing he would look foolish to the one she loved. Yon no Kimi was ashamed and sad about this state of affairs. She herself felt it was cruel to have been so overwhelmed by the deep attachment she had come to have for her seducer; and she imagined that Chūnagon also thought it cruel. The latter, though, was resigned to the situation, for he felt he had no reason to reproach her and he behaved as though he saw, heard, and knew nothing. This gave rise to feelings of jealousy in Yon no Kimi.

Chūnagon went in secret to visit the Prince, taking with him only the nephew of the priest as his guide and four or five other people with whom he was on intimate terms, such as his wet nurse's children. It was around the ninth month, and the autumnal mountain landscape with its rich brocade of colors moved Chūnagon. Yet as they made their way into unknown distant regions, he became lonely and sad, feeling uneasy that his parents would worry about what had become of him. He seemed embarrassed as he realized that if he felt this forlorn on a journey he knew to be a temporary one, he would feel so much more so when he took this path for good as planned:

> Odd indeed it is
> That my tears on their course
> Already depart,
> For this mountain path I take
> Is not my last from this world.

The guide was sent ahead, and so they were expected at the Prince's house—the preparations finished, everything cleaned and dusted, and everyone in fresh clothes.

Chūnagon entered the gate, and while word of his arrival was conveyed to the Prince, he carefully adjusted his clothes, and then went inside. He was wearing, hanging loosely from his shoulders, a red lined robe of beaten cloth[83] over a grayish-white spangled hunting robe; and this over bloused trousers of float-patterned damask, embroidered here and there with all the autumnal grasses. He was so radiantly, brilliantly handsome that even had the messenger of Paradise, in his cloud palanquin, come to fetch one, one would want to remain in this world and continue gazing at Chūnagon.

"Can such a person as this exist even in this age of decadence, when all is deplorable and in decline?," exclaimed the Prince in amazement, fixing his gaze on Chūnagon as he gradually got himself settled. The Prince, who had once looked fresh and handsome, seemed to have been made haggard by his religious devotions. His complexion was white, his head was very clean-shaven, and he was of noble mien. He seemed younger and more clean-cut than Chūnagon had imagined him. Gradually, the two lost all reserve as they spoke together, and the Prince marveled at how Chūnagon had come to excel so in learning and everything else. Since the Prince knew in his heart that Chūnagon would guide his daughters until they were grown and could go out into the world, he was kind and candid. He told about all that had happened to him in the past: his trip to China, his witnessing

---

[83] The cloth was placed on a fulling block and beaten with a mallet until it shone.

the sad and dreadful death of his wife, and his inability to
abandon his extraordinary daughters. He spoke of the incred-
ible rumor that had circulated about him and of how he had
thus become involved in the painful turmoil of this world. He
explained that since his daughters remained an obstacle in his
path out of that world, he had been unable to hide himself in
an even more obscure place than the one in which he found
himself at present. As he spoke, the place did not seem to be
all that austere; and those watching him—elegant, charming,
in an easy, contemplative attitude—found it difficult to hold
back their tears.

"Is that what happened?," wept Chūnagon. "I too am
thought, unlike others, to have no cause for depression or
regret." He told the Prince that since childhood he had been
unusual, had been different from others, and that now that he
had at last come to understand the situation, he found it
difficult to remain in society. The Prince was able to infer the
true source of Chūnagon's problem from all he had said, and
he wept. "Though it's natural that you should regret your
condition," he said, "it won't last for long. Everything that
has occurred is the result of events in your former lives and
not in this one. You should, in any case, endure the circumstances of this life. It would be very childish and completely
lacking in understanding for you to lament and resent others.
This world is not something of which you should grow weary.
Further, I believe that you are destined to attain a very high
position. Though I won't go into detail, there will come a time
when you will realize the import of my words. But let's not
go on speaking too much like physiognomists."

Chūnagon did not understand what the Prince had seen in
him, why he, who was such an unusual person, should attain
a high position. "About your daughters," he said, "however
unreliable I may be, I will look after them as long as I remain
in the world. You need not worry about them any longer."

"I have never let it be known that I have these two daughters," the Prince replied. "It must be so fated. But it is not because I want to have them presented at court, as most parents would, that I have made sudden and unsolicited reference to them. Since the girls live here alone, I cannot abandon them and turn my back on the world. Without anyone to visit them, it is unlikely they would go on living here. This has worried me. Still, I would never tell them that my dying wish is that they should end their lives on this mountain or anything of the sort, for one's fate is predetermined. Such a wish might occur to me, but it would probably not be fulfilled because of karma. I do not hope, even, that they comport themselves without contention and with dignity; this too I simply leave to fate. Yet it pains me to wonder whether my departure from this world still lies in the distant future. This troubles me." He wept and could not restrain himself from speaking until it grew light.

Chūnagon sat beside this fine and beloved Prince; and since the Prince spoke clearly and well even about China and Korea, Chūnagon felt as though all had grown clear from the depths of hell to the ends of heaven. Chūnagon was content, and his grief over his unusualness vanished. He was deeply touched by many things and could not bring himself to leave.

The Prince showed Chūnagon many Chinese classics no longer available in Japan, and was astonished to find that Chūnagon seemed no less learned than he himself, who had been confident no one, not even in China, was his equal in learning and understanding. What a marvelous person! When the Prince presented Chūnagon with themes and had him compose Chinese-style poems, he created poetry even more interesting and moving than that of China; and his calligraphy was beautiful. "What a fabulous person! He must be a spirit temporarily in the guise of a man." Aware of Chūnagon's strange fate, the Prince studied him with curiosity.

Two or three days passed with a dreamlike quality. The Prince constantly admired Chūnagon and even neglected his

Buddhist austerities. It seemed that Chūnagon wanted to hear the seven-stringed koto, and so late one moonlit night the Prince played ever so plaintively and enticingly. When, after some time, he put the koto down, Chūnagon picked it up, and the Prince immediately heard the same tune played again.

"How amazing! You've picked up the playing of these lingering notes in just the same way as I've taught it to my forlorn daughters, whom I mentioned earlier as an obstacle in my path out of this world. Might it be that I, a hermit used to hearing the mountain wind on Yoshino peak, did not hear the notes correctly? But, then, I'm glad that you have gone out of your way to see me, and I should not be speaking to you coldly." So saying, the Prince went to his daughters' room.

"Since our guest has come to visit and is staying for a few days, do speak to him here," said the Prince. "He appears to be an extraordinary person. Though others may think it strange that you should so suddenly receive this man here, I don't believe he would ever be guilty of misbehavior." He instructed them to put their room in order. When the mood was most touching, with dawn approaching and the moon veiled by mist, Chūnagon was summoned. He arrived, radiant and exuding an indescribable perfume, but the Princesses, who had been near the threshold gazing at the moon, felt embarrassed and withdrew inside.

"Stay," coaxed the Prince. "Just behave as I have asked you to. Why, in this unusual hut, should we treat him in the usual ways of the world? Nothing will happen to make you uneasy." And he walked away.

The Princesses' apartment, situated deep inside the main hall,[84] was of a laudably special simplicity. It seemed the home of someone for whom the Prince cared greatly. Both inside and outside it was quiet, and there seemed to be no one about. Only the moon reflecting in the water was bright. Chūnagon sympathized with the Princesses as he wondered what they

[84] *Shinden.* See note 7, above.

must feel, living in such a place, spending their time gazing out of the window lost in their thoughts. He wondered whether these women from China, unlike Japanese women, might lack deep emotion or be unaware of the profound pathos of life? He wanted to know them. Since no one spoke, he recited:

> To Mount Yoshino,
> To turn away from the sad world,
> Far have I come.
> Yet will no one speak with me—
> Not a sound will anyone make.

"It is unfeeling of you." He looked very fine and moving as he gazed blindly at the scenery and wept. If at the capital many hearts burned with love for Chūnagon, how much more fascinated were these girls, unaccustomed as they were to seeing even ordinary people. Since there were no ladies there who could have unhesitatingly recited a poem in answer to Chūnagon's, nor could the Princesses do it, they felt embarrassed and helpless. But it was unacceptable to be long in answering, and so the elder sister, remaining on her knees, inched a little closer to where Chūnagon stood.

> It asks how I am,
> The wind blowing ceaselessly
> Through the pines of this peak;
> But when to my senses I return,
> I find there is no one there.

Though she spoke but faintly, she impressed Chūnagon as graceful and charming. One so refined as this was rare even in the capital. Chūnagon was all the more tantalized as he wondered which of the sisters this was.

> Though I be no more
> Than the sound of the wind
> Blowing through the pines,
> Strangely it disquiets me
> Just to ask how you are.

Chūnagon did not flirt with her in the usual manner, but instead spoke very warmly of how, being deeply impressed by the sadness of life and wishing to retire from the world, he had come to Mount Yoshino. Perhaps the Princess had begun to feel comfortable with him, for she occasionally replied to him not coldly. She seemed so lovely and considerate. "She is wasted on me," thought Chūnagon, "but I wonder if Saishō has not yet learned of her existence. If he knew he would surely fall deeply in love and do all he could for her." When he first thought of Saishō, he felt sorry for himself, and then he smiled.

The moon was completely veiled in mist. The chaotic hum of the insects, the flow of the water, the sighing of the wind, the call of the deer—all these sounds added to the pathos of the surroundings; one could not help being moved to tears.

"I'm not used to staying outside the bamboo blinds like this," said Chūnagon, as he quietly slipped in. "It's terribly uncomfortable. Don't be so inconsiderate."

The Princess, startled and confused, lay face downwards.

"Please don't treat me so coldly," said Chūnagon. "I would never presume on you. I am unworthy, but however unusual it may be, I would like you to think of me as but another sister." Calmly and with charm, Chūnagon tried to console her, but it was natural that she should feel flustered, as though it was a dream. The younger sister had come to join her sister, and they were now together.

The ladies serving the Princesses wondered what was happening, and some seemed nervous. They regretted that the Princesses were so disconsolate, living on and on in this sort of place. So hearing that this fine and peerless man was there made their hearts throb with emotion. Yet because their clothes were worn, they were embarrassed and fled to an inner room. The Princesses were thus left alone. They wondered what had happened, distressed that no one came. There was nothing in Chūnagon's behavior, however, that was ill-tempered or fashionably vulgar. He seemed simply charming. The elder Princess, thinking her agitation might be excessive, spoke of her feelings. "What you refer to as intimacy between a man and a woman, isn't it just what we have here?," she reprimanded Chūnagon. "It is shameful what others will think."

"Don't worry about that," replied Chūnagon. "As long as I am of this world, I want to do all I can for you to demonstrate that my intentions are good. I acted as I did because I was uneasy, thinking our relationship much too uncertain and the barriers between us too many. I thought we might simply be frank and unreserved with each other."

After a while the Princess began to feel better. The younger Princess was overwrought and had buried herself beneath her robes. Her sister, feeling sorry for her, concealed her behind a curtain-screen.

"How unfeeling and withdrawn you are. My feelings are the same towards both of you," said Chūnagon reproachfully.

Now the elder Princess looked ready to follow her sister behind the screen, and so Chūnagon, behaving the way a man normally would, restrained her and lay down beside her. There he promised her his affection not only in this life but in lives to come. There was nothing the least objectionable about him. How could the Princess help but realize his good intentions? Yet she was deeply embarrassed. Never having known such a man, she felt odd and worried, and her distress and embarrassment increased with the light of dawn. With her slender figure wrapped in only a white unlined summer robe, she seemed as delicate as if she had slipped from a picture. Her hair was extraordinary, lying naturally very full over her tunic. Her face, charmingly concealed, was very white and lovely. She was inexpressibly dignified and beautiful. Chūnagon was curious to see if she was like a Chinese woman, distant, different in any way from other women, and he trembled with excitement. She was graceful, and Chūnagon wanted never to take his eyes from her. He promised his heartfelt support even more strongly than before. It goes without saying that his appearance was splendid.

At dawn, each thought the other exceptionally lovely, but since it was growing light, Chūnagon left. He sent his morning-after letter,[85] recalling how very beautiful she had been:

> We have just parted,
> But so troubled did you seem
> I would return.
> Oh, to pluck it and make it mine,
> The white chrysanthemum.

It was written in the usual manner of such letters. That the Princess's ladies considered it to be just such a morning-after letter showed in their faces. Chūnagon had been charming and loving, and so the Princess had somehow managed, however reluctantly, to speak with him; but now she felt wretched, embarrassed, and even ill as she wondered what had really taken place. She did not answer Chūnagon's letter. Her ladies thought it disgraceful, but the Princess put an end to the matter by insisting that no answer was required.

When it grew dark, Chūnagon returned. He and the Princess spent the night talking, gazing at the moon, and playing the koto together. Chūnagon had quite lost his heart to the girl and was loath to leave her. After a number of days passed in this manner, the Prince learned of their intimacy, but he was untroubled. "Very good—they're talking to each other," he simply said. Thus there was nothing to keep them apart.

Chūnagon could not go on like this indefinitely, however, for he had not yet taken holy vows. "How worried and upset my parents must be. Yon no Kimi's father probably feels resentful and grieved, too. Only Yon no Kimi herself would understand."

With so much on his mind and unable to bear remaining

---

[85] A letter customarily written after a man had returned home having taken leave of his beloved that dawn. To not receive such a letter was to be told in effect that the man was no longer interested.

hidden away here, he decided to leave. He presented the Prince with hempen robes, priests' gowns, night clothes, and bedding so that he would be warm as he listened to the sound of the wind blowing through the pines on the peak. To the attendants, high and low, and the Princesses, he presented not only many red polished silk and brocade robes, all of extraordinary shades of color, but also silk and damask cloth. The Prince, on being presented with so extravagant an array of folding fans and other objects of unusual appearance, said: "I've given such things up and have no desire for them." But Chūnagon looked so noble and handsome that the Prince felt abashed in his presence, and it was difficult for him to refuse the gifts as he had intended. He was relieved to have entrusted to Chūnagon his daughters who had kept him from the path out of this world. He spoke about his intention to go far into the mountains and immerse himself in Buddhist devotions from then on.

"There is nothing to keep you from that any longer. I am thinking of moving your daughters to the capital," Chūnagon said.

"People will talk," replied the Prince, "and it will be awkward for you if you suddenly were to do that now. Even if they were to remain here, I would be free of worry if I thought only that you would not abandom them." They exchanged promises, and for gifts the Prince presented Chūnagon with all the medicines and similar items he had brought back from China that were not to be found in Japan.

Even after Chūnagon repeatedly promised the Princess endless affection, he was reluctant to leave:

> My heart uneasy,
> Crushed by grief as by a storm,[86]
> When I no longer hear

---

[86] The word *arashi* is a *kakekotoba* in this poem. It means "tempest" and also functions as *araji*, "not to have" (an easy heart).

The familiar sound of the wind
Blowing through the pines of this peak.

The Princess, for her part, felt that she would be lonelier than ever when she would not see the dazzling and charming Chūnagon:

The passing years
Have accustomed me to the sound:
The wind in the pines.
Now, whenever it blows,
It will but add to my grief.

She was so beautiful Chūnagon wished he could show her to a real man, unlike himself. Reluctantly, he left.

The hills and fields had gradually turned the deeper hues of autumn. It moved him to think that so many days had flown by. On his return, he went to see his father first.

"I thought you would be gone for two or three days as usual, but when I didn't see you for so long I was worried and thought of you constantly. Where did you go? To leave the everyday world and go wandering about secretly is a very frivolous thing to do," Sadaijin said. Since he had hardly eaten anything for days, he now shared a meal with Chūnagon. Chūnagon was fated to be unusual, his father thought, but it consoled him that even with his defects he was a fine person and mingled in society. His father's expressions of delight touched Chūnagon deeply. Chūnagon was gorgeous, and one never grew weary of looking at him. He looked so exceptionally handsome that his father smiled, keeping his gaze constantly on him.

"Udaijin has been grieving for days," said Sadaijin. "In addition to his anxiety over his daughter's condition, he has been concerned that your heart is going astray. Why do you permit such a view of yourself? For appearances' sake, you should behave in a seemly manner." He urged him to pay

Udaijin a visit, but with tears filling his eyes, he then said: "As long as I live I shall always want to see you near."

At Udaijin's home everyone had been worried, for Chūnagon, leaving word that he would be away for four or five days, had remained in concealment somewhere for as many as ten without sending any word. Unable to understand this, they lamented. Udaijin ate nothing and grieved. Yon no Kimi was miserable, knowing she was the cause of all this. Since Chūnagon was disconsolate and did not want to remain in this world, Yon no Kimi was distraught, wondering what he had decided.

Saishō, not knowing what Yon no Kimi felt, thought Chūnagon's absence a good opportunity for visiting her. Since he wept, consumed with longing for Yon no Kimi, the weak-willed Saemon led him to her, night after night. Though Yon no Kimi thought some aspects of these encounters cruel, she did come to realize the true depth of Saishō's love. Her own feelings for him were considerable, and so she yielded to him. Fretting, her body swelling, she looked so lovely. It was natural that Saishō, who stealthily caught faint glimpses of her, should be overcome with love. They parted night after night, both in tears, and Yon no Kimi's anxieties grew. This distressed Udaijin, and he could find no respite from his worries.

When Chūnagon returned, Udaijin bustled about having the house cleaned. He even insisted that the ladies deck themselves up in finer clothes than usual.

"Why are you lying down like that?," he asked his daughter, forcing her to sit up and having her get all dressed up. Yon no Kimi felt awkward and distressed. When they heard Chūnagon enter, Udaijin hid himself and peeped into the room. He thought Chūnagon had grown a little more radiant while he was away. His sparkling charm seemed to touch all about him. He quietly seated himself and moved close to Yon no Kimi.

"In the mountain region where I thought I'd stay a short

while," he said, "there were books I wanted to read, and I couldn't return until I had finished looking at them. I wondered if, out of worry, you might send someone to search for me, and I thought I would just see if you would do that while I was there. But as time passed I sadly realized you would not and returned in shame."

There was no appropriate reply Yon no Kimi could make. She turned farther away from him and hid her face. When it became apparent that she was not going to answer, Chūnagon said: "Is that how it is? You always find me distasteful. I wondered if your feelings for me mightn't have changed because of my being away so long." Casting a sidelong glance at her, he stopped voicing his grievances, but just sat there lost in thought. Yon no Kimi was miserably unhappy.

From the edge of her sleeves to the hem of her skirt, Yon no Kimi was charming and supple. Her hair hung full and rich, and streaming down to the hem of her robe, it was so beautiful that to say she looked like a picture would not do her justice. Surely one would never tire of gazing at such magnificent beauty. Chūnagon had spoken to her only so much as was seemly, and did not approach her familiarly. Udaijin, who stood there watching, felt very chagrined. And yet Chūnagon and Yon no Kimi looked so well together. Were anyone else placed next to her he would certainly not look so fine.

When Yon no Kimi and Chūnagon used to lie together, they had spoken lovingly and exchanged vows. Though the relationship had not been that of a true husband and wife, they did care for each other deeply. But Yon no Kimi had changed, and it was reasonable that she no longer loved him very much. And Chūnagon, embarrassed and self-conscious, also felt estranged. They had grown very much apart.[87] Chūnagon realized that Yon no Kimi cared little for him because theirs had not been a real marital relationship, and he could not

[87] *Naka no utoku mo.* See note 79, above.

reasonably be bitter. He was ashamed, despising his own manly reflection in the mirror.

"If a gentle and refined woman felt love and affection, she would love her husband even if they only spoke to each other dispassionately," he thought. "She must love someone else much more than me." She was, for some reason, unfeeling; yet it was futile to reproach her. "It doesn't matter. I realize this life is but temporary, and even the painful should not pain me."

Chūnagon frequently walked in the snows of Mount Yo-shino; just as the snowflakes failed to melt away, neither did Udaijin's resentment at these absences. Days and months thus passed fleetly by, and the time came for Yon no Kimi to be moved to the room where she was to give birth to her child. Her father was worried and had sutras chanted and prayers said without interruption. Sadaijin thought the entire matter of the pregnancy odd, since he knew the child could not be his son's, but he had additional prayers said so that others would not find anything amiss. Perhaps it was the result of all these prayers that Yon no Kimi, who had suffered without respite for some time now, gave birth with ease to a charming girl. The child was so lovely that Udaijin imagined her rising in the future to the very highest position one could possibly wish. He was delighted. It was unbelievable the way he fussed over the birth ceremonies, adding every possible beautiful touch. Sadaijin too appeared to take extraordinary care even in arranging the rites in the bathing room. Udaijin had been waiting for this and briskly joined in the activity.

The girl closely resembled Saishō, and Chūnagon suspected she was his. His heart was in turmoil. He and Saishō had been so friendly and congenial together; now how strange and foolish Saishō must think him. Chūnagon was ashamed and hurt. He thought about it so much his heart ached. When the mother of the child, still feeling the aftereffects of all she had just been through, put on her floss silk robes, tucked herself in snugly, and lay down to sleep, he went to her.

"I want to ask you something," he said. She started at hearing his voice and looked up. Even under normal circumstances, Chūnagon seemed embarrassed, finding it difficult to meet with people in general. Yet now, even with all he had been considering, he smiled and said: "What do you think of this poem?"

> The child's visage,
> A memento of another
> Who dwells in our world.
> Shall I look after her?
> Shall I love her as my own?

He made Yon no Kimi feel so embarrassed that she could not say a thing. Understandably she hid her face. There was nothing Chūnagon could do. If he had intended to go on living in this world, he would have made her hear out his reproaches, but he saw that it was pointless. The fault lay in his own unusualness, and he felt there was nothing left to think or say. His tears fell.

"With everyone bustling about in celebration, someone may see that I am weeping, and that would be unfortunate," he thought, as he left, saddened. Even then Yon no Kimi remained so miserable that she was close to fainting. People could not understand why she felt this way.

Everyone shared in the joy as they bustled about, Udaijin's wife attending to the bathing room and Sadaijin's helping with the child's first bath. Though some noticed that Chūnagon did not look at all enthusiastic, they assumed it was just his usual composed and sober manner.

At Sadaijin's celebration of the seventh night after the child's birth[88] all the noblemen and courtiers gathered; only Saishō did not come because he was ill. Unknown to others, he had been worrying about Yon no Kimi's delivery. Even when all

---

[88] Birth ceremonies (*ubuyashinai*) were traditionally conducted on the third, fifth,

had gone well, as he had prayed it would, it was as if he were some outsider that he was told of the birth, and being far away, the news did not dispel his anxiety. Unable to contain himself, he went to Saemon's room.

"You know what the ties are between Yon no Kimi and myself. Arrange a meeting just for tonight, fleeting as a dream," he urged her. Though Saemon thought it futile, Saishō was so very distressed that she went to Yon no Kimi to see what she could arrange. Everyone had left. The older ladies were supervising matters in the kitchen, and the mothers of the ladies of nobility, busy with the gifts, had gone to their own rooms. Yon no Kimi had taken a hot bath that evening and was resting with a few ladies nearby. Saemon realized this was actually a good opportunity, and so, dimming the lamps, she led Saishō in unseen.

Yon no Kimi considered it a bad time for Saishō to come, but the mutual fate that was forced on them was, alas, unavoidable now. In the dim light, Yon no Kimi, dainty, slim, and lovely, looked thoroughly white.[89] She was dressed in white robes, the floss silk cloth that lay about her recalling the cloth tied around the flowers for the Chrysanthemum Festival.[90] Her hair hung beautifully long. Saishō thought her truly lovely like this. Exuding a wonderful perfume, she seemed particularly enticing. He spoke to her hesitantly. Amorous and sensual, he spoke of many things, trying to convince her that he was deeply in love and to touch her heart.

seventh, and ninth nights after a child's birth. Banquets were held, and members of the family sent food and clothing to the separate quarters specially prepared for the delivery. For details, see Nakamura 1965: 60–73.

[89] For the delivery and for several days after the birth the mother was dressed completely in white. See *ibid.*, pp. 29–31, for details.

[90] The Chrysanthemum Festival was held on the ninth day of the ninth month. On the preceding day, floss silk cloth was wrapped around chrysanthemums, and people believed that they could achieve longevity if, on the morning of the festival, they wiped themselves with this now dew-soaked and fragrant cloth. See Fujiki 1960: 190–91.

His words and manner would have swayed a rock or a tree. Not strong of heart, Yon no Kimi wept. She looked most touching, and Saishō could not bring himself to part from her.

Outside, the celebration was at its height, and Chūnagon sang "The Sea of Ise,"[91] beating time with a baton.[92] Saishō heard his delightful and charming voice. "Curious," he thought. "Why, when he's married to someone so lovely, is he not intimate with her? He's handsome and graceful, yet he always looks so serious, so somber, as though deeply troubled by something. I wonder what has moved him so—whether he's not in love with someone else." There was much he wanted to know about Chūnagon.

During the ceremonies Chūnagon had taken off his outer robes to present them as gifts, and since it was very cold, he decided to slip inside and put on some others. When he stole into Yon no Kimi's room, there was a strange commotion behind the curtains, and he peeped in; someone seemed to have gotten up and slipped out. But in his hurry, he had dropped his fan and some thin paper.[93] Yon no Kimi was so startled she did not even think of hiding it. Chūnagon walked quietly up to her. The fan had fallen near her pillow; he walked over to the lamp and looked at it. A scene of snow falling on bamboo was painted on red paper stretched over a lacquered frame. On the reverse side someone had jotted down some interesting lines. They were in Saishō's hand. Just as he had suspected, thought Chūnagon. Intending to slip in here, Saishō had not come to the banquet. Chūnagon might have been resentful, but he did not feel so jealous.

    [91] This is a line from a *saibara* (*NKBT*, 3: 386, no. 10): "At the clean shore of the sea of Ise, / Between the tides, / I would pick the seaweed, / I would gather the shells, / I would gather the pearls."

    [92] *Hyōshi*, a baton-like instrument with which, in several types of songs, the main singer beat time.

    [93] *Tatōgami*, a piece of thin paper that was folded twice horizontally and four times vertically, and kept in the folds of a robe. It was used either as a tissue or for jotting down a draft of a poem.

"It's probably natural," he thought, puzzled, "for a man to behave this way. It's true that under the circumstances, Yon no Kimi was easily accessible this evening, but this was not the first such incident, and there surely must be a go-between who knows about it. Saishō probably sent word that he wanted to come tonight. But that she let him—such a lack of reserve at a time like this—indicates that she's very much in love with him. If I leave her to Saishō's love, I can abandon this world without any compunction on her account, and that makes me happy; but somehow I'm sure I will feel worse than I expect to. I suppose Saishō too will feel that way.[94] Often it was quiet, and I was not here. But of all times for Yon no Kimi to be so unreserved! On this special occasion when there was so much commotion, if someone had seen her, it would have been unfortunate for both of us. I wonder what to do about our relationship now. People would think it rash if I stopped seeing her altogether. Yet it's foolish to go on pretending I don't know what's happening while the two of them seem to be meeting untroubled by the possibility that people might see them."

Though there was musical entertainment and one thing and another, Chūnagon was too preoccupied to take part. When all the celebrations for the child were over, he went to Mount Yoshino as usual and consoled himself there. It would be tedious to describe these events in detail, so let us pass on.

Saishō grieved over his secret affair with Yon no Kimi, difficult as it was for them to meet, but he consoled himself by exchanging love letters and arranging trysts with her at every possible opportunity. In his usual amorous manner, his love knew no bounds, but it was not to be expected that he could care for only one woman. Besides, it would be very

[94] The meaning of this last section is unclear. I follow Suzuki in assuming that *hazukashiki hito*, "the splendid" or "beautiful one," refers to Saishō, and in interpreting the remainder as Chūnagon's supposition that Saishō will feel concern or anxiety about him because of Saishō's relationship with Yon no Kimi.

awkward if Chūnagon learned of their relationship. So he decided to seek other mistresses.

Naishi no Kami at the Sen'yōden was very beautiful, and Saishō thought that if he were in love with her he would be free of the anxieties he faced in his relationship with Yon no Kimi. Once again he went to the Sen'yōden and, in tears, told Lady Saishō no Kimi all about his love. How could he slip in under cover of darkness? One night, when a strict abstinence was being observed and Naishi no Kami did not go to the Nashitsubo to attend the Crown Princess, Saishō stealthily entered the Sen'yōden.

Naishi no Kami found this very unexpected and was taken aback. Nevertheless, being a prudent and restrained sort, she seemed to stay absolutely still. Saishō wept and was distressed; he did not leave even when it grew light. It was an unusual situation that both found awkward. But since there was nothing they could say to keep the ladies from coming in, they lowered the curtains all the way and pulled down the bamboo screens around Naishi no Kami's platform under the pretext of her rigorous abstinence. Only two of the ladies knew what was happening, and they were most distressed.

Meanwhile, the thought that he would now see Naishi no Kami's highly acclaimed beauty, as he had ardently desired, made Saishō forget everything. She seemed tall to his touch, but that could not be regarded as a defect. Her hair hanging down loosely was thick. The face he saw with difficulty was just like Chūnagon's but much more refined. Hers was a lucid beauty, and her grace and elegance surpassed his. Yon no Kimi was refined, endearing, thoroughly lovely in every way, and none could equal her in those respects. But Naishi no Kami's beauty had an unworldly radiance that dazzled the eye.

His prudence completely gone, Saishō reproached her. Though Naishi no Kami was gentle, refined, charming, and seemingly frail, she would not yield. Saishō's heart was in turmoil: he wept without respite as the day passed, and he grieved that the night too seemed to have come to an end.

"My father will come when the period of abstinence is over, and Chūnagon will surely be here as well. There will be trouble if you stay. If you truly love me, think of Shiga Bay[95] and go. That would make me very happy," she said in a delightful voice just like Chūnagon's.

Saishō was captivated and even more reluctant to leave.

> You say we'll meet again.
> But on what am I to rely?
> On empty promises?
> How then can I go, vanish,
> Like the moon at the mountain's edge?

"How absurd!...." But before he could finish speaking, Naishi no Kami replied:

> I but amuse myself,
> Asking that you send me news
> On the winds of Shiga Bay.
> To future meetings with you
> I give not a single thought.

"Please understand." She spoke charmingly. There was nothing more Saishō could say without being unkind, and so he walked out, an empty shell, leaving his soul behind.[96]

Saishō did not receive any letters from Naishi no Kami after this. She never answered him and remained as remote as the clouds. He was annoyed and disappointed that she had slipped away from him. He was constantly at the palace, feel-

[95] A reference to a poem in the *Goshūi wakashū*, XIII, Love III, Ise no Taifu (*KKT*, 3: 686): "At Ōmi Sea / Difficult will it be / A meeting to have. / So send me your love on the wind; / It blows from Shiga Bay." There is a play on the word Ōmi, which is both a place-name and a term for meeting another. The same pun is used below, in Naishi no Kami's poetic reply to Saishō.

[96] This image is drawn from the previously cited poem by Lady Michinoku (see note 67).

ing distracted and hoping to find the opportunity of seeing her. On one such occasion he saw Chūnagon coming. His features were identical to Naishi no Kami's. She was more elegant and refined, but Chūnagon surpassed her with his fashionable airs and winning charm. Tormented beyond endurance by his love, Saishō wept copious tears. Chūnagon thought it very odd.

"Ever since we were young," explained Saishō, "there have been no barriers between us, and we've grown very close. In all that time my distress has only grown; I don't think I can go on living like this. Whenever I see you I feel as weak as a woman and weep." And he wiped away the tears. "No one is like the pine that lives a thousand years. Yet it seems sad that, like the dewdrops on the branch, all must fall, some sooner, some later."[97] Chūnagon spoke to him kindly, even though in his heart he was troubled by the thought that Saishō must think him a fool.

Saishō was constantly wretched. Even in his affair with Yon no Kimi, who shared his feelings and loved him, only their hearts had been free to meet. If he had not showed restraint and had been willing to risk public notice, and people learned of their relationship, it would have been very sad and embarrassing for Yon no Kimi. Because they were both cautious, their meetings were few and fleeting, dream meetings. As for Naishi no Kami, since she had slipped away she seemed to be more out of reach than ever, and Saishō was tormented by his love for her. He truly found no escape from his torment either at the pillow or at the foot of the bed.[98] He felt forlorn, both

[97] The allusion here is to a poem that appears in both the *Wakan rōeishū*, II, Miscellaneous, Evanescence, no. 798, Ryōsōjō (*NKBT*, 73: 256), and the *Shin-kokin wakashū*, VIII, Sorrow, no. 757, Priest Henjō (*NKBT*, 28: 170): "Dewdrops on the branch, / To the root of the tree / Will they fall? / Pattern of our lives is this, / For some linger while others fall."

[98] The last phrase is an allusion to a *haikai* in the *Kokin wakashū*, XIX, Miscellaneous Forms, no. 1023 (*NKBT*, 8: 316): "Tormented by love, / In the middle of the bed, / Helplessly I lie, / For no escape is there, / Not at the pillow nor the foot."

his sleeves wet with tears. He wanted very much to see Chūnagon, whom he thought of in connection with both Yon
no Kimi and Naishi no Kami. He realized it was rash of him,
but unable to contain himself, he went to Chūnagon's home.
When he arrived he was told that Chūnagon had gone out. He
stole a glance in the direction of the Nashitsubo and proceeded to walk there; he wanted to go in, but it was pointless, and
grief overcame him with special force. He inquired where
Chūnagon had gone, and when told it was to his father's
home, Saishō went there.

He sneaked into the room in the Western Pavilion where
Chūnagon usually was. It was a very warm day, and Chūnagon was relaxing, his robes scattered about. When he caught
sight of Saishō, he retreated to a room further inside the
house.

"You have come at a bad time. I'm not properly dressed for
seeing anyone," he said, and paid no attention to Saishō when
he told him to be at ease and remain as he was. Since there
were no women about, the unconcerned Saishō went right in.

"I really look shabby," Chūnagon said, smiling as he sat
down.

"I've been feeling unwell, and so it's been a long time since
I've seen you. I really wanted to visit you very much and felt
forlorn. I came especially to see you and you ran out," Saishō
said reproachfully.

"What could I do? I'm not fit to receive you," Chūnagon
replied.

"Since we're both suffering from the heat, I think I'll do the
same as you've done," Saishō rejoined, taking off his robes.
"That's fine, then," said Chūnagon, spreading some cushions
out in a cool spot and lying down to rest. He let Saishō come
near, and they chatted.

Chūnagon was wearing a white unlined summer silk kimono over red silk trousers. Relaxed, his face flushed with the
heat, he looked even more handsome than usual. The shape
of his hands, the fullness of his hips clearly visible under the

trousers that encased them, his white skin—it was as though he had rolled about in snow—were unbelievably lovely.

"How beautiful he is! Should there be a woman like this I would languish for love of her," thought Saishō, his passions aroused as he gazed at Chūnagon, and he lay down beside him. "It's too hot," said Chūnagon, annoyed, but Saishō paid no attention. They talked until it grew dark. A good breeze had sprung up, with a hint of autumn in it.[99] Saishō would not let Chūnagon rise. He told him, full of reproach, that no one would take any of his messages to Naishi no Kami, and that if the love he had felt for many years was unrequited he would leave this world. It was very moving.

"He probably has said the same things to my wife," thought Chūnagon, "and being only a weak woman, she couldn't help being swayed. How distressing. Even when he secretly visits a woman, he is miserable if she does not respond with the same intensity of emotion he feels. And it is not only Yon no Kimi[100] he loves, but Naishi no Kami as well. How full his heart must be." Chūnagon was deeply distressed.

> I do suspect
> You love not only one.
> Compare them then,
> The love that was fulfilled and
> The grief of unrequited love.

Chūnagon smiled to conceal his feelings. His composed, splendid appearance when seen from afar was nothing compared to the way he looked now.

Chūnagon moved closer to Saishō and was warm and affectionate with him, thus comforting Saishō about both his loves. Saishō wondered if Chūnagon knew about his relationship

[99] The phraseology here recalls a poem in the *Kokin wakashū*, IV, Autumn I, no. 169, Fujiwara no Toshiyuki (*NKBT*, 8: 136): "Autumn has come. / Not yet quite perceptible / Is it to my eyes; / Yet by the sound of the wind, / I know that it is here."

[100] Yon no Kimi is indicated here by a phrase that literally reads "the love that though fulfilled was not actually pledged," that is, the love in which there was no true marriage even though it was consummated. This expression is carried on into the following poem.

with Yon no Kimi, for he seemed so very pleasant. But putting any feelings of remorse out of his mind, he embraced Chūnagon still more firmly.

> All the others
> Have I already forgotten;
> I do not compare them.
> So attached am I to you,
> So intense my love for you.

Even before Saishō finished speaking, Chūnagon became annoyed. "I can believe that," he said. "It's because you think of me in connection with both of the ladies you love." He tried to rise, but Saishō would not let him. "You must have lost your senses. I have something to discuss with my father, but I decided to take a rest first since it was very hot. If I don't get up and put in an appearance straightaway, he'll think it odd. I'll go and be right back."

Chūnagon arose. What could Saishō have been thinking of? Upset, he could not stand to be separated from Chūnagon now. In the grip of his passion he seized Chūnagon.

"What are you doing? Have you lost your mind?," snapped Chūnagon in disgust, but Saishō paid no heed. Though Chūnagon treated his pursuer coldly and though his determined appearance certainly was manly, he could do nothing when Saishō seized him, and his heart grew weak. "What is happening?," he wondered. He wept tears of shame.

Saishō was amazed at what he had discovered. The love he felt for Yon no Kimi and Naishi no Kami now combined into a single feeling of tenderness and pity for Chūnagon. This was no time to wonder questioningly about Chūnagon's odd behavior. That was something for another, more suitable occasion. Now that he had learned the whole truth about Chūnagon, Saishō felt that no one had ever moved his heart so much, and this inner turmoil saddened him. Chūnagon, seeing that Saishō appeared unable to understand, was won-

dering what Saishō thought of him. It was because he had
gone on living in this sad world that his painful secret had
been uncovered, he thought, and as his tears fell he looked
very beautiful and touching.

"What am I going to do now that I can't bear to leave you
for even a moment?," wept Saishō. The night passed, and he
still did not look as though he would get up to leave.

"Even if I were to reproach him for his behavior," thought
Chūnagon, "I couldn't act manly and strong, for now he
knows I am not what I should be. Though infuriating, there
is nothing I can do even if he chooses to use this night as an
unusual topic of conversation and tell others about me. It
must be the result of karma in previous lives, just as the
Yoshino Prince told me." Yet he found it hard to part from
his lover. Touchingly he said: "My appearance is unusual, but
since our hearts have found one another, if you behave in such
a way as not to embarrass me in public I shall know you truly
love me. I live quietly,[101] and so if we act nonchalantly it should
not be difficult for us to meet like this."

He spoke very sweetly and soothingly to Saishō and then
sent him away. Even so, though it seemed quite reasonable,
Saishō felt he could not leave for even a moment. Yet sad as
he felt at the separation, after pledging his love time and again,
he finally tore himself away.

Chūnagon was left with the feeling that it had all been a
dream. "Why don't I leave this world? As long as I stay, it will
certainly be embarrassing to go out and mingle with others in
front of Saishō." But he felt forced to remain when he recalled
how anxious his parents had been when they did not see him
for even a short time.

When Chūnagon went to his father, Sadaijin gazed smiling-
ly at him as usual and looked very pleased. "Were you here

101 I have omitted a clause here, the meaning of which is unclear. A possible
reading might be "and since I am not one to be considered of such station as to have
lots of people always milling about me."

last night? I ask because Saishō came especially to see you. He said he had some questions about something he was studying." Chūnagon became agitated.

"Udaijin is very upset that you stay away all night. Do behave so as not to antagonize people." Chūnagon was embarrassed, and it was natural that he reply: "I don't think my behavior is such that people can reproach me." He breakfasted with his father, and just as he was leaving he received a letter from Saishō:

> What am I to do?
> Already my yearning for you
> Has grown so intense,
> I feel on the verge of death.
> How I wish to be at your side!

"I must see you this evening, my darling." In view of his unusual position, Chūnagon had to answer and consent to the meeting. In his customary serious manner he carefully wrote:

> To everyone,
> You are dying, you are dying,
> So you often say.
> Yet it appears to me
> Your life will be a long one.

His calligraphy was beautiful, and it seemed even more so to Saishō that morning. But he wondered if in not mentioning a tryst that evening Chūnagon was saying there was not to be one. Forlornly he wrote again:

> It does not matter
> How often I have spoken
> Of dying in the past;
> For never yet have I felt
> As intensely as I do now.

Chūnagon was at Udaijin's home when he received this letter.

It was a nuisance, but since he did not want to hurt Saishō's feelings, he wrote:

> Far greater than yours,
> The turmoil in my heart.
> Better think of that,
> The sorrow borne by someone
> Unlike any in this world.[102]

Saishō had been eagerly awaiting this response, and when he read it he naturally wept even more as he hastened to Udaijin's home.

"Not only would people see us and think it odd," thought Chūnagon, "but if I go out and greet him there will be no way to avoid a meeting tonight." It really was all such a nuisance. So very firmly he shouted to Saishō outside: "I've been feeling unwell since morning and can't see you. I am sorry that you've taken the trouble to come."

This made Saishō resentful and sad, and even though others were watching him, he was unable to hide his emotions or restrain himself.

"There is something I must tell you. Just come to the door," he cried.

"If I weren't feeling so ill I would certainly speak to you when you've come especially to see me," Chūnagon replied, not going out. "It's just that now the pain in my chest has nearly reduced me to unconsciousness."

Saishō was miserable but was forced to endure his suffering. He supposed that the two whom he loved, Yon no Kimi and Chūnagon, were probably together. Though he was intimate with both and could not part from either, his lingering would seem strange, and so he returned home and spent the night lamenting, feeling more dead than alive.

Chūnagon found the thought of mingling shamelessly with

---

[102] This poem appears in the *Fūyō wakashū*, Love IV (ZGR, 14: 70).

people and possibly seeing Saishō disagreeable; and so, using his illness as a pretext, he did not go out. Saishō was resentful and called on Chūnagon day after day to ask why, only to return downcast, his visits in vain.

Finally Saishō heard that Chūnagon had come to court. He was excited. Seeing him at last, he felt tense, like someone who has found a beloved one he has not seen for years but has never stopped yearning for. On meeting his gaze, Chūnagon's face turned crimson. He composed himself and remained aloof and serious. Saishō was unable to approach him familiarly. Chūnagon seemed very distant, and Saishō again felt unsure and downcast.

Chūnagon was summoned by the Emperor. When he arrived, the Emperor had him come close as usual and asked, as he always did, that Naishi no Kami be presented. He scrutinized Chūnagon, noting that his face was so very beautiful one could gaze at it forever. "I've heard," he thought, "that Naishi no Kami looks very much like Chūnagon. If he were well made up and had longer hair, he would be like a goddess descended from heaven, but better for not being so grand, so excessively beautiful. No one is so charming and radiant as he." Once again, he felt he had to see Naishi no Kami, and made Chūnagon feel he had no choice but to have her sent to court.

While Chūnagon was close to the Emperor, he acted serious and respectfully restrained, having learned a lesson from his experience with Saishō. He firmly told the Emperor that his sister had no thoughts of the sort usual to women of the world. The Emperor gazed tirelessly at him and for the longest time would not let him leave. It occurred to Saishō that the Emperor might notice, as he himself had, that Chūnagon was a woman and that, despite Chūnagon's unusual guise, the Emperor would certainly never glance at another girl after that. The Emperor was looking constantly at Chūnagon and though they seemed only to be talking and friendly, Saishō

could not get this thought out of his mind for days. He was
worried and upset.

Saishō was waiting for Chūnagon when the latter finally left
the Emperor, and accompanied him to the place where they
usually rested. Chūnagon could not manage to get away, and
he stayed on, making it look as if they were on night duty
together. Whenever Chūnagon and Saishō served, the courtiers, with renewed spirit, would gather at the post for the
night watch, and then all night it would be very noisy and
unpleasant. That evening Saishō and Chūnagon seemed to
have private matters to discuss and they disregarded everyone
else, so the courtiers scattered. Before they had gone far
enough, though, Saishō, his appearance very touching, began
to weep and reproach Chūnagon. Had people happened to see
him, they would have thought the situation very strange.

"My dear," said Chūnagon, reproachful in his own turn, "if
you really love me don't act this way when people might see
us. If meeting each other presented difficulties and if opportunities for us to come across one another were unlikely, then
you might feel this way. But when we come face to face night
and day, what rare event is it that causes you to act like this?
It seems to me that you are treating my unusual and shameful
condition particularly lightly, and this is very unkind."

"It hurts me to hear you say such things," replied Saishō.
"Meetings certainly are hard to arrange; I do see you like this,
but you keep your distance and look uninterested. It distresses
me so."

Chūnagon could not but be moved by Saishō's pained
expression. But it was difficult being constantly upset by
Saishō. He did not want his unusual condition known to the
world, and so he promised to see Saishō, but only when it
would not look unseemly to people. This too Saishō found
hard to bear.

"Though I knew all that was happening, I thought, how
could I with my unusual person, show myself to be suspicious

of anyone," Chūnagon said, alluding to Saishō's secret meetings with Yon no Kimi. "But since I am continuing to act as though I know nothing, you should console the poor girl at appropriate times when there is no one about."

Saishō pitied him, but since Chūnagon had spoken without rancor, Saishō did not want it to seem as though he was concealing anything, and he told about everything in detail from the beginning. He said that since he had found Chūnagon, his heart could no longer be soothed by Yon no Kimi.

"How cruel he is to say such things now about someone he loved so passionately before. He seems as fickle as the color of the dayflower," Chūnagon thought, as he looked at Saishō. "I don't think he will ever allude to my strange condition as long as he loves me, but when his love wanders to another he will reveal my secret." He was worried and unhappy to think that he was inescapably bound to such a person.

Things went on in this way. Saishō followed Chūnagon like a second shadow, to the palace and everywhere else. Chūnagon continued to act as though the type of tryst Saishō desired was hard to arrange, but at the same time he always spoke to him very tenderly. When they did meet, Chūnagon, aware of his inescapable ties to Saishō, yielded to him, but once they were apart he acted as if they were not at all on intimate terms and as if their meetings were terribly difficult to arrange. This saddened Saishō all the more. At times Chūnagon urged him to go to Yon no Kimi, who loved and yearned for him, and dispassionately he arranged suitable opportunities for the two to meet. Saishō thought it natural that he see Yon no Kimi, as Chūnagon so very extraordinarily and kindly intended him to, but since he had already given more than half his love to Chūnagon, his love for Yon no Kimi now seemed ordinary.

He passively endured the separation enforced by Chūnagon, and his sense of helplessness about it all grew. He did not even feel like seeing other women to console himself during the separations. His intimacy with Yon no Kimi would never be enough to distract him from the suffering Chūnagon thus inflicted on him. He was loving and kind when he went secretly to see her, which he did more frequently than before, for now he had lost all fear of discovery by Chūnagon and shrank only from others' eyes. Yon no Kimi felt that they had grown remarkably close and was very yielding and desirable. But Saishō felt his heart throb most for him who made him suffer.

Chūnagon was now aware of all that was happening between Yon no Kimi and Saishō. It was a strange situation, he thought. It was both dreadful and extraordinary, and he lamented it. Yet now more than ever he would not let Yon no Kimi know that he knew about it. In any event, he probably would not remain in the world long, and thus he spoke kindly to her.

Chūnagon had gone to the house of his wet nurse in the sixth ward, since it was that time of the month again, and of course, Saishō could not keep himself away while Chūnagon was in residence there. Concealing himself behind a brushwood fence nearby, Saishō looked around. A light rain was falling, and the night sky, darkened by clouds, was lovely. The rattan blinds had been rolled up, and Chūnagon, dressed in layers of violet and white Chinese figured silk over red, was gazing outside. In the light of the setting sun he looked more radiant than usual, his chin resting on his hands, his arms as lovely as polished jewels. He wiped away his tears.

> An autumn shower
> Gently fills the evening sky
> And moistens the air.
> Yet no less wet are my sleeves
> Drenched by my bitter tears.[103]

"Why should I be so sad when I am not likely to be long of this world?"[104] Even in painting, no brush could capture the

[103] This poem is similar to one in the Winter section of the *Fūyō wakashū* labeled "the first Daijōdaijin (Chancellor) of *Torikaebaya*" (ZGR, 14: 28).

[104] This sentence draws on a poem in the *Kokin wakashū*, XVIII, Miscellaneous

loveliness of Chūnagon gazing idly out, murmuring thus to himself.[105] Saishō became more agitated than ever, and he quickly approached and said:

> Darkness envelops me,
> Descending from clouds and grief.
> Tears and autumn rain fall.
> Though wet am I, had I not come
> How might I have seen you?

This was so sudden that Chūnagon was taken aback, but moved by the occasion he said:

> Alone I sit,
> Gazing distractedly
> At the rainy sky.
> But not because I wait for you
> Are my sleeves wet with tears.

Saishō had not finished telling Chūnagon that it was cruel of him to hide so that no one would discover his secret and to sit alone gazing outside lost in thought. "I've decided that I can't go on living at all if you are always this cruel." He left nothing unsaid. Since there was no need for him to feel any reticence in this secluded place, Saishō had lain down on top of Chūnagon, and, weeping and laughing, they spoke of many things. One could never repeat it all. They did not even realize that it had grown light.[106] They both sat up, and Saishō looked at Chūnagon. Chūnagon's unapproachable, brisk manner and firm bearing were certainly manly, but now, with his confused, yielding, unrestrained behavior, he was most graceful

---

II, no. 934 (*NKBT*, 8: 291): "Why am I distressed? / For like the seaweed soon cut / By the fisherman, / Unlikely is it that I / Long will remain in this world."

[105] This might be an allusion to a poem in the *Horikawa gohyakushu*, cited in Suzuki 1973: 91: "The maiden's beauty, / Though in a picture painted, / No brush can it capture. / Oh, to whom will she show it, / Her flowerlike appearance!"

[106] A similar phrase appears in a poem in the *Zoku goshūi wakashū*, Miscellaneous II, Lady Ise (*Kokka taikan*, 1: 487): "Beaded blind, / Unaware of dawn's approach, / Within it we lay; / Do I not wish it were so, / Even if but in a dream!"

and lovely, looking desperately sad and heartrendingly appealing.

With Yon no Kimi, Saishō was constantly burdened with the guilt of his illicit affair; and though they shared all intimacies, he felt nothing special for her. Chūnagon, now completely different from the person he had grown to know so well as a male, was so touchingly lovely. He was delightfully yielding and playful, lovable and gentle. Saishō thought it so sad that when Chūnagon was out in public, he sometimes looked at him almost dispassionately. He wanted with all his heart to hide Chūnagon away somewhere and consider him his own.

"I've seen you in your usual male guise for years, yet when I look at you now you seem more beautiful than the most wonderful of princesses," he said repeatedly to Chūnagon, whom he considered quite his own. "Since you are actually a woman, won't you conceal yourself and remain hidden away as one? I'm not able to see you as I wish if you remain in your male role, and this troubles me. Since olden days it has been customary in this kind of relationship for the woman to submit to whatever inconveniences a man creates, no matter how wrong they may be. For your own sake, too, it's most unnatural for you to disguise yourself as a man."

Saishō, wanting fervently to consider Chūnagon his own, spoke of this night and day. It was, of course, reasonable. But for Chūnagon, accustomed as he was to a man's life, to be suddenly confined indoors like a woman would have been unnatural. He could not even contemplate it. Night and day, Saishō tearfully reproached him, unburdened himself without restraint; and many days passed, more than usual, for one of Chūnagon's monthly absences.

It pained Chūnagon to imagine how upset Udaijin must be again, and he sent a letter. "I remain secluded here because recovery from my usual ailment is taking longer than it normally does. I am depressed, wondering what is to become of me in the end."

Though I live on,
It is empty, worthless,
This life I lead.
But when I think of leaving it,
Oh, the grief that fills my heart!

"The customary thing for him to do would be to entrust himself to our care, whatever his ailment," thought Udaijin. "I can't understand his going off to a separate place like this from time to time. What kind of marital relationship can they have?" Udaijin grieved, and others worried, talking about it in whispers.

Only Yon no Kimi herself understood his absence, since she was aware of her own guilt, and she felt pained and embarrassed. She felt sorry for Chūnagon because her father now took delight in saying nasty things about him. Then too her beloved Saishō was not so anxious to be with her as he used to be. Yon no Kimi went on brooding over one thing and another. Then a letter from Chūnagon arrived, and Udaijin, naturally eager to read it, ripped it open at once. "How unfortunate!," exclaimed Udaijin in tears, his bitterness forgotten. "I don't see why he should be so seriously ill. In this degenerate age he is so splendid, and yet he writes too much of matters unsuited to him. It's most inauspicious. His calligraphy is far beyond anything others can produce." He read the letter again and again and urged Yon no Kimi to write a reply, one that would move him with its affection. She seemed very self-conscious:

Beset by sorrows,
So dreadfully distasteful
I feel my life to be.
Yet even I have not vanished
But gone on living till today.

She wrote charmingly, but the contents did not seem to interest Chūnagon. He definitely did not want to let Saishō

read the letter and did not open it wide. But Saishō, thinking
that it looked like an answer from Yon no Kimi, snatched it
from Chūnagon and read it. Suddenly his heart began to
throb. Though he did in fact love Chūnagon more than anyone else now, when he saw the letter, his face changed color
and he grew serious. He looked very grave.

"And I'm to rely on such a person," thought Chūnagon,
looking at him, "change my appearance to a woman's, and
bury myself away indoors with him!" He felt forlorn.

Saishō, however, felt he could go on living a thousand
years [107] now that he was with Chūnagon. He gave himself over
to pleasure night and day to the point of indecency, pledging
his love even in lives to come.

When a good many days had gone by in this manner,
Chūnagon wanted to leave, but Saishō detained him, reproaching him repeatedly: "You'll probably stay away again
and act as though I am of no concern to you." Still they could
not go on like this indefinitely, and so Chūnagon managed to
make Saishō leave, and he himself went traveling about to
various places.

While the two were going about their lives in this manner,
sometime after the tenth month, when the time had come for
Chūnagon to go as usual to his hideaway [108] at his wet nurse's,
he felt peculiar. It did not occur to him that he might be
pregnant. He was constantly uneasy, wondering why he felt
as he did. Since he did not feel the need to go to his hiding
place this month, he went to Udaijin's home. Yon no Kimi cut
an elegant and refined figure. While Chūnagon was there, all

[107] This expression is used in a similar way in a poem in the *Goshūi wakashū*, XI,
Love I, Fujiwara no Saneyori (*KKT*, 3: 676): "When trust there is, / So heartened do
I feel / That if I might / My life would I prolong, / Thus to remain one thousand years."
[108] Literally "the village of which there is no sound." The expression *oto nashi*
("without sound") appears in a poem in the *Kokin waka rokujō*, II, Towns, no. 468
(*KKT*, 9: 335): "Tormented by love, / I raise my voice to call out; / No sound does
it make. / I wonder which one it is, / The village without sound?" *Oto nashi* is also
used in a poem in the *Shūi wakashū*, XII, Love II, Anonymous (*KKT*, 3: 483), the
last two lines of which ask: "Where would it be, / The soundless waterfall?"

other cares vanished from her mind. He was moved to see how she tried to attend him without leaving his side, and he thought: "I just want her to recall me kindly when I'm no longer here." So he spoke with her attentively and tenderly. Her father was happy to see this and bustled about, turning all his attention to prayer arrangements and other such matters. Yon no Kimi too was pregnant again, but she thought it would look bad if people learned about it so soon after her last child, and so told no one.

With Chūnagon feeling ill and staying indoors, Saishō, inhibited by the troubling presence of others from finding his usual relief, was unable even to write letters that would ease his anguish. He languished on until the twelfth month. Chūnagon was not so ill as to stay in bed, and he went regularly to his father's home. Since he did not eat enough, he had become very thin. The sight of an orange or a tangerine was enough to make him nauseous. This puzzled his father, who was constantly arranging to have prayers said for him. Chūnagon was beginning to add things up.

"A pregnant woman's condition must be like this," he thought. "Apparently Yon no Kimi feels the way I do." Profoundly unhappy, he felt he should hide himself away, leaving no trace behind. He was inconsolable, but his circumstances were such that he could not reveal to anyone that he was pregnant. He was even too embarrassed to approach his parents. Then should he inform Saishō and marry him?

The intensity of Saishō's love increased as long as he could not see Chūnagon, and he was reproachful, finding the situation so unbearable that he seemed unable to restrain himself in public. For Chūnagon this was most embarrassing. But aware of his own strange fate, he found it difficult and heartbreaking to forsake Saishō, and so went to meet with him at his wet nurse's home. Saishō was waiting for him. Chūnagon was embarrassed to reveal his pregnancy, but because he had been a man all this time, he boldly spoke up nonetheless: "The months pass, though with increasing grief; and our pledges seem regrettable, and even loathsome."

When Saishō was told the amazing news, he wept and spoke of their deep ties. "If our union has produced a child, do, as I asked from the first, consider taking on the appearance of a woman so that we may be married. It's hard for both of us if you remain a man. When we're young it's all right to meet at the palace, but when we're adults, noblemen of the third rank or higher, we can't take night watch even though we may be at the palace. We will never be able to meet in our homes as long as you stay a man, since you worry about others noticing us. There will be absolutely no way for us to satisfy our desire to see each other. So do as I ask and discard your pretense now. How can you go on otherwise? Make up your mind and change back to a woman immediately."

Chūnagon was very ashamed. He had consoled himself with the thought that he had been fated to be as he was, living as a man. But if he revealed that he was a woman and confined himself indoors as Saishō's wife, it would, he thought, be sad indeed. Since he would not want anyone to know about what he had done, he would have to shut himself away without letting even his parents know, and this would grieve them.

"Ever since I realized I was unusual," he thought, "I have very much wanted to forsake the world, but I have put off doing so because of what my parents might think and have gone on living this way until now. It pains me greatly that, having let someone else know of my strange condition, I have placed myself in a situation from which I cannot extricate myself."

Though nothing should have troubled the bright, charming Chūnagon, he was somehow bewildered, and holding his sleeve up to his face, he wept bitterly. Though it was strange when one realized that Chūnagon was unusual, when one saw him it seemed that even a recognized beauty with hair seven or eight feet long would be insignificant by comparison. Because he was actually a woman in man's guise, Chūnagon looked different. He was attractive, lovable.

"It's natural for you to feel sad, but it's all karma," wept Saishō, trying to comfort him. "Don't brood so."

And he repeated that Chūnagon ought to change his appearance into a woman's and retire indoors that very day or the next. Chūnagon felt he would have to do precisely that, since he could not go on as he was. He had many recollections of the world he had frequented, all touching events, and at first nothing could cheer him. Then he thought that Saishō must truly be concerned about him, for his tears had flowed so profusely, and he had expressed himself to the fullest.

Saishō wrote passionate love letters whenever he was separated from Chūnagon, but he could not be satisfied with only one woman.[109] Chūnagon noticed that he seemed to be stealing away to Yon no Kimi when he was not with him. Since it was around this time that Yon no Kimi became pregnant again, it certainly appeared that he loved her very much, the repeated pregnancies testifying to the depth of their bonds.

At this realization Chūnagon told himself: "Even if Saishō loved me with all his heart, I would still go far into the mountains and hide. I would give up the Imperial favors bestowed on me and my office and rank, and devote myself to the contemplation of my future life. There can be no regrets though I leave the world.[110] Certainly Saishō is different from

---

[109] "He could not be satisfied with only one woman" is a loose translation. The text reads: *utsu suminawa ni wa arazu. Utsu suminawa* refers to an inked marking string used to strike straight lines. The term appears in a poem in *Shūi wakashū*, XV, Love V, Hitomaro (*KKT*, 3: 511): "No concern have I / Now for this one, now for that. / Like the straight line / Cut by the Hida artisan / Is my love for you alone." The *Manyōshū*, XI, no. 2648 (*NKBT*, 6: 215), includes a very similar poem: "No concern have I / Directed now here, now there. / Like the straight line / Cut by those from Hida, / I have but one path of love." Hida is an area known for its woodcutters and carpenters.

[110] The meaning of this sentence is unclear. It might also read: "There would be no regrets even though I have changed myself (my person)."

others in charm and elegance, but to be fated to entrust myself
to such a person and stay indoors leaves much to be desired.
Moreover, he is unreliable, very fickle and lustful. Even now
when his love for me seems second to none, he secretly
continues to bear great affection for Yon no Kimi. Add to this
the fact that if I were to do as he asks, I would see his ardor
lessen; he would grow used to me until I was no longer special,
and he would become unfeeling. How mortifying it would be!
I would be a laughingstock."

He continued to think about the situation: "To do as Saishō
has asked is still distasteful to me. But I cannot go out again
in my present condition and continue to mingle in society. So
I shall hide from the world." Having made up his mind, how
sad he felt when he saw his parents or went to court. He had
taken them for granted, sparing them few thoughts, but now
that he was to remain with them for only a month or two, even
the sighing wind made him feel sad and forlorn.

Unaware that Chūnagon's appraisal of the situation was
different from his own, Saishō thought he would now be able
to keep him indoors as his wife, and his inner turmoil slack-
ened. At the same time Yon no Kimi seemed sadly grieved and
miserable about her pregnancy. Unable to justify herself by
speaking up about the trials of her marital relationship, she
just continued to lament:

> The sorrows I feel,
> I who have pledged vows with more than one,
> Add not to them.
> Do not create and freeze
> These icicles within my heart.[111]

"I feel the loneliness of the late winter nights."

Saishō, facing her as she spoke, observed how elegantly
lovely and fragile she was, as she concealed the source of her

---

[111] This poem contains a couple of *engo*, or associative words. *Tsurara*, "icicle,"
is associated with *tsurasa*, "sorrows"; and *musubu*, "to form" or "harden," with
musubu of the same character but meaning "to add," "tie on," "attach."

troubles. She, who had for so long moved his heart, touched him as no other.

"Should even Chūnagon seclude himself as my wife, there is no reason why I should refrain from seeing Yon no Kimi. Indeed, I'll take them both as wives," Saishō thought, and his heart throbbed in anticipation. So happy was he that both his sleeves were drenched with tears of joy. Since he would have regretted being considered unfeeling by Yon no Kimi, he somehow contrived various means of going to her.

"It is just as I suspected," thought Chūnagon, "he loves her. If he gives me cause for anxiety like this, he isn't putting his whole mind to the question of what ought to be done in my case. Unfortunately, it seems that his love for Yon no Kimi is growing." But though Chūnagon was resentful, it would have been awkward to reproach Saishō, and besides, his feelings were not of the usual sort. So enduring feigning unconcern, he went on grieving, and in this state it seemed he would never feel well again.

Toward the end of the twelfth month, Chūnagon went to his father's home. Though everyone was bustling about, Sadaijin felt it would be improper if they did not meet every evening. He had eagerly awaited Chūnagon, and when he happily gazed at him, his heart ached to see him haggard and depressed when he was so handsome and at the prime of life.

"Why do you look so poorly? Do you still feel ill?"

"There is nothing particularly wrong. It might come from having been sick so long."

"This is shocking. We must begin to have prayers said again," said Sadaijin, and summoning the appropriate people, he told them what he required—incantations, prayers to the gods, prayers for the washing away of sin and defilement, and so on.

"My," thought Chūnagon, "since he loves me so, how will he feel when I have disappeared without trace?" Unable to stand it any longer, he wept, though he tried to hide it.

"I thought it my misfortune that you and your sister were so unexpectedly different from what you should have been. I wanted to end my life," said his father. "Now you have attained high office and rank, a position in which you go out and mingle in society. Everyone says what a fine figure you cut in public. I myself am nothing special, and I have achieved my reputation through yours; that has soothed my grief. I felt it must have been fated. But just when I was about to lay my sorrow to rest, I find that you are terribly distressed, and this, even more than your lengthy ailment, upsets me. I cannot go on living." Sadaijin wept, and Chūnagon felt unbearably sad.

"There is nothing to worry about," said Chūnagon to comfort his father. "Because I am unwell I am causing you to grieve. But it is not a matter of my life, as I would prefer. It is only that I worry that you may never see me again." He managed to stay through the meal. Sadaijin was happy and content as he dined with his son. His mother, however, was unconcerned and asked about nothing.

When the old year had ended and the new one had begun, Chūnagon felt like a sheep being led to slaughter.[112] How long was he to go on living like this, he wondered. The ox carts, the curtains in them, the yokes and shafts—all were freshly and beautifully decorated for the new year. Even the footmen had coordinated the colors of their robes, and they were given adornments. Of course, Chūnagon himself was specially dressed for the occasion. From his over-garment down to the lustrous pattern of his innermost robe, he sparkled like the surface of the pond in which the ice has melted.[113] Having taken special care with his clothes and appearance, he first

[112] The commentator in the *Kakaishō*, XIX (A commentary on *The Tale of Genji*; see Fujimura 1950, 1: 473–74), speaks of this image of sheep being led to slaughter as an illustration of *mujō*, the impermanence of things. The passage is cited in Suzuki 1973: 102.

[113] An allusion to a poem in the *Kokin wakashū*, I, Spring I, no. 12, Minamoto Masazumi (*NKBT*, 8: 107): "Melting is the ice / In the wind of the valley. / In each ice-free crack / The waves are showing through: / The first flowers of spring."

went to his father's house and paid his respects to his parents. He seemed much more radiant this year than ever before. Unable to restrain themselves, they wept, though to do so was inauspicious.

When Chūnagon went to the palace, everyone was stunned at the sight of him. Saishō also came, looking more splendid than anyone else. "It's going to be hard for him to become a woman now that he has become accustomed to mingling in society, looking so marvelous, and now that he is held in such high repute," he thought on seeing Chūnagon. His heart ached, but though he kept his eyes fixed on him, Chūnagon was on the whole aloof and rigid, and Saishō was unable to meet with him.

Chūnagon then went to Naishi no Kami's apartments, where many courtiers and noblemen had gathered. They sat down and received him. It was awkward and trying to be with them, but what could he do? They prevailed on Saishō to play the lute, and Chūnagon sang "The Plum Branch."[114] His voice was beautiful.

Saishō had transferred his affections to Chūnagon and had been content. But now he recalled how unexpectedly cold Naishi no Kami had been toward him, how she had firmly ended his attempted affair with her by rejecting him. So with a troubled heart he left.

Chūnagon earnestly attended all court gatherings at which officials discussed government affairs. The Emperor considered what he said more valuable than the advice of the older, higher-ranking noblemen who sat before him. The rare Imperial favor shown him was the greatest obtainable in this world.

That year the flowers in full bloom were more beautiful than ever, and at the beginning of the third month the cherry

---

[114] From a *saibara* (*NKBT*, 3: 107, no. 28): "The nightingale perched on the plum branch. / All through the spring it was bright. / All through the spring the nightingale sang. / But still the snow falls. / Oh, so beautiful there. / The snow falls."

blossoms at the Shishinden[115] had to be seen and admired.
Scholars in all fields were summoned, and they put their
hearts into composing poems on themes they thought would
be interesting. When the day of the poetry contest came, and
they were given the chosen theme, even the compositions of
the scholars who had won special recognition did not attain
the level of Chūnagon's poem. Needless to say it was unique
in Japan, but even in China there was nothing like it, said
everyone, from the Emperor on down, and reading Chūnagon's poem aloud, they created quite an uproar. The Emperor
summoned Chūnagon and singling him out for distinction
over the other worthy men, he removed his robe and made
Chūnagon accept it. In the way Chūnagon delicately executed
his formal bows stepping down from before the Imperial
presence, and in his careful carriage, he seemed more splendid
than ever. Even the beauty of the flowers was overshadowed
by him, and everyone looking on wept. His father was deeply
affected by the sight.

"What a magnificent figure he cuts. I was needlessly upset
about him. No one knows he is really a woman. It seems he
can very well go about as he is." Naturally, he shed more tears
of joy than anyone else. Of Udaijin's joy it is needless to speak
at all. The joy in both Sadaijin's and Udaijin's hearts was equal.

When it grew dark a concert began. Chūnagon, thinking
that he would probably never play the flute again after this
day, put his whole heart into the music that at previous occasional concerts he had been unwilling to play. The notes rang
out, splitting the heavens. They set one and all a-tingle and
were indescribably lovely. In ability and appearance he was
so absolutely splendid that he did not seem to belong to this
world. People believed that someone with all this brilliance
would not live long,[116] and that was inauspicious. The Em-

---

[115] The text has Nanden, a less common name for this palace building.

[116] It was commonly believed that anyone too beautiful or magnificent would be
taken by the gods and thus die at an early age.

peror was pleased. He had felt that Chūnagon's office and rank were not suitably high. Since Chūnagon had demonstrated that he would excel in all things that day, the Emperor, as a sign of his good intentions toward him, appointed him Major Captain of the Right.[117] The Emperor considered Saishō superior too, and made him an Acting Middle Counsellor. The honor done them and the joy they experienced were exceptional.

After Chūnagon had received his appointment and it had grown dark, his father left the palace behind his son. Chūnagon, in his capacity as head of the Imperial Guard, waited and received his father. His splendor sent shivers through all who saw him; but though he had been honored, his heart was darkened by grief. "Never will I cease to lament that I am different from others. In the eyes of the world I have been magnificently promoted, yet I must vanish without trace."

His father, however, was unaware of his sorrow and proceeded to see him to Udaijin's home. The latter had been awaiting Chūnagon, and the uproar and joy there was even greater than if he had seen his own daughter made Empress. How happy he looked!

Saishō was not all that delighted by his promotion, for he felt he had been especially honored out of compassion, that the promotion had been conferred on him in the wake of Chūnagon's. "Chūnagon is extraordinarly handsome and gifted. For someone like that to remove himself from the world is certainly difficult, as I can see by putting myself in his place." He spent the entire night in such thought, and when it grew light he wrote a congratulatory letter.

> In your happiness,
> Donning robes of the clouds,

---

[117] Udaishō. He was appointed to one of the six divisions of the Imperial Body-guards, which were responsible for guarding the innermost part of the palace and were divided into two groups, the Right and the Left. The Major Captain was the highest-ranking officer in the division.

Purple in hue,[118]
Will your feelings have changed?
Will you forget the vows we shared?

Although there was great commotion over the celebration,
both indoors and out, in his heart Chūnagon was worried and
as a result, found Saishō's concern both comical and touching.
"I should congratulate you first," he wrote.

My cares multiply.
When these robes I remove,
Exchange for others,
What, I wonder painfully,
Is then to become of me.

Seeing this, Saishō became sympathetic. It was reasonable and
touching, and so the amorous Saishō felt none of the joy of
his own promotion, and he wept.

What with the bustle accompanying his promotion, Saishō
had less time than ever to meet with Chūnagon, but as he
calculated the month and day when Chūnagon was due to
give birth, he consoled himself with the thought that Chūnagon would soon be his.

Chūnagon began to feel constrained by his pregnant condition, and he knew that though it was truly hard to give up his
present life, he could not go on as he was. He often went on
night watch at the palace feeling very forlorn. Saishō came
also, and they met and talked at their usual resting place.

Saishō was secretly sending answers to someone's letters.
He would hand them to a messenger, intimating that they
were love notes. Chūnagon was saddened to notice that when
Saishō hid the letters, he seemed to be holding things back
from him; and that when he did not hide them, he seemed to

118 The color of one's robes varied by rank; purple denoted the rank of Major
Captain. "Robes of the clouds" means gods' or goddesses' robes; thus one who had
become part of the realm above the clouds, or the Imperial Palace, was likened to
a god or goddess.

feel sorry for the sender. Chūnagon was thus quite aware that they must be from Yon no Kimi.

"Come now, let me see whose letter that is," he would say. Amused that Saishō could think of no reply, Chūnagon at last playfully snatched one from him. Saishō could not hide it then, for he did not want to appear to be keeping secrets from Chūnagon. The handwriting on the purple paper, the ink so very pale that one could not be sure if it was there or not, was unmistakably Yon no Kimi's. It seemed to be an answer to a letter that read something like "You must be happy about Chūnagon's promotion."

> More for the one unknown
> Than for the one others can see,
> Sleeves of my nightrobes;[119]
> Hearing of his promotion,
> Could I remain unmoved?

"The ink is too light. I can't see anything at all. Whose is it?," said Chūnagon, concealing his displeasure at what he read. And he held it out to Saishō.

"What does it say?," said Saishō, relieved.

"Well it's unclear and I can't make it out," said Chūnagon, putting an end to the conversation. In his heart, though, he thought: "Whether man's or woman's, the heart is an unreliable thing. On the surface Yon no Kimi seems young and graceful and innocent, but she has behaved disgracefully! I can resign myself to anything they do, but when it comes to my reputation and the way things look to others, I find it very cruel. If even my wife acts so badly, I wonder what the hearts of all the common people in the world are like. It pains me to imagine. But I need not show myself in the least displeased." He betrayed no sign of his displeasure to Yon no Kimi.

---

[119] Yon no Kimi's husband, Chūnagon, is the sleeve others can see, and Saishō is the one unknown.

Chūnagon thought that he would remain as he was for that month, since he would soon be giving birth; and so he went to his father's home day after day and served on night watch at the palace. He had done this for years, but he had never paid attention to or begun a conversation with the noblemen and courtiers unless there had been some special reason for doing so. People had thought that this was his only defect, that though he was unique and splendid, he never thought of others as human beings, keeping his distance and acting superior. But recently he had been paying attention to everyone and behaving very affectionately. Lovely court ladies had once found it difficult to approach him, but now Chūnagon kindly listened attentively to them. This behavior worried people all the more.

Chūnagon was on night watch, and the moon had not yet risen, for it was after the twentieth, a time of the month when the moon does not appear until very late. Like the plum flowers hidden in darkness, his presence would not have been known were it not for his perfume.[120] Chūnagon remembered the one who, on the day of the Gosechi ceremonies, had recited: "A meeting with you—always hard to arrange."[121] When the courtiers and everyone else had gone to sleep, he stealthily approached the Reikeiden.

> Where did it go,
> The moon I saw in winter?
> I know not,
> So very dark is it
> On this hazy spring night.[122]

Just as he charmingly recited the last line, someone drew near.

[120] An allusion to a poem in the *Kokin wakashū*, I, Spring I, no. 41, Mitsune (*NKBT*, 8: 112): "In darkness of spring night / Unreasonably hidden: / The plum flower. / Your color I cannot see / But your fragrance you do not hide."

[121] See the poem recited by the Lady of the Reikeiden on p. 36, above.

[122] Because the moon here is being compared to the lady, this poem also has the following meaning: "Where are you, / You whom I saw in winter? / Because I know not, / Gloomy and dazed am I / Like the darkness of this summer night."

As I gazed at it,
The moon slipped away from sight,
I too knew not where;
Regretfully I wondered,
Had it forever vanished into the mountain?

From the response he realized it was the same lady he had known before. In his desolation, he had walked on without going specially to see her. He had assumed she would not remember him very well. But her feelings for him had not changed. As a result, he found it hard to go on his way, and he approached her.

Book Two

WHEN THE fourth month came round, Chūnagon found himself hampered in his activities because of his pregnancy. He forced himself to behave nonchalantly, but even going out secretly pained him. This distressed Saishō, who as a result could not see him as much as he wanted.

"Why have you gone on like this until now? How dreadful it would be if people, noticing something strange about you, were to suspect," he said to Chūnagon.

There was an enchanting place in the vicinity of Uji that belonged to Saishō's father, and Saishō made all the necessary preparations for hiding Chūnagon there. He thought he could surely keep him in seclusion, and was impatient and reproachful that he had not yet come with him. Chūnagon had resolved that he would not give in. Were he only without child he would have been able to hide at the home of the Yoshino Prince.

"To give birth near one who is like a manifestation of the Buddha would be thoughtless and inappropriate," he told himself. "I would also be sorry to show myself in an unseemly and startling light to the Princesses, who seem so timid. There is my wet nurse, of course. I'm close to her, but if I overcame my reluctance, asserted myself, and alienated Saishō by showing him my resentment, and then had to turn to her to receive help in my condition, I would be so embarrassed that my grief would only increase. What am I then to do? I wonder. My future troubles me so. I guess I'll just have to go along with Saishō for the duration of my pregnancy, simply turn my back on the world, and hide. It would be disgraceful to be helped by anyone else in this bothersome pregnant state." Having thus reconsidered, Chūnagon promised Saishō he would go with him and fixed the date for their departure. Then he went, for the time being, to see the Yoshino Prince.

Ever since his first visit, Chūnagon had been helpful and supportive in every possible way, seeing that proper care was given to every corner of the Prince's residence and providing for the Princesses.[1] And not only did he take the trouble of making the long trip to see them, but he was discreet in the way he traveled. The Prince was not a little impressed that a man so young and radiant possessed such a generous heart. He now happily awaited his visit, and when Chūnagon arrived he was less reserved with him than ever and spoke with him of everything. Yet, although Chūnagon did not openly reveal his cares, he was more pensive than usual and spoke more of depressing matters.

"Even though you feel this way, it probably won't be so very bad. It's only a temporary discomfiture," the Prince said, weeping, and he prayed with deep devotion, employing the Goshin method[2] and other such austerities.

Chūnagon, as always, also saw the Prince's daughters and, weeping, told them moving and interesting things. "Even if I change my appearance to something other than it is now," he said, "I will certainly return here as my final home. Until then, do not forget me. I probably won't be able to come for about

[1] What I have translated as "every corner" more literally reads "until the door of the priests' quarters became cramped." It is unclear what this refers to. It may be an allusion to some poem now unknown.

[2] *Goshinpō*, a ritual of the Shingon sect for the removal of all obstacles and the protection of the body and soul of the follower. It involved magical finger signs and mystic formulas.

three months. If my life does not last until then, this visit may
indeed be my last. But if I do live longer than I expect, please
behave a little less coldly toward me when I return."

When Chūnagon had first begun to visit them, the Princesses had been reserved for a while, thinking his behavior
strange and, on such short acquaintance, too familiar; but
then they felt that since he was a most sensitive man they could
rely on him as a close friend. Now, seeing his thoroughly forlorn expression, they were bewildered and saddened; everyone wept. Even while he was there Chūnagon was uneasy, for
he wanted to see his parents and to have them see him. He was
sad still when he was about to return home:

> I will come again
> And hide here my wretched self.
> Yoshino Mountain.
> O wind, in the pines of the peak,
> Do not forget to blow for me.[3]

"What strange circumstances I find myself in."

> Be not long to return.
> Remember that we are here
> On Yoshino Mountain,
> In the wind blowing through the pines,
> The stormy wind that is our grief.[4]

No matter what was to become of him, Chūnagon would
not go back on the promises he had made to the Princesses,
but in view of the length of time that he would not be visiting
them, he made preparations for all they might possibly need
until autumn or winter. The Prince, aware of what Chūna-

---

[3] Because the wind here refers to the Princesses the last two lines of this poem also
contain the meaning, "Princesses, you who hear the wind blowing through the pines
of Yoshino peak, do not forget me." This poem appears in the *Fūyō wakashū*,
Miscellaneous II (*ZGR*, 14: 93).

[4] *Arashi*, "tempest," and *matsu kaze*, "wind blowing through the pines," are *engo*
here, and there is a play on *arashi* and *aru rashi*, "appear to be."

gon's problem actually was, prayed for him often[5] and gave him medicines.

For days Chūnagon stayed with his parents from morning until night. They were happy; but each time they smiled, Chūnagon wept and could not stop. It pained him to think how bad his father would feel, for though his father helplessly reproached Chūnagon, he illogically also thought him such a splendid person. He saw Yon no Kimi looking very lovely and distressed as she grew larger and larger with child, but this had no longer pained him[6] once he had set his heart on leaving this world.

"I am puzzled that I feel nothing toward Yon no Kimi but the tenderness that developed during the months and years I grew attached to her, when now it seems she thinks me much inferior to Saishō. I realize that in my inability to dislike her, even after her affair with him, I am different, but now more than ever I must show no attachment."

The curtains, newly changed for summer, looked exceptionally cool, more so than Yon no Kimi. Wearing an everyday cloak of blue and yellow silk brocade over a light purple robe lined in blue, she seemed lost in the mass of robes, delicate, graceful, alluring. Yon no Kimi's daughter was like a doll made for a game. She was captivatingly adorable as she gradually began to grasp at things.

"No matter what becomes of me," Chūnagon said to himself, "as long as I still live I will see my parents to the end. But this is perhaps the last time I will be here with Yon no Kimi. There is no reason for me ever to return." Hence Chūnagon even stopped to look at the ladies-in-waiting he had not noticed before.

"Will you think kindly of me when I am no longer of this

---

[5] The text reads: "he frequently used Goshin." See note 2, p. 110, above.

[6] The phrase used here is from a poem that appears in both the *Shinchokusen wakashū*, XIV, Love IV, Ariwara no Shigeharu (*KKT*, 5: 122), and the *Yamato monogatari* (*NKBT*, 9: 308, Section 143): "Oh, to forget, / So the heart desired, / The sadness within; / No longer need it suffer / What elsewise would it pain."

world?," he asked, drawing closer to Yon no Kimi. His embarrassed blushes were most lovely and radiant.

> It is unlikely;
> Yet if my sorrows permit,
> And I outlive you,
> You will remain in my heart;
> Tenderly yearning for you.

Yon no Kimi looked young and charming as she hid her face.
But when Chūnagon recalled that she had written the poem
about "the one unknown,"[7] he became displeased, telling
himself that she did not love him as she did Saishō, and he
turned his back on her entirely. Yet though he appeared to
have lost all feeling for her, that day he loved her with all his
heart. What a foolish heart his seemed to be.

> If I could believe
> You would truly yearn for me,
> Think of me fondly,
> With what tender thoughts of you
> Might then I leave this world.

"Unlike others," said Chūnagon, his sleeve over his face, "I
am unable to show myself to advantage. In my heart I have
loved you very much, and for years I assumed it was the same
as everyone else's love; but the actual situation and my feelings were two different things. As a result you concluded that
my love for you was less than what another felt. I am ashamed
and sorry. But be that as it may, even when others might think
me a fool and my shameful reputation spread, and even when
I, unable to understand it all, become depressed and feel I shall
not go on living in this world long, even then I love you with
all my heart. There may indeed come a time when you will no
longer feel that the way I spoke was so disagreeable."

What could Yon no Kimi say? She was understandably

7 See p. 106, above.

embarrassed and sad. She perspired profusely. Chūnagon felt sorry for her, and again comforted her.

"I won't go to my father's at all today," he thought. "When I see him my resolve weakens, and I find it unbearable."

He decided to go to Naishi no Kami's. He dressed with special care and moved unusually close to Yon no Kimi.

"I'm going to court, and if I must I will stay for the night watch; otherwise I'll be back," he said, and to her ladies he added: "Serve her well. It troubles me that she always seems so gloomy."

He was on his way out, but Yon no Kimi's daughter looked so lovely lifting up her hands and following after him that he came back and suddenly bent down beside her.

"Oh, why," Chūnagon thought, "was I fated to be so unusual? Though to everyone else we must look related, I will probably be a complete stranger to this child." As he gazed at her he was moved to tears for no particular reason. He embraced her and left, looking more wonderful than ever. He was nineteen years old. Yon no Kimi would have been three years his elder. Chūnagon's charm was undeniable. As he waited for his forerunners to come, he paused at a corner of the veranda and, looking about, leisurely recited "The Voice of the Nightingale in the Bamboo Grove."[8] His voice was very beautiful.

When Chūnagon arrived at the Sen'yōden, not many ladies were about, and Naishi no Kami was having the wild pinks in her garden trimmed. Wanting to watch, she had had only a three-foot portable curtain drawn up in front of her. While Chūnagon was quietly chatting with her, the ladies, embarrassed before such splendor, slipped behind the curtain and hid.

"I haven't been feeling well since autumn of last year and

[8] This poem appears in the *Wakan rōeishū*, I, Spring, Wisteria, no. 134 (*NKBT*, 73: 81): "Deep in the dew drops on the violet wisteria, / The color of the remaining flowers. / Within the smoke of the green bamboo grove, / The voice of the nightingale."

have been very depressed," said Chūnagon. "I feel that my life is coming to an end. But when, conscious as I am of the pain of being unusual, I decide once and for all to quit this world, I think of what our parents will feel, and I worry that there are but the two of us to care for them. Then the trepidation in my heart grows as I imagine how you would feel were I no longer here."

Tears swam in his eyes as he spoke. Naishi no Kami felt the same way. Having matured and become aware of the relationships between men and women, she had overcome some of her excessive shyness. She still felt shy in the company of others, but since there were only the two of them, brother and sister, she felt close to him and affectionate. When Chūnagon wept and spoke of matters that concerned them both, Naishi no Kami too was saddened.

"I have been so depressed. I've wondered about myself as the months and years passed," she said, weeping. "There probably is no one else so unusual and wretched as we. It is pointless to speak of this again now, but I am not a person who should go out into society. I too have felt that I would like to hide all trace of myself on some distant mountain just as you have said, but I have gone on living, acting as if I had no such thoughts. But I can't go on like this. More and more I realize how strange a fate is ours."

Chūnagon listened, convinced that she was expressing her true feelings. He could only dimly perceive her behind the pale purple brocade curtain, but from what he saw, the figure dressed in an ordinary cloak woven in blue and yellow threads over a red robe lined in blue looked beautiful. "Ah, I should have looked like this from the start," he thought, and even now, resolved to quit the world, he felt wretched—and not for the first time.

Naishi no Kami thought Chūnagon's bright and radiant face much more lovely now that it had grown thin. He appeared very masculine when he acted firmly in public, but worried and depressed as he was now, he seemed slender and sweet.

"How strange we are! I should have been as he is," Naishi no Kami thought. Looking at each other, the two spoke of many infinitely touching and sad matters that made them weep profusely. Chūnagon, anguished at the thought of leaving, stayed until dark. Then, saying, "Who is here? You seem to have very few ladies with you. You should have many come to stay with you," he left. Naishi no Kami watched him go, and she was troubled as she noticed that he seemed somehow strangely different from usual. Intending to spend the night in service at the Sen'yōden, Chūnagon instructed his attendants and forerunners to report in the morning and then dismissed everyone.

Before long, Saishō, in shabby attire, was waiting in a wicker ox-cart[9] at the Northern Gate. As if in a dream, Chūnagon secretly slipped out and got into the cart. On the way to Uji he was overcome with gloom, wondering why this had happened to him. The moon rose clear, and the scenery along the road was beautiful. When they reached Kohata, an area of lowly mountain folk who would not notice anything unusual about them, Chūnagon threw off his reserve. He had with him only the flute he had been attached to since childhood. To part from it would have grieved him above all else in this world. Depressed as he was, he played beautifully, the sounds quite indescribable. Saishō kept time with his fan and sang "At Toyora."[10]

It was a charming place at which they arrived. Since Saishō

[9] *Ajiroguruma.* These ox-carts, the roof and sides of which were woven of such materials as cypress or bamboo, were used only for informal occasions by higher-ranking officials (the Great Ministers, Major Counsellors, Middle Counsellors, Minor Counsellors, and Major Captains), but were used regularly by those of the fourth or fifth rank (Chamberlains, etc.).

[10] From a *saibara* (*NKBT*, 3: 401, no. 34): "In the Enoha well, / Before Temple Kazuraki and / To the left of Temple Toyora, / Are jewels like dewdrops. / Real white dewdrops are plentiful. / Our country will prosper, / Our home become rich. / Abundance, abundance."

wanted Chūnagon to live there, he had had everything inside
the house beautifully arranged. It would not do for Chūnagon
to be without ladies-in-waiting in attendance, and so Saishō
had sent two of his wet nurse's daughters and some very
young children, who would know nothing of what was to
happen, to live in the house. They had already settled down
in their new home, awaiting Chūnagon's arrival.

Chūnagon had misgivings the moment he alit from the cart.
Wretched, he thought, "No, I'll return home," but he could
not. Now that Saishō had managed to get him here, he would
not let him go back. Despite himself, Chūnagon was wretched, and so the night passed.

The next morning Chūnagon opened wide the lattice doors
of the house and looked about. Even then nothing seemed to
be real. Saishō, happy now that his desires had been fulfilled,
had Chūnagon's hair washed and let loose. It was thick
though short, resembling a nun's shoulder-length locks. He
plucked his brows and blackened his teeth, making him look
like a woman. He seemed more radiant this way than he had
as a man; he was very lovely. Saishō thought enthusiastically
that it had all been worthwhile, and he was happy; but
Chūnagon kept worrying about what was to become of him.
Gloomy and dazed, he was plunged in grief, not even arising.

"The way you are now is normal," Saishō tenderly rebuked
him. "Did you think the way you looked for years was reasonable? It was because of your fondness for going out and
mixing freely with people that you deliberately made yourself
look like a man. Though you were splendid, you can't go on
as someone you are not. It may be strange for you, but a
woman is what you should be. Even if your father learns
about it, he won't think it wrong."

The embarrassed Chūnagon knew this was true. "It's probably a good thing if I am as I should be," he consoled himself.
"Even if I'm not as I was before, I shall still be able to meet
with anyone as long as I remain alive."

Chūnagon's short locks looked most uncomely for a woman. Among the medicines he had received from the Yoshino Prince was one that would make hair grow three inches overnight. He had brought it along, thinking that he might need it, and every day he washed his hair and applied the medicine. In the meantime, Saishō let no one see him, and he devoted himself to this sensuous and alluring woman. Chūnagon in turn gave himself over to Saishō's care. He felt dazed and would often cry quietly. Many days passed in this manner.

Meanwhile in the capital, on the morning after Chūnagon's visit to Naishi no Kami, his forerunners came to the palace with the ox-carts. "Our master gave orders for us to leave late last night," they said, inquiring for him everywhere, but Chūnagon was not to be found. Surely, they thought, he has gone into hiding as he always does for five or six days every month. But he was not at his wet nurse's either. Then they thought he might be at Yoshino, for when he had first visited the Prince he had remained in seclusion there for over ten days, but more days than that had elapsed. All those who would have been his attendants were in the capital, and someone said, "He was at the Yoshino Prince's home around the first of the month, but he stayed for only two or three days and then came back." It was very sad.

"He was very depressed about the world," thought Sadaijin, "but he was probably also distressed about his abnormality. Even so, I never thought that someone in such an enviable position would turn his back on the world without a very special reason. Since the winter of last year he seemed at times particularly strange. Why didn't I suspect anything when I noticed it?" It would be a gross understatement to say that he wept and grieved.

Now Chūnagon excelled in all things. He had no parallel in all the world. When he came in and sat facing his father, Sadaijin forgot all his cares, and the problem of his old age receded into the far distance. As he dwelled on how wonderful

it had been to see Chūnagon, Sadaijin quite lost his senses and
seemed like one dead. Obviously there was much commotion
in his home. It was extraordinary. Everyone recalled Chūnagon's unparalleled figure and face. What could have happened?

Many days passed, but there were no rumors about his
having taken religious vows. Everyone thought about and
discussed this sad affair. Even the Emperor and the Cloistered
Emperor lamented the loss of such a shining light in the world.
They wondered what reason Chūnagon could possibly have
for vanishing. Prayers and incantations were read on mountains and in temples, and everywhere, publicly and privately,
there was frenzied activity as all prayed that he might return
unchanged. They trusted that with so many prayers, no matter
what the problem, there would be more than enough miracles
to fill the world. But as this was going on, days were passing
without any news. Even those who had caught but a glimpse
of Chūnagon's splendid figure yearned for him and were sad.
Making their way into the fields and hills, they searched for
him, but the sun that should have been shining was so covered
by clouds that they lost their way in the darkness.

With everyone so sad, we can imagine how much more
intense Udaijin's grief was. When Yon no Kimi recalled that
on the day Chūnagon had left her, he had said he wanted to
hide himself away from the world, she was so overcome with
sorrow that she seemed to be losing her senses. Udaijin was
no less grief-stricken than Chūnagon's father, but though he
wept with longing for Chūnagon, at the same time he also
reproached him.

"He certainly was not a terribly loving person," Udaijin
thought. "He ought to have found it impossible to go off like
this when he had a young daughter and when he saw that his
wife's condition was a source of anxiety."

Rumors about Chūnagon's amazing disappearance got so
out of hand that Saishō's relations with Yon no Kimi were

spoken of as the cause of his growing weary with the world and hiding.[11] It was freely bandied about that the daughter born to Yon no Kimi seemed to be Saishō's child. This reached Sadaijin's ears, and he thought that disgraceful though it was, it might indeed be possible.

"Chūnagon is wise and sensible. When someone learned of his unusualness, he wondered how he could then mingle in society and so hid himself away," realized Sadaijin. Saddened, he wept. "He went away without saying anything about his reasons, keeping the burden all to himself."

In his anxiety, Udaijin came to see Sadaijin. When the two were face to face, Udaijin wept with all his heart, for Chūnagon had abandoned Yon no Kimi just as Udaijin had anticipated he would; Chūnagon's love for his daughter had not seemed very deep. It was very trying for Sadaijin, and deeply grieved as he was, his conduct was certainly not that of a nobleman. Perhaps his good sense was affected, but he now told Udaijin everything people were saying.

"At first Chūnagon trusted Yon no Kimi as someone to be respected, as someone without equal, and yet recently at times he has been strangely depressed about his life. It seems to me now that that is probably what happened."

At this Udaijin's tears ceased, for he was stunned at the amazing information and ashamed that he had come to visit; he returned home. There he told his wife what Sadaijin had said, and the word "amazed" could not adequately express what she felt. The wet nurses of Udaijin's other daughters felt no sympathy for Yon no Kimi. It was most regrettable, they thought, that Udaijin should have considered Yon no Kimi unsurpassable and their mistresses markedly inferior to her. When they heard, however vaguely, about Yon no Kimi's affair, they wrote detailed accounts: "Chūnagon disappeared

[11] The meaning of the term *ushinge ni*, which appears in the text here, is unclear. Suzuki 1973: 121, note 13, suggests "in seeming to be thoughtful" or "prudent" as a possible literal translation. Thus Chūnagon's excessive thoughtfulness contributed to his worldweariness and decision to hide.

because he was disgusted by Saishō's affair with his wife. The daughter born to Yon no Kimi is Saishō's child. Chūnagon thought the child his own and was very happy, but when she was born he saw that she was the very image of Saishō, not a feature different, and he grew suspicious. Then, at the seventh-day celebration, he discovered Saishō lying beside Yon no Kimi." They dropped these notes where they would be found. Udaijin's wife saw them and showed them to her husband. Stunned, Udaijin carefully inspected his granddaughter. "True. She's exactly like Saishō," he thought.

It was too regrettable and mortifying for words. The quick-tempered Udaijin renounced Yon no Kimi forever and would not see her at all.

"This is most unpleasant. You are not to remain in this house. Now that things have come to this, it is pointless either to take care of you or to admonish you. There is our reputation to consider, as well as what Sadaijin will think. It would be very embarrassing if Chūnagon too were to hear I condoned your behavior even though he had abandoned the world. He will know at least that when I learned of the situation I thought it shameful indeed."

How was Yon no Kimi to feel then in her heart? She brooded terribly, her grief dulling her feelings more and more. There was no way Saemon [12] could console her, and she gazed at Yon no Kimi sadly. Saemon now had no one else but Saishō to turn to, she felt, and though it was painful, she wrote five or six moving pages about how the life appeared to be ebbing out of Yon no Kimi as she brooded over this regrettable affair. Saemon then found an attendant who had come as a messenger from Saishō before this, and she gave him the letter, instructing him to give it without fail to Saishō. The messenger delivered it to Uji.

There, some twenty days had by now idly flown by. Since Chūnagon was helpless to do otherwise, he had gradually

[12] The wet nurse's daughter. See p. 43.

settled down. Yet he continued to feel sad about what his
parents would be experiencing. He himself felt as though he
must be dreaming, and his sorrow and pain grew. Many days
passed as he lay in bed, unhindered and peaceful, and as a
result he was rested. Perhaps it was the effect of his medicine,
but his hair looked as though it had been stretched; gathered
together, it hung down gracefully. He had also had his brows
shaved off; he was dazzlingly lovely now that he had settled
down, and looked quite like a woman. He was all the more
radiant. Distress and despondency showing in his face, he
relied on Saishō completely and clung to him. He realized that
he had to be like this, and his gentle, feminine manner did not
suggest the man he once was. Charming and graceful, in every
regard he was all that Saishō had desired.

"Since long ago, both night and day I have fervently wished
to have just such a one as my wife. The Buddha has answered
my prayers," thought Saishō happily. "Somehow I shall not
let him regret this or recall life as it was until now." He
accordingly arranged everything so that Chūnagon would be
comfortable.

Chūnagon had once sat alongside the men at his father's
home, and he now often reminisced about what had been said
and done then. Saishō, however, amiably interrupted these
recollections: "Are you fond of that sort of thing?" The embarrassed Chūnagon did not like to hear such words, but he
managed to feign indifference.

It was during this period that Saishō saw the letter from
Saemon. So that there would not be the slightest barrier between them, he brought it in and showed it to Chūnagon,
saying: "Public opinion and Sadaijin's feelings are very awkward and troublesome matters for me too. I wonder what Yon
no Kimi really feels. No doubt she is miserable to be unwanted
because of me. It's all very sad."

Chūnagon replied: "Yon no Kimi and I had a troubled
marriage because she was joined to me and I was unusual, but

when I think about it, it was your fault and yours alone that this has happened. It was because you sought to gratify your excessive lust everywhere. Sometimes, when I think about it, I find you quite loathsome. If it hadn't been for you, Yon no Kimi and I might have gone on as we were, even though it was a limited relationship." Weeping, he looked so charming as he voiced his grievances that Saishō wanted to go on gazing at him forever. Though uneasy about leaving Chūnagon's side for even a moment, he was sorry that Yon no Kimi was so distressed, and he therefore left for just one night.

"What am I to do?," thought Chūnagon when he was alone. In his misery he spent the days weeping, drenched in tears. When night fell and the bright moon shone clearly on the surface of the Uji River, his reminiscences never ceased, and his heart felt full to bursting:

> Reflection of the moon,
> Shining clear in Uji River,
> Now here, now gone.
> Never did I think my life
> Would become as uncertain.[13]

Saishō felt uneasy on his trip, and he arrived at the capital with the image of Chūnagon still in his mind. The night was already far advanced when he slipped stealthily into the house. Saemon met him and, sobbing, told him about Yon no Kimi. "She appears on the verge of death. It's hard to tell whether she is alive or not. I feel so helpless and sad, and there didn't seem to be anyone I might consult but you." This was logical, and so Saishō said he would see Yon no Kimi. Saemon could not very well refuse him at this stage of affairs, however stubborn she might be.

[13] There is a *kakekotoba* in Uji, the name of the river, and *ushi*, "to pain" or "grieve." *Kage* here refers not only to the reflection of the moon, but also to Chūnagon's own person. Thus there is the underlying meaning that he did not think he would be so pained and become so frail as to be uncertain whether he lived or not. This poem appears in the *Fūyō wakashū*, Miscellaneous II (*ZGR*, 14: 91).

"You will see her in her last moments," she said, and ruled by an imprudent heart that found no alternative, she led Saishō to Yon no Kimi's room. In the dim light she looked more fragile and heartrending than ever, almost as if there was nothing left of her. She was lying down, her long hair hanging loosely and her belly immensely swollen with child. Even unfeeling warriors or barbarians from far away on the continent, had they seen her, would surely have been affected. How much more deeply affected then was Saishō, who loved her! The moment he saw her, his eyes dimmed with tears. He lay down beside her and grasped her arms.

"Come now, come now," he said, waking her.

"My, my!," she exclaimed, languidly looking up. "What's this? When our relationship has grown more and more complicated, have you come again like this?" At this wretched thought, Yon no Kimi broke into weeping, her life's breath on the verge of giving out. This was understandable and very sad, and Saishō too found it unbearable, his eyes dimming with tears.

"How terrible," he said. "This is fate. Do not brood so. If you live, surely you will have your parents' pardon. The sin of dying while pregnant is very great." Even after he fed her hot water with a spoon, she still seemed on the verge of death. To say that Saishō was sad and pained at this would surely be an understatement.

"As long as it becomes no worse, her condition is nothing to worry about," he said, having lamps brought so as to see her better. The way she shyly hid her face was infinitely elegant and charming. Saishō thought how dreadful his grief would be if Yon no Kimi were allowed to die pointlessly. He lay beside her all night; nor did he feel he could leave her when it grew light. Quietly he summoned the servants and gave instructions that prayers be commenced, and he remained with her. Yon no Kimi felt uncomfortable as she wondered what to do; yet to be trusting would be foolish.

Saishō was uneasy lest Chūnagon at Uji might feel unsettled
and worry about their relationship, but it was also difficult for
him to abandon Yon no Kimi in her sad plight. So he wrote
long letters to Chūnagon while he remained with Yon no Kimi
for five or six days and, weeping, cared for her. She was
terribly sad, thinking Saishō ought not to be with her, but
there was nothing she could do. She continued on the verge
of death, and Saishō, sad and mournful, unable to abandon
her, did not leave her side for so much as a moment, but cared
for her with all his heart. His misery seemed infinite.

It was both privately and publicly lamented that Chūnagon
had disappeared, and rumors attributing this to Saishō's affair
with Yon no Kimi persisted. It pained Saishō to hear them.
That Sadaijin had no doubt heard these tales and considered
them true was also troubling and embarrassing. As a result,
Saishō felt abashed and did not go out in society. He had
prayers of all kinds said and took care of things in every
possible way. Then, weeping, he left instructions and returned
once more to Uji.

Very few people were about, and Chūnagon, large with
child, seemed to be feeling oppressed and pained. He was
lying down, lost in thought as he worried sadly about anything and everything. On seeing him, Saishō wondered why
he had spent all this time away from him. It was natural yet
sad that Chūnagon should think Saishō remarkably unfeeling.
So here again Saishō's tears fell on his already wet sleeves as
he spoke consolingly. He told Chūnagon all about Yon no
Kimi's condition.

"He seems to love her very much," Chūnagon could not
help feeling, "to be so concerned and to feel such compassion
for her. It seems he writes to her. He must not love her any
less than he does me. To be relegated the way I am to the
uncertain position of sharing Saishō's affections will make me
ridiculous in people's eyes."

Chūnagon himself had not stopped loving Yon no Kimi,

and since he felt it was not his place to criticize Saishō, he affected an unconcerned air. Yet within his heart he thought: "Even if he loved me more than anyone else it would not mean much in light of the lustful nature he once displayed. And when one adds to that the fact that he is divided between Yon no Kimi and me, his love is quite worthless. But for the time being I'd best not turn my back on him and leave." Though he looked like a woman now, his heart—the heart of a man— was resolute. Seeing Chūnagon's composure, Saishō thought he had achieved all he desired and was extremely happy.

In the meantime Sadaijin, accustomed to Chūnagon's occasional disappearances, continued to wait anxiously for his return. Roughly two months had passed, and they had still found no trace of him in any guise at all. "Even if he turned his back on the world and took holy vows," thought the distraught Sadaijin, "we should still be able to find him, since we have made such a thorough search. Surely he would not be in some distant province, but there is no place within the boundaries of this region that we have not investigated. Though the thought surely has not entered Saishō's mind, isn't it possible that some of his disgruntled messengers, concerned that he is worried and has lost interest in the woman [14] he secretly visits because of Chūnagon, may have done something terrible to Chūnagon?" At this point he ceased even to weep with longing for his child and lost himself in thought as though stupefied. Everyone in his home grieved as well and cared for him.

Naishi no Kami recalled what Chūnagon had told her the evening he left the palace: "He had decided that day was to be his last. Had I known I would never have let him leave. I should have said that I would go with him. We were not close when we were young, but ever since I entered into court service he has come and looked after me whenever he was at the palace. I felt this was an honor, and it made me secure and

[14] This is Yon no Kimi.

happy. How terrible that he has disappeared when there were only the two of us.[15] In what corner of the world has he hidden himself? On what field or mountain has he concealed all traces of himself? Chūnagon was most thoughtful and behaved as though he felt everything very deeply, and though a woman, he made up his mind to do as he did.

"I was a male and succumbed to my inclinations for a woman's life when I was young and have gone on living as one. But to persist now, to be cared for by others, and to remain hidden from the world are wretched and lamentable things to do. Our father seems to be dying as a result of his cares. Since his life will soon end, he will not be able to find Chūnagon. Others seem to be chasing vague rumors. They don't have their hearts in the search. Even though the investigation is difficult, where, outside our world, could he be? I will not remain as I am. I will dress as a man and search for him. Then, no matter what he looks like, when I find him we will return together. If I am unable to find him, I too will change my clothes, become a monk, and hide all traces of myself on some distant mountain. Others will probably be willing to look after my father. For years I have been cared for as a woman, and it's not to be expected that I could suddenly appear in society and give orders and look after others. But if I were to remain as the woman I am now and to outlive Chūnagon, I could not go on in this world."

Night and day, Naishi no Kami was lost in tears. If she too simply disappeared, rumors would run rampant. It would have been much too terrible to speak of this to her father, and Naishi no Kami, looking very forlorn, thus spoke to her mother.

Chūnagon's disappearance has made me feel all the more forlorn because I do not have many brothers or sisters. It is natural that I should feel sad. Father's grief seems to be driving

---

[15] I have omitted a short passage following this sentence, the meaning of which is unclear. A possible interpretation might be: "He mingled as a man, but, understanding this, he wanted to mingle as a woman."

him to his death. It would be most regrettable if I, a man, were to simply look on and do nothing about it. I would like to take on my true male appearance and do all I possibly can to find Chūnagon." In contrast to her usual manner, Naishi no Kami spoke now in a manner appropriate to a man.

"Oh my!," exclaimed her mother, amazed, wondering what was happening. "What madness is this? Where would you go to search for him when you are so delicate, so completely like a woman?" And she wept and wept.

"Truly, this is the situation: people say they're searching the mountains and provinces, but they just gossip and certainly don't have their hearts in it. Chūnagon and I were fated to be brother and sister. If I put my heart into it, why shouldn't I find him? He probably thinks that I'm not searching. If I do search, he'll never be able to stay hidden, no matter how far he has gone. Though he and I grew up separately, he never behaved toward me as if we had done so. He was much more than just compassionate and courteous. It's hard to hold out against such love."

"What ought to be done?," said her mother, weeping along with Naishi no Kami when she saw how unbearable it was for her. "If this is how you see it, it is apparently fated. Let it be as you wish."

"In the event that people suspect that I have disappeared, simply pretend I'm still here," said Naishi no Kami, pleased. "Probably no one will know whether I'm here or not since, being unusual, I am never seen by anyone but four or five ladies. Don't tell Father for a little while either. If he asks, tell him I'm not feeling well. Don't let anyone see that anything in the least unusual is afoot. Father probably will not come here to see me anyway; he seems to be much too weak. Then too, because Chūnagon's mother is with Father and many people are around, I haven't been going there; so it's not likely anyone will suspect that I am not here."

Naishi no Kami forbade her servants and all others who

came near her to tell anyone about any of this. Then, putting
on a hunting robe and trousers over her clothes, she summoned
one of her wet nurse's children, an assistant of the Imperial
Princess's, to come behind her curtains and cut her hair. When
her tresses had been put up into the usual male's topknot, both
her mother and the wet nurse were astounded. But since her
true appearance would have been precisely this, it suited her
perfectly. She was so splendid that, though amazed, they all
consoled themselves with the thought that whatever she might
think of would be wonderful. The assistant was particularly
amazed at having been suddenly summoned and at seeing this
transformation, when she had been in the Princess's service
along with Naishi no Kami for years without ever even having
heard Naishi no Kami's voice. In a man's headdress, hunting
cloak, and trousers, Naishi no Kami betrayed none of the
awkwardness one might expect of a person wearing something
new and unaccustomed. Rather the clothes suited her very
well. She looked exactly like the missing Chūnagon. Even
when the two had been conversely male and female their faces
had been mirror images. Now, with Naishi no Kami dressed
just as Chūnagon had been, it seemed quite as if he had simply
returned. It was most astonishing.

"If only Sadaijin could see her right now. It is wonderful to
be cared for, as she would be if she were somehow to continue
living as Naishi no Kami, but for her father's sake, how happy
he would be if he saw her as Chūnagon." Both her mother and
the wet nurse consoled themselves with the thought that Naishi no Kami's transformation into a man was something over
which they should rejoice rather than lament.

"Don't ever let anyone see you sad or looking out of the
ordinary. Just be as you are now," said Naishi no Kami repeatedly as she left.

Naishi no Kami thought that she should not return if she
did not find Chūnagon. Needless to say, this made her overwhelmingly sad when she thought of her parents. Then there

was the Imperial Princess, whom she had grown used to seeing night and day and who was perhaps pregnant. Naishi no Kami's distress at leaving her was quite indescribable, and she felt as though some force was keeping her from going. "My father is so ill that I don't know when I may be able to come to the palace again. It is so depressing."

> Were I to vanish,
> Quit this sad uncertain world,
> How would you feel?
> Would you think of me fondly?
> Would you yearn to have me there?

The Princess's response was touching:

> If, of all others,
> You alone whom I love best
> Were no longer here,
> Know that in this world
> I would not linger on.

After looking at the Princess's reply for a very long time, Naishi no Kami wrapped it just as it was in some thin paper. Then, late on a moonlit night in the sixth month, she left, taking with her only three of her wet nurse's children and seven or eight retainers, strong and reliable soldiers, plainly dressed such as would arouse no suspicions.

She was very frail and had never stepped outside the inner-most section of her room, yet she had lost no time donning the robes befitting a man and leaving. Everyone who saw her was amazed. As she quickly purified herself, she told the servants not to reveal anything. They thus behaved as though she was still there, and none of the others knew that she was not.[16]

This now-male Naishi no Kami thus started out without having considered in which direction she was going.

---

[16] The meaning of this sentence is unclear. My translation is based on the tentative suggestion offered in Suzuki 1973: 134.

"Chūnagon frequented the home of a priest on Mount Yoshino, and he swore that was to be his final home. He might be there," said one of her wet nurse's children.

"That may indeed be the case. The others generally raise such a hue and cry about their search that it seems rather pointless, since Chūnagon, if found, would never come out and say it was he," thought Naishi no Kami as the party headed for Mount Yoshino.

In the intense midday heat they crossed the Uji River and cooled themselves on the far shore under the shade of a large tree. There were lovely areas near the river. They strolled about in these charming places they had never seen before. From beside them there came the single voice of someone chanting sutras, but no one was to be seen. Naishi no Kami thought it a particularly charming place and approached a small brushwood fence. The rattan blinds of the house within had been rolled up, and Naishi no Kami was startled to think that someone indeed lived here.

Quietly she looked in. In the front garden a stream flowed here and there like the threads of a cobweb. It looked as though it had been painted in a picture. The rattan blinds were rolled up to just the right height, and bright new silk summer curtains had been put up. Some fourteen or fifteen neatly dressed young girls were brightly clad in red trousers over unlined underrobes dyed red and blue; they wore their sashes loosely and seemed to be fanning themselves. There was a woman, too, whom Naishi no Kami could see faintly through the curtains. She appeared to be wearing silk summer trousers of the same red color over an unlined red silk brocade robe. She gazed out absently, looking very troubled. The complexion of her downcast face was radiant, as if luminous, and the way her hair hung down on her brow made her look very charming, as though she had been painted in a picture. One wanted to gaze at her forever. She appeared both beautiful and troubled. The look in her eyes was so striking it made one jealous.

As Naishi no Kami looked at her, she felt the woman was like someone she had seen before. In fact, she seemed to resemble Chūnagon. Her heart in turmoil, Naishi no Kami gazed at her. With her troubled and dreamy expression, she was more beautiful than anything imaginable. Her features were radiant. She seemed indeed to be Chūnagon. When Naishi no Kami considered that she herself had become a man, it seemed possible that Chūnagon had come to be a woman. She wanted to approach the woman at once and ask if somehow she was really Chūnagon, but since she had no grounds for thinking she might be, she feared being reproached. So she waited and looked on. Perhaps the woman inside sensed that someone was there, for the rattan blind was lowered. Naishi no Kami's disappointment knew no bounds.

It was unendurable. "If that's Chūnagon dressed like a woman, then he'll probably eye me curiously and recognize me." Naishi no Kami, wanting to be seen, strolled up to the small brushwood fence. The ladies in the house sensed that, curiously, someone seemed to be about. Lowering the rattan blinds, they looked out from behind them. An indescribably handsome and elegant man, a most refined man, came into view. Bewildered and with no clue to his identity, they kept their eyes on him. He was someone who had been in society, someone very splendid, the kind of person who would not be unknown. Yet he was not someone Chūnagon had ever seen before, nor, what was more, did he seem to be of any lesser station than Chūnagon himself. It then occurred to Chūnagon that this man was the mirror image of himself when he had been a man.

"On the evening that I felt was my last in the world," he thought, "Naishi no Kami wept and seemed so unhappy. This man reminds me very much of the face she had turned aside then."

It never occurred to Chūnagon that Naishi no Kami would change her appearance. "Oh, that such a handsome man should exist in the world!," he exclaimed. He found the man so dazzlingly handsome he naturally could not take his eyes from him.

"It seemed there was no one else so beautiful as our mistress, but someone does exist," a girl near Chūnagon thought, as she looked hard at the man. Then a realization came to her, and in her amazement she called to the others inside, pointing Naishi no Kami out to them. "Good heavens! It seems to be Chūnagon, who has disappeared from the world and whom everyone is busy looking for. I guess no one knows that he's come here. They say he's made his father grieve. If only I could tell them that he is here."

Hearing the girls speak to each other as they did, Chūnagon felt both moved and uncertain, and his tears fell, whereupon he retreated farther into the house.

Naishi no Kami lingered for a while, but no one made a sound, for one of the ladies had given a warning: "The mistress said that those going in and out of the house are not to let it appear that she is here." Without any excuse to do so, Naishi no Kami could not simply approach and pay a visit. Disappointed that she could do no more, she stepped out and asked whose home this was. Someone replied that this was the domain of the Minister of Ceremonies, Saishō's father. This made the situation especially difficult, and so, when she had heard the reply, Naishi no Kami could not even allude to the troubling glimpse she had caught of the lady.

Even if the woman was someone other than Chūnagon, Naishi no Kami wanted to be with her whose lovely visage remained in her mind; suddenly it became difficult to leave even the neighborhood where she was. So when the evening breezes began to blow, Naishi no Kami was sorry to leave. "Even if I had been out in society I would have wanted just such a woman for my wife," she thought, the lady's visage still in her mind. "I had thought the Imperial Princess infinitely lovely, but this woman is even lovelier than she." So attracted to this lady was her heart that she made such a comparison.

Pity for Yon no Kimi, whom he cherished, seemed to make Saishō uneasy, and he went to see her again. In the meantime, at Uji, as the last month of his pregnancy drew near, Chūnagon arose less and less often, and quiet and lonely, would gaze blankly at nothing.

"It seems I must remain as I am. There is nothing I can do. And how wearisome it is, too!," Chūnagon realized. "Saishō has divided his love and given deeply of it to Yon no Kimi, no less so than to me. He's here five or six days, then secludes himself with her for as many. I'm not used to this sort of thing. To go on constantly waiting and thinking is not to my liking; it worries me. But to change myself once more into the man I was before is impossible. When I deliver my child, I shall go to Yoshino and become a nun." The thought comforted him.

Saishō, however, knew nothing of this resolve. He was relieved now that Chūnagon was calm, and grew confident that Chūnagon would continue to stay with him this way. That Yon no Kimi had come so close to death grieved Saishō, and he accorded her a not insignificant portion of his love. Then, because he was reluctant to be seen out in society generally, he did not go wandering about. So feeling easy at heart, he went to and from these two places, loving both Chūnagon and Yon no Kimi.

Saishō for years had lamented that his desires had not been fulfilled as were those of others in the world, and feeling these desires were now satisfied, he was relaxed and happy. Yet at no time was his heart ever completely at ease. When, with troubled heart, he returned to Uji, Chūnagon seemed to be distressed and in suffering. In his anxiety about what would happen, Saishō felt his life force draining from him no matter where he was. He lay down beside Chūnagon and spoke to him. "Do listen to us," Chūnagon's attendants then said to him. "This afternoon Chūnagon, about whom there has been such an uproar since his disappearance, was here!"

Saishō was amazed and, smiling, asked: "And what happened?"

"Dressed in hunting robes he stood at the small brushwood fence, but it was such an awkward situation we didn't make a sound, and so he wearied and left." It was strange.

"Is it true? Did you see him? Who are they speaking about?," Saishō asked Chūnagon.

"Since they are speaking as they do about the man who was here, a man I feel I have never seen before, possibly my own person has left me," answered Chūnagon, smiling and weeping.

"You still want very much to be the man you were before," said Saishō reproachfully, embarrassing Chūnagon as usual. "Nevertheless, what was the man like?," Saishō persisted.

"Imagine him as looking like me. Surely he cannot be an agreeable man then," said Chūnagon, ending the discussion.

Naishi no Kami had gone to call on the Yoshino Prince. First she sent in a messenger and instructed him to say that someone was there from Chūnagon. With Chūnagon's disappearance from the face of the earth and the resulting commotion over his search, the Prince had grown increasingly sad and uncertain since Chūnagon's last visit. He was happy now, wondering whether this was the same man who used to come as Chūnagon's messenger. "In here," he called out and had the messenger shown in. When a handsome man who looked exactly like Chūnagon entered, the Prince was startled. "What is this?"

"About two months have passed since Chūnagon hid himself from the world. Someone told me that he occasionally visited you, and that he had said he considered this his last resting place in this world. As a result I came here, wanting to learn if by any chance he had left some word. I am his brother," said Naishi no Kami.

"Since autumn of the year before last, Chūnagon, having made a promise that extends not only to this world but to future lives, has been coming here and inquiring about various subjects. But this year when the first days of the fourth month had passed, he spoke as though depressed about the world in general, and he did not say when he would return this time. He made but one promise: 'It will be very difficult to go on living through the end of the sixth month and the beginning of the seventh, but if I should, I will certainly send word before the end of the seventh month that I am still in this world, even if it is by the blowing wind, who will be my messenger.' I suppose there is something about which he must be most careful during this period, and I think of him every morning and evening when I invoke the Buddha's name, though he is probably still in the world. But you must truly feel sad and depressed with this present anxiety."

"We don't have any other brothers and sisters," said Naishi no Kami, reassured by the Prince's words and weeping. "Because there are only the two of us, I feel forlorn and often weep in sorrow. I am in despair, for he has hidden himself without even letting me know where. And it is especially sad that our aging parents are dying of grief."

The priest's sleeves too were damp with tears. "I do not seem to be very strong-minded. Even my daughters have become obstacles to my devotions. The Buddha himself explains that parental love is very strong. It would be even more so in the case of a child as splendid as Chūnagon. Your parents' grief is most natural. In any event, Chūnagon will surely come to see me. Do not brood," said the Prince reassuringly. Marveling at Naishi no Kami's extraordinary features, he tilted his head and looked at her. "She certainly seems to be the one who is destined to have a bond with my daughter," he thought.

At last the Prince was happy and reassured. He entertained Naishi no Kami with a feast appropriate to the place and was most hospitable. He spoke of much that has happened since olden times, and this comforted Naishi no Kami.

"It is very disagreeable suddenly to change myself into a man, look like Chūnagon, and act as though I've exchanged places with him before anyone has realized what has happened," she thought. "Now that I have taken on this masculine appearance I see no reason why I should have to stay indoors like the woman I was before. There are not so many days left until the time Chūnagon said he would send news of himself. And it is unlikely that rumors will be spread about my having left the capital and come here. I'll stay in the meantime and wait for word from Chūnagon."

"Splendid," said the Prince when she told him her intentions. "Do stay on and wait. Chūnagon would never break a promise."

Naishi no Kami was overjoyed, but since her mother would be alarmed and distressed that she too might have disappeared along with Chūnagon, she sent her a detailed account of what was happening: "I have come to a place where Chūnagon said he would send news at the beginning of the seventh month, and I shall remain here until I have grown more accustomed to my new appearance. Go on in the same way as I instructed you when I left and told you not to worry. Simply act as though I were still there, and if a letter comes from the Imperial Princess, send her a reply saying I am ill."

Naishi no Kami's mother had been heartsick when she considered what was happening. So uneasy had she been that it seemed her heart was floating away. Then, when the message came from Naishi no Kami, she was happy, if apprehensive about the girl being so far away for so long. "How sad that both Chūnagon and Naishi no Kami should have these unusual appearances," she exclaimed, weeping. "As long as I am still alive," she wrote, "do not think of leaving the world and becoming a priest. To forsake me and leave me with no one to rely on would be a sin." She sent this letter, along with many gifts of robes and other things.

Naishi no Kami stayed at Mount Yoshino attended only by

one of her wet nurse's children and a servant. She had been living as a woman, and so she now studied subjects suitable for a man. She thought the Prince a very good and learned teacher, and she told him about the unusual guise she had adopted up to that time.

"I heard Chūnagon hint at a similar grief," said the Prince. "This confusion lasts a little while when one has gone at all amiss. It would be good if Chūnagon would also assume his original appearance. Reading his physiognomy, I consider that he should attain the position of Empress Dowager."

Naishi no Kami was obsessed by the figure she had glimpsed at Uji, and it pained her even to speculate whether she would ever see the woman again.

> Yoshino Mountain:
> Upon your road I embarked,
> Mind free of thoughts;
> Only to be lost in thoughts
> Of a woman like my sister.[17]

Naishi no Kami had seldom left her curtained chamber, but now she was on this mountain, her whereabouts unknown, under unforeseen circumstances. It was all very strange for her. She was so sad to spend night after night far from the Imperial Princess that she could not fall asleep. At such times the image of the woman she had glimpsed at Uji flashed through her mind, mingled with the waves of the river. She yearned for her terribly, wanting to see her once again. Weeping, she said:

> I barely glimpsed her;
> Wind blowing at the shallows
> Of Uji River.
> How long before we float together?
> How long before we can meet?

---

[17] *Imose yama*, the opening line of this poem, refers to Mount Yoshino and, because *imose* means "brother and sister," also to the one who resembled Naishi no Kami's sister.

At Uji, Chūnagon was looking extremely distressed. The months had passed, and the time set for his delivery was fast approaching. As a result, Saishō did not leave him for even a little while, troubled, wondering what he was to do. In appearance Chūnagon was so radiant and charming one wanted to gaze on him forever. In attitude and behavior, having been accustomed to cutting a fine figure in public, he was not so frail and gloomy as a woman would normally be, but cheerful and happy. Because his heart was experienced in the ways of the world, even when he worried and grieved he was not so completely overcome as a woman ordinarily would be. When he had to weep he would, and when something amusing was said he would smile.

Now this most affable and charming person was truly sad and distressed, and Saishō, observing his state, was worried, wanting somehow to assure him an easy delivery, even if it meant taking his place. Perhaps it was the result of Saishō's wishes that at the beginning of the seventh month, considerably after the anticipated date, a beautiful boy was born. Saishō's joy far surpassed the usual for such occasions. It was touching the way he himself put to sleep and cared for both mother and child. Not for an instant did he take his eyes off the child. He summoned a wet nurse he knew well. "If it were known that I had such a child by this woman he would be pampered by all manner of wet nurses. How sad that all must be so hidden and secret," he thought regretfully.

For the time being he did nothing but devote himself to caring for the child, not leaving him for even a moment. "This is the destiny of two people who loved each other deeply in a previous life. How wonderful it would have been if you had become a woman long ago; we might have lived like this without any cares all that time," he said, bringing to the mother this child whose radiance and beauty shone forth more each day.

"How true. And how strange I was," recollected Chūnagon.

Lightly he spoke of that seventh night after Yon no Kimi's child was born when he had come across Saishō's fan. Both Chūnagon and Saishō were amused and moved.

More than ten days had passed since the delivery, and Saishō thought with relief that things would probably go on that way. Observing that Chūnagon seemed distraught, Saishō had not been wholly confident that Chūnagon might not resume his masculine guise, but when he saw how much Chūnagon seemed to love the baby, constantly embracing and caring for him, Saishō began to be convinced that Chūnagon would never forsake his child.

"Yon no Kimi feels that though she is still in the world, it is no longer the same one she once inhabited, and she is sad and broods," said Saishō. "I believe she should also be giving birth about this time. I don't think she'll live much longer, and it worries and grieves me. It's my fault and no one else's that she's unwanted. It's heartless to act as if it were no concern of mine. I had intended to stay and look after you until at least the celebration of the fiftieth day after the child's birth, and it would worry me terribly to be away even for a short time. How would it be if I brought her here secretly? I know you have cast her off, but . . ."

Chūnagon was taken aback, but he acted like he was unconcerned. "It's natural that you should feel the way you do. But I was her husband, and there is no one I would be more embarrassed to reveal myself to as I am now than her," he replied, blushing in his loveliness.

"I see. I simply contemplated this move because I did not want even short absences to worry you," Saishō dissembled, smiling.

Thinking Chūnagon now calm, Saishō, out of compassion for the sufferings of Yon no Kimi, for whom he yearned, again shifted his affections and went into hiding with her. As he looked after her, he seemed free of care.

Yon no Kimi's father, having made his dreadful vow, would

not even set eyes on his daughter. Her mother had withdrawn in the face of the great love her husband had held for his child from her earliest days, and so perhaps she did not have any special affection for her. "What an unexpected and unenviable situation Yon no Kimi has found herself in!," she sighed, imagining herself in her daughter's place, but even so she did not come and stay with her. Since her sisters had not been shown anything like the same kind of love as Yon no Kimi, they were critical and did not think the public uproar over their sister's affair particularly regrettable.

Yon no Kimi's plight was thus touching and sad. She had no recourse but to hide, rely on Saishō, and be cared for by him. His pity for her as she looked so sad and wasted was unbearable. Even during the day he would slip in to remain constantly by her side, speaking consolingly and pledging his fidelity. Since there was nothing for it, Yon no Kimi did not resist. Saishō found her so very charming as she meekly accepted his comforting. He was always with her during this period. For some time he did not go to Uji, for if Yon no Kimi went into labor during the night after he had gone and was far away, he might never learn of her urgent condition.

Letters from Saishō came many times each day; and though there was no cause for anxiety, they did not make Chūnagon happy. "Apparently I am fated to go on like this. My heart was filled with sorrow, but to the world at large, I had attained such glory as none could stand beside me. Despite my reluctance, I have been made to seclude myself like a woman; I even have a rival. I surely should not have to go on waiting anxiously like this for Saishō to come to me. Udaijin will probably disclaim his daughter for a time, while everyone is making such a fuss about the affair, but then since she is his favorite daughter, he will approve of her love for Saishō, and she will surely have the advantage over me. No matter what happens, my identity apparently cannot be revealed; and I will find myself worrying to the point of counting the nights till he comes, like the watchman at the Uji River Bridge who counts the whitebait in the wicker net.[18] But I can't go back to being a man. I'll take my thoughts far into Mount Yoshino and contemplate the life hereafter." Chūnagon gave himself over to his ruminations; but it was hard for him to abandon his son, and he keenly felt the obstacles to leaving this world.[19]

Seven or eight days passed, and Saishō came to Uji as usual. With a show of frankness he told Chūnagon of his sorrow at Yon no Kimi's forlorn circumstances, as Chūnagon listened halfheartedly. If Saishō had concealed more or had found other things to speak of, that would have been fine. But he kept nothing back.

Chūnagon told himself that he would not have to go on seeing Saishō for years and years to come, and so treated him graciously. No one could have thought Chūnagon imperfect then. Saishō felt his love steadily increase and was deeply moved. Still, Chūnagon might think his love shallow, for he was fickle, ever smitten by each and every one.

"He'll probably stay a little while as he usually does," thought Chūnagon.

In the evening, however, someone came from the capital and whispered to Saishō: "Yon no Kimi seems to be in much greater pain than usual. It looks like she may be ready to give birth."

"What would Chūnagon think if, after having been away so long, I unexpectedly returned to Yon no Kimi before the day was over?," thought the restless Saishō, his heart in turmoil. He felt perplexed, not knowing what to do. But then he and Chūnagon would be together for a long time, and Chūna-

---

[18] There is a *kakekotoba* in *yoru* here; it is read with both the meaning "to approach" and the meaning "nights." It is possible that this reflection may have found its inspiration in a poem in the *Kokin wakashū*, XIV, Love IV, no. 689, Anonymous (*NKBT*, 8: 238): "On her narrow mat, / Beneath her own nightrobe, / Lying there alone; / Does she wait for me tonight, / The Lady of Uji Bridge?"

[19] The last phrase is taken from the poem by Mononobe no Yoshino cited in note 73, p. 47.

gon would come to understand. As for Yon no Kimi, however, if he were not to see her once more and she were to die, his grief would know no end. So explaining his reasons to Chūnagon, he left hurriedly.

"It is quite natural for you to feel as you do," said Chūnagon calmly. Because he himself had been resented by women when his heart had been a man's, he had not then felt the unhappiness or uneasiness of jealousy. Though he spoke calmly, however, he now thought: "How wretched it is to have become the woman I now am. Even the Buddha claimed woman is sinful. Udaijin always disliked me, and at times Yon no Kimi looked reproachful. Is this my retribution for those days—that I am to experience, in her place, the misery of being forsaken by a man?" He thought feelingly of past and future, and because he had no one with whom he could speak freely, he grew distressed, his feelings pent up in his heart.

The following morning a letter came from Saishō. "Poor abandoned Yon no Kimi looks pitiful. I am near her and will stay and try to keep you abreast of her condition to the end. I returned to the capital worried about her, and now my heart is uneasy about you; I am concerned about our son, too."

Chūnagon ignored this and replied: "Even if one broods terribly, there is an end to it. Why does Yon no Kimi seem so pitiful?"

"He was familiar with men and so never seems resentful. How refreshing!," thought Saishō foolishly when he saw the reply.

At Uji, Chūnagon was carried away with the desire to find a way of sending someone to Mount Yoshino. His child's wet nurse was experienced and trustworthy. "If she loves my son dearly," he thought, "I will tell her about myself, and she will probably not reveal what I have told her."

"Though we do not know each other so well," he said to her wistfully, with affection, "if you think my son dear, you will feel for me, I think. I would like very much to be able to rely on you. I am sure you will listen to me and not let others know what I have told you."

"Of course I will," said the wet nurse happily, thinking such trust wonderful. "Even if it means casting my life away."

"I do not want the attendants here to know about this, even less Saishō. I think you might devise some plan to enable me to send news to a priest in the remote regions of Mount Yoshino," said Chūnagon. He was overjoyed when she replied that that would be easy.

"Has all been peaceful these past months?," Chūnagon wrote. "I have wondered sadly how you have been. Time has passed uneventfully and peacefully for me to this day. I look different from the person you once knew. I would like somehow to come to you." Sealing his letter carefully, he added, as he gave it to the wet nurse, "Be sure this is delivered."

Since no one at Uji knew what Chūnagon's previous appearance had been, nor who he was, everyone now concluded, having heard the Yoshino Prince had daughters, that possibly he was one of them. It was the beginning of the eighth month when they arrived at this conclusion. The wet nurse selected an attendant whom she apparently knew well to serve as messenger, and having given him explicit instructions, sent him to the Prince.

At Yoshino, Naishi no Kami was studying, for this seemed unexpectedly interesting. She thought with pleasure how delightful it had been to have come across this charming Prince. What's more, the Prince's daughters seemed to be out of the ordinary, and Naishi no Kami wanted to see them. She was hesitant, however, lest she suddenly lose her head and make advances toward them in this priestly place. She calmed her heart with the thought that she would be able to see them again anyway, since she was now on very familiar terms there.

One evening when Naishi no Kami was fretful and naturally anxious, for the time when Chūnagon had promised to send news of himself was passing by, an agreeable-looking man arrived. "I have a letter to deliver," he said. When asked where it was from, he replied: "Please give this letter without fail to the Prince."

The Prince took the letter, looked at it, and saw it was from Chūnagon. It was extraordinary, and the Prince showed it to his guest, Naishi no Kami. To say that she was happy expresses but a fraction of what she felt. Her mind was in turmoil when she saw the words "I look different." "Apparently he has become a priest," she thought. "He would not hide himself away unreasonably." Her heart throbbing, she called the messenger to her. "Where is this person?"

The messenger did not reply. "I would tell where," he thought, "but I was not instructed to do so."

Naishi no Kami asked him again, but charmingly this time, and it seemed quite wrong to hide the information. "I know that it's in the vicinity of Uji," he said.

"Where in Uji?"

"I understand it's in the domain of the Minister of Ceremonies," he replied. And Naishi no Kami then realized that it was really so, that the one she had seen there had indeed been Chūnagon. She was happy and very moved.

Naishi no Kami sent a reply along with the Prince's. "Having decided to search for you one day in the sixth month, I left the capital. I stopped at Uji and then came to inquire of the Prince. He told me that you had said you would send news of yourself. Trusting that you would, I have been hiding on this mountain. But what are your circumstances? May I see you somehow? Are you some place where I can visit?" Naishi no Kami wrote in great detail and gave her letter to the messenger together with the Prince's reply. She also gave the messenger a set of robes and the horse she had ridden. "Take this horse, and you will arrive at Uji in no time. Be sure to return with a reply."

Happy at this unexpected and delightful windfall, the messenger rode off. He arrived at Uji and delivered the letters. "I would like a reply to the message I have just presented," he immediately said to Chūnagon. Chūnagon glanced at the Prince's reply. Then he saw the other letter. "So," he thought, "that man about whose identity I wondered was Naishi no Kami, who had left the capital to search for me, her appearance changed. I am so sorry that that never occurred to me." It was so strange and moving he could not look at the letter. "It's fate that my appearance is different from my previous one, and that hers is too." Weeping, Chūnagon wrote a detailed reply.

"I would like to speak with you directly at length. I am in this vicinity. Send word with this messenger of a visit from you," wrote Chūnagon.

Reading Chūnagon's answer, the delighted Naishi no Kami felt as though she was dreaming. "After I have seen and learned of Chūnagon's present state, I will send news to Father," she thought. Secretly she went to Uji with the messenger as her guide. She stopped at a nearby house and sent word of her plan to visit.

Saishō was distressed that Yon no Kimi was feeling poorly, and he remained with her.[20] Chūnagon therefore spoke to the child's wet nurse: "My brother has come secretly. I would like to meet with him in secret; no one should know. If someone in the know told Saishō of this, it would be most painful for me. I don't want anyone to know about it."

"That is easily done," said the wet nurse. "I will make it look like someone is coming to my room after returning from the capital, and then under cover of darkness I will bring him in. You may come to see him when it has grown late."

"In that case, do arrange it that way," said Chūnagon.

Chūnagon was not closely attended by the children of Saishō's wet nurse or by any others in the house, and they especially did not come near him when Saishō was away. So

---

[20] There is some speculation that there is a missing passage after the words *kokoro madoite* in this sentence. For the sake of continuity in the translation, I have added the words "and he remained with her."

under cover of the faint evening light, the wet nurse easily led Naishi no Kami inside to her room at the front of the hall and then waited for the others to settle down to sleep. When it had grown late and everyone was asleep, Naishi no Kami, guided by the wet nurse, quietly made her way to the western extension of the main building, and there the wet nurse left her. Quietly Chūnagon went there too. Both Naishi no Kami and Chūnagon felt as though it was all a dream, and neither spoke a word. In the bright moonlight, Chūnagon's hair cascaded lustrous and full, and he looked most beautiful. As he sat there, an endearing and tearful woman, Naishi no Kami wondered who he really was. And with Naishi no Kami now an indescribably refined and elegant man, neither felt the other was real.

Naishi no Kami told Chūnagon all that had happened: she had worried, and not knowing his whereabouts, had deliberately inquired about him; she had left the capital and gone to Uji where there was someone strangely like Chūnagon; her chagrin was unbearable, and she had thought that by chance that person might see and recognize her; she had left with no idea what the situation actually was. All this she explained in detail. Then she asked how it was that Chūnagon looked as he did.

The embarrassed Chūnagon was hard put for an answer, but with one so closely related as Naishi no Kami he did not have to keep everything locked in his heart. "For years I grieved about my unusual appearance, but there was really nothing I could do. I had to settle down quietly," Chūnagon told her he had thought; and he vaguely described having to change appearances because of an unforeseen and painful matter; he spoke of his sorrow and of his having hidden himself. Naishi no Kami understood what had happened.

"Until now you apparently had to be a man, but how can you go on like this now unknown to others?," she said. "How am I to tell Father?"

"That's just it," replied Chūnagon, weeping. "It seems to me that on no account can I simply go on like this. It was disgraceful to have been seen when I was in the unusual guise of a man. But now that I'm a woman I can't reveal myself and be cared for by others. Shamefully, that is exactly what must be the case with Saishō, who realized I was unusual, and so I have completely entrusted myself to him. Wondering whether I had to, I have lived on till now. But I feel I should not continue as I am; yet I can't again change into the man I was before. Since there seems to be no place for this unusual person, I think I shall become a nun and hide all trace of myself on Mount Yoshino."

"My dear," said Naishi no Kami, "do not speak of such things. Neither you nor I should give up the world as long as our parents are alive. It's because you hid yourself that I left our father, who was losing his senses, and came to look for you. Really, why should you have to seclude yourself like this? Besides, now that your appearance is different it would be of no interest even if rumors did arise. I left instructions at home for everyone to act as though I was still there. Since I was never known to anyone anyway, it is likely that no one knows whether I'm there or not. Surely then it would be best if, just as you are, you were to take my place as Naishi no Kami. Even if Saishō comes to see you, that should not be a problem. If you behave as though the relationship with him were beginning now for the first time, in the eyes of society it will appear quite seemly."

Chūnagon made no reply at all to this. "If only I might be someplace unknown to Saishō," he said.

"That would be very bad," replied Naishi no Kami. "Although Saishō's character is as it is, and he is not of truly high rank, he is not of inferior station. In any case, go first to the capital and do as Father tells you."

"I don't want you to tell Father what has happened. Just

tell him I had trouble managing my unusual person." Chūnagon's embarrassed appearance did not at all recall the behavior of one who had for years been a strong and resolute man.

The night was almost over before they finished talking, and so Naishi no Kami quietly left and made her way to the capital. When she arrived, memories of her departure, when she had decided that this was her last time in the city, came sadly to mind. She let no one know of her return.

As the days and months passed, Sadaijin had many prayers recited at every possible mountain and temple, brooding that this was the end. Then, in a dream one night, the night of Naishi no Kami's return, a priest, worthy of respect and pure, came to him and said: "Do not grieve so! The affairs of both Chūnagon and Naishi no Kami are settled. In the morning when it grows light you will learn of their circumstances. In previous lives their paths were crossed, and in retribution a goblin [21] changed the boy into a girl, the girl into a boy, and caused you no end of sorrow. A very long time has passed for the goblin, and as a result of your having entered on the path of the Buddha and having had many prayers said as the years have gone by, the situation has been completely remedied. The man will be a man and the woman a woman, and they will be made to prosper as you wish them to. The mental anguish you suffer is but a small part of the retribution from former lives."

"In the many months I have been ill," said Sadaijin to his wife, the mother of Naishi no Kami, after this dream, "I did not know what was happening around me. I have not been able to see Naishi no Kami. Just now in a dream this is what I saw," and he related his vision. Surprised, his wife told him all that had happened.

"And I did not even know Naishi no Kami had left the palace

[21] A *tengu*, a minor deity, part man and part bird, winged, with a long beak or nose. *Tengu* were considered not so much evil as mischievous. They were believed to live deep in the mountains. See Piggott 1969: 61–62.

and gone out into the world," he thought, amazed, but happy that there was truth in what he had seen. At length he realized that dawn had come. Then someone approached his wife and whispered something in her ear. "This is probably in accordance with the dream," said the surprised Sadaijin. Everyone was still asleep. He requested that Naishi no Kami come to him, but even then he thought: "Chūnagon has been accustomed to mingling in society since childhood. He cut a very fine figure. But when I think that Naishi no Kami was weak and secluded, unseen by anyone, I feel she will probably be inferior as a man."

When Naishi no Kami came before him, her father rose, turned up the lamp, and looked at her. It was as though Chūnagon's radiant figure had been reproduced in another. Naishi no Kami's somewhat taller and more slender build was superior to Chūnagon's. That Chūnagon was a bit small and tended toward the short side had been a defect in him, but he had still been young. Naishi no Kami was somewhat more imposing in stature and seemed, indeed, without imperfections. Her father gazed at her as if in a dream. But she brought to mind the one whose whereabouts were unknown, and this was so unbearable that Sadaijin wept aloud.

"Well then, what did you find out about Chūnagon?," he asked when he had calmed himself.

"He no longer looks like a man as he did before, but has become a woman," replied Naishi no Kami. "He told me that since it pained him that he was so unusual, he thought he would try changing himself to his original sex and so go into hiding for a while. Until his hair has grown longer and he is more feminine he does not want to be seen by anyone. I will, of course, arrange things in accordance with your wishes."

Sadaijin did not ask for further details. "Ah, so my dream was true!," he thought, so happy that he wept with joy. "Splendid. We will tell everyone that Chūnagon is Naishi no Kami, and it will be well for you to take his place," he said.

"Since I have been secluded for years," she replied, "I can't mingle in society as a man. I will again probe Chūnagon's feelings and, for a little while, we will keep it secret that I have become the man I am. First I will meet with Chūnagon, and then I will come back to see you."

When it grew light Naishi no Kami left. Sadaijin, refreshed and happy, had no regrets. He rose and ate a little rice. "When will she go to see Chūnagon at Uji?," asked his wife.

Chūnagon's happiness had lingered on after his meeting with Naishi no Kami. He had felt as though it had all been an amazing dream. But now he was in a quandary: it would be very strange if he took his son with him, but if he left him behind it would be too sad. Nevertheless he thought: "Since the bond between parent and child can't be broken, I will probably come across him again. No matter how dear this suckling child is to me, how can I, who was once so celebrated in society, go on spending my days merely waiting for a man to visit me in this place where there is so little sign of life?" Remembering how he had gone through life as a man, Chūnagon thus resolved to leave. With an air of nonchalance, he tore up and burned every unimportant letter that might prove troublesome, gazing at his child all the while. The boy was so very lovely. Chūnagon had watched as he learned to speak, stared at people, laughed, and his heart had been touched.

Saishō returned to Uji, apparently for his usual short period of time. Chūnagon thought this was to be the last time they would be at Uji together, and so did not behave curtly. He had taken special care with his appearance and sat there looking incomparably lovely. He wore a blue and yellow garment lined in blue over a red unlined undergown and a blackish red robe also blue within.[22] Chūnagon had grown thin after the delivery, but now that he had recovered he was all the more

---

[22] "Garment" here translates *uhagi*, the outermost robe when a number of layers were worn. This and the following robe mentioned (*kouchigi*; see note 60, p. 39, above) are women's clothes, and the entire description is appropriate only to a woman.

lovely, exuding radiance. His hair was lustrous and seemed to reflect the rays of light. The tresses, just short of his seated height, flowed out in profusion like an open fan spread wide. The way the strands fell about the hem of his robe seemed truly more beautiful than if his hair had been eight feet long. There was not a single imperfection in the way his tresses, like woven cords, stopped at his cheeks and fell in back. One glance at Chūnagon seemed to sweep away Saishō's most dreadful worries, and he forgot his grief.

"Ever since you gave birth, you are more radiant than ever," said the contented Saishō. "Why did I think you beautiful when you went about as a male? You are far more beautiful as you are now. If you were permitted to go out and mingle in society looking as you do now, everyone who saw you would lose his heart."

In excellent humor Saishō stroked Chūnagon's hair. He now forgot his concern for the sufferings of Yon no Kimi, about whom he had worried so much he would have exchanged places with her. And with nothing else on his mind, he lay down and chatted with Chūnagon.

Then a messenger came again. "Just now Yon no Kimi looked as though these were really her last moments. She seems to have fainted," he reported.

It was terrible for Saishō to be constantly going back without warning to Yon no Kimi. He felt sorry for Chūnagon and thought things ought not to be this way. "Come to tell me when she is about to deliver," he instructed. Immediately afterwards the messenger came running in to report, and Saishō found it unbearable.

"I will just go to be with her until something decisive happens, whatever it may be. Since it seems unlikely she will live long, I simply will not have myself appear unsympathetic. I can do this because you are a good judge of things and are cheerful and happy and not unreasonable and begrudging. I shall see Yon no Kimi to whatever end she comes, and after you have

seen what my love for you is like when this is over, then
reproach and criticize me if you can." He seemed pained as
his tears fell.

"Since I do not want to go on like this, why should I be
upset?," thought Chūnagon, looking at him. "Even before
now I have felt that Saishō did not love me and was not one
to put my faith in. I expected he would probably forsake me
like this. It seemed to me that while I was going through my
pregnancy it was better to go along with him than to be looked
after by people I didn't know. Had I thought, though, that I
would go on being like this, I would be sorry now and taken
aback by this situation." He could only smile radiantly and
say: "You know how I feel; these explanations every time you
go off are rather tiring. It's best for me not to know anything."

This was more threatening than if he had teasingly reproached Saishō. "All right, my dear," said Saishō, "I'll go if
you frankly say, 'Go quickly.' "[23] He stood, unable to move
from the spot.

"Now go quickly," said Chūnagon. "At a sorrowful time
like this you must lose no time."

Saishō constantly looked back at Chūnagon before making
his way out of the room, but Chūnagon would not let him see
that he had turned pale and bore up with a nonchalant air.
But when Saishō finally did leave, Chūnagon held his son in
his arms and stayed awake all night, weeping until dawn.

The next morning Saishō wrote: "During the night Yon no
Kimi finally gave birth. Her condition, however, does not
seem promising. I will stay on a little longer to see what is to
happen and come to Uji immediately afterwards."

"I received your letter," replied Chūnagon. "It does not
seem to have been as wretched as you have told me. I recall
with sadness the delivery of her first child."

Chūnagon thought this would be a convenient time to leave
Uji and decided to write to the Prince about his intentions.

[23] The meaning of this last sentence is unclear.

Then all day long he held his child in his arms and secretly wept. At dusk Naishi no Kami went to the place nearby as usual. Because she had sent word of her intended visit, she was shown into the wet nurse's room in the usual way.

While Chūnagon waited for the others to settle down to sleep, he felt restless and agitated, but he did not let even the wet nurse see his state. He kept his eyes constantly on his child and was overwhelmed by sorrow. Sadness flowed straight from his heart. When it grew late and the others had settled down to sleep, Naishi no Kami was led into the western extension as on the first occasion. When informed, Chūnagon felt uneasy and agitated. "Hold the child for a little while," he said to the wet nurse. When the nurse took the child in her arms, he awakened and cried. As he gazed at his son, Chūnagon felt as though he was leaving part of himself with the child, and he slipped out of the room on his knees. More than anything else it is the darkness of the path of love for one's child[24] that can make one reconsider decisions and dull one's determination, but perhaps Chūnagon had a strength of resolve left to him from the days he was accustomed to being a man.

"There are circumstances to be considered for a little while, and so we will not have you go to the capital," said Naishi no Kami. "Before coming here I arranged this course of action by telling Father you would be at Mount Yoshino."

With them were only the daughter of Naishi no Kami's wet nurse and three other women who had been in close attendance. The moon was bright, and Chūnagon went out with them, stealthily hiding in the shadows. His child's face was still with him and he wanted to turn back, but he got into the carriage. While new drivers constantly replaced the old, Chūnagon spent the entire next night in the carriage. The next day they arrived at Yoshino.

[24] This phrase is from the poem by Fujiwara no Kanesuke cited in note 78, p. 52, above.

The Prince had been informed of what was happening, and since his own quarters were unsuitable, he had prepared the place where his daughters lived. Chūnagon stepped out, and when the Prince saw him face to face in the light of day both he and Chūnagon were radiant and felt joyful and moved, as though it had all been a dream. From Sadaijin anxious and troubled letters came so often one might think he was not far away. Then the local people, having been told to do so, all gathered and presented Chūnagon and Naishi no Kami suitable gifts from the vicinity.

Chūnagon was calm, having left behind the depressing relationship with Saishō that had made him constantly unhappy, but he yearned for the face he had grown used to seeing night and day, one that was clearly going to grow up to be most beautiful.[25] He gazed distractedly into the distance. Ashamed lest his suddenly changed woman's appearance might strike others as strange, he did not even meet with the Princesses. He lay there quietly, lost in thought. Looking at him, Naishi no Kami understood that Chūnagon was probably miserable with Saishō gone. "It must be dreary," she said, "to have to be separated anew from Saishō who knew your appearance to be unusual. What do you think? Have you decided what you are going to do?"

"I made undesirable and incomprehensible vows with Saishō," replied Chūnagon, weeping, "but how was I to go on like that? Though it pains me, I have forsaken my innocent young child because it would have been strange to bring him along. This alone grieves me." The sight of Chūnagon in this state was very moving.

"It is truly natural that you feel this way. The relationship of mother and child is a tie hard to break," said Naishi no

<hr />

[25] The expression *yamaguchi*, the entrance to a mountain path or the beginning of something, which appears here in reference to Chūnagon's and Saishō's son, and which I have loosely incorporated into the phrase "going to grow up," is used similarly in "The Wind in the Pine Trees" chapter of *The Tale of Genji*: "It was clear that she was entering on the path of becoming a beautiful woman" (*NKBT*, 15: 201).

Kami, but she thought: "Chūnagon wants very much not to tell Father about his relationship with Saishō, and he apparently wants to break with him. I am distressed when I wonder what is to become of their relationship. I too have rather casually changed from the person I was accustomed to being, and in coming to Yoshino I have been long separated from the Princess, whom I had never left for two nights. She was clearly pregnant, but I have gone on roaming unknown mountains and valleys and have not looked after her. It's quite mad. But for all that, I feel inexperienced and embarrassed, having suddenly come out into the world, and I will be patient in this male form until I'm accustomed to it. When Chūnagon takes my place serving the Princess he will naturally be able to arrange for me to meet with her. When the Princess gives birth or at other times, surely if I send word to Chūnagon, I will be able secretly to help her."

Having thus convinced herself, Naishi no Kami felt cheered, and she told Chūnagon all about what had happened between the Princess and herself. "I'm worried about her. Please secretly look after her in my place."

"Though it's hard to go back home again, obviously I love my parents, and now, with this matter of the Princess, there is surely no escape. I must return," replied Chūnagon. While he continued to speak of these things, he thought: "When I think that Naishi no Kami will have to mingle in society in my place, her appearance will not be much of a problem. But with regard to the affairs of the world generally, she will make mistakes and be awkward." Sophisticated in these matters, Chūnagon nevertheless instructed Naishi no Kami without an excessively knowing air about affairs of state he knew of and had had carried out, about what this and that person had told him, how one should reply, and so on.

Because she was in seclusion and studied feverishly, as if bereft of her senses, Naishi no Kami soon learned to play the koto and flute and practiced calligraphy. She played both instruments in precisely the same way as Chūnagon. No one could tell that this was the music of someone other than Chūnagon. And when Naishi no Kami copied Chūnagon's penmanship so as to write like him, her calligraphy did not differ from his in the slightest. And how could their voices differ when not only were they similar to begin with, but Naishi no Kami had long been imitating a woman, while Chūnagon had grown accustomed to acting like a man. Indeed, it seemed fated, this amazing bond between brother and sister.

As time rolled on, the two spoke of both public and private concerns. On one occasion Chūnagon brought up the matter of the woman he went to see at the narrow corridor of the Reikeiden, and he described the whole situation with Yon no Kimi. "Udaijin was resentful toward me all the time. Secret intrigues aside, as long as I remain in the world he probably will continue to resent deeply my not visiting Yon no Kimi. She's superb in every respect. There's not the slightest thing wrong with her. But the incident with Saishō was something I had not expected. He has no restraint with regard to her. He has decided that she is his, and he looks after her. So it will be difficult for you to care for her as I did in the past."

As Naishi no Kami became more familiar with the Prince's daughters she found them superb, all one might desire. On long, lonely nights they were a comfort she could not forgo. She grew used to speaking to them at appropriate times, but unaccustomed as she was to being a man, she did not want them to see how very naïve she would appear at first.

The Prince left everything to fate and did not keep his daughters near him. He seemed to want to purify his heart even more in preparation for his holy path and did not inform his daughters of the distinction between the one whose appearance was exactly like Chūnagon's and the Chūnagon who had been with them before. The Princesses therefore did not think there was anything different, and as a result of their familiari-

ty with the first Chūnagon they were not at all wary. Naishi
no Kami was bewildered at their amazing and unexpected
intimacy, and felt as though she was dreaming. An infinite
tenderness and deep love grew in Naishi no Kami's breast. It
was indescribable. As she grew familiar with the Princesses,
she found them graceful, refined, radiantly beautiful, ideal.
She was vexed that she had even thought contemptuously that
having been brought up by a priest so far removed from the
world and so virtuous, they probably would not be like the
people who moved in society.

Meanwhile, at Uji the wet nurse thought it strange when
Chūnagon did not return before it grew light. Even when she
raised the lattice, Chūnagon was still nowhere to be seen.
When others inquired suspiciously, the startled wet nurse
could say nothing, and she searched thoroughly every nook
and cranny of the place, even where it would not occur to
people to investigate, but Chūnagon was not to be found.

While she was still thoroughly bewildered, Saishō returned,
and she reported that Chūnagon was absent. As soon as Saishō heard this, darkness enveloped him; his heart was in
turmoil, and he could understand nothing. "But what happened? How did she seem these last few days? Did someone
from her home come to visit her?"

The wet nurse herself still seemed upset and unable to tell
him what had happened. "She did not look as though she was
going to hide like this. When you were with her she appeared
carefree enough, but when she was alone she secretly wept
night and day, never taking her eyes from her child. It pained
me to see her then, and I wondered whether there might be
someone in the world about whom she was unhappy or worried. But I did not see any sign at all that she might have been
thinking of disappearing like this."

There was nothing for Saishō to say. "Chūnagon was treated with the utmost care," he thought. "But while he was so
perfectly hidden away here, I was devoting myself to helping

Yon no Kimi; I didn't calmly settle down here with him. My
heart had a tendency to stray to Yon no Kimi at the capital.
Chūnagon probably did not really get used to not seeing me
much, and found the situation strange and unsatisfying. Yet
when I saw him, he looked at ease and without any cares. I
would never tire of looking at him, so beautiful was he then."

He simply could not stop longing for Chūnagon. In no time
at all, he became so distressed he lost all sense of past and
future, and his grief was unbearable. He felt he would never
see Chūnagon again. In his helplessness and grief he wanted
to leave this world, but he was stopped by the thought that
this would then be the last time he would see the innocent and
smiling face of his son, who seemed unaware of what was
happening. Still, Saishō realized that he was bound to find it
more and more difficult to abandon the child, and that his
sadness would increase.

"How great his determination must have been to have forsaken such a child!," thought the stunned Saishō. He was
incapable of addressing himself to the question of why such
a thing had occurred, and he was crushed and terribly vexed.
He felt Chūnagon had been truly heartless. Chūnagon had
cast off his robe where he had lain, and its lingering fragrance
brought to mind the one who had just been there. Saishō
pulled it on and wept bitterly. Had this been a dream, the
ominous feeling it produced would have remained with him
on awakening.

Chūnagon's appearance and behavior were utterly charming and full of radiance. He was affable in troublesome, painful, or sad times, but had a most affectionate nature, and he
took the trouble to speak gently. Saishō's heart could not
contain all he felt. That people would see him and think him
mad did not trouble him. He stamped his feet on the ground.
Weeping did not sate his excess of emotion, and he lay down,
overcome with grief.

The ladies-in-waiting sorrowed that he looked so pitiable,

and that there was nothing they could do. "Someone must have conspired with Chūnagon and helped him leave. Then, too, someone must have known he was hidden here, but how could that be?"

Though he thought about this, Saishō was baffled. He wondered whether Chūnagon might not have left a poem or something for him to accidentally see, but Chūnagon was not one to be devious or to linger on.

"A certain man living in the neighborhood looked out his window and saw a most handsome and elegant young nobleman furtively hand a very lovely woman into a cart and go off. He was suspicious about who it was," a lady-in-waiting told Saishō. She had heard this from someone else.

"It was only a little odd to think that Chūnagon, having grown used to conducting himself as a man, had decided he would leave alone, but this story of a man and woman leaving together is even stranger!," thought Saishō. He felt even more perplexed now and nothing could cheer him.

"I have long grieved about various misfortunes, but they were nothing compared with my grief now. Capricious in my lust for all women, in the end I find myself thus forsaken, and as the days pass I lament this sad affair and condemn myself." Only the sight of his child's face sustained him, though his tears fell all the more. Under normal circumstances, Saishō would have gone on composing and reciting moving poems, but when he thought about it he felt heartbroken, pained and downcast.

In the meantime Yon no Kimi had given birth to another beautiful daughter. She was very weak, however, and now she was losing consciousness, for she no longer wanted to get well. One could hardly tell whether she was alive or not.

"I shall surely die without having seen Father again and before he rescinds my banishment," thought Yon no Kimi, overcome with tears.

Seeing her intense grief, Yon no Kimi's mother wept and wept, and told Udaijin about her daughter's state. "If Yon no

Kimi lives, then you may bear society's censure, but . . . ," she said to her husband. Udaijin was stern. He had sent Yon no Kimi away, intending not to help her. But even so, as the months had passed, he had longed sadly for her. He simply felt distracted and lost. It was unbearable even to hear about her.

"I cannot endure it any longer," he said. "Surely whatever happens is the result of our karma in former lives. How regretful and sad I would be if I stayed away and did not see her when she was dying." And Udaijin went to see his daughter. Lovely Yon no Kimi, looking more dead than alive, was lying with her long hair spread magnificently about her. No matter how hateful a man might be, he could never carelessly dismiss her from mind. So much the more, then, did the sight of her affect a parent who held her dear.

"Why did I behave so perversely toward her? How she must feel the pain of being disowned!," thought the sorry and saddened Udaijin. "My dear, I have not helped until things have come to this pass. You are infinitely dear to me, but in my grief and anxiety when I heard about your amazing affair with Saishō, I disowned you. A regrettable thing. Well, I would like nothing better than to have you live and to look after you. Let the gods take my life instead."

He wept aloud in his grief and obliged Yon no Kimi to take the hot water he ladled up for her. Though Yon no Kimi felt as much dead as alive, when she heard her father's voice she forced open her eyes and looked at him. Her father was touched and pained to see her tearful eyes fixed on him. Reciting every possible prayer and holding her firmly in his arms, he felt at a loss.

Then, gradually, Yon no Kimi seemed to be regaining consciousness. Breathing with difficulty, she said: "I pray you, make a nun of me."

Udaijin felt it would be unfortunate to do such a thing. "As long as I live, do not think of such a thing," he said, and weeping with grief, he stayed with her and helped in every possible way. Yon no Kimi was delighted and touched. Then, perhaps because she had weathered her weakness and drunk some warm water, her condition improved greatly. After an impatient wait, Udaijin took her home with him and cared for her there, never leaving her side for so much as a moment.

In the meantime Saishō, overcome by depression, had forgotten both past and future. If the situation had remained as it had been, if Yon no Kimi still depended on him, she would probably reproach him for not coming and not having left anything behind for her, but Saishō's absence now was timely, for she thought he was not coming because she was with her father. Udaijin had a number of wet nurses attend to Yon no Kimi's newborn daughter and found the child an unending delight. Sadaijin had sent no word at all; Udaijin thought this sad and trying, and his pleasure was somewhat spoiled.

Naishi no Kami and Chūnagon could not simply remain secluded as they were on Mount Yoshino, no longer mingling in the world. Besides, their parents were most impatient for their return. Realizing that they must go back, they were about to set out secretly. But Naishi no Kami, feeling uneasy about leaving the Prince's daughters for even a little while, asked the elder Princess if she would come with them. It was sad and desolate living on Mount Yoshino, but the Princess was hesitant about leaving the shade of this familiar mountain hidden away from the world and putting herself under the sway of someone with whom she was not well acquainted. And she was not the only one involved. She was loath to leave her younger sister behind, and yet she hesitated to take her along. If she did not live out her days in this remote spot in the house near the foot of the mountain, it would be hard to see her father, and she would worry about him when she realized how far away he was. Furthermore, it seemed to her that even if she did suddenly appear in society in such a splendid place as the capital, she was different from the people there and inexperienced; she would be ridiculed, and her hardships would increase. And if she then came back to the mountain, she would be put to shame by what the pines would think. She thus unexpectedly gave up any thought of leaving, and it seemed she would not come along.

Naishi no Kami reproached her, and the Princess was naturally moved to tears:

> Weary of the world,
> To escape the pain I came
> To Mount Yoshino.
> How can I leave this cherished place
> To return to that bitter world?

"Please think of me. Even though I am here . . ." She left her sentence unfinished. Her response was very tasteful, elegant, and graceful.

> Weary of the world,
> Others too have thought, "No more,"
> And left for a mountain.
> Yet I hear that even they
> Could not remain forever there.

"It is all right for you if you stay, but it shames me," said Naishi no Kami reproachfully.

However, Naishi no Kami then had another thought: "If I were suddenly to take this girl with me, I would in due course have to tell Her Highness about it. Then she might suspect that was why I came here, and that would be very trying. Indeed, it would be precipitate to take her along now. I'll go back without her this time, prepare a place for her to stay, and then come back for her. Since we are leaving in secret this time, our departure will be quite unnoticed. I'll come for the Princess after I have arranged things so that, were the Prince to see the arrangements, even he would be somewhat surprised." And Naishi no Kami left.

Under cover of darkness, the brother and sister arrived at

the capital. Naishi no Kami led Chūnagon to the curtains[26] where she used to be and presented herself to her father. It had long been a source of grief to him that he could not exchange his children. Now, when he saw her, those regrets passed away. In his joy, tears dimmed his eyes, and he could not see how she looked.

Chūnagon was beautiful. This charming and radiant woman's hair was lustrous and full. Sitting there, looking so very splendid and delicate, he was like a dream. Naishi no Kami was an indescribably good-looking man, and seemed unreal standing there, composed and handsome. It was natural that Sadaijin should be worried, wondering in what way they might change again.

After speaking of what had happened over the last few months, he said: "Your appearances, which should have been as they are now from the start, have been most peculiar until this time. You should remain like this and not deviate from your proper roles. It would be quite a problem if you were not alike in appearance. It is amazing that you were apparently fated to be exactly alike. From now on, Naishi no Kami, you will go about in public as Chūnagon. No one will see anything at all different in you. Anyway, what difference does it make if you do look a bit different? No one will discuss it or argue about it. As for Udaijin's daughter, Saishō went to some pains to stay with her and help her, but her father withdrew his censure and took her home. In his heart he will think of you differently, but public opinion will make it inconvenient for him to say so. It is for the good of all." Sadaijin sighed, and Naishi no Kami's heart throbbed.

The former Naishi no Kami[27] had said that she had been suffering from an ailment these past days, and as a result a messenger arrived from the Imperial Princess.

---

[26] The text reads *michō no mae*, "before the curtains." This may be a mistake for *michō no naka*, "within the curtains," which seems to be more appropriate here.

[27] From this point on I shall refer to Chūnagon as Naishi no Kami, since he has

"How is Naishi no Kami?," he inquired. "The Princess has been unwell too and would like Naishi no Kami to come at once if she is well enough."

"Say that you went into hiding with the Yoshino Prince because you found Yon no Kimi's unexpected and confusing affair with Saishō disagreeable," said Sadaijin to Chūnagon, who was saddened by this news of the Princess. "Go to the palace immediately."

Though his father thus urged him on, Chūnagon felt quite inexperienced and shy. Of the numerous rumors people were spreading, one was most widely circulated and most plausible: "Chūnagon lamented over the affair between Saishō and Yon no Kimi. Having gone into hiding with the Yoshino Prince, he intended to turn his back on the world. Then he became intimate with the Prince's daughters, and in the end he was unable to carry his project through. Yet he abandoned all thought of returning to the capital because of his unhappiness over the affair between Saishō and Yon no Kimi. Learning of this, Sadaijin wept, and sad and resentful, pressed Chūnagon to return: 'Don't you want to see once again the face of a parent who is even now in his last hour?' Unable to refuse, Chūnagon had no recourse but to leave Mount Yoshino."

The joy at Chūnagon's return was boundless. The Emperor too learned of his return and was tremendously happy that at all events he had remained in the world and had not taken the holy vows. When the Emperor summoned him, Chūnagon came to court.

Chūnagon had dressed with great care and as soon as he stepped out onto the veranda on his way to his carriage, everyone was uproariously jubilant. Chūnagon felt most awkward. Forerunners, rear guards, and others who had served him for years and who had grown close to him had felt as

now assumed the female role, or on occasion as "the former Chūnagon." Similarly, Naishi no Kami now becomes Chūnagon or "the former Naishi no Kami."

though plunged into darkness during his absence, and so when they caught sight of him and took their places again, their feelings were indescribable. They even shed tears.

Chūnagon, nonchalant and calm, entered the palace. As he arrived at the seat appropriate to his station, everyone looked at him with curiosity. When he came before the Emperor, the latter looked at him for some time, convinced that Chūnagon had become even more breathtaking during these long months past. A radiant beauty and charm were added to his other features. Gazing at him, the Emperor thought: "Oh, how woeful it would have been for mankind had such a person taken religious vows." His tears fell.

> Though above the clouds,
> Plunged into darkness we felt;
> The court without you.
> As we floundered about,
> Not a ray of light could we see.

The grateful Chūnagon replied:

> Realm above the clouds,
> My Emperor its clear shining moon.
> For love of you,
> I could not remain there,
> Lost forever in the valley.[28]

As Chūnagon spoke, the Emperor gazed at his dazzling appearance. "He has gained both in manliness and in refinement of beauty," he mused.

Chūnagon then went to the Imperial Princess. He remained far from her, outside the bamboo blinds, and an attendant slipped out on her knees and with great curiosity spoke to him. "Does Naishi no Kami's ailment still trouble her?[29] Since

---

[28] A *kakekotoba* in this poem is *sumu*, "to be clear" and "to live." *Tani*, "valley," refers to Mount Yoshino.

[29] The *senji* here is an attendant in the service of the Imperial Princess. She is unaware that this Chūnagon is the former Naishi no Kami.

the Princess still seems unwell too, do have Naishi no Kami come if she's all right. The Princess often looks anxious and in pain. So urge Naishi no Kami to come."

Chūnagon's heart throbbed. It seemed that the one with whom he had been familiar night and day would from now on be far away, as remote as the clouds. When suddenly an image of her, more distressed and distraught than ever, came to his mind, Chūnagon was unable to restrain his tears. He then left, feeling awkward and having said very little; but for a short while, he stopped to gaze in the direction of the distant Princess.

> Round and round they spin,
> Recurring in my thoughts,
> Those old days I miss:
> The days I grew to know you,
> The days of *shizu* cloth reels. [30]

When Chūnagon returned home, he saw Naishi no Kami lying near the front of her curtain, quietly and absently looking out, apparently lost in thought. Chūnagon looked at her, thinking sadly that her appearance now as she wiped away her tears was more radiantly beautiful than it had been. He wondered, as she rose, how she truly felt about things. When Chūnagon told her what had happened when he went to court, she was sad, recalling how she too had once been there.

It was difficult for Chūnagon to go on neglecting Yon no Kimi any longer, and he wanted to see her; but it was most distasteful to him that Saishō had clearly been passionately intimate with Yon no Kimi, and he was disinclined to go to her. It was a sore point. It would have been more distasteful, however, if he were thinking of taking only this one woman

---

[30] "Kuri," "reel" or "wind around," is an *engo* (associative word) with *shizu no odamaki,* the reel on which one spun the fibers for this particular type of cloth. The image is taken from a poem in the *Ise monogatari* (*NKBT,* 9: 131, Section 32): "Oh, to spin the reel / For old *shizu* cloth again— / If only I might!— / And to turn the present / Into those days of old."

as his wife; but unbeknownst to others, he was thinking about the Imperial Princess. If he could install one of the Yoshino Princesses in his home as his wife, and if he were to be generous to Yon no Kimi along with the other Yoshino Princess and the Imperial Princess, then Chūnagon wanted to meet with Yon no Kimi. Desirous, therefore, of learning something about Yon no Kimi, he consulted Naishi no Kami and then wrote a letter. "Because I cannot write all about the reasons for my absence, I will let you learn them yourself."

> Have you forgotten me,
> Accustomed to my absence now?
> For your sake it is
> That I have not quit this world,
> But left instead the mountain road.

Now Udaijin heard that Chūnagon had appeared in public, and he was confused about what had happened. If Chūnagon had resolutely turned his back on the world and taken religious vows, Udaijin could have consoled himself with the thought that Chūnagon's heart had been far from worldly affairs. But that Chūnagon had ceased to write when he had not entered the religious life chagrined him terribly. He wondered how Chūnagon would behave from now on, and his heart was distressed. He had waited for a letter from Chūnagon, and the moment he received one his tears fell.

"Surely there is nothing so sad for a woman as to learn that she is forgotten by the one with whom she first exchanged vows," he said to his daughter. "But this is not all. There are dreadful rumors about that shameful affair with Saishō and about Chūnagon's total neglect of you. Be that as it may, it would seem that Chūnagon's feelings for you are only deep enough for him to correspond with you. But there's nothing for it. Answer his letter."

Though Yon no Kimi felt that to do so would be quite

unsuitable and had no inclination to write, she could not refuse
to do so. Her father sat down beside her and told her what
to say. Though she did not want to do it, she lowered her head
in fright and wrote:

> "No more," you said,
> And gave up caring for me;
> So it seemed to me.
> Since then, days pass while I fade,
> Unsure whether I live or not.

It was a refined and charming poem, so enticing to Chūnagon that he set it aside to show to Naishi no Kami. Yon no
Kimi's countenance and appearance had been charming, and
the letter brought moving memories to Naishi no Kami of the
time when she had often seen her calligraphy. Both Naishi no
Kami's heart and Chūnagon's were distracted when they
thought about Yon no Kimi, with whom they were bound in
an indissoluble bond of love.[31]

Chūnagon wondered how the Imperial Princess and the
cheerless and sad Yoshino Princess were. But even so he felt
he could not go on without seeing Yon no Kimi. Accordingly,
he decided to pay her a visit after it grew dark. Udaijin suspected that Chūnagon might indeed come, and he busied
himself arranging the furnishings in the house and adding
attractive touches to his daughter's appearance.

"During the time I was hidden away in that very sad period
when I was disowned, Saishō was never unkind to me,"
thought Yon no Kimi. "I opened my heart to him. I grew used
to seeing him. I was cared for by him. I feel sorry and ashamed
that he should now wonder if I have rejoined Chūnagon.

---

[31] The epithet *shinobi no mori*, "woods of longing," appears in this sentence, but
its usage is unclear. It may have referred to a specific area near the capital. One text
has it as *shinobu no mori*, in which form the name or expression appears in poems
in such anthologies as *Shinchokusen wakashū*, *Zoku goshūi wakashū*, *Shinshūi
wakashū*, and *Shinzoku kokin wakashū*.

Chūnagon would never be intimate with me and look after me, and yet I feel ashamed after having been estranged for months. He was so handsome his beauty embarrassed me even when we had become accustomed to seeing each other constantly. Meeting such a person face to face intimidates me, and I do not wish to see him. But this is not an affair that has just begun, and so I can't leave it to my own decision. What shall I do if he comes?" Feeling awkward and pained, she wept.

Yon no Kimi was moved that her father himself cared for her, had her hair combed, and perfumed her robes. With beating heart and in a state of anguish, she considered what was to happen next.

The night drew on. Acting in such a way as to conceal the fact that the surroundings were unfamiliar to him, Chūnagon stealthily entered the house. He looked breathtaking. Delicately and languidly he stepped into the dim lamplight, the absolute image of the former Chūnagon. Everyone had been resigned that they had seen the last of him; but when they saw him now unchanged, they marveled, weeping, as if it were all a dream. Chūnagon, saying as little as possible, inquired for Yon no Kimi, but she was suddenly unable to move.

"Oh my!," sighed the fretful Udaijin. "It's precisely because you behave this way that others say disagreeable things." Frightened and feeling more dead than alive, Yon no Kimi slipped out on her knees. Ashamed that she had thought she would never be able to meet him face to face again and remembering that he had cruelly left her, she felt that this was all unreal. Since she had been weeping, she looked elegant and fragile, slender and sad in the faint light.

"She is truly splendid," thought Chūnagon, even more captivated and elated. "I understood just how unusual I was," he said, "but since you reproached me I thought I might be able to turn my back on the world and tried to. I made my way far up to the peak of Mount Yoshino; but my anxiety for you was unbearable, and my compassion for our young child an unsurmountable obstacle to my leaving. My behavior was shameful. So I reconsidered. Though my sin is still great, it would give me much joy to know that you are not worrying."

It would have occurred to no one that this was anyone other than the former Chūnagon. Since there was no way for Yon no Kimi to reply, she simply said:

> I hear 'twas not grief
> Made you turn your back on this world,
> But one like the wind.
> She blows through the treetops,
> The Yoshino Mountain pines.

Yon no Kimi was young and lovely. "Indeed I can make a similar response," replied Chūnagon, smiling and affable:

> 'Tis as it should be
> That you wait for the treetop.
> Yet giving up hope,
> Did not waves of fickleness
> Come surging over Pine Mountain.[32]

"This grieved me, and I thought there was no place for me."

As he spoke, Chūnagon was so much more superb than he had been that Yon no Kimi felt embarrassed. "Why did I speak up thoughtlessly?," she mused on seeing signs of his displeasure. Bathed in nervous perspiration, she looked so lovely that the greatest of sins might all be forgiven.

Yon no Kimi and Chūnagon had been used to being very close and simply passing the time by speaking tenderly with each other. Since Chūnagon seemed the same, Yon no Kimi

[32] The treetop refers to Chūnagon himself. His use of "waves of fickleness" alludes to Yon no Kimi's clandestine relationship with Saishō. The last line has its origins in a poem, also referring to Mount Sue no Matsu, here translated simply as Pine Mountain, in the Kokin wakashū, XX, Court Poetry, no. 1093, Anonymous (NKBT, 8: 328): "Where you it concerns, / Should it ever fickle be / This heart of mine, / Then shall waves come surging, / Submerging Pine Mountain."

assumed things would go on the same as before. But Chūnagon showed an amazing change of heart in his sexual treatment of her now, and she was even more embarrassed than
when Saishō had first lain with her. She was still more upset
that she could not protest. Her reaction was obvious, and
Chūnagon mused sadly that she must find him truly odd.
When he thought of Saishō's lack of restraint, acting as
though Yon no Kimi were his, he felt he could not be frank
with her. And yet he could not leave it at this. He felt no less
a tenderness for Yon no Kimi than for any of the ladies he
loved, but at the same time he could not forget the dearness
of the Princess who, though free from care and buried away
in the snows of Mount Yoshino, would, sleepless, be thinking
of him. This was a profound love.

Still shy, Chūnagon could not remain with Yon no Kimi in
the daytime. They were reserved in their relationship, and at
night Chūnagon still appeared to be resentful. Though a man,
when formerly he had spoken passionately with her, close up
he had been supple, slender, and lovely. He now had the same
charm and the same appearance of youthful beauty, but she
wondered whether this man was not indeed different. Again
and again she considered her situation strange and incomprehensible; it was unbearable for her. She sighed:

> The one I knew,
> He whom I was wont to see,
> You seem not to be he.
> Is it I who am different?
> Or is it you who have changed?

Chūnagon thought it amusing and natural that there should
be aspects about him at which she would wonder.

> Your heart's confusion,
> A heart that has been given
> Not to one alone;

Therein may lie the reason
You think me not who I was.

He spoke these lines, imitating the former Chūnagon's manner, and Yon no Kimi was apparently unable to tell the difference.

As the days flew by and the months passed one after the
other, the son born to the former Chūnagon and Saishō grew,
looking constantly more beautiful, and at last he began to sit
up. Saishō stayed at Uji, gazing at his son, never taking his eyes
from him.

"Chūnagon was so indescribably lovely it was well worth
gazing at her," he thought. "She gave the appearance of many
graces. She was calm, but seemed to think her lot a sad one.
Yet she did not neglect her son as one might expect, but held
him in her arms and cared for him. Where then and in what
guise has she gone? Where, without seeing or knowing about
her child, has she hidden herself?" Saishō's tears flowed night
and day, and turned the color of blood, and he thought that
it was his fate that his life should soon be extinguished.

"I hear that Chūnagon was discovered in the capital,"
someone said, repeating to him a comment he had overheard.
"He has been to the palace, among other places."

Saishō was greatly perplexed on hearing this. "Then she
returned to the world and did not take vows," he thought,
feeling quite rejuvenated. "Even so it's odd. She'd been accustomed to going about as a man, and so no doubt wanted to
be one again. But she was so splendidly feminine that it is most
unusual and unparalleled in this world that she should decide
to become a man again and leave. Yet what has happened?"

He might have been able to piece out more about these
matters under normal circumstances, but not in his present
distress. In any event, he wanted very much to see Chūnagon,
if only to get a glimpse of her, to know how she looked. At
last he came to a decision, and taking his son, he left, meaning

to stop first at his father's house in the capital. The noblemen were having a conference to discuss various matters, so Saishō attended, imagining that Chūnagon would surely be there. Just as he had supposed, Chūnagon was apparently coming, his forerunners positioned colorfully in front of him. When Saishō saw his beloved's figure, he thought: "It is quite natural that anyone accustomed to splendor should be discontented when hidden away in seclusion."

Chūnagon did indeed look splendid and radiantly beautiful, even enhanced by a youthful charm. Saishō felt his eyes grow dim but kept them fixed on Chūnagon.

"How odd Saishō must find this," thought Chūnagon as they looked at each other. Feeling the color of his complexion change, Chūnagon firmly composed himself. Saishō wanted some opportunity to speak with Chūnagon and learn her feelings. With this thought alone in mind, his eyes remained fixed on her. But Chūnagon understood what Saishō must be thinking, and he saw to it that Saishō should have no chance to stop and speak, pretending not even to recognize him; and when the conference came to an end Chūnagon left quickly.

"Perhaps she has indeed quite forsaken me," thought Saishō when he saw this. "But she should be thinking how splendid her son was and wondering how he is." Reproachful and sad, he made a public spectacle of himself as he left weeping bitterly. He spent the night lost in thought, and when it grew light he felt he could bear it no longer:

> I have seen you.
> Yet my tears I cannot check;
> Upon my sleeve they fall.
> If only I might drown myself
> Deep in Uji River!

Though he could not write everything, he filled this letter with his reproaches. When Chūnagon saw the letter, he realized that Saishō had taken him to be the former Chūnagon, a situation he found both amusing and pitiful. He therefore showed the letter to Naishi no Kami. Saishō had always anticipated that Chūnagon would change back to his male form. He used to chide Chūnagon: "You seem to want to meet people face to face rather than keep in seclusion like a woman. You seem to long for the good old days."

Naishi no Kami was upset, sorry to think that Saishō was probably deeply hurt. But the present Chūnagon could not explain that he had not been the other one. It was sad and shameful that in his heart Saishō should think Chūnagon strange. Yet in order to try to establish Chūnagon's innocence as someone who had never been out in the world, Chūnagon would not reveal Naishi no Kami's affairs and permit others to think her indiscreet.

"Simply let him think as he does," Chūnagon urged, "and as for a reply, you must compose it, for he is a perceptive person, and will surely be suspicious if I write it."

Naishi no Kami was ashamed and sorry to write something Saishō would see, but being frail, she had no alternative. Nor was she in a position to refuse. So she wrote only in the margin of Saishō's letter:

> My heart reproached you,
> You, capricious as a boat,
> Afloat on the river.
> Oh, how the days passed for me,
> Wretched at Uji River.

Her calligraphy was so beautiful it dazzled the eye. Chūnagon glanced at it only long enough to see that it was in her lovely handwriting, and sent the letter to Saishō. Saishō was expecting it, and when he received it he thought sadly that it was natural for Chūnagon to feel as she did. It grieved him terribly that it was his own neglect of her that had made him distaste-

ful to Chūnagon, and he was overcome by sorrow. He wrote
a reply in which he apologized profusely and immediately sent
it with a poem:

> Ever growing grief!
> I understand why you left;
> Wood cast adrift.
> My misery knows no end,
> Oh boat on Uji River![33]

[33] Here and in the two preceding poems the author uses the same pun on *uji* as
earlier (see note 13, p. 123, above). *Nageki*, meaning "sorrow" or "grief," is used
in this poem as an *engo* with *nageki*, meaning "wood cast adrift."

Book Three

AT THE END of the eleventh month Naishi no Kami went to the palace. The Imperial Princess naturally felt that she had lost contact with Naishi no Kami to a surprising degree. She had thus been saddened and waited anxiously to see her again soon. Even as she proceeded to the palace Naishi no Kami wondered what the Princess would think. Feeling sorry for her, Naishi no Kami looked ill at ease, for she did not know what to say. The Princess, apparently in great pain, was lying down. She looked so small she seemed to have no body within her robes. She appeared very oppressed. Her belly was swollen with child. It grieved Naishi no Kami to see her in this condition, and she lay down quietly beside her. She remembered the time when she had thoughtlessly grown familiar with Yon no Kimi, and she was moved. It would never have occurred to the Princess that this Naishi no Kami was different from the one she had known before, and so she was unreserved in speaking of her anxiety and despondency during these many days past, and Naishi no Kami was pained.

Naishi no Kami wanted to explain the situation in detail, but it was, of course, an embarrassing one to speak of, and so she pondered for a little while. "I have been worrying for days," she said, "wondering how you were. I wanted to come and see you at once, but I was quite absorbed in Chūnagon's affairs, which had become confused in many ways. I am sorry it has taken me until now." Since she seemed identical to the former Naishi no Kami when she spoke, the Princess harbored no suspicion at all.

That night Naishi no Kami and the Princess chatted about what had happened during the past few days. "I was uneasy when we were separated for so long. I did not even receive a letter from you," the Princess said, moved to tears.

Naishi no Kami was deeply touched and pained. She too naturally felt the pathos of the situation, and so she wept and spoke tenderly with the Princess. To the Princess it seemed that Naishi no Kami's charm and desirability had increased more than in all the years before. Feeling ever so comforted, the Princess looked lovely.

When it grew light, Naishi no Kami drew out a letter Chūnagon had asked her to present secretly to the Princess. The latter had no idea of what it was; but she opened it, and there was Naishi no Kami's handwriting. The Princess did not understand, but she read the missive: "I cannot possibly tell you how great is the turmoil in my heart."

> Your lovely image,
> The one I grew to know so well,
> Is with me ever.
> Oh, how sad these days and months
> I have spent without you near.

"Because Naishi no Kami has come to you I am sustained by the thought that this gloom of many months will at last clear." The Princess looked carefully at the letter. It was odd, but there was nothing she could say, and so she broke into tears.

Her attendant, Senji, was the daughter of the late Emperor's wet nurse and an intimate of the Princess's. Since the Princess had no suitable wet nurse among her own servants, she was deeply attached to Senji. Senji now drew near the curtain, and the Princess left it to her to relate her unbearable distress about days past.

"The Princess's condition has been a source of anxiety these past months," said Senji, weeping. "Because we did not know whom to go to to inquire, what preparations to make for her condition, and how to cope, the Princess was worried and waited for you to come. Though it may seem that I serve the Princess constantly, I naturally leave her every night to return to my own home. You are the only one who never left her for a moment from the time you first came, and so naturally you would be aware of her unusual condition.

"Throughout these past months, the Princess has been unwell, and while we grieved, she was uneasy that you stayed at your family home for so long. During that time we realized what this most strange and incomprehensible condition was. We had no inkling about any affair and were amazed, but we knew what was usually done in cases of pregnancy and had the Princess perform the ceremony of donning the maternity belt.[1] However, I can't say for sure how she came to get pregnant. This kind of situation does not arise unless someone has introduced a man. Because I cannot inquire without knowing anything more definite, I worry alone. So I wanted you to come at once. I thought perhaps you knew about it. I was so uneasy I thought that even if you did not, we might discuss the problem, sympathize, and lament together, and so I waited impatiently for you to come."

Naishi no Kami felt there was nothing she could say, and she was silent for a while, lost in thought. However, since she had grown used to being a man, she was accustomed to reasoning things out and pondered what ought to be done. If she claimed that she had not even known about the Princess, the Princess would be very sad.

[1] This ceremony, during which a sash (*iwata obi*) was fastened about the pregnant woman's belly, was held in the fifth month of pregnancy. It was a congratulatory ceremony in which the father formally recognized the child as his. For details, see Nakamura 1965: 24–28.

"As long as the Princess's condition is so unstable, I will truly sympathize and do all I can for her," she thought, weeping. "It's awkward that the Princess is lying there listening intently, but the time will soon come when she will understand what's happened."

"I did indeed notice something unusual about the Princess," she said, "but I could not speak of something that would never even have occurred to me, and so I did not tell anyone. I simply did not realize that she might be pregnant, and this matter of Chūnagon's disappearance took me by surprise; I left for home, forgetting everything else. When I was there I fell gravely ill, and days and months passed when I could do nothing. I was very anxious about the Princess, but too depressed even to write, and so the months went by.

"When my uneasiness began to slacken, I was anxious to return at once. 'I had a dream that revealed to me that the Princess was possibly pregnant,' Chūnagon secretly told me at the time, 'but I've not been able to determine whether this is true or not. Since I feel that it is, I beg you to go to her at once and help her.'

"It was then that I finally understood the Princess's condition, and I wanted to come directly. Since you feel as I do and also understand the Princess's plight, I'm glad I have you to rely on rather than having to worry alone."

As she spoke, Naishi no Kami seemed quite the same as the one of months ago. People had never seen the former Naishi no Kami face to face, for she had been reserved and used to serving the Princess within the curtains, and so Senji could not think her other than the former Naishi no Kami. Senji assumed that she was, and that she had conspired with Chūnagon and guided him to the Princess. After having worried alone for months, Senji felt strengthened. And when she discussed various matters concerning the time of delivery with Naishi no Kami, the latter was more reasonable than she had ever been. In the past she had spoken faintly and in few words; but now it was charming the way she expressed herself audibly and clearly. One wanted to go on listening to her, so lovely was it.

"When is she due to deliver?," asked Senji.

"Chūnagon said he thought it would probably be around the twelfth month," replied Naishi no Kami.

"If that's so, why, it might be any day now!," cried the startled Senji.

The Princess had been reclining, intently listening. "Astonishing! I don't understand. Senji has been lamenting for days, but I thought it would all be cleared up when Naishi no Kami came. But what incomprehensible things she's saying! Why should she speak like this when I have never met with Chūnagon even in a dream?"

The Princess then thought: "Indeed the situation is one she can't speak about, and she's apparently pinning the blame on Chūnagon." But then again she thought: "But what of the letter I had from Chūnagon a moment ago?" She pondered the matter, but it was all unclear and she could not understand. Nevertheless, she thought: "There's nothing different about her, yet all the same she does not look like the one with whom I was intimate. That one had had a delightful youthful beauty and behaved with an easy intimacy. This one, however, is infinitely charming and has an appearance one would like to gaze on forever. What is happening here?"

"What has happened to the one with whom I have exchanged vows? Might he be called Chūnagon now?," thought the Princess, though she still did not understand. "In that case, though, who is this one? I had not heard he had many brothers and sisters."

The Princess, depressed and fretful for days, had waited for Naishi no Kami, and now that she had come the Princess wondered whether she was someone different. Shame and sadness overcame her, and, weeping, she pulled her bedclothes over her head. Naishi no Kami thought this natural, but there was nothing she could say and no way she could console the Princess. So she too wept as she lay down beside her.

When it grew dark, Chūnagon came to see Naishi no Kami. She confided all to him telling him about the Princess's condition, about Senji's grief, and about her conversation with the Princess, and Chūnagon wept too. When the early part of the night had passed and everyone was quietly sleeping, Naishi no Kami stealthily led Chūnagon into the Princess's apartments. Both he and the Princess felt it was a dream. Chūnagon did not know what to say, but they could not simply remain there in silence forever.

"If I told her all about our circumstances, she would not consider it some curious tale to be repeated. So why should I hold off?"

Chūnagon then told the Princess about everything from the beginning. The Princess found the recital curious and astonishing.

"Then he did not feel utterly unable to part from me," she thought. "If he loved me he would never have been able to leave me as he did. When he realized that I was in a helpless and painful state, would he have left me and gone to mingle in society? Would he entrust my affairs to someone else and be so unfeeling? Also why did he not tell me everything when he went in search of the other Chūnagon? I could never have given away his secret. I was worried the many days he was not here. I remembered him both yearningly and reproachfully. I thought of him with tenderness. He is truly so splendid that he should not be buried and hidden away in the guise of a woman. In the end he had to become a man as he did. But while I was in this condition, he should not have handed me over to the care of someone else. He should have looked after me himself. Yet he forsook me in my wretchedness."

The Princess, weeping in silence and pondering the problem, realized both Chūnagon's lack of feeling and her own misery and shame. It was reasonable and touching, and Chūnagon realized how she felt. Weeping bitterly, he spoke of his neglect these many days, but the Princess did not seem to be listening to what he was saying. Weeping, he soothed and humored her. When it seemed to be gradually growing light, Chūnagon prepared to go, but it was hard for him to leave the place he had grown used to day and night, asleep and awake. He was desperately sad:

> In my visits to you,
> Am I to be secretive,
> Stealing in and out,
> As if this were not the place
> Where, night and day, our intimacy grew?

"This is not as it should be; I would like at least to come and help you secretly. Even though some will think it strange, they will not all consider it improper. You ought to feel that there is some stronghearted person to help you," said Chūnagon.

> Would you have gone off,
> Neglected me so long,
> As already you have,
> Had you felt this to be the place
> Where, night and day, our intimacy grew?

"It seems useless at this point to reveal our relationship and so let fly rumors of your fickleness," said the Princess, moved to tears. These words were naturally more upsetting than if she had said much more in reproach.

"All right," said Chūnagon. "It is no good speaking to you. A subsequent meeting would probably not be more difficult than this one, but it is depressing that we should be so distant when we have been intimate day and night, awake and asleep. If you were the Empress I could not attend you, but you are now in a position that permits intimacy, and I would be your intimate guardian, for I am a close relation of Naishi no Kami. I would serve you well." While Chūnagon spoke it had grown light, and so he left.

Chūnagon did not love the Imperial Princess as much as he did the Yoshino Princess and Yon no Kimi, but the feelings he had developed for her over the many years he had known her were not insignificant. Thus on subsequent suitable occasions, Naishi no Kami, concealing him well, arranged for him to meet with the Princess. The latter was chagrined that he suddenly loved her so little. She was in anguish, thinking that the rumor of his inconstancy was widely known, and that this was her wretched fate. Meanwhile, her delivery was imminent, and with the passing days and months she had grown very restricted and unable to conceal her condition. In this state she did not rise at all, but remained in bed depressed. With the exception of Naishi no Kami and Senji, everyone thought her ill. Her father, the Cloistered Emperor, and the Emperor too were informed, and everyone grieved.

It was natural that the Emperor should worry about her illness, and still not having forgotten the love he had had for Naishi no Kami long ago, he very much wanted to see her as she attended the Princess. Thus he decided to go to the Nashitsubo, using as a pretext a visit of inquiry about the ailing Princess. Without sending any advance notice of his intended visit, the Emperor inconspicuously went to the Nashitsubo one tranquil afternoon. Quietly he concealed himself behind a curtain and looked in. The Princess was resting, a thick white robe pulled over her from the top of her head on down. Naishi no Kami was a little distance from her. She was wearing eight unlined robes of pale violet and an outer garment that seemed to be of a brocaded fabric. As though to make them longer, she pulled at the edges of the sleeves of the outer lined robe, which was somewhat similar in color to the others, and covering her mouth, lay down near the Princess. Suddenly she seemed very lovely to the Emperor. Her charm engulfed the area around her. Her face was the image of Chūnagon's, whose unparalleled nobility, elegance, and grandeur, which bespoke his fine lineage, increased as he grew older.

As the Emperor gazed on the indescribably alluring Naishi no Kami, her appearance was infinitely pleasing, one that would obliterate the most dreadful cares. For many years the Emperor had wished to see her famed countenance, but he had never had the occasion. It vexed him that he had not seen her till now, and he felt he could not think calmly. It would not be difficult for him to pay court to her at present.

"She is lovely and flawless, but her father has kept me from her by resigning himself to her being the Princess's attendant and considering her superfluous and unneeded," he thought.

The Emperor was concerned lest hearing about his attachment to the girl, Sadaijin might even now place her in seclusion in his own home. Despite himself he was nervous and agitated. He wondered whether this was his fate. Calming himself, however, he looked at Naishi no Kami again.

A letter wrapped in thin white paper lay unopened beside the Princess. Naishi no Kami was bending over slightly and reaching out to take it. She moved her hand gracefully, and her hair, as it cascaded forward when she inclined her head, was of a dazzling luster. However, the Emperor guessed that it was not very long. It looked as though it might be but the length of her seated height. Yet it was not so short that it flawed her. Indeed, spread out on the hem of her robe, it looked more beautiful than tresses over eight feet long.

"How irksome this waiting," fretted Naishi no Kami, hiding the letter. "There was no answer this morning, and so the Princess speaks sullenly, but . . ." The Emperor could have had no doubt about the identity of the writer. He must have realized that it had been sent by Chūnagon, since he would have had occasion to speak with the Princess.

When the Emperor had been standing there for some time,

Senji's younger sister, who was called Chūnagon no Kimi, entered. "The Emperor came here. Where is he hiding?," she said. While she looked about, she lowered the curtains. The Emperor then came out from behind the curtains and sat down, behaving as though he had just come in. Whenever the Emperor came, it was normally Senji who attended him and spoke with him, but she was confined to the women's quarters with a cold. As a result, there was no one to come forward at once to attend him. Rather the ladies waited on him while remaining out of sight. The Emperor felt as though the face of the Naishi no Kami he had just glimpsed was still with him.

"Is Naishi no Kami in attendance here?," he asked, wanting to hear her voice and see the way she moved. There was nothing she could say, but since she seemed to move a little, the Emperor went on: "The Princess's illness seems to be continuing indefinitely. What is her condition? Was the Cloistered Emperor informed of how she is? Are there no prayers being recited for her?"

Naishi no Kami could not think of a suitable response, but she was worried and could not very well put an end to the conversation. "She has been suffering from this condition for several months; the cause of it is unclear," she said simply, thus evading the issue. "Recently she seems to be feeling unwell frequently. Perhaps it is evil spirits." As she spoke, she seemed so like Chūnagon that the Emperor listened to her in amazement. Were she to go on for a thousand years, he would never tire of listening to her.

The Emperor stayed for quite some time, asking questions to which Naishi no Kami had to reply. She felt it would be awkward if she said too much, however, and so time and again she only stirred. The Emperor grew impatient, but since it would appear odd for him to stay on pointlessly, he took his leave, saying: "It is careless to have allowed the Princess's illness to go on indefinitely. Prayers should certainly be said."

Even then he felt as though the face of the Naishi no Kami he had just seen was still with him. The Princess was not very close to the Emperor, but he was not negligent about the Cloistered Emperor's affairs, and so he decided to be especially kind to her.

The Emperor's visit naturally brought to Naishi no Kami's mind the old days when she was with the Emperor night and day, conversing with him without reserve. Both of the same heart, they would amuse themselves playing the koto and flute. Now she had barely heard his voice, separated as they were by the curtains. Deeply moved, she felt as though it was all a dream:

> They have not changed,
> Neither sky above the clouds,
> Nor light of the moon.
> Court and Emperor the same,
> I alone am not what I was.[2]

In the twelfth month Naishi no Kami was uneasy, for she thought that the Princess was due to give birth around this time. Even if the Princess were to be moved from the palace, the long-worried Cloistered Emperor might well visit her and realize that she was pregnant. That would be dreadful, Naishi no Kami thought, feeling most constrained. Thus, though there was no precedent for delivery at court, there was nothing for it but to leave the Princess there. Fortunately, it was a period of few religious observances, and Naishi no Kami thought there would be no problem with rituals for impurity, and so even now, when the Princess was experiencing her pains, they did not inform the Cloistered Emperor. Rather Naishi no Kami, Senji, and two or three other suitable ladies who were aware of the circumstances, stayed in constant

[2] The poem recalls one by Ariwara Narihira that appears in the *Kokin wakashū*, XV, Love V, no. 747 (*NKBT*, 8: 250): "Is there not the moon? / Is not the spring the same / As the one of old? / Oh, would that I too might be / The one I used to be!"

attendance. Thus—in anxiety—the days passed. Around this time, Chūnagon often came secretly. On the pretext of visiting the ailing Princess, he would serve on night duty nearby. It upset the Princess, however, to think that now people might suspect the truth.

The Emperor, with the face of the Naishi no Kami he had recently seen still with him, thought he could not go on living unless he saw her again. Thus when Chūnagon came to court, he summoned him as usual, and during their conversation spoke of his never-ending love for Naishi no Kami.

Now that Naishi no Kami was a woman, it was no longer necessary to hesitate and avoid the subject, but since this had been the practice from the beginning, Chūnagon said: "Naishi no Kami was extremely reserved and found it painful to be seen by anyone unknown to her. Thus, probably so as not to hurt her feelings, her father resigned himself to her being only a court attendant. Now, however, she has grown more mature and has come to understand feelings between men and women. She probably is not so shy. I will speak to Father about this again."

The Emperor looked closely at Chūnagon. He saw his fresh, clean, handsome appearance, one that seemed flawless and mature. Suddenly he recalled Naishi no Kami's face so like Chūnagon's in every respect, and he would have wept had he not resolutely put it from his mind.

"Though I have hinted about my love to Sadaijin many times, he rejected me in no uncertain terms and put an end to the discussion. Since it is hard for me to insist, take me in secret to the Sen'yōden!"

"I would not like to have him see her for the first time in such a casual way," thought Chūnagon. "When she goes to him I will have her appear in splendor and in public." He thus said nothing at all in response to the Emperor and respectfully withdrew.

Chūnagon told his mother what the Emperor had said and

added: "Now that we have returned to our original sexes there is no need to be reticent. Since the Emperor is so inclined, I will simply have Naishi no Kami go to him."

"Now how would that be?," said his mother. "It would be embarrassing to let her go when we have refused as we have up to now. Since she is serving in the same palace as he, it would be splendid if the Emperor met with her secretly at first, and if, as he desires, she then became his concubine or Empress. Otherwise everyone will wonder why your father changed his mind about something he has refused until now. It would be strange." Chūnagon, recalling the fact of his sister's relationship with Saishō, wondered whether it would do to present her publicly to the Emperor. He regretted the situation and was unhappy about it.

The Imperial Princess did not suffer so much as had been expected, and she gave birth to a very beautiful son, the image of Chūnagon. Those, like Senji, who knew whose child he was, looked on the Princess with deep emotion and embarrassment. However, since this state of affairs could not be made public, Naishi no Kami's ladies-in-waiting made secret arrangements to take the child from the palace, and they proceeded to Sadaijin's home, Chūnagon no Kimi holding the child in her arms.

Chūnagon had secretly informed his mother of the situation, and the child was given into her keeping. The mother was deeply moved and happy, and she told her surprised husband the truth about what had happened. He selected an outstanding wet nurse and had her attend the child, who was given the greatest of care. In public Chūnagon deliberately asserted that a son had been born to him by someone he had been secretly frequenting.

Udaijin and his family found the situation strange. "Until now he has behaved as though nothing was happening. When could such a thing have occurred?," they said.

As in the past, Chūnagon did not remain with Yon no Kimi

during the day. He went to her under cover of night and left when it grew light. With the exception of those times when he was on night duty at the palace, he never stayed out late into the night.

Chūnagon was unable to go to the Yoshino Princess routinely because of the great length of the journey, but in the tenth and eleventh months he went for four or five days. After that he felt he would soon be ready to receive the Princesses in the capital.

After her delivery, the Imperial Princess had hovered close to death, and it seemed she would not live long. At rare intervals she would say helplessly: "If only I might see Father one last time. I could then become a nun." There was no need for secrecy now, and her attendants had no qualms about telling the Cloistered Emperor. "Though she has been severely ill, I have not looked after her. I will move her to a cheerful place and see that she's cared for and have prayers said for her," thought the Cloistered Emperor. He informed them he would have the Princess moved to his own palace within the year.

The Emperor heard about this intended move, and he found that at the thought that the Princess might take Naishi no Kami away with her, he became strangely sad and upset. Thus when Sadaijin came in, he said to him: "The Princess is still not well, and so she is leaving for her father's home. Will Naishi no Kami be going along?"

"Yes, that is no doubt what she will do," Sadaijin replied. "I know that ever since Naishi no Kami went to her, the Princess has found it hard for them to be separated for even a moment."

"That is reasonable," said the Emperor, "but won't it be uncomfortable for her when the Cloistered Emperor will constantly be with his daughter? The Cloistered Emperor is past his prime in years, but he is very up-to-date and young at heart. Indeed you might not think it bad that he see Naishi no Kami, but I find it unreasonable that you would forsake my cause, and I resent it. Naishi no Kami is not an ordinary Imperial concubine or an attendant in the Emperor's or a Prince's bedchamber, but is in the usual court service; so it would be best if she remained at the palace as she is, even though the Princess leaves. If the Princess takes her away it will be terribly lonely about the court. Young courtiers gather at court because they find ladies like Naishi no Kami attractive and want to frequent them."

"Indeed Naishi no Kami does not necessarily have to go and stay with the Princess," replied Sadaijin. "Because the Cloistered Emperor was not with her, he was worried and told me to have Naishi no Kami be her guardian in his stead. As long as the Princess is in the Cloistered Emperor's home there is no reason why Naishi no Kami should have to be in attendance on her. She ought to return home. However, since she really must fulfill her service obligations at court, she will leave around the beginning of the new year."

"That is splendid," said the Emperor, overjoyed. "Now I will not worry that you have refused so long to have your daughter presented at court. I'm sorry that I have not yet had a daughter, but I shall love Naishi no Kami in place of a daughter. There is no point in your doubting whether I still feel the same way I did before about loving her." Tears flooded the Emperor's eyes.

Now that Sadaijin saw that the Emperor's feelings for Naishi no Kami were sincere, he was very happy. "Time and again this was what you had desired and it makes me tremendously happy to feel that what you have wished for all these years is finally to be fulfilled. I had resigned myself to the fact that Naishi no Kami was a lowly and useless person, and so did not follow your wishes. I am grateful and happy that even now your feelings for her have not changed." Sadaijin wept tears of joy.

"It's odd that her father still does not think of having her presented to me publicly as a bride," thought the Emperor. "And when I caught a glimpse of her the other day, she was hardly the reserved person he described. It would be regrettable for a daughter who has been well brought up to have an excess of feeling and to make a spectacle of herself in public." The Emperor still found the situation strange.

When the Imperial Princess left the palace, the Cloistered Emperor stayed constantly at her side. Because of her shyness at this, Naishi no Kami did not remain with her. Chūnagon was dejected, since it would be difficult for him to see the Princess; but by now Senji and Chūnagon no Kimi had grown to know him well, and he secretly sent letters to her through them.

The Cloistered Emperor was constantly with the Princess—not only because it was novel for him, but also because he had been uneasy in the past months. Nevertheless, when the Princess gradually began to feel better, she was dead set against remaining in the position of Crown Princess. She wanted to become a nun and devote herself to her future life. She had explained this to the Cloistered Emperor many times, but quite naturally he thought it sad and regrettable, and since there was no Crown Prince, he would not permit her to do so.

Oh, yes, I remember now. Saishō attached himself to Chūnagon like a shadow. "If only there was some opportunity, I would speak to him." He thought of nothing else and walked about, concentrating on finding his chance. People thought that, though their relationship had been good in the past, it seemed somewhat cooler now due to the affair over Yon no Kimi. Chūnagon felt that if he approached Saishō and treated him with familiarity, he would be unable to answer should Saishō reproach him, and so he behaved coldly. Saishō found this most irritating and dissatisfying, and was saddened. Even toward Yon no Kimi he no longer felt the resentment he had in the past.

This led Saemon to think: "Chūnagon doesn't visit Yon no Kimi openly, but he does come every night as he used to, and so it is natural that Saishō would be rather irked."

For Yon no Kimi, too, even in the early days that she had spent merely conversing with Chūnagon, it had been unpleasant being scorned by him because of the regrettable affair with Saishō. And now she felt it would be more embarrassing if he became aware that she was keeping even inconsequential secrets from him. She thought it would be cruel of her to do so. She thus did not consider writing even a single line in answer to Saishō's letters; yet he did not seem to resent it very much. "How strangely proper Saishō has become," she thought.

Chūnagon was planning to receive the Yoshino Princess in the capital as soon as the old year gave way to the new, and so he had an impressive mansion of three or four wings built on three sections of land in the second ward near the Horikawa River.[3] It was magnificent. Yon no Kimi, as his wife, would naturally move in, but Chūnagon still felt displeased about the matter with Saishō, and he wondered how it would appear if he received her publicly. But she was so superb that he felt he could never neglect or abandon her in the future. The Yoshino Princess he found exquisite, and she was of thoroughly good lineage, refined and sensible, elegant, supple, noble. In these respects no one could compare with her. But for a pleasantly melancholy, youthful, and charming appearance, Chūnagon thought there were probably few to compare with Yon no Kimi. Chūnagon could not decide who was the more beautiful, the Yoshino Princess or Yon no Kimi. But then somehow Yon no Kimi's regrettable affair with Saishō would come to mind, and he would feel a sort of sadness welling up within him. The Imperial Princess was merely noble; when Chūna-

---

[3] I use "section" here for a *chō* of land (3.5 acres). This parcel was thus about 10.5 acres. The second ward extended between First and Second avenues, which ran east-west across the northern portion of the capital; and the Horikawa River flowed north-south through the eastern portion.

gon conversed with her she did not appear elegant or tasteful. Chūnagon was embarrassed to think this way of all three ladies.

The new year came, and all was fashionably lively at the court as usual. Those serving there gathered together and enjoyed themselves as if they were without worries. Untouched by the bustle of the season's banquets, the Emperor for days and months felt that the visage of the Naishi no Kami he had glimpsed was still with him, and his heart was heavy. When things quieted down after the first days of the year and their accompanying bustle had passed, he secretly lingered about the Sen'yōden. He heard the faint sound of a thirteen-stringed koto. As he stood there contentedly for a while, someone played "The Song of the Nightingale" twice and then stopped. That the instrument had been strummed exactly as Chūnagon had played it led the Emperor to think how marvelous the bond between this brother and sister was.

The hanging shutters had been pulled closed over the lat-ticework, but a wooden door at a corner of the building had not yet been fastened, and the wind blew it open. The delighted Emperor entered quietly, and no one knew he had come in. He hid in a dark spot and watched two ladies apparently playing *go*. Naishi no Kami was reclining within her curtains with the koto as her pillow. She was strumming the instrument in a desultory manner and gazing intently at the lamp. Incomparably beautiful, she seemed absorbed in the poignant sadness of things. The Emperor realized how extraordinary it was that, though they had been living in the same palace, he had gone on thinking of her as someone far away with whom he had no relation.

"Even if people suspect something, I feel I can't let this night pass without going to her," he thought. "I am so impatient. If only the ladies near her would go to sleep."

Naishi no Kami continued to think longingly of the past. "Oh how I felt when I left my son, thinking it would be the

last time I would see him. He was innocent and smiling as we
looked at each other." So intense was her yearning and sorrow
at recalling these things that she composed a poem:

> Always brooding,
> Uncommonly engrossed am I
> In my sad thoughts.
> Yet what pains me most of all:
> My fate in this world!

The tears pouring down her cheeks embarrassed her, and
she lay there, her robes pulled over her head. The ladies playing
go stopped and seemed to go off to sleep.

"Bring the bedding," said one, taking the lamp away and
placing it at a distance. "The wooden door there is not fastened," she added, and then someone came toward the spot
where the Emperor was standing. He was afraid she might
discover him, but he remained quietly hidden in the dark.

"Odd. It seems like someone is about. I have a funny feeling," said the lady, quickly going to her sleeping quarters after
having fastened the door.

Everyone was asleep, and when the Emperor looked there
was no one near Naishi no Kami's curtains. Without hesitation
he approached her quietly. He pushed aside the robes with
which she had covered herself and lay down beside her.

Since Naishi no Kami was not yet fully asleep, this startled
her. She thought Saishō had come to see her, having found his
opportunity. It did not occur to her that it might be someone
else. It was vexing, but she did not move to pull her clothes
over her. While he eagerly moved her clothes aside, the Emperor, weeping bitterly, proceeded to tell her about his chagrin
at her father's deliberate refusal of his request and about how
he had first faintly seen her when he called to inquire about
the ailing Imperial Princess. This astonished Naishi no Kami.
"This is someone other than Saishō," she thought. "I was
thoroughly unhappy and annoyed when I thought it was he,

but this is the Emperor, and if he were to learn of my lamented change of sex he would wonder what it was all about. And if he discovers that I have been so foolish and am no longer pure, he will find me despicable and forsake me in the future. I am upset and ashamed. Naturally it pains me that Chūnagon wanted me to be the Princess's guardian for him when he was concerned about her situation. I wanted very much to find some way not to stay in the world and to go into seclusion. It is regrettable that I appeared so much in service at the court.

"Why, when the Princess left, did I not go along? Around the beginning of the year Father wanted me to continue serving in the palace, and the ladies also felt it would be lonesome if I left. But why was it necessary? I shall remain here as I am until the Rinji Festival in the third month,[4] but when that is over I'll return home." She was wretched as she thought in this vein, and she wept profusely.

"Do not feel this way, my dear. It is fate. If only you were to feel as I do no harm would ever come to you." The Emperor's appearance as he spoke and wept defies description.

Even when Naishi no Kami was like a man, gallant and strong, she had been unable to escape when Saishō took her. So she was all the more vulnerable now that she was an ordinary woman. She did not want to appear inconsiderate; but the Emperor would not yield even to coldness, and she was as unable as ever to extricate herself. There was nothing she could do about this act of violation. It was embarrassing and painful. She wanted to raise her voice and call for help, but the Emperor would not feel obliged to restrain himself just because others saw him. And even if someone did hear her and, suspecting something, came in, nothing could be done,

---

[4] As the name suggests, the *rinji no matsuri*, or Special Occasions Festivals, were not regular annual festivals but were scheduled at some special or extraordinary time. The festival involved here was held at the Iwashimizu Shrine in the third lunar month (Suzuki 1973: 207).

the Emperor being who he was. And since he appeared un-
alarmed, it was hopeless.

The Emperor found Naishi no Kami to be much more
exquisite, much more lovely at close range, than when he had
seen her from a distance. He felt it would be depressing to be
away from her during the daytime and did not want to leave
her for a moment.

"Oh, god! What is this?," he cried, realizing that Naishi no
Kami was apparently not a virgin, and a sense of disappointment mingled with his other feelings. "This is why her father
kept me away from her and why he covered up by placing her
in an unusual position. Because the problem was serious, he
would not have been able to speak up with the truth. It was
unseemly and embarrassing, and so he refused me by making
excuses," the Emperor realized. "Even so I wonder what the
circumstances were. What kind of person was it who pledged
his troth to her? No one, after catching a glimpse of her, would
end his relationship with her. Therefore her father, knowing
that such an affair was going on, must have forbidden it. And
in that case perhaps he was a thoroughly frivolous young
man," thought the Emperor, regretfully.

Even a fundamental flaw, however, would not have seemed
worthy of notice to the Emperor now. Naishi no Kami's
appearance was exquisite. The Emperor felt that any trans-
gression she might have committed had been expunged. Weeping, he pledged that they would never part even in lives to
come. The Emperor's face did not betray the fact that he might
suspect something about her, but it was quite clear to Naishi
no Kami that he did. Unable to do anything, she felt her tears
mingle with drops of perspiration. Because the Emperor was
indeed worried that the ladies in attendance might become
suspicious, he decided to leave. But even then so earnestly did
he pledge his love that none could imitate him:

> Whether we shall meet
> At Mitsuse River crossing,

That I do not know.
Yet would I have my pledges to you
Last unto our future lives.[5]

"I feel a vow for this life alone to be a shallow thing. Yet it saddens me to wonder what will happen in lives to come," said the Emperor, the tears streaming down his face. Naishi no Kami was all the more at a loss for something to say, and she felt very humble.

"I shall not be able to leave without having heard a single word from you yet," said the Emperor, hesitating to leave. Having no alternative, Naishi no Kami said:

I too know naught of them,
These meetings in lives to come;
For mine are the vows
Of one unsure, in this life,
Whether to go on living.

Worried lest the Emperor suspect that this was the voice of Chūnagon that he had been accustomed to hearing, Naishi no Kami spoke unevenly and quietly. It was charming, and the Emperor wanted to go on listening to her. He felt he could not part from her for even an instant. However, with a sense of leaving some of himself with her, and repeating his pledges over and over, the Emperor left through the side door he had used the night before. Only one lady named Chūjō no Naishi had attended him. She had waited for him anxiously, and when it had grown light, her weary head had drooped and she had lain down. The Emperor now roused her and returned to the Seiryōden. Even after he quietly entered his bedchamber, the extraordinary feel and appearance of Naishi no Kami remained with him. He wanted to see her now too,[6] and the

---

[5] On the Mitsuse River, see note 71, p. 45, above. Ōse, "meetings," is an *engo* with *kawa*, "river," since the second character of ōse read separately means "rapids" or "current."

[6] The phrase used here appears in a poem in the *Kokin wakashū*, XIV, Love IV, no. 695, Anonymous (*NKBT*, 8: 239): "The one I loved so, / How I want to see her

tears streamed down his face. Since there was no one to deliver this morning-after letter, the Emperor gave instructions that Chūnagon come immediately. He waited for him impatiently.

Naishi no Kami's appearance was such that even the lustful Saishō forgot everything when he was with her, both his love fulfilled with Yon no Kimi and the grief of his unrequited love with the former Naishi no Kami.[7] The Emperor had never seen anyone quite like her, and so it was quite natural that he should find the situation unbearable.

Hearing that Chūnagon had arrived, the Emperor summoned him. When Chūnagon stood before him looking incredibly splendid, the Emperor was ashamed to speak about Naishi no Kami. From his robe he withdrew a letter folded so that it looked large, and acting as though it was of no special significance, he said: "Some time has passed since I had your father consent to my sending a letter to Naishi no Kami. Today, however, is auspicious, and I am sending this message. Do show me an answer to it soon. I am asking this of you in particular, for if I send it with the usual court servant and your father is not there, Naishi no Kami will be distrustful, and a response from her, otherwise a simple matter, would be difficult." Taking the letter, Chūnagon departed. Because the Emperor's manner had seemed strange, it occurred to Chūnagon that perhaps he had seen Naishi no Kami.

"Naishi no Kami said that she has been ill since last night," a lady called Dainagon no Kimi told Chūnagon when he arrived at the Sen'yōden. "She is still resting."

"You have not told me why she is ill," said the surprised Chūnagon. "What kind of ailment is it? Has she caught cold?"

This exchange made Naishi no Kami uneasy, and so she got up. "I am confined because I have pains in my chest," she said.

---

now, / To see her flowers; / On the mountainside they bloom, / The pinks in her rustic hedge."

[7] The author here reverts to the phraseology of Saishō's poem on p. 83.

Her face was red, and she looked as if she had been crying.

"Perhaps the Emperor has indeed been with her," thought Chūnagon, wanting very much to know what the letter was about. He approached Naishi no Kami and gave her the missive. "I was summoned by the Emperor this morning, and when I presented myself he told me to give this to you myself and not send it through anyone else. He said you should look at it now because he wants an answer from you at once."

With all her heart Naishi no Kami had wanted to handle things in such a way that what had happened with the Emperor the night before would remain unknown. But when Chūnagon spoke to her, she assumed he must realize what had occurred, and she was embarrassed. She felt she could not show her face; but to be immature and bashful would not be in keeping with her situation, and so, blushing, she accepted the letter. She did not, however, unfold it, though Chūnagon urged her to write a reply.

"The Emperor told me there should definitely be an answer. If I return without one and he has waited in vain, as his special messenger, I certainly will not be able to face him."

"My, but you speak like someone other than yourself," said Naishi no Kami, smiling. "Still, it is natural that I should hesitate to compose an answer when I know that his Imperial Majesty will find it strange to see familiar handwriting. And if I acted the clever one and wrote a letter without Father's knowledge, he would be disappointed in me, even though the Emperor said he wanted a reply without fail. Therefore tell the Emperor only that I have indeed received his letter."

"I realize there are difficulties in answering at once," said Chūnagon. "But what about looking at the Emperor's letter?" He appeared nonchalant, but Chūnagon seemed to want to see the Emperor's message. Understandably, the blushing Naishi no Kami, thinking it risky to open it, hid it from him. And so Chūnagon left.

The Emperor had been waiting for the expected answer to

his letter, and he was disappointed to have waited in vain. His distress at being away from Naishi no Kami was unbearable, but he forced himself to behave nonchalantly. "She should not behave so coquettishly, as though this was some ordinary affair," he said. Overcome with gloom and dejection he sent another letter to Naishi no Kami, though he did not tell Chūnagon about what had happened the night before.

"I saw a silhouette dimly lit by lamplight and wondered if it was hers. It was an extraordinary figure such as I have never seen. It never leaves me, and I am distressed in my yearning for her. I have considered carefully what to do. Her father distinctly forbade me to go to her, and I felt it imprudent to pretend that I didn't know he had and become intimate with her. It is because of this that I hold back. Despite myself, however, I have never felt like this; my inexplicable feelings are doubtlessly fated to be. At least in you beats a heart sympathetic to mine; you shall be my guide and lead me tonight to the one I merely glimpsed last night," said the Emperor, weeping.

"It is just as I imagined," thought Chūnagon. "I can't believe he only caught a glimpse of her from a distance. She too seemed strange. There must be some reason for that."

In any case, Chūnagon was happy to see that the Emperor was overcome with love for Naishi no Kami. He did, however, think it regrettable that she had been unexpectedly seen and had had no time to make preparations. Certainly she lacked nothing to enable her to enter the court in the usual way and attain the position of Empress.

"I will first deliver this letter then," said Chūnagon, withdrawing.

Since the Imperial visit to Naishi no Kami was not something one could conceal, Chūnagon told Sadaijin about the Emperor's strange state and about what he had said. Though Sadaijin was displeased to think that the Emperor had had relations with Naishi no Kami, he was nevertheless happy. He had long been dissatisfied with Naishi no Kami's circumstances, and so this development with the Emperor was cause for considerable joy. Pretending to know nothing of what had happened, he presented her with a court lady's robes and ornaments of more than usual beauty. He even arranged for lovely household items of daily use. For years Sadaijin had expended much effort on her behalf, but he had regretted her court service where no one saw and praised her. He was overjoyed that the Emperor was visiting her now.

The Emperor's undying love for Naishi no Kami grew. She was unflawed and would be perfect as Empress. However, he was dissatisfied about one thing that weighed on his mind: he was concerned how it would be to have as Empress someone who had already had a relationship with another man. Still, he told himself that the affair had not been widely bruited about. "Surely only two or three people who knew the circumstances well remember that it took place, but they have not come to court as concubines or attendants in my bedchamber. I think I will see her secretly first in her capacity as a court attendant, but after that I'll trust to my feelings. There's really nothing to stop her from being Empress."

The Emperor felt no constraint, and so after he had pledged his troth to Naishi no Kami, he went to her even during the day. Before long, Naishi no Kami went to visit him at night as well. The Emperor loved only her and ignored all others. This overjoyed her parents and brother.

The splendid mansion Chūnagon was building in the second ward was finished. The Yoshino Princess was to move in around the middle of the third month, and so, about the tenth day, Chūnagon went to see the Yoshino Prince. Chūnagon was sorry that the holy man would find his surroundings even lonelier after the Princess had left, and he tried to console him. He presented the Prince with the produce of an estate he owned in the area and made arrangements so that he would live well and not feel neglected.

"This goes very much against my original plans, and I find it most regrettable," said the Prince. "Because of my concern for these daughters whom I could not leave, I have gone on until now living in a dwelling near the world, seemingly unaware of its sadness and transience. Since I want so much to seclude myself in calm and unconcern on a mountain devoid of even the song of birds, it is contrary to my desires to receive these favors from you."

The Prince returned everything and hastened to prepare himself mentally for retiring far into the mountains. The Princess was sorry. Though she was going to the capital, she was inexperienced, and it would be annoying to be laughed at. If that happened, she thought, she would return here, to the mountain path from which the misery of the world could not be seen,[8] and make this house her final dwelling. She would be happy, indeed, if the place were to remain unchanged over the years and not be permitted to fall into disrepair. She continued to be depressed by the thought that their home might fall into ruin, but it was not like her to play the part of the wise one and speak of this to the Prince, and she said nothing.

On the appointed day, splendid moving ceremonies were performed. Since they could not leave the younger sister behind at Yoshino, they took her along when they left. The Princess was still reluctant about the move, wondering what was going to happen now. But her father had decided what she must do.

"Why should you try to return to this cottage again?," said the Prince, weeping. "This meeting will be our last, for I shall not be going to the capital. Out of concern for you who were obstacles to my path but dear ones I could not leave, I have naturally long neglected my works toward my future life. From now on I shall devote myself in contentment to these efforts:

---

[8] The expression used here is from the poem cited in note 73, p. 47, above.

At this departure,
So far apart will they be,
Our destinations.
Alas, I know not when
We shall meet face to face again.

"Today we should abstain from anything inauspicious,"
said the Prince, wiping away his tears.

Not knowing when
We shall be meeting again,
This parting of our ways.
Hard is it for me to go,
As weeping, weeping, I depart.[9]

Holding her sleeve over her face, the elder Princess could not
bring herself to make her departure. The younger Princess said:

Father or sister,
Which one I accompany
Matters not at all.
For whether I stay or whether I go,
A painful parting awaits me.[10]

The younger Princess had no need to leave, but it was only
natural that the elder should feel lonely with no one to rely
on during even a short separation. Consequently, the Prince
thought he would let her accompany Chūnagon at once and
abandon himself to his devotions, putting them out of mind.
He did not even permit the old ladies who lived in the house
with him to stay and wait on him, but had them go with the
Princesses.

Chūnagon went in the same carriage as the Princess. Ten
ox-carts, displaying the sleeves and skirts of the ladies within,
and then children and lower servants followed in procession.
Their appearance as they came from the thatched hut deep in

---

[9] *Naku*, with its meaning "to weep" and "to lack," is a *kakekotoba* here.
[10] This poem appears in the *Fūyō wakashū*, Parting Poems (*ZGR*, 14: 39).

the mountains where they had led such a solitary life was majestic and impressive. Many suitable courtiers of as high as the fifth and sixth ranks attended them. In addition, the lady attendants had found a number of agreeable persons among their relatives to serve the Princess. The younger Princess's carriage followed somewhat behind the others, and she had only three ox-carts from which the sleeves and skirts of the ladies hung out. Here too there were many appropriate persons, forerunners and the like, and the elderly ladies had come in secret as part of the younger sister's retinue. The Prince had happily seen them off, thinking the sight rewarding. It was as though no trace of them had been left behind, and his heart had become clear. He felt forlorn but happy, for now he could devote himself completely to his religious devotions. The desire he had cherished for years had been realized.

Chūnagon and the Princesses stopped along the way to spend the night at Nara, arriving at the mansion in the second ward the next day. The splendid residence was built on three square sections of land and had been divided into three wings by inner walls. The one in the center was to be the principal residence. On the side facing Tōin Avenue, Chūnagon planned to receive Yon no Kimi secretly. The other side, facing Horikawa Avenue, was for the use of Naishi no Kami were she to leave the court, and the Imperial Princess would live there too. Because the Yoshino Princesses had arrived in such an impressive and splendid manner, everyone at Udaijin's home was very sad. It was surprising and painful for them, but they did not reproach Chūnagon, for he seemed quite blameless.

Yon no Kimi had become pregnant around the tenth month. This time there was no doubt whose child it was, but even so she felt timid and deliberately hid her condition. When the truth was discovered, everyone was surprised, and her people began having prayers said for her. They informed Sadaijin about it, and since this time Chūnagon was definitely the father, Sadaijin was overjoyed and had prayers said. Udaijin was in raptures when he heard about it.

Chūnagon, too, though he deplored Yon no Kimi's pledges of love to Saishō, felt his compassion and pain for her grow. But he regretted that it would have to be Yon no Kimi, with her complicated feelings, who became pregnant. The young boy growing up at Sadaijin's home was the true aristocrat.[11] "Since we have not disclosed the identity of the child's mother, it is natural that everyone should assume he is not a very important person. And why doesn't the Yoshino Princess, with whom there would be no problems, become pregnant?," thought Chūnagon, regretting that there were no signs that she was. He planned to bring his son to his mansion and place him in her care, but his parents would not let the child leave them for an instant and were even reluctant to let Chūnagon see him.

Naishi no Kami had been pregnant since spring. Her condition increased the Emperor's boundless love. Since none of his many consorts had yet given him a child and there was no Imperial Prince, prayers had been said on mountains and in temples. When Naishi no Kami conceived, the Emperor's joy knew no bounds. If the child was a boy it would be an honor for Sadaijin, and for Chūnagon too.

Now Saishō would not have gone on grieving and yearning as the days and months went by if he had simply felt he did not know where Chūnagon was.[12] But why would she change herself when she had fully become a woman? Why, though she might regret becoming a woman and find it hard to discard her male guise, would she go back to being a man again? She might have thought him hateful, unfeeling, and not worth looking at, and so have forsaken him, but Saishō wanted to let her know that he blamed her for the waywardness she

[11] The boy referred to is the son of Chūnagon and the Imperial Princess.
[12] This would be the former Chūnagon, that is, the female Chūnagon of Saishō's recollections, since Saishō is unaware that the brother and sister have exchanged roles.

displayed in leaving their child, knowing that she would not see him again. However, since people now wondered why there was such tension between Chūnagon and himself, he could not approach Chūnagon unless he had something special to say.

When they went to court, Chūnagon still treated Saishō with particular coolness, firmly keeping his distance. There was no way Saishō might approach him and speak when Chūnagon looked as though he did not think they had ever even exchanged vows. Saishō dispatched letters, but though Chūnagon sent replies that evinced no hesitation, he would not reconsider their former relationship. The stunned Saishō was sorely grieved. He was overcome with sadness even in society, and he completely lost his fickle passions. He had become serious. Were Yon no Kimi to vanish he would not fret unduly and grieve as he always had before.

Saishō was amazed when he heard of Naishi no Kami's fate and her present splendor. Though she had coldly sent him away and deceived him once, she resembled Chūnagon so much that it was hard to tell them apart. As a result he was not pained, for he was consoled by being able to see Chūnagon in her place. Naishi no Kami, however, regretted that she had risen to such an unparalleled position when she thought what a silly fool Saishō would remember her as being.

As the days and months passed, Saishō watched his son grow ever more beautiful. "How could I console myself if I did not have such a son as this?," he thought. "How wonderful it would have been if Chūnagon and I had brought up the child together, consulting each other and sharing the same feelings."

Dissatisfied, sad, overcome with grief, he did not go out. Day and night he would not let the child leave his side and spent the days playing with him. When he thought about this, it struck him as so foolish. "Even though I feel shattered because Chūnagon left me, nothing will come of it. While shying away from society, for months now I have been behaving as though she were a stranger and abandoned Yon no Kimi, who was so full of feeling, who appreciated and shared deeply touching moods with me, and returned my love," Saishō could not help recollecting. Bored, lonely, and with nothing to console him, he wrote a detailed letter to Saemon. "I have been worried for months and would like to find out for myself how she is. I will therefore come secretly in a woman's cart. If this is inconvenient, come here. There are no ladies about and you need not feel any reticence."

Saishō had not contacted her in a long time, and Saemon, thinking that he had given up Yon no Kimi because of her own heartlessness, had felt bad. Thus, when she read this extraordinary letter, she was moved by his account of what was obviously painful to him, and she found it hard to bear. She informed him that she had been disturbed these past months too and had wanted very much to speak with him, and that though she feared gossip, she would come in secret. Saishō was overjoyed. He sent an inconspicuous cart to fetch her and waited for her to arrive. Saemon told only Yon no Kimi about her projected visit, and then, pretending to go to her own home, she left.

Saishō felt extraordinary. "I was unwell for months and my suffering unendurable," he had thought constantly, "and so I did not go out and lived in seclusion, lost in my own thoughts. Yon no Kimi had gradually grown intimate with me, but she gave me up because of my heartlessness and inconstancy. As a result I am quite aware of how very wretched my life is. I have not a thing to reproach her for, and I am sad. Yet must it end without one more meeting, just once?"

He had felt thoroughly resigned then, but when he received Saemon he recalled the past, weeping bitterly, and looked serious. "I hear that these days there may be occasions when I can visit. Do arrange something when it's possible," he told Saemon.

She felt truly sorry for him and said, weeping: "For all those years Chūnagon's love for Yon no Kimi did not seem shallow. On the whole he spoke of her as an extraordinary and very special person, and he spoke with her tenderly. But he seemed surprisingly ill at ease when it came to the kind of intimate, complete love consummated by other fashionable young men. Theirs was like the relationship of two ladies who only talked instead of making love. I felt ashamed but it pained me to see you so intense and impatient, and being softhearted, I took you to her.

"However, Chūnagon's behavior since he has come back from Yoshino this time has amazed me. He hides pointlessly, as though he were afraid, and seldom stays during the day. But his love for Yon no Kimi in private is much more intimate than it was, and on top of everything else, she became pregnant last winter. His love for her has apparently grown all the greater. When Yon no Kimi's two daughters were born, Sadaijin did not appear to be happy, and when Chūnagon saw them, he left for distant Yoshino. But this time, perhaps because he cannot possibly be mistaken about whose child it is, he seems worried and tends to remain near Yon no Kimi. Udaijin is overjoyed too. Yon no Kimi has decided that it would be totally heartless if he or Chūnagon were to learn of the slightest impropriety, and so she said that though she might see your letters, she would never consider sending you an answer. Since she won't contemplate even this, there's all the more reason why my taking you to her is unthinkable.

"Though Chūnagon's love for Yon no Kimi is deep—he still thinks of your affair with her as cruel to him—he has chosen the Yoshino Princess to be his first wife. He considers Yon no Kimi in second place, as one whom he has grown to know over the years and whom he finds it difficult to stop loving. When I see this state of affairs, I feel that if she had remained as Chūnagon had wanted her to be and had never erred, he would have loved her deeply, and in terms of general reputa-

tion no one could have competed with her. When I think of
the worries that dog her because of you, I regret the past and
its unfortunate vows. I am thus unable to take you to her."
To Saemon's young mind, it was saddening to see Yon no
Kimi fated to be surpassed by the Yoshino Princess, and so it
was natural for her to speak in this way.

To this Saishō simply replied: "It is quite normal that Yon
no Kimi herself should not wish to see me, but why do you
too feel so strongly? I never thought you would." As he listened to what Saemon went on to say, beginning with Yon no
Kimi's pregnancy, he found much of it hard to understand and
was quite bewildered. Once more he thought about the one
whom he had just recently started to forget a little, until he
grew depressed again. He said little and seemed very troubled.
"It has grown late. Others will think it strange," he said. Then
he added, as he sent her back: "Return to her." Saemon, of
course, felt bad, wondering whether Saishō was pained by her
coolness, and again and again she looked back over her shoulder as she left.

Chūnagon was at the mansion in the second ward, and so
Saemon told Yon no Kimi in secret about what had transpired. Though she wept, Yon no Kimi had quite abandoned
all hope of seeing Saishō. Chūnagon was in every respect
beyond compare, and his love for her had increased. Since she
had become pregnant, he seemed to love her even more. His
affection appeared no less than Saishō's. Though embarrassed
and frightened, Yon no Kimi had been attracted to Saishō,
who had seemed so earnestly in love with her in the beginning.
But now she wondered what others might say or think, and
what her father might feel in his innermost heart. She did not
consider that Chūnagon and Saishō might be comparable.

Saishō pondered all that was not only unusual but increasingly incomprehensible to him in many ways. All through the
night he tossed about and drowned in a river of tears, meditat-
ing until it grew light. "If only somehow I could approach

Chūnagon, speak to her once, and look at her," he thought, wanting to go out.

One day, when it seemed that Chūnagon would be at court, Saishō went there. Acting nonchalantly, he fixed his eyes on Chūnagon, and Chūnagon, of course, returned his glance. Chūnagon acted so serious and severe that Saishō was unable to approach him naturally and was most disappointed. Since Naishi no Kami's pregnancy, Chūnagon had been constantly at the court, and Saishō followed him about like a shadow, watching for a chance to draw near.

Chūnagon thought all this quite comical, but he was preoccupied now with the younger Yoshino Princess's future and wondered how to deal with the problem. Perhaps it was because Saishō, having forgotten both his love fulfilled and his unrequited love,[13] now seemed to have lost practically all his fickle passions and to have become serious, that Chūnagon at times thought: "Shall I let her become his wife? When he sees her, even if he has an inconstant heart drawn to everyone he meets, he will be unable to neglect her." But then, when he recalled what had happened between Saishō and Yon no Kimi, he thought: "It would be absurd for the Princess to be unreserved and familiar with him." And he did not speak his mind.

It was after the twentieth day of the fourth month, and the Kamo Festival was over, a period of idleness at the court.[14] Chūnagon, recalling what Naishi no Kami had told him in the course of a conversation about the narrow corridor of the Reikeiden, went to linger there awhile. The lady there had never forgotten the nights when Chūnagon had spoken endearingly to her.[15] Even when he had quite disappeared

---

[13] Yon no Kimi and Naishi no Kami.

[14] The *Kamo matsuri* was a major event in the lives of the aristocracy. The festivities took place at the Kamo temple on the day of the bird in the fourth lunar month. For a detailed description of the festival, see Ikeda 1967: 556–60.

[15] Chūnagon as recalled here was then the female Chūnagon. "The lady" is the younger sister of the Emperor's concubine.

from the world, she had secretly remembered him with longing and sadness. This evening as she sat intently gazing out,
lost in thought, she was surprised to realize that the figure
clearly visible in the dark was Chūnagon. She resented the
months that had passed without any word, and though with
throbbing heart she wished to speak, she felt she could not.
Yet wanting him to know that she had seen him, she sighed
and murmured:

> Unlikely is it
> That anyone is there
> Who will remember me.
> Yet, oh, I cannot forget
> The moon I glimpsed that night.

Chūnagon realized that the lady who had said this must be
the one of whom Naishi no Kami had spoken. It was charming
that her mood was so in tune with Chūnagon's, and he drew
nearer.

> With these words indeed,
> No one do you surprise.
> Would I forget it,
> The moon that together
> We gazed upon that night?

Even someone used to hearing him constantly would never
have been able to distinguish his voice from the former Chūnagon's; and, of course, it did not occur to the lady that this was
someone different. Charming as always, Chūnagon stood
speaking of one thing and another. The lady had grown used
to seeing him on evenings like this in the past, and since she
assumed that this time he would likewise not behave in the
licentious manner usual to the world, she had taken no pre-
cautions. However, since her appearance was unexpectedly
agreeable and she looked very lovely, giving the impression of
high birth, Chūnagon found it impossible to leave. Quietly,

therefore, he entered her room and pushed the door closed. The lady was startled and at a loss what to do.

"How impertinent of you!," she said scornfully. But Chūnagon was quiet and apparently composed. He calmed her, and gradually her reserve melted away. There was nothing she could do about the situation. Overwhelmed by the uneasiness she had felt these past months, she had attracted his attention by reciting the poem, and she wept, chagrined now that she had done so.

Chūnagon compared her to the ladies he knew, Yon no Kimi, the Yoshino and Imperial Princesses. Though she was not in their class, she was not disagreeable on the whole, and she did not seem to belong to the ranks of the experienced female court attendants either. Chūnagon was pained. "I feel sorry for her. How inconsiderately I have acted!," he thought, speaking now to her tenderly and with considerable feeling.

They did not have long to wait before the dawn's light appeared. It was natural that the lady then seemed ashamed. Chūnagon had become restless, and quietly he pushed open the door. The light of the moon, still in the dawn sky, filled every corner of the room. Chūnagon of course was splendid, and the lady was lovely. She had positioned herself with the sliding door behind her and sat leaning against it. It was hard to leave her, and for some time Chūnagon delayed.

At that moment Saishō was as usual shadowing Chūnagon and spying on him. Chūnagon appeared to be saying something, and so stealthily Saishō hid in a corner and listened, conscious of Chūnagon's voice. He felt happy, and strained his ears to listen. Chūnagon was saying tenderly that because theirs was a long-standing relationship, they had exchanged vows, but that from now on, fearing that people might see them, he would be unable to follow the dictates of his own heart and meet with her freely.

The lady wept bitterly. How lamentable that their relationship should come to an end like this. But even if they gave in to their hearts, opportunities for meeting would be rare. They spoke together with a troubled air, and Chūnagon seemed unable to take his final leave.

"What is going on here!," thought the intently listening Saishō. "These past months he has been talking, however casually, to a number of court ladies. He is not so serious-minded, as he was for years. People have been whispering that some nights, especially when he is on duty, he stays and speaks to ladies like Chūjō no Naishi in the service of the Emperor or Saishō no Kimi who used to serve Naishi no Kami. I assumed that this was impossible, and that it was only supposition. It never occurred to me. I feel as though it is all an amazing dream hearing him speak like this to the lady. Can this be someone else and not Chūnagon?" Wanting to see with his own eyes, Saishō peeped in, keeping out of sight.

> The light of the moon,
> As though harboring my love,
> Lingers into dawn.
> Until we meet again
> See in this a remembrance of me.[16]

This was recited by Chūnagon, and hearing him quietly taking his leave, the lady responded:

> Always so wretched,
> This life I have been leading.
> How can I go on,
> How long remain in this world
> Gazing at the moon of dawn?[17]

She seemed terribly upset. However, since it had gradually grown light, Chūnagon left, apparently not listening to the

---

[16] There is a *kakekotoba* here in *ari*: *kokorozashi ari*, "to have love," and *ariake*, "dawn." This poem appears, in slightly different form, in the *Fūyō wakashū*, Love II (ZGR, 14: 62).

[17] As in the preceding poem, *ari* functions as a *kakekotoba*: *yo ni ari*, "to be in the world," and *ariake*, "dawn."

end. Saishō caught sight of him then, and there could be no mistaking the fact that it was he. The amazed Saishō was unable to think calmly, and he seized Chūnagon's sleeve as he was going out.

"Who is that?," cried Chūnagon, and having no idea who it might be, he looked back and saw that it was Saishō. Chūnagon regretted that it was Saishō rather than someone else who had discovered him in this imprudent situation, but pretending that nothing was out of order, he stood still.

"You do not think of me as someone to whom you once pledged your troth," said Saishō, weeping profusely. "Unexpectedly you acted as if you didn't know me and left me abandoned. I resent this. I did not intend to reproach you like this, but my dissatisfied heart makes me fret despite myself."

"What lady have you just parted from that you seem so unable to control your gloom?," said Chūnagon, smiling. "There is something I would like to speak to you about calmly. But though it was suitable for us to talk together like this when we were young and of low rank, now that both of us have risen to a grade where it is most improper, I cannot. Of course, you naturally think me unfeeling. Since I have been neglectful, I shall make it a point to come to see you."

Though we have said that he was the very image of the former Chūnagon, that was true only when one glimpsed him from a distance. However, when he spoke to Saisho close up like this, he clearly looked like a man. In his amazement, Saishō stood with Chūnagon's sleeve in his grasp. He had not seen Chūnagon this clearly since they had parted at Uji; and since it had finally grown quite light and the sky was clear, Saishō inspected him carefully. On his upper lip were the unexpected signs of a moustache.

"Oh, no! Who is this? And what has happened to the one who was Chūnagon before?," pondered Saishō, baffled. He stood for a while staring at Chūnagon. The latter, aware of what Saishō must be thinking, was amused; but even so he felt uncomfortable. It had grown light, and feeling unfit to be seen, Chūnagon walked away and went to the Sen'yōden, where he woke the ladies and went in to see Naishi no Kami.

Saishō's extraordinary love for Chūnagon had been rekindled, and he felt even more distressed, yearning for her more. "If only I could calmly meet with her again, discuss all that had happened, look at her. Surely this Chūnagon belongs to the same family as the one I knew," he thought, at his wits' end.

At dusk, in the cool evening breeze, he went to Chūnagon's mansion in the second ward. It was at a time when Chūnagon was usually with Yon no Kimi at Udaijin's home. Few people were about, and it was quiet. Saishō was on the verge of returning home, disappointed, when he heard the faint and extraordinarily beautiful notes of a seven-stringed koto carried on the wind. His heart stirred, and he stood for a while, listening. There was also a thirteen-stringed koto accompanied by a lute. Both were equally lovely, but the intermittent notes of the seven-stringed instrument sounded very foreign.

Irresistibly drawn to it, Saishō turned back. Quietly he slipped in among the luxuriant pampas grass beyond the fence to the south of the center gate and looked in. Two lattice dividers between the pillars to the south and east of the main room were raised; apparently the musicians were playing there. It was very lovely, and Saishō wanted to see them.

"If only I could catch a glimpse of whoever is playing," he thought uneasily.

As if having awaited a lull in the early summer rains that had been falling for days, the evening moon shone brightly.

"It's beautiful outside. No one will see us. Let's look out," said a youthful voice. Rolling up the blind, a lady seated herself on the veranda outside the room. Saishō watched her in delight. The lady wore a worn white unlined kimono that tended to split at the seams and a sort of shapeless skirt. She seemed to be an attractive young lady. Only two of the ladies who had been inside came out and sat on the veranda. The one who had been playing the thirteen-stringed koto had been near the raised rattan blind, but now she quietly slipped toward the veranda. She was slender, and by the length of her hair and the shape and appearance of her head, seemed young. Those who had played the seven-stringed koto and the lute seated themselves on the lower level of the house frame.[18] Bathed in the bright moonlight, the ladies sat facing in the direction of Saishō, and he could see them very well.

The lady of the seven-stringed koto was a bit farther inside than the others. Lying stretched out on her side, she pushed away her instrument and lost herself in thought as she gazed intently at the moon. The expression of her eyes, the appearance of her brow and head, the hang of her hair—all was elegance and grace. Such was her refinement and radiant beauty that Saishō felt that in a world where he had seen so many women, he had never, until now, observed one so lovely.

"I wonder if she is the Yoshino Prince's daughter." Even someone of high rank, though reputed to be beautiful, would probably not be very refined after having been brought up far from the world, Saishō had thought disdainfully and had felt no desire to see her. Now he was sorry, as he stared at her intently.

"She resembles Naishi no Kami at the Sen'yōden," he recalled. "Naishi no Kami seemed slightly, though not in an unseemly way, tall and large to the touch. I was not disappointed, but it would have been better if she had not been so tall. But this one is slender and seems almost to have no body at all. She is uncommonly elegant-looking and dainty." Though fickle passions had left Saishō's now-serious heart, they suddenly flared up again, and he wanted to know this woman. The other lady was leaning on her lute as she looked

[18] The koto-player was the elder Yoshino Princess, and the lute-player her sister.

out at the area near the house. Her plumpish, charming, and young appearance was beautiful.

"These ladies are so lovely in so many different ways. Of the many women I have known, I thought Naishi no Kami, Yon no Kimi, and the lady of the Uji Bridge[19] who has disappeared were all three incredibly lovely, each in her own way. However, the lady with the koto, though she may not look so young and charming as Yon no Kimi, seems to excel in delicacy and refinement. And the lady with the lute surpasses everyone when it comes to her charming and youthfully lovely appearance."

Saishō lost all sense of time and forgot his grief over Chūnagon as he stood watching. The moon had risen bright and clear, and the notes of the lute that rang out, clearing the heart of all darkness, did not sound of this world. They were so lovely that even the heavenly maiden who descended to earth in appreciation of another Major Captain's flute would have taken note of them.[20] Then the lady with the seven-stringed koto rose and played softly. Her playing was consummately artful. Not only were the melodies that she played under the clear night moon lovely—plaintive melodies that soothed the heart—but it was unusual that she should have learned the technique, for the art had completely died out in Japan and no one seemed to know it.

Saishō wept. What more could trouble a heart that had gone through so much as his? He was overcome with sadness. He naturally wanted to know how the Yoshino Princesses would look and behave if he drew near. Because he still want-

[19] This refers to the female Chūnagon. Legends about an Uji Bridge lady seem to have predated the *Hashihime monogatari* (Tale of the Lady of the Bridge). There is one recorded legend of a woman who had been relatively unjealous, who had been loved by a man, and who, after her death, became guardian spirit of the bridge (Suzuki 1973: 233). The lady of the Uji Bridge also appears in the poem cited in note 18, p. 142, above. Of course, the most well-known reference to the lady appears in *The Tale of Genji*, which has a chapter by that title.

[20] In *Sagoromo monogatari* a male deity descends to earth in appreciation of Sagoromo's flute music (*NKBT*, 79: 46). The author has perhaps got the sex of the deity confused.

ed to see Chūnagon, he felt that it would not do to overlook these ladies who were connected with him. But it would be unfortunate if people happened to hear that Saishō was a person of fickle passions, and so, on consideration, he decided that it would not do for him to approach them.

"Were it to be the younger sister that I approached and spoke to, I know she would not keep at arm's length or be unaffectionate," he thought in distress, irritated that his desires had been frustrated as usual. "Yet a passionate act like that in Chūnagon's mansion would be bad. What shall I do?"

The moon hid behind a mountain peak, and the lady with the seven-stringed koto went inside. The lady with the lute, still gazing at the area around the house and speaking with the lady of the thirteen-stringed koto, seemed to smile. They were all speaking of the mountain village at Yoshino, of the things that had moved them, of the times when the flowers and the maple leaves were in beautiful color, of the snow—unimportant, trifling matters. Though Saishō might have stayed indefinitely, he realized it would be troublesome if someone noticed him peeping, and so he left quickly. Even then he felt as if his soul (which amazingly he still retained though he thought he had lost it in his love for Chūnagon) had as usual entered a lady's sleeve.[21]

Saishō was dissatisfied and chagrined that he had not let the Yoshino Princesses know that he had seen them. He now seemed grieved, on top of everything else, about the Princesses as well. He had had a number of loves, but the ladies' feelings had been different from his, and they had left him. Thus as the days passed he had slept alone, with only the night as his companion. This might do for a little while, but it was an unsatisfactory situation, and he recalled the lady with the lute in the moonlight. If only he might be close to her and speak with her. She had looked innocent and beautiful. "If only I could somehow approach her and speak to her! I wonder

[21] On this expression, see note 67, p. 42, above.

what Chūnagon has in mind for her." With his love for the younger Yoshino Princess, Saishō occasionally comforted his empty and bewildered heart.

Chūnagon was slowly beginning to change his mind about Saishō and the younger Yoshino Princess. "Shall I marry the younger Princess off to Saishō? Naishi no Kami pretends nothing is amiss, but she is worried about the child she had by Saishō. Without a link of the sort made possible by Saishō's visiting the Princess, how could Naishi no Kami get news of her child?"

One day somewhat past the tenth of the sixth month, when the artificial lake at Naishi no Kami's wing of the mansion in the second ward was enticing, and it seemed cool at the pavilion built overlooking the pond, Chūnagon proceeded there with both Yoshino Princesses. Courtiers and noblemen were whiling away the day there amusing themselves with such pastimes as composing Chinese poems and reciting Japanese ones. When the moon appeared, Chūnagon sent an invitation to Saishō. As messenger, he sent his mother's nephew, a man named Hyōe no Suke, who was a keeper of the Imperial Archives.

> That you come to call
> For the sake of your host,
> I would not expect;
> But will you not come here,
> To visit with the moon?

"Chūnagon told me to serve as your attendant," said Hyōe no Suke when he had given Saishō Chūnagon's poem.

"What is this?," thought Saishō, not knowing what to do, so overcome with excitement was his agitated heart.

> Moving it may be,
> The atmosphere at your home,
> Moon shining clear above.

But it is to see the host
That I would like to come.[22]

"Go first and tell him that I will come shortly," replied Saishō. Then wearing a fragrant perfume and a starched cloak with a special design, he proceeded to Chūnagon's mansion.

The light of the moon flooded every corner of the pavilion over the pond. Wearing a graceful cloak, Chūnagon was softly humming a melody and playing the flute to amuse himself as he waited. He presented his guest with a lute and strongly urged him to play. However, Saishō recalled the lady in the moonlight whose music had been so lovely. "How am I to play so?," he thought, and would not touch the instrument.

"Then am I to be denied what I especially invited you for," said Chūnagon, playing the flute, and so Saishō consented to perform a little. The lovely notes rang out clear and high. The music of Chūnagon's flute was superb, of course. Saemon no Kami played the thirteen-stringed koto, Saishō no Chūjō the flute, Ben no Shojō the pipes and Hyōe no Suke sang "Mushiroda,"[23] keeping time with his fan. His voice was lovely. Though not a lavish musical entertainment, it was elegant and enjoyable. Saishō's heart, however, was filled only with the sounds of the seven-stringed koto he had heard the other night.

"It would certainly be amusing to include the music of the ladies on a night like this," he suggested. Chūnagon thought Saishō would admire the elder Yoshino Princess much more if she played the seven-stringed koto. The wine cups were passed around many times, and everyone grew befuddled with drink. The night was growing late. Saishō had only the one thought in mind and seemed quite unreasonable.

[22] There is a *kakekotoba* here on *sumu*, "to be clear" and "to live." The first sentence may therefore also be read as: "No matter how moving the home in which the moon lives . . ."

[23] From a *saibara* (*NKBT*, 3: 408, no. 47): "The cranes living in the Itsunuki River of Mushiroda, of Mushiroda, / For one thousand years already have they played together, / For one thousand years already have they played together."

"What can I expect? Would perhaps the lady of the Uji Bridge be within this bamboo blind?," he said, wanting very much to know whom the blind concealed. Though the ladies had put up a curtain in addition to the rattan blind and had tried to keep their skirts from rustling as they moved about, Saishō sensed their presence nearby. The ladies he had seen the other night were beautiful, but he was in a strange situation, for they might have noticed him, and he could not speak up. When some people left, Saishō edged up to Chūnagon.

"Why should you have invited me particularly? Might it be that you have some fine gift for me?"

"Why should I let the opportunity pass?," replied Chūnagon, smiling. "If you were to receive some extraordinary gift, the resentment you have felt all these days might be quite dispelled."

> If it be not
> That maiden of Uji Bridge
> I knew long ago,
> Then nothing at all is there
> That can my resentment dispel.

"In whatever life, how could I ever forget her?," said Saishō, wiping away his tears.

> Sleeping alone,
> Her sleeve spread for her pillow,
> She wearied of waiting.
> In her grief, the bridge maiden
> Drowned herself in Uji River.

"There is hardly need for a gift, then; I'll think no more of giving you anything," said Chūnagon, looking strong and resolute. The startled Saishō wanted nonetheless to know clearly what the situation was. It was difficult for him to forgo this evening's gift from his host even if it was not to be the lady of the Uji Bridge, and he acted more intoxicated and grieved.

"I cannot leave at all tonight. I will spend it in front of this bamboo blind. It's useless to complain, isn't it?"

"That would be a most inappropriate place to stay. Come over here," said Chūnagon, leading him within the blind. Then accompanied by his wife, the elder Yoshino Princess, he retired to an inner room.

"Who might this be?," thought the excited Saishō, approaching. "Will it be the lady of the Uji Bridge?" Inside the curtain reclined a lady, looking very timid. He suddenly felt that she was most beautiful. "It appears to be the lady who was playing the lute in the light of the moon the other day," he thought. Though he was not sorry about that, he did tell himself that it was not the one he knew at Uji, which made him feel dissatisfied and sad. Even on seeing the lady within the curtains, he felt like the one who saw the moon over Mount Obasute and was inconsolable.[24] However, the lady was ideal. She was charming, youthful and apparently adorably gentle. Saishō's heart, fickle as the dayflower with its quickly changing colors,[25] did not forget the many loves he had once known. But he felt more than half his grief soothed away as he spoke to the lady at great length, as always, about the love he had felt for her since he had first seen her dimly in the moonlight that night. It had already grown late, and Saishō felt as though what remained of the night had passed in no time. He did not leave the lady.

Chūnagon was surprised to learn about this. He sent water for washing and rice gruel. Lady attendants, after fixing their clothes and appearances, went to attend Saishō. When the sun was high, Saishō wakened from his sleep and looked at the Princess. Not more than twenty years of age, she was young and beautiful. There was not an unsatisfactory aspect about

[24] This refers to a poem that appears in both the *Kokin wakashū*, XVII, Miscellaneous I, no. 878, Anonymous (*NKBT*, 8: 278), and the *Yamato monogatari* (*NKBT*, 9: 328, Section 125): "As I gaze at it, / To find comfort for my heart / Am I unable: / Moon that in Sarashina / On Mount Obasute shines."

[25] On the dayflower image, see the poem cited in note 49, p. 31, above.

her. Each feature was perfect. She was radiant and charming, and one wanted to gaze at her forever. When Saishō looked at her, knowing she was in no way inferior to the incomparable Chūnagon, he felt his grief lessen and was happy. As she spoke, the Princess seemed timid, but she was not so shy as to make one uneasy. She was perfect. Her words too had a lingering charm. Saishō found them worthy, all he wanted them to be. They spent the entire day talking.

Just then a messenger came to Saishō from Chūnagon. "I should come to apologize for my rudeness last night under the influence of liquor; but I'm agitated and confused, and it would be best if you came here," wrote Chūnagon. Saishō went to him. Chūnagon's face, though still untidy after his night's sleep, was beautiful to see. He spoke quietly, but Saishō was disgruntled because he made no mention of the waves of the Uji River.[26]

"Having been abandoned by you, who thought me wretched and useless, I have hesitated and not been able to ask why, in all these months, you've never inquired about your innocent child," said the weeping Saishō. "The love you felt for me was out of the ordinary; you waited for me to come and were glad when I did. What happened? I feel this is unreal, and in my grief I wonder whether I've lost my senses again, but there is nothing I can do now. As for the child whom I look after in memory of the one who has vanished, since I am a man I of course cannot be with him each and every moment. On days when I have little time and can't see him, I worry very much. I would feel easier, however, if from now on I might have him stay here in the care of the younger Princess. Though it is improper, I speak as I do because it concerns a child I feel no one should ever abandon."

"One would, of course, feel that way," said the pained

[26] This is an extension of the image of the Lady of the Uji Bridge who, according to the poem Chūnagon had earlier recited, had drowned herself. Saishō is of course alluding to the former Chūnagon.

Chūnagon. "I realize that your request is reasonable. But there's nothing to say, for what happened is not my fault, nor was it your sin. I feel that if it were not for the younger Yoshino Princess, there would be no way to dispel the resentment you have felt for months. Though pairing you two up might have seemed unexpected and sudden to you, I felt sure you would not find her unsatisfactory, yet here you are, lost in the darkness of concern for your child."

"If I did not feel thus consoled, I could scarcely go on living," said Saishō. He did indeed feel most comforted by the younger Princess, having spent his days in grief and tears when he thought of familiar Uji without Chūnagon.

Thereafter Saishō went to Chūnagon's home on all suitable occasions. With the same interests at heart now, they played the koto and flute and studied together. The younger Princess continued to see Saishō, too, and she was overjoyed, for there was nothing displeasing about him. Her love for him was apparently deep. Chūnagon therefore was also pleased.

Rumor had it that Saishō was seeing the younger sister of Chūnagon's wife, the Yoshino Princess. It was said that Chūnagon had brought them together as man and wife. The relationship between Chūnagon and Saishō, supposedly distant because of Saishō's affair with Yon no Kimi, was very good. Chūnagon had an excellent disposition; he thus acted differently than people in their incomplete understanding expected he would, and for this too they seemed to admire him. Saishō thought time and again that it was inconvenient to have the reputation of being such a fickle and passionate man, but he had still not learned from experience. The image of the lady who had played the seven-stringed koto in the moonlight the other night was still with him, and though behaving nonchalantly, he sought a suitable opportunity for seeing her. The Yoshino Princess, however, was cool to him, and he did not seem to have the ghost of a chance. He was disconsolate.

In the seventh month Naishi no Kami informed the Emperor that it was the fifth month of her pregnancy and withdrew to the mansion in the second ward. Chūnagon's joy knew no bounds. In this condition Naishi no Kami naturally recalled her first child at Uji. She had never forgotten how, as the days and months of her pregnancy accumulated, she had felt flurried and depressed; how, leaving her government business half undone, she had had to seek seclusion, and how, continuously grieving, she had waited anxiously for Saishō to come, she, the lady of the Uji Bridge. Now related to Chūnagon, Saishō was always there when Chūnagon was at home, and he went about, speaking freely with the ladies.

Long ago, Naishi no Kami and Saishō had amused themselves so familiarly that it had been embarrassing, and they had spoken together without any reservations at all. In the end, even her unusual person had been completely known to him, and their vows to each other had been deep indeed. And, of course, there was the innocent, smiling face of her son. When Naishi no Kami remembered all this and when she heard Saishō's voice, she was saddened, and her tears often flowed. However, she thought it would appear strange if people saw her and wondered, and she wiped them away.

Yon no Kimi was to give birth at the mansion in the second ward, and she went there at the end of the eighth month. Chūnagon came to the house constantly, and since he cared for her with all his heart, he was all one might desire. Yon no Kimi still felt awkward about the daughters she had had by Saishō, and she did not take them with her. Chūnagon did not ask why. Udaijin, therefore, supposed that what people had been saying about these children being Saishō's was true.

At the beginning of the ninth month Yon no Kimi gave birth to a son. The joy of Sadaijin and Chūnagon was boundless. This time there was no cause for doubt about whose child it was, and the birth ceremonies were held publicly. Sadaijin was so ecstatic that he kept running into things.

When Naishi no Kami learned that Yon no Kimi had given birth, she recalled various things that had happened in the past. "I learned that Saishō secretly visited her on the seventh night after her first child was born, and I heard about her second child's birth while I was in seclusion at Uji, unable to do anything and very worried." In private, she concentrated on recollecting such matters, feeling it had all been an extraordinary dream. The child born to Yon no Kimi this time bore no resemblance at all to his elder sisters but looked as though someone had exactly copied Chūnagon's face. The grandfathers were very moved and happy.

When this was over, Chūnagon devoted himself fully to caring for Naishi no Kami in her pregnancy; without much pain she gave birth to an Imperial Prince. Since there had been no Crown Prince for years, prayers had been recited night and day. Perhaps this birth was the fruit of such supplications. Everyone was amazed, considering it a rare blessing that the child had appeared from the womb of this brilliant lady, daughter of Sadaijin and sister of Chūnagon.

One can imagine what the ceremonies after the child's birth were like, even if we do not speak of them. Sadaijin took charge of the celebrations on the third night, the steward of the Imperial Princess on the fifth, Imperial courtiers on the seventh, and Chūnagon on the ninth. All vied with each other and put all their hearts into serving at these ceremonies, which were splendid. In addition to the usual observances there were various entertainments that were grand indeed. Nevertheless, Naishi no Kami at no time forgot the occasion of her first son's birth at Uji. The young Prince was very beautiful. He was large and had a sovereign's nobility. But when Naishi no Kami thought of the time she had had the child in secret, she was sad and wept bitterly. In her heart she thought:

> With all my heart
> Would I like to forget,

But hard it is.
Why was the child born to remain,
Constant reminder in this world? [27]

At that time new government officials were appointed, and Chūnagon, concurrently serving in his military capacity, became Great Minister of the Center.[28] Promoted in turn, Saishō became a Major Counsellor, and in his happiness he recalled the past. He remembered, as though it had just happened, how, when he became a Middle Counsellor, Chūnagon had seen Yon no Kimi's poem about the "one unknown," [29] and how, though it did not show on his face, Chūnagon had seemed to be pensive. At this Saishō felt his joy tempered, and he wept.

Saishō had taken his son from Uji to the mansion in the second ward and placed him in the younger Yoshino Princess's keeping. She found the child darling, held him in her arms, and cared for him. Saishō was pleased. The boy's wet nurse had vaguely understood that the lady who had unexpectedly disappeared might be the daughter of the Yoshino Prince. Thus, when the Princess suddenly appeared as the wife of Saishō and received the child, the wet nurse thought she had discovered that this was the lady whose whereabouts had been unknown and for whom Saishō had grieved. She was happy and moved, planning to go to her one day soon and speak of past months. The Princess found the child so lovely she could not be shied away from him even by the wet nurse, and so the nurse was able to see her in the dim light. She was not, how-

[27] There are two sets of *kakekotoba* in this poem. *Yo* means not only the "world," but also a "relationship between a man and a woman," here the relationship with Saishō, which she would like to forget. From *wasuregatami* come the two meanings a "memento" and "difficult to forget."

[28] Naidaijin. Though Chūnagon is promoted here, the original continues to refer to him by the title attained at his last promotion until he is again promoted at the conclusion of the tale. There appears to be no particular reason for this inconsistency on the part of the author.

[29] See Yon no Kimi's poem on p. 106. The former Chūnagon is being discussed here.

ever, the lady she had seen at Uji. This was regrettable and hard to understand; but the Princess looked beautiful, and she treated the child with an affection rather greater than a real mother's.

In this way, she consoled her comfortless, yearning, and saddened heart. When Saishō was away, the wet nurse stayed constantly with the younger Princess, and they chatted. The Princess was charming and spoke with apparent guilelessness. The wet nurse was happy, and she wept as she spoke frankly of how beautiful the boy's mother looked when she had left her child.

"How touching!," said the Princess, weeping. "It would pain me greatly to leave this child when I have but seen him like this. How his mother must have sorrowed to leave him and seek seclusion!"

"I thought she might have been one of the Yoshino sisters," said the wet nurse secretively. "When you came here it did not occur to me that you were not she, and I had planned to see you as soon as possible. Then, even though you turned out to be someone else, you were more lovely and extraordinary than the one of old, and I was very happy. Yet the gloom in my heart is never lifted, and I wonder where she has gone and what has become of her. Could Chūnagon's wife, your elder sister, perhaps be the child's mother?"

"It's embarrassing that I've appeared to you to be oblivious of all this when you had such different thoughts in mind," laughed the Princess. "There are only Chūnagon's wife and myself. We have no other sisters. And Chūnagon's wife could not be the lady of Uji. How is it that you mistook us for another? Because the incident was unusual, it is regrettable that you suspected both my sister and me," said the younger Princess, looking charming and beautiful. Even so, the wet nurse at no time forgot this matter, about which she could not do anything.

Accompanied by many pleasing and felicitous events, the

new year replaced the old. Until now there had been no Crown
Prince, and the Imperial Princess had occupied that position;
but now she planned to withdraw from that position under
the pretext of her endless illness. Thus, in the first month of
the year, at the celebrations of the fiftieth day after the child's
birth, the boy was raised to the rank of Crown Prince, and the
Princess was retired to a nunnery and called the Cloistered
Princess.

Chūnagon, using as his excuse Naishi no Kami's deep love
for the Cloistered Princess, visited the Princess faithfully. The
Cloistered Emperor, her father, seemed satisfied about how
things had turned out. Naishi no Kami's son had become
Crown Prince, and she herself received an Imperial decree
ordering that she become Imperial concubine. Shortly thereafter, in the fourth month, she was elevated to the position
of Empress. The ceremonies were of course extraordinary.
Everyone seemed pleased, for the installation of an Empress
should have taken place long ago, and they had waited very
anxiously for it.

Saishō, being now in Chūnagon's favor, became High Steward to the Empress.[30] He remembered when long ago Naishi
no Kami had had him put his trust in the Bay of Shiga,[31] and
he was moved. Sadly, it did not occur to him that the Empress
was the lady of the Uji Bridge.

The Uji boy now spoke very well, ran about, and played.
When Saishō saw him, he recalled the unforgettable situation
with the former Chūnagon. "I still can't fully understand what
happened at Uji. Perhaps the younger Yoshino Princess does,"
he thought. He tried to find out what had transpired many
times, but the younger Princess appeared not to know either.

"Roughly when did Chūnagon arrive at Mount Yoshino?,"
the uneasy Saishō asked.

[30] Chūgū no daibu. Reischauer 1937: 101 translates this as "Master." Saishō held
this position concurrently with his position as Major Counsellor.
[31] See Naishi no Kami's poem on p. 80, above.

"Well, I know that he came from time to time after he was promoted to Middle Counsellor," she replied.

"When did he start visiting your sister regularly? How did it begin?," questioned Saishō.

"Was it the year before last? I don't really know," said the younger Princess in an attempt to cover up, and then she said no more.

"For years I was lost in grief, and in the end I fell ill and my life seemed to be coming to an end," Saishō reproached her. "But ever since I first happened to see you the desire to live grew in me as never before. I keep absolutely nothing from you and think of you as my supreme love. Yet though you know what has happened, you keep a barrier between us. I find your behavior deplorable and displeasing. If you felt for me but a fraction of what I feel for you, you would tell me what I am concerned about and what I want to know just as you know it."

"What do you mean, I keep a barrier between us?," said the Princess, smiling. "You certainly maintain a barrier and do not seem to speak of things as they are. I can guess at what is in your heart but cannot speak of it."

This was quite reasonable, and Saishō laughed. "I don't feel restrained with you, but because the matter is one I can't speak of, it naturally seems that I am reticent. Even though I haven't spoken of it, if there is something you vaguely understand, it would be best to speak up. And then I will tell you what happened from the beginning."

"Since what you know within your heart is hard to speak of, how can I relate what I only vaguely understand? Look into your own heart and simply consider what is there," said the Princess, laughing. Her appearance was most pleasing. She was a delight to see, and Saishō was happy.

"If she were not as she is, how very much more sad I should be," he thought.

"No one told me in so many words, but the situation does

seem to be along the lines I vaguely understood," thought the Princess. She supposed it was vexatious for Saishō. He must truly find it worrisome, strange, and incomprehensible. Yet she thought: "If I were suddenly to speak of this unusual matter, it would be a source of anxiety for everyone." Thus resolved, the younger Yoshino Princess said nothing. Saishō was disappointed and reproachful, and he spoke to her and cajoled her in every possible way.

"You must simply believe that there were reasons for it," she said. "Even if you learned of them, since it is difficult to draw water from a spring that is no longer in the field,[32] the pain in your heart would but increase. Besides, it is pointless to sully another's name and reputation."

Saishō was very displeased that she would not tell him, but there was nothing he could do. "While I am to think the lady's whereabouts completely unknown, the Princess knows but will not say," he thought, disgruntled.

In no time the months and years passed and were replaced, and the Empress gave birth to two or three Princesses. The Emperor was convinced that she had been fated to become his wife. Generally, everyone forgave her her transgressions; and the ladies close to the Emperor seemed resentful only that they were not so fortunate. When Udaijin's second daughter considered that she had come to court before anybody else, she found it embarrassing that Sadaijin's family was there and seemed most prosperous. She therefore left the palace and returned home.

"In the old days," thought the Empress when she learned of this, "I paid for my relationship with Yon no Kimi, for Udaijin reproached me night and day. Then, as the lady of the Uji Bridge, when I gazed out lost in thought, it must have been my retribution that I was convinced Saishō lacked feeling for

[32] The image of the spring in the field comes from a poem in the Kokin wakashū, XVII, Miscellaneous I, no. 887, Anonymous (NKBT, 8: 280): "Old spring in the field, / Its water now is tepid. / But they who know, / Know what once it used to be, / They still draw water there."

me because of her. Again it is due to me that this lady, out of resentment, has secluded herself in her old home. Despite the deep bonds between Sadaijin's and Udaijin's families, mutual feelings of bitterness never seem to cease. This is the fate of their relationship, which ought to have been one of profound emotional ties."

Chūnagon had three sons in a row by Yon no Kimi. The one who had been raised at his father's home was growing up too, and he was permitted to go to court to learn its manners. The childless elder Yoshino Princess was impatient for the birth of a child of her own, and so she considered this boy her own and loved him especially. The child went regularly to visit his mother, the Cloistered Princess. Old Senji looked on him with much tenderness. On the grounds that the boy was related to the Empress, that Chūnagon had deep feeling for the Cloistered Princess, and that the boy was thus very close to her, Senji introduced him behind the bamboo screens, and there he enjoyed himself greatly and was most affectionate. Though the Cloistered Princess was generally reserved, she succumbed to a natural mother's love [33] and looked on his handsome, mature face with great tenderness.

The younger Yoshino Princess gave birth to two daughters and a son. Chūnagon's wife, the Yoshino Princess, being partial to the younger girl, placed her and the Cloistered Princess's son to her right and left and treated both affectionately.

Saishō's son, the boy who had been secretly born at Uji, had grown up, and so he went to court and circulated as freely as did the son of Chūnagon and the Cloistered Princess. When the Empress saw him she was saddened. He was in no way inferior to the Crown Prince or to her daughters, and each time she saw him she felt moved and sad.

One quiet, lazy spring day, the Empress's elder daughter and this son of Saishō in their play came to the Empress's resi-

[33] The expression used here, the darkness of her heart, is from the poem by Fujiwara no Kanesuke cited in note 78, p. 52, above.

dence. They looked very much alike, though the Uji boy was a bit more radiant and of unsurpassable charm. So splendid was he that he stunned the eye. The Empress was moved, for it was hard for her to bear seeing him. On this occasion there were not many people about her, and so she felt at ease and called the children behind her bamboo screen. Her elder daughter came in, but the Uji boy did not.

"Do come in too. I won't hurt you," said the Empress.

Quietly and humbly he sat formally on the veranda and thus visited her from behind the screen. When the Empress saw how very beautiful he was, she recalled the night she had left him, thinking that it was to be forever, as she handed him over to the wet nurse and secretly went on her way. She felt as though her departure had just now taken place, and was very sad. Thinking the boy must find her behavior strange, she forced herself to conceal her sadness, but the tears welled up, for it was unbearable.

"Do you know about your mother?," she asked, weeping. "What did your Father tell you?"

As the Uji boy had gradually come to understand more about life, he had felt uneasy wondering what had become of his mother. Both Saishō and his wet nurse had apparently spoken of her, weeping and yearning for her night and day, but her whereabouts were unknown. The Empress looked young and beautiful, and she wept and was very moved as she inquired about his mother. It then occurred to the Uji boy that perhaps she was his mother, and he was suddenly filled with emotion.

"The Empress is not like what I expected my mother to be," he thought. "She is also not someone whose whereabouts are unknown or who could be mistaken for someone else." He pondered seriously in an adult manner, but said nothing.

The Empress was sad as she wondered what he was thinking. She gazed at him intently, and holding her sleeve up to her face, wept profusely. The boy lowered his head and felt his own tears fall. He looked touching to the Empress, and she edged a little closer and stroked his hair.

"Your mother is related to me, and it pains me to see that she seems unable to forget you and yearns for you," said the Empress. "This is why I spoke as I did. Saishō probably thinks your mother is no longer of this world. Do not tell him that I have spoken to you of her. Know in your heart that she is alive, and come regularly at suitable times. I will arrange for you to meet her secretly."

The Uji boy appeared to be moved, and he sat with his head bent. He was so handsome that the Empress found it hard to part from him. But her younger daughter came running in. "Well, let's go," she cried, and pulled him away.

The Empress was disappointed and sad. Outside the residence, still weeping, she followed the boy with her eyes as he left. Then she lay down. Was he eleven years old now? The boy's hair hung softly down to his shoulders, and he looked beautiful. The way he sat up formally in deference to Princes and Princesses was touching.

> If to the same nest
> They always do return,
> Children of the crane,
> Why then is that one alone
> Far from this part of the sky?[34]

The Empress wept profusely.

The Emperor had come, and when he quietly peeped through a crack, he saw the Empress sitting facing a young boy and weeping as she spoke with him. The Emperor found this strange, and without making a sound, he went on watching for some time.

"I see," he thought. "So this is what it is. I thought there might be something. That boy is the Empress's child. I had heard, curiously, that Saishō was lost in a river of tears night

[34] "This part of the sky" refers to the Imperial court.

and day, and that without saying who this child's mother was, he brought him up, never leaving his side. Now this makes sense. Some years ago Naishi no Kami said she had been ill for a long time. She did not go to see the Imperial Princess, and for roughly half a year she remained in seclusion. Apparently, it was at that time that she gave birth to this child."

Taking into consideration the boy's age, the Emperor had no doubts. For years he had been uneasy, and though he had behaved nonchalantly, he had been distressed not knowing with whom Naishi no Kami had exchanged vows. He was happy to have found out.

"Since her father knew who her lover was and would not permit the relationship, I wondered what kind of low-born person he was. I felt he must be frivolous and inferior. But even an Emperor—if he was the least bit imperfect—could not compete with someone like Saishō, and even if Sadaijin did not permit such a relationship, nothing could be done.[35] Saishō is an extraordinary person—in appearance and personality and in every other respect. Theirs was thus a relationship of two people who loved each other very much. Sadaijin no doubt was hesitant to permit the affair because, unfortunately, it ran against what he, in his vanity, wanted for her, wishing that she become Empress. He was also hesitant because Saishō was thoroughly fickle and unreliable and did not seem to love Naishi no Kami, for he had gone to Yon no Kimi among others. Both Saishō and the Empress are probably distressed about each other in their hearts," the Emperor thought compassionately.

Wanting to know more, the Emperor stepped out beside the Empress as though he had just arrived. The Empress wiped away her tears and rose.

"For many days," said the Emperor, smiling, "I did not give any thought to the matter, but you no doubt thought me absurd for not noticing until now that the boy who plays with

---

[35] The meaning of this sentence is unclear.

our daughters resembles them very much. Chūnagon, who is an official of high rank,[36] and Saishō have now become higher noblemen, and I thought there were no longer good-looking people. But their children are many, and they seem no less handsome than their fathers.

"The world is coming to its end. Yet there seem to be many fine people. Of these the Uji boy and Chūnagon's eldest son by Yon no Kimi have been especially outstanding recently. It is odd that I have heard no open rumor of who the mothers of the Uji boy and Chūnagon's first son are. People have whispered, however, that the mother of Chūnagon's first son may be the Cloistered Princess. That may indeed be so. The refined elegance and charm of his character are surely such that it might be true. Yet apparently nothing is said about who the Uji boy's mother may be. I wonder why. Is it that, though some probably know, no one will tell me?"

Looking at him, the Empress realized that he might have observed her talking with the boy and become suspicious. It was painful for her.

"Well, I do not know about the boy's mother," she said. "As for the mother of Chūnagon's son, what you say is cruel and, for the Cloistered Princess, most inconsiderate. Couldn't it be someone other than she? How could she have had the child without my knowing it, since I was in her service then?"

"People say you are the only one who might be expected to admit that you know. But since your not telling won't inconvenience anyone very much, it's all right. I will not know about it then. But do you know about the mother of the Uji boy? I would like to know more about that."

The Empress, unable to reply, blushed and turned away. She looked incredibly lovely then. Even if she was guilty of great transgressions or faults, her appearance was such that if one but looked at her they would all vanish. And since she had given birth to many children as the months and years had

36 *Ason*, officials of the fifth rank and higher.

passed, the Emperor's love for her seemed to grow deeper and deeper irrespective of what went on in her heart. Why would he love her less? The two lay down and rested.

The Uji boy had gone away, very moved at what had happened. "I saw someone I think might be my mother," he confided to his wet nurse. "Do not say anything though. She told me not to tell my father." He spoke with deep emotion, tears filling his eyes. His wet nurse was surprised.

"What?," she said, moved and sad. "Where is she? How do you know she is your mother? What did she look like?"

"She was young and beautiful, more charming, more noble than Saishō's wife, the younger Yoshino Princess. She did not in fact tell me that she was my mother, but she did say: 'Remember that your mother is alive,' and she wept and wept." Looking very moved, he said no more about where she was.

"Your father yearned and grieved for her night and day, and I would like to tell him that she is alive," said the uneasy nurse. "For what reason did she hide herself like that? Why did she see you?"

"She told me not to tell my father. But when I meet with her again soon, I will ask, and if she tells me I may, I'll tell my father then. For the present say nothing to him."

The nurse looked at him. "He's not a child," she thought. "He looks very handsome and mature."

Oh, yes, now I remember. The lady at the Reikeiden would have been grieved if Chūnagon were to forsake her in the future, and so on suitable occasions he would speak with her in secret. She subsequently gave birth to a beautiful daughter. Since Chūnagon had no daughters other than those born to Yon no Kimi,[37] he was troubled and wanted to receive her at his mansion in the second ward. However, the Imperial concubine at the Reikeiden was constantly lamenting that she did not even have a daughter, and since the child was lovely and her own sister's, she was very attached to her and could

[37]Actually these two daughters were Saishō's.

not let her go. Chūnagon acquiesced, and he permitted her to look after the child properly. The Empress had received so much love from the Emperor that others were displeased, and so when she went to court there were many embarrassing and awkward moments. But now, at the birth of her niece, Chūnagon felt sorry for the Imperial concubine of the Reikeiden and showed her great kindness and assistance, and she now hid whatever displeasure she felt.

The months and years passed and were replaced by new ones. Sadaijin took the tonsure, and Udaijin became the Chancellor.[38] Chūnagon became the Minister of the Left and Regent. Saishō was made both Minister of the Center and Major Captain. Their sons had their coming-of-age ceremonies, and all were called Middle or Minor Captain. The Emperor abdicated, and the Crown Prince became Emperor. The second son of the Emperor and the Empress became the Crown Prince. Yon no Kimi's eldest daughter, who had been brought up by the present Regent, went to court as an Imperial concubine and was installed in the Fujitsubo. Afterwards, the girl brought up in the Reikeiden came to court as a concubine of the Crown Prince. All these people turned out as splendidly as one could wish, and they were content in every way. Yet throughout all this, as the months and years passed, even as all the world changed, never were Saishō's sleeves dry of the bitter tears shed over the affair of the waves of the Uji River[39] that had ended without his ever knowing where his lover had gone. As the Uji boy, now a Middle Captain of the third rank, grew, Saishō saw that he was superior to the others in appearance and capabilities.

"What were her feelings when she resigned herself neither to see nor to know her son and to go into eternal seclusion?," he wondered.

I am told that he felt sorrow, pain, and longing, and was overcome with grief.

[38] Daijōdaijin, the Prime Minister who presided over the Great Council of State.
[39] There is a pun here on *nami*, meaning "waves" and "tears."

Reference Matter

APPENDIX

Relevant 'Mumyō zōshi' Passages

The translation, with one minor exception noted toward the end, is based on the text in Tomikura Tokujirō, 'Mumyō zōshi hyōkai' (Tokyo, 1972), pp. 213–15.

'TORIKAEBAYA'

"In the *Torikaebaya*,"[1] someone then commented, "words are poorly linked together, and there is much that somehow creates a weird and overwhelming feeling. The story that was concocted seems a rather curious one. There do appear to be surprisingly moving aspects. The poems are good. Yon no Kimi is splendid. She is an ideal and good person. Naishi no Kami is also a fine person after she becomes a male. Then, in the latter half of the book, these people have many children. The young noblemen and courtiers remain indoors at the palace on a day of abstinence, many people gather there and speak of *monogatari*. The judgments of the rainy night in *The Tale of Genji* are recalled, and matters both very extraordinary and interesting are brought up. However, they fail in their imitation, and very ridiculous things appear to be said. The female Chūnagon looks very splendid, but it is shocking that

[1] The *Ko torikaebaya*.

he does such things as shake loose his hair[2] and give birth to a child. Furthermore, the matter of his menstrual periods is very unclean. It is most touching when the lieutenant general of Yon no Kimi's mother becomes a priest.[3] Likewise touching is Saishō's wearing a straw coat on a snowy morning. The time when the female Chūnagon dies and then is revived is frightful indeed. A mirror is brought in, and everything [pertaining to the female Chūnagon's fate] is clearly seen in it. Such unreal occurrences are quite disturbing."

'KAKURE MINO'

Then someone said, "Speaking of an unusual story, there is *Kakure mino*.[4] It should be worth reading, but it has many excessively unpleasant aspects. The language is very old-fashioned, and, perhaps because the poems are not good either, it is far surpassed by the *Torikaebaya*, which we discuss in the same category. Few people look at it now. The idea behind it should have made the contents worthwhile in many ways; it should have had emotional appeal, interest, and novelty. Regrettably, it does not have any of these at all. I wish there were someone to produce an *Ima kakure mino* like the splendid *Ima torikaebaya* recently created. Surely even nowadays there are people who can create works worth reading. They say a variety of works are produced these days. I have looked at a few, and one could consider them rather more moving than the old works."

'IMA TORIKAEBAYA'

"I have looked at many tales predating *The Tale of Genji*, beginning with *The Tale of Utsubo*, and all seem to possess

[2] That is, undo the male topknot.
[3] This character does not appear in the extant version, nor do the other events mentioned here.
[4] This is a lost tale apparently dealing with the actions of someone who became invisible when wearing a special straw raincoat.

little of value. As one would expect, they deal with the olden days and are old-fashioned. The word usage and poems are not great, and this is probably because they do not attain the level of what was seen in the style of such works as the *Manyōshū*. Why then would something like the *Ima torikaebaya*, of which we have just spoken, be superior to the old works? An imitation of anything is certainly inferior to the original, but this *Torikaebaya* is not distasteful and seems to be of interest. Its language and poetry are not bad either. There do not seem to be any overwhelmingly frightful sections. In the original the female Chūnagon's situation was loathsome, but all is fine in this version. One does not feel it to be an offensive and absurd plot that such a sex reversal occurs. It is assumed that it is truly [the female] Chūnagon's fitting retribution, and when he bitterly laments the position he finds himself in it is very heartrending. Naishi no Kami is also very good. Both the section in which Chūnagon changes back into the female he originally was and gives birth to a child and the one in which Naishi no Kami becomes a male are very well written in this work. In the old tale the brother and sister of the beginning section vanish and then reappear from nowhere. This is not very realistic. In this new version they appear after having taken each other's place. As the intended conclusion, one can appreciate that this role reversal should indeed have been like this.

"Yon no Kimi is hateful in this *Ima torikaebaya*. On the surface she appears to be very gentle and lovely. She recites: 'A lovely spring night. / Yet because it is I / Who gazes upon it, / The moon has darkened, become / The shadow of my distress.'[5] Considering that she thus feels such utter grief while possessing a husband who, wondering what is to happen, is so serious and faithful, her hard heart is unbecoming. Her reciting 'More for the one unknown / Than for the one others can see, / Sleeves of my nightrobes; / Hearing of his promo-

---

[5] See p. 42, above. See p. 42, above.

tion, / Could I remain unmoved?' is certainly very distasteful.[6]

"Saishō is certainly very inconsiderate. If his feelings are so shallow, why should he continue to indulge his insatiable lust? It is very bad when he imprisons the female Chūnagon at Uji and feels easy, assured that she will remain with him no matter what happens. What could he have felt, then, even when confronted by the amazing situation of having had the female Chūnagon flee from him after she had undergone such a change in appearance? Later, when Naishi no Kami becomes the male she originally was and mingles at court as Chūnagon, the female Yon no Kimi recites: 'The one I knew, / He whom I was wont to see, / You seem not to be he.'[7] Yet Saishō does not realize that this is someone different, even though he sees him so clearly and directly. His situation is thoroughly helpless. Even if Saishō did find this male Chūnagon's appearance unusual, just compare his behavior to the appropriate, discreet, and unmoving attitude of the male Naishi no Kami when she lived quietly at the Sen'yōden."[8]

When this was said, someone added, "After the situation changed for Saishō and he became the younger Yoshino Princess's husband, he wandered absentmindedly around the mansion of the second ward, overcome with thoughts of the place where he had left behind so many regrets.[9] Such actions as this are terribly unworthy.

[6] See p. 106, above.

[7] See p. 172, above.

[8] The text mistakenly reads Reikeiden instead of Sen'yōden.

[9] Here I read *omoishirarete*, as does Suzuki (1973: 426), rather than the negative *omoishirarede*, as suggested by Tomikura. The place is Uji, and the regrets are over the missing female Chūnagon.

Works Cited

The place of publication is Tokyo unless otherwise noted. The following abbreviations are used in the Notes:

KKT Nakatsuka Eijirō, ed., *Kōchū kokka taikei.* 28 vols. 1927–31.

NKBT Takagi Ichinosuke et al., eds. *Nihon koten bungaku taikei.* 102 vols. 1957–68.

ZGR Ichishima Kenkichi, ed. *Zokuzoku gunsho ruijū.* Vol. 14. 1907.

Cranston, Edwin A. 1969. *The Izumi Shikibu Diary.* Cambridge, Mass.

Frank, Bernard. 1958. "*Kata-imi* et *kata-tagae:* Etude sur les interdits de direction à l'époque Heian," *Bulletin de la Maison Franco-Japonaise.* n.s. 5: 1–246.

Frye, Northrop. 1971. *Anatomy of Criticism.* Princeton, N.J.

Fujiki Kunihiko. 1960. *Heian jidai no kizoku no seikatsu.*

Fujimura Saku, ed. 1950. [*Zoho kaitei*] *Nihon bungaku daijiten,* vol. 1.

Fujioka Sakutarō. 1974. *Kokubungaku zenshi 2: Heianchō hen.*

Fujiwara Teika (1162–1241), comp. *Shūi hyakuban uta awase,* in *Gunsho ruijū,* vol. 11. 1893.

Fūyō wakashū, in ZGR, vol. 14. 1907.

Genji monogatari, in NKBT, vols. 14–18. 1964.

Gosen wakashū, in KKT, vol. 3. 1927.

Goshūi wakashū, in KKT, vol. 3. 1927.

Hamatsu chūnagon monogatari, in *NKBT,* vol. 77. 1964.

Hisamatsu Sen'ichi. 1971. *Shinhan Nihon bungaku shi,* 2: *Chūko.*

Ikeda Kikan. 1932. "Nihon bungaku shomoku kaisetsu, 2: Heian jidai, jō," in *Iwanami kōza: Nihon bungaku,* vol. 8.

————. 1967. *Heian jidai no bungaku to seikatsu.*

Ise monogatari, in *NKBT,* vol. 9. 1957.

Katayori Masayoshi. 1938. "*Torikaebaya monogatari* no kisoteki kenkyū," *Kokugo to kokubungaku,* 15.1 (May): 53–82.

Kokin waka rokujō, in *KKT,* vol. 9. 1929.

Kokin wakashū, in *NKBT,* vol. 8. 1958.

Kokka taikan. 1931. Ed. Matsushita Daisaburō and Watanabe Fumio. 2 vols.

Miyada Waichirō. 1940. "*Torikaebaya monogatari* no kenkyū, *Koten kenkyū,* 10, special autumn supplement, pp. 133–44.

Morioka Tsuneo. 1967. *Heianchō monogatari no kenkyū.*

Morris, Ivan. 1969. *The World of the Shining Prince.* Baltimore, Md.

Nakamura Yoshio. 1965. *Ōchō no fūzoku to bungaku.*

Nomura Hachirō. 1944. *Chūko bungakushi ron.*

Piggott, Juliet. 1969. *Japanese Mythology.* London.

Reischauer, R. K. 1937. *Early Japanese History: Part A.* Princeton, N.J.

Seikai dai hyakka jiten. 1955–58. Ed. Hayashi Tatsuo. 32 vols.

Shika wakashū, in *KKT,* vol. 4. 1928.

Shinchokusen wakashū, in *KKT,* vol. 5. 1928.

Shinkokin wakashū, in *NKBT,* vol. 28. 1968.

Shinmura Izuru, ed. 1971. *Kojien.*

Shūi hyakuban uta awase, in *Gunsho ruijū,* vol. 11. 1893.

Shūi wakashū, in *KKT,* vol. 3. 1927.

Suzuki Hiromichi. 1968. *Heian makki monogatari ron.*

————. 1971. *Heian makki monogatari ni tsuite no kenkyū.*

————. 1973. *Torikaebaya monogatari no kenkyū.*

Takano Yutaka. 1956. "*Torikaebaya monogatari* no seiritsu nendai ni kansuru kōsatsu," *Heianchō bungaku kenkyū,* 1.1 (Dec.).

Tomikura Tokujirō. 1972. *Mumyō zōshi hyōkai.*

Wakan rōeishū, in *NKBT,* vol. 73. 1965.

Waley, Arthur. 1960. *The Tale of Genji.* New York.

Yamato monogatari, in *NKBT,* vol. 9. 1957.

Zoku goshūi wakashū, in *Kokka taikan,* listed above, vol. 1.

The authorized representative in the EU for product safety and compliance is:
Mare Nostrum Group
B.V Doelen 72
4831 GR Breda
The Netherlands

www.ingramcontent.com/pod-product-compliance
Lightning Source LLC
Chambersburg PA
CBHW030631030726
47497CB00006B/1729